# THE
# INSIGNIFICANT GIRL

www.amplifypublishinggroup.com

# The Insignificant Girl

**For more information, please contact:**
Mascot Books, an imprint of Amplify Publishing Group
620 Herndon Parkway, Suite 320
Herndon, VA 20170
info@amplifypublishing.com

Library of Congress Control Number: 2021922218

CPSIA Code: PRV0722A

ISBN-13: 978-1-64543-852-6

Printed in the United States

For Skyrish. My half-Scottish, half-Irish
love of my life.

# THE
# INSIGNIFICANT
# GIRL

## TOM FITZGERALD
Author of *Defector in Our Midst*

# PROLOGUE

# BEIRUT, LEBANON, 1978

The dank parking garage grew colder—yet he waited. Levi raised the binoculars to his eyes and focused on the concrete stairwell at the end of the garage. He tapped his fingers on the steering wheel to the melody in his head, then checked his watch for the third time. He glanced down at his tightly woven shoelaces and shook his head.

Two years earlier, at his apartment in Tel Aviv, he had knelt down to tie his shoes when one of the laces snapped apart in his hand. His elder brother Micah had barked at him, "You're on your own, Levi! You won't make me late for the bus again."

The two brothers used to take the city bus every day to the Israeli Boxing Academy, where Micah trained. That day, after yelling at Levi, Micah turned and rushed out the door. Levi quickly unlaced the broken shoestring, dashed to his closet, frantically yanked the shoestring from a worn shoe, and laced up his shoe. Levi shot out the door and sprinted down the street. As he rounded the corner, he inhaled a thick cloud of black exhaust that was still lingering in the air from the departing bus. He coughed on the fumes as he held his arms up and waved them to no avail. The bus continued to accelerate as Levi stood and watched dejectedly.

Suddenly, as the bus crossed the intersection, it erupted into a massive orange fireball. The behemoth vehicle lifted two feet off the ground in a thunderous explosion. Levi shielded his eyes from the brightness as the heat from the blast caused the hair on his arms to singe. Pieces of the bus whirled past his head. He dropped to the ground to avoid the flying wreckage. The smell of sulfur and burnt hair filled his lungs. His ears were ringing. All sound was muffled, and it felt as if he had cotton balls stuffed in his ears. He looked down past his bleeding, glass-covered arms at his mismatched shoelaces, and he began to cry. The river of tears carved a meandering path through the thick soot and blood that covered his face. Micah was gone.

It was such an insignificant thing at the time—a broken shoelace. For Levi, it was what drove him. It was what brought him to the musty parking garage in Beirut. Levi wiggled his feet inside his securely laced leather boots and raised the binoculars to his eyes again only to see an empty stairwell. He glanced down at his watch again; his target was later than usual. The tapestry of violence that had begun with an explosion that slaughtered a bus full of innocent people would complete its weave here—in a vacant parking garage, with the assassination of the bomb maker, Jaafar Venzi, who blew up the bus. Or so he thought.

Levi's life had been spared that day at the bus stop, but forty-two others, mostly young adults in their twenties going to work, were massacred. On the morning of March 11, 1976, five militants had landed their Zodiac rubber boats on a beach north of Tel Aviv. An American photographer, Gail Rubin, had the misfortune of taking pictures on the beach that morning when the radicals landed their boats ashore. They asked the innocent girl where they had landed. When she told them where they were, they realized they were forty miles away from their intended target. Gail Rubin was brutally murdered that morning as the radicals had to improvise a new plan. They made their way to the nearest bus stop and chose a bus at random.

Micah boarded that bus forty minutes later without his brother.

Levi peered through the binoculars and waited for Jaafar to appear at the bottom of the concrete stairs. On Levi's signal, his partner would flip the switch to a detonator, and the man they had been tracking for nine months would be destroyed. Levi looked through the field glasses again. His heart skipped a beat as he took a deep breath—his target, Jaafar, was finally descending the flight of stairs. Without hesitation he turned to his partner.

"Now!" Levi shouted.

He heard the "pop" of the mechanical switch as the detonator was engaged. In sixty seconds, the bomb would explode. From his peripheral vision he noticed movement from the opposite end of the garage. Levi lowered the binoculars and jerked his head around. He felt his stomach sink as panic set in.

Levi spun around toward his partner. "What in the hell is she doing here?!"

Jaafar's spouse and her two small children were now walking closer and closer to the car that would soon explode. The young children, Malcolm and Raji, were twenty feet behind their mother. Levi had two options: watch the target and his entire family die in front of him or try and save the children. There was no kill switch. His mind flashed back to his brother, who was killed on the bus that day. The man whose death he was here to avenge.

Every young man has their idol, and if it was 1976 and you were a young lad living in Israel, it was Micah Miles. He was the heartthrob of every girl and a larger-than-life idol to most boys. He was charismatic, good-looking, and a national hero. If he was on top of his game, there was a good chance he would have been the first Israeli to ever bring home a gold medal from the Olympics. He had the fastest hands in boxing, which reminded many boxing enthusiasts of another charismatic boxer with fast hands who had taken the world by storm twelve years earlier: Cassius Clay. Cassius had proclaimed to the heavily favored World Champ, Sonny Liston,

"You can't hit what you can't see!" Most would remember Cassius by his other name, Muhammad Ali.

Levi enlisted with the Israeli army the day after Micah's funeral. Almost immediately, he caught the attention of his superiors. He was recruited by Israel's highest intelligence agency, Mossad. It takes a peculiar mindset to join the ranks of Mossad, and Levi had what they were looking for. Within two years it had come full circle. For the past nine months, Levi had been tracking the man considered to be the master planner of the bus massacre, an Iranian named Jaafar Venzi.

Levi opened the car door and bolted toward the children. Their mother was too far to be saved. He sprinted toward the boy and his sister. The scene left an indelible imprint on his mind: The little girl had a yellow flowered dress with white shoes and a lace ribbon in her hair. The boy was dressed in sneakers and khaki shorts with a plaid striped shirt. As Levi ran toward them, he caught the attention of Jaafar. He spotted Levi running toward his small children and then scooping them up under his arms. Instead of trying to save his wife, Jaafar turned and ran as fast as he could toward the stairs. Levi tried his best to shield the children from the impending blast and then dove behind a large cargo van. Three seconds later, the sound from the massive explosion reverberated throughout the concrete parking structure. It was deafening. Levi looked at the boy in his arms; he was bleeding, but alive. Debris and metal that had been blown underneath the cars had injured the boy. Levi turned the small girl over to assess her condition. Blood was dripping from a large gash above her left eye. Levi pulled a red bandanna from his pocket and tied it tightly around her head. The girl opened her eyes and stared at Levi. He was unprepared for the emotion that filled his heart. Her eyes were iridescent gold, almost translucent. *How could such beauty come from such a monster of a father?*

The little girl reached out and touched the *kippah* on his head, mumbling, "Where's my mommy?"

Levi's heart sank. His lips tensed as he replied, "I don't know." The image would forever be imprinted on him. The kids would survive, but Levi needed to flee the scene. He left the children lying on the hard surface. Smoke filled the air, which made it difficult to see. He had neither the time nor the visibility to check the status of his target. He limped back to his car, which his partner had already pulled from the stall. He hopped in the passenger side, and they sped down the ramp. The small boy regained consciousness and grabbed his sister's hand as they watched Levi's vehicle speed away.

Levi yelled at his partner, "I thought you checked on his wife?"

"She must have changed her itinerary. I called the school this morning." He briefly looked at Levi as he steered their car toward the garage exit. "You shouldn't have done that Levi. You may have blown this entire operation that we have worked on for so long."

Levi looked up and squinted as he stared him in the eyes. His ears were still ringing from the sounds of the blast. He gritted his teeth. "I don't kill children."

"Did you save them?"

"Yes. They'll be fine."

"And the target?"

There was a long pause before he answered. "Jaafar ran back to the stairwell when he saw me. This may have all been for nothing."

They pulled the vehicle out of the garage and turned onto the heavily congested road. Clouds of smoke continued to billow out of the garage. Behind them lay a thread that would be woven across entire continents and generations for a girl that lay bleeding on the concrete clasping the hand of her older brother. A thread that had started with an exploding bus and would end decades later with the creation of a magnificent tapestry. Permanently woven into the fabric of the tapestry would be Levi, his brothers, an unknown nephew, and a not-so-insignificant little girl named Raji.

# PART 1

# CHAPTER 1

## PARK CITY, UTAH, SPRING

H is bloodied hand left a smudge on the polished chrome handle as he pushed the door open to the condo. His sense of foreboding had long vanished, but he called out for her anyway. It was the optimist in him.

"Jen, are you here?"

His eyes scanned the posh resort room. Outside the huge expansive glass window, he watched the snowboarders outfitted in colorful pants and jackets carve their way down the mountain's snow-packed slopes. He pulled the half-melted bag of ice from his swollen eye and tossed it in the stainless-steel sink. A loud clanging sound rang out when the bag slammed against the morning's coffee mugs and saucers. His eyes darted back and forth, taking inventory of the room for anything out of place. The wooden floor, made from reclaimed oak from a cotton mill in Mississippi dating back to the 1850s, creaked beneath him on his deliberate walk toward the master suite. The heavy knotty alder door was open, and rays of bright sunlight danced against the wood-clad hallway walls. Myk entered the room and froze. The canopy bed had been made, with its crisp linen white duvet drooping over the sides and the gray and teal decorative pillows perfectly placed against the high-gloss mahogany headboard. His surroundings blurred as he stared at the middle of the bed. A sheet of white paper was folded in half and propped up like a lone tent in the vast wilderness. Written in perfect penmanship on the outside of the paper was his name. Without taking another step, he stood and stared. His shoulders and head sunk, his stomach churned, and ever so slightly, he shook his head back and forth as he closed his eyes. Like the others, she had left. He knew better—he should have never left his gun behind. Perhaps that would have made the difference. She had even stuck with him during his twelve-month prison term. And now, only two weeks after his release, she was gone too.

# Three hours earlier

Myk and Jen had stood in the lift line, shuffling their way closer to the chairlift up the mountain. The opening of the ski resorts had started with great ambitions of maintaining some semblance of social distancing the first season after the COVID-19 pandemic, but by the end of the ski season it had long been forgotten. Myk glanced ahead to the man he had been inconspicuously keeping an eye on. To all those around him, there was nothing about the man that would have appeared out of the ordinary. Myk continued his conversation with Jen as if nothing was wrong. The lift-chair swung underneath them to whisk them to the top of the mountain. Myk watched as three of the four skiers got off the chairlift, but the man he was watching stayed on and was looping back around. "Shit," Myk mumbled as he took a deep breath of the cool mountain air. All doubts of what was about to happen vanished from his mind. The man who failed to get off the chairlift was an assassin. The only surprise was how little time had transpired before his enemy put a hit on him. Prior to his one-year prison term, Myk had received a threat from an anonymous caller. He was warned to "let sleeping dogs lie and leave the investigation alone." Myk did nothing of the sort. His first day after being released, he picked up his investigation right where he had left off.

It was the last day of spring skiing, and yet the man who Myk was watching was bundled up in a heavy winter ski jacket that had the Park City Ski Patrol logo emblazoned on it. Myk wore a lighter, cooler Spyder zip-up vest over a thin sweatshirt because of the warm skiing conditions. Myk would have gladly welcomed the assassin making a reckless miscalculation, but, as fate would have it, Jen had convinced him to leave his gun in the locker back at the lodge. It was the last day of their three-day ski trip, and she had pleaded with him, "It's our last day Myk. There have been no incidents since we've arrived. Just relax and enjoy the day—do it for me."

He had forced himself to leave his weapon behind. She was different. She was worth the risk. He had never been as vulnerable with anyone as he had been with Jen. Somehow, she opened him like a tornado on a trailer roof. He stood his ground and carried his gun with him as he left the condo. But her silence and body language got the best of him. He had finally acquiesced and left his weapon in a locker at the ski lodge. Jen's eyes beamed with gratitude when he told her what he had done. He looked up as the chairlift seats continued to move toward each other and saw the man nonchalantly reach inside his jacket pocket. The radiant look in Jen's eyes when he told her he had left the gun would soon be replaced with unmitigated fear. The assassin was now seventy yards away.

Myk hastily explained the situation that was developing as he leaned toward her ear. "The man in the Ski Patrol jacket in the chairlift on the other side has a gun. He's going to try to shoot us. When I—"

She tried to interrupt him, "How do you—"

"Jen, I don't have time. Listen to me. When I give you the signal, I need you to jump off the lift. There's enough fresh powder snow that you'll be fine; just keep your knees bent when you land. Give me one of your ski poles. I'll distract him, and that will allow you enough time to jump."

She looked across to the assassin in the bulky jacket and asked,

"Myk, are you sure?"

"Absolutely."

"What are you going to do?"

"I'm still working on that part. If I don't kill him first, I'll find out who sent him." Myk managed a smile. "I told you I was getting close to them, didn't I?"

Myk knew he was onto something. The appearance of an assassin confirmed it. As the man in the chairlift came closer, Myk discreetly removed the basket at the end of the shaft of the ski pole. He grasped the pole and looked at Jen. "Are you ready?"

She nodded with tears in her eyes while her hands trembled. "Myk—I am so sorry. I never should have asked you to . . ."

"It's okay, Jen," he interrupted. Then, with a sudden urgency, he exclaimed, "Jump. Now!"

As Jen fell from the chairlift to the powdery snow below, Myk launched the ski pole like an Olympic javelin thrower. The snow erupted around Jen in an explosion of white flakes as she crashed into a huge pile of snow. The assassin flinched as the ski pole penetrated his board pants and gashed him across his thigh. He pulled out his weapon and took aim. Jen landed safely and scrambled to her feet, skiing her way into the cover of the dense forest.

The man fired off several shots at the empty chairlift. Myk had quickly hopped off the chair and grabbed the bar below the seat and was hanging on underneath the chairlift while using the seat as a shield against the shots. He drew the fire of the assassin while Jen escaped into the thick of the aspen trees. The assassin couldn't get off a clean shot at either of them. His boss would not be pleased. The chairlift moved farther and farther away. Myk dropped from the chairlift to the snow below. The killer finally had a clean shot and took aim but was too late again. Myk dove behind the massive support pole of the chairlift as sparks from the ricochet pinged off the metal pole.

Myk peered around the pole to check if the assassin was still there. He began buckling his snowboard. The hunted was now the hunter. This was his first chance at gaining solid intel on who had put the hit on him, but he would need to capture him alive. As Myk finished strapping on the snowboard, he saw the assassin jump from the chairlift and start his way down the hill. Myk slid his snowboard out of the open slopes and into the cover of the trees. He was flying down the hill, carving and dodging his way around the huge, leaf-barren aspen trees as he tried to catch up. The assassin turned and spotted Myk descending through the tree line. He fired off six rapid rounds. Shards of bark and wood splinters exploded around Myk as he flew through the trees. He looked up and saw the assassin going full speed down the slopes while the panicked skiers cleared a path for the crazed man firing a gun. Myk couldn't let him get away, but he would never catch him if he stayed in the slow, thick snow in the trees.

Myk turned out to the quicker, compact snow of the groomed slopes to gain more speed, rarely using the edge of his board to slow down. He pointed it straight down the hill and let it fly. Myk noticed the assassin had pocketed his gun so as to avoid the attention of the crowds at the ski lodge. He coaxed his board to go faster as the assassin bounded up the steps to the oversized wood deck and through the doors to the lodge. Myk flew recklessly down the slopes, dashing around some startled skiers. He approached the lodge at full speed and quickly turned the board on the edge of his heels to stop. A massive wave of snow came flying from underneath the board, spraying snow at the patrons that were on the deck eating lunch. He shouted out, "Sorry!" as he unbuckled his board and sprinted up the steps to the lodge.

Myk slammed through the doors and felt the warm air inside the lodge whisk across the cold skin of his unshaven face. He immediately spotted the assassin, who was now sprinting toward the parking lot. The lunch-going crowd peered down from the upper deck at the commotion below as the assassin shoved children and servers out of his way. The historic lodge was supported by massive hand-hewn redwood timbers with huge hammer and beam trusses forty feet above. The extraordinary building had housed the first trek of silver miners who founded the town in the late 1800s. No doubt those early pioneers would have been astonished to see their blue-collar town turned into a world-class resort for the elite. Desperate, Myk snatched a large food tray from a table, took two quick steps, and hurled it at the man with all his might. The large plastic rectangular tray sailed vertically, end over end, like a bad Frisbee throw. The hard food tray smacked the hit man in the back of the neck and sent him face first to the floor.

The assassin spun around to his back and fired off three rapid shots at Myk. One of the bullets ricocheted a foot from his ear. The loud sound of banging gunshots sent the lunch crowd of skiers into a frenzy. They scattered in all directions, like bugs fleeing the wrath of a child with a magnifying glass. In the pandemonium, the assassin stumbled out of the lodge and ran to the small parking lot in front of the Monaco Ski Resort. Myk was right behind him and gaining ground. The assassin ran across the street and weaved his way through a row of cars. Myk darted through the exit doors and ran after the fleeing assassin as fast as he could. He could see the man was heading toward the front entry of the ski resort, so he changed course. If he used the shortcut through the side entrance, he could catch him in the lobby. Myk's calculations were right. The assassin was entering the front entrance at the same time Myk went through the side entry. He would confront him in the wide-open, opulent lobby.

The assassin never saw what hit him. He had been looking behind him when Myk tackled him running full speed, like a defensive right end sacking the quarterback from his blind side. The assassin let out loud groan as the two men crashed into the large check-in counter of the front lobby. Resort guests scattered away from the two fighting men while a few teenage boys simultaneously snatched their phones and shuffled backward to record the fight from a safe distance. Myk landed two quick blows to the man's midsection and then caught him square in the jaw with a solid right hook. The dazed assassin stumbled backward, caught his balance, and countered with a roundhouse kick with his right foot. Myk caught the man's foot midair and held it in place while he kicked the assassin as hard as he could in the groin. The man doubled over and twisted to the floor in agony. Just as Myk was ready to pounce, the man spun and pulled out his Glock. Myk quickly dodged out of the assassin's aim, shifted his weight to his right foot, and kicked the gun out of his hand. The Glock slid across the hardwood floor that had faded blue lines of six-foot social distance reminders painted on it.

Myk turned and lunged for the gun. As he grabbed the gun and spun back, the assassin bolted out the front door. Myk gave chase as the resort guests remained captivated. The teenagers, with exciting fight footage and aspirations of instant fame on YouTube, followed behind. Myk slammed through the front door just as the assassin ran from under the porte cochere and into the street. Myk raised the gun, took aim at the killer's leg, and yelled at all the bystanders to take cover. He squeezed the trigger just as the assassin turned headfirst into an oncoming truck. His body sailed through the air like a limp rag doll being tossed from a playful dog's mouth and landed on the hard, icy area alongside the road. The group of three boys who followed looked away from their phones that were recording the action and uttered in unison, "Whoa!"

Myk cursed as he ran toward the assassin, whose right leg was contorted at an angle human limbs were not meant to bend. The right side of his face was bloodied and mashed, and the man began to spit up blood. Myk bent down and asked, "Who do you work for?" The assassin turned, and Myk noticed blood oozing from his eye socket. "Who sent you?"

The man gasped, and Myk heard a gurgling sound coming from his lungs.

Myk got closer and leaned in. The man opened his mouth and managed to utter two words: "Heinrich Mueller." He began to convulse for a few seconds before his body stiffened and then became motionless.

"Shit." Myk searched the man's pockets and pulled out a set of car keys and a pack of gum, but nothing that would help identify him. He heard the sound of sirens in the distance, then pulled out his phone and dialed the number for his agency.

Director David Adelberg ran the Triple Canopy agency. Adelberg had previously been the director of the FBI before stepping down after he embarrassed the US Congress's Intelligence Committee. Adelberg had ruffled the feathers of the committee's leader, who responded by coming after Adelberg with a vengeance. The leader had tried for years to manufacture dirt on Director Adelberg but could never get anything to stick. Then, Director Adelberg made the mistake of calling an audible. His top agent, Myk Miles, had a direct line on a high-profile target they had been tracking for years. If they waited for approval, they would surely lose the top man on the FBI's most wanted list. Adelberg gave the green light for the operation, and Myk and his team eliminated a mass murderer that had eluded authorities for a decade. It was just the thing the Intelligence Committee was waiting for to finally get rid of Adelberg.

But things didn't turn out as the Intelligence Committee had planned. They subpoenaed Myk, who told the committee's leader over the phone that he would testify that Director Adelberg gave him direct orders to proceed with the operation. Myk told them he even had a recording of Adelberg's orders to him. That was all the committee needed. They went on all the networks and began prosecuting Adelberg in the court of public opinion. Had the committee done their homework on Myk, they would have easily learned that Myk would have walked through fire for David Adelberg. But the

Intelligence Committee was full of self-important politicians that loved to hear the sound of their own voices, so they took Myk's bait and ran.

There was no chance Myk would ever turn on Adelberg—he was like a father to Myk, who had been raised by a single mother. Since Myk had already decided to take the fall for Adelberg, he thought he would have some fun while he was at it. He came up with a plan to embarrass the committee. When the Intelligence Committee called him to testify in their highly publicized hearing, Myk walked the plank for Adelberg. He told the members at the Intelligence Committee hearing that Adelberg gave him explicit orders not to carry out the operation. He testified that he disobeyed a direct order from Adelberg and carried out the mission independently. The committee was left speechless while a nationwide audience watched.

The next day, social media exploded with the pictures of a wide-eyed committee with ghost faces staring blankly. Myk served twelve months at Fort Leavenworth Military Prison and was treated like a celebrity his entire sentence. His girlfriend, Jen, was a frequent visitor and was given very liberal visitation rights. Adelberg retired a few months later with a full pension and benefits. He was hired the same year at double his previous salary by Triple Canopy, an exclusive private intelligence company that only worked for the US Department of Defense. Myk was brought on board Triple Canopy immediately after serving his time in Leavenworth.

Director David Adelberg answered on the second ring.

"Director, it's Myk."

"I thought you were on vacation."

"I am. I'm in Park City. I must be getting close because they sent an assassin while I was on the slopes with Jen. Luckily, they sent a guy from the B-squad though . . . dumbass tried to shoot us from a chairlift."

"Are you and Jen okay? Any collateral damage?"

"We're fine. No damage that I know of."

"What happened?" Adelberg asked.

"Apparently our guy never learned to look both ways before you cross the street. He got obliterated by a truck."

"That's unfortunate. Did you get anything out of him?"

"He only managed to give me the name Heinrich Mueller before he died. No ID, of course, but I've got his gun and a set of car keys." Even though the car was probably stolen, or had a fake registration. Myk looked up as a swarm of red and blue sirens approached. "The authorities just arrived. I'll need to call you back."

"Okay. Good work, Myk. I'll get a forensics team up there shortly. Don't let the locals touch anything. Something has come up in San Francisco, so I'll need you to catch a flight tomorrow. I'll get your itinerary sent to you tonight."

"Okay." Myk had been scheduled on a flight to Oregon tonight; it was going to be the first time he met his uncle Levi. He'd have to reschedule. Now though, he slid his phone into his pocket and pulled out his identification, which he held high above his head as he walked to greet the first officer on the scene. Myk saw the officer swipe the touch screen on his front dash as he slowly exited his patrol car. The patrol car tilted as the middle-aged, overweight sheriff stood up.

Myk reached forward and handed the sheriff his identification. After a quick glance he studied Myk's face and peered at his identification. He handed his ID back and asked, "So Mike, our department is getting flooded with 911 calls about gunshots and a brawl. What's the situation?"

Myk replied, "My name is pronounced 'Mick'—"

The sheriff turned his palms up as he interrupted, "My apologies, Agent Miles."

"No worries." Myk shrugged his shoulders. He was used to the pronunciation of his name getting botched. "It's a tough name. Czechoslovakian. Myk is short for Mykel."

"Ahh, okay," the sheriff grunted. "I see that you're with Triple Canopy eh?"

The Department of Defense had a long list of contractors to use when they didn't want to get their hands dirty from any blowback. Each of these private contractors had their own specialty. If they needed intelligence gathering, a call was placed to a company called G4. For low-level security or bodyguards, Orion was brought in. But the most dangerous and difficult missions only went to Triple Canopy. By current Department of Defense standards, missions contracted to Triple Canopy were deemed impossible. Triple Canopy employed only the elite performers of the Special Forces and the Navy Seals—the best of the best.

Myk put his identification back in his pocket and replied, "Big Brother is sending their forensic team. I don't think they'll find anything." Myk pointed to the corpse. "Guy was an assassin."

The sheriff's eyes widened as he looked Myk up and down. "So it's true—y'all at Triple Canopy are the badasses from Special Forces!"

*There's a mangled body lying next to us and he wants to strike up a conversation about Triple Canopy?* "Somebody's gotta dirty their hands nowadays, right?" Myk replied.

The sheriff chuckled. "Ain't that the truth, brother! Well, God bless you, Myk!" The sheriff rounded the vehicle and walked toward the dead assassin. He looked at the corpse and asked, "What happened?"

As Myk began to brief the sheriff, he felt the phone in his pocket vibrate from a text. He glanced at the screen and began to worry about Jen. For the next ten minutes, Myk gave the authorities every detail he could remember and then began a slow jog back to his condo.


Myk remembered when he had told Jen what he did for a living. They talked in bed until an hour before dawn the following morning. Then they moved the conversation to his balcony in their bathrobes to watch the sky change from black to dark indigo and then to light auburn until finally, the bright morning sun filled the sky and chased them back indoors.

Relationships were highly discouraged in his line of work. He would not be a man that could come home and talk about his day at work. "I am fine with that, Myk," Jen had told him. He would be gone for long stints to hostile parts of the world, and he would not be able to tell her where he was. "You're worth the wait, Myk—besides, it'll give me the time and freedom to further my career!" she had told him. His career would be a mystery to her. "That's okay, Myk, it'll give us stories and adventures to talk about when you retire!" she had replied with a grin. The more he'd divulged to her, the more she was drawn in. He'd told her that even her life could be in danger. "I don't care—I love you!" He'd told her that he was fiercely independent—to a fault. She chuckled. "You think I don't already know that!" It was something he took pride in, until his therapist convinced him that it wasn't healthy to be completely independent. Jen agreed. He'd confessed to her that he was a broken man. "My love will heal you," she had said as she placed her hand on his heart. He had never been so open and vulnerable with a woman before. She was different. Yes, they all wanted to "fix" him, but she was genuine.

Myk sat on the bed, hesitant to read the note Jen left. Part of him wanted to toss the letter in the trash unread. He stared at the letter and contemplated what he should do. He was already feeling the pain of her departure. He set his pride aside, leaned over, picked up the note, and began to read. She explained that she had never been so terrified in her life—her trauma on the ski lift helped her see things clearly. She apologized for overestimating her ability to cope with fear and death. The thought of facing that on a daily basis while he was away on missions and never knowing if she would see him again was something she couldn't cope with. She went on to say that when he had explained what he did for a living she'd had no concept of what that meant in real life until today. She could never ask him to give up his occupation for her, and after what she witnessed today, she was confident the country was in good hands. Once she had gotten to safety and caught her breath, she was awestruck by what she had just witnessed. In the face of such imminent danger, she sensed no fear in him. It was incomprehensible to her that a man could be so fearless.

Myk crumpled the note in his palm and tossed it in the trash can. He pulled his cell phone out of his pocket and dialed his uncle Levi and told him that he had been called to an urgent matter in San Francisco. Their first-ever meeting would need to be delayed a few more days.

# CHAPTER 2

# SAN FRANCISCO, CALIFORNIA

Myk waited until his suspect had descended halfway down the escalator before he stepped on and began to follow him. Myk wore a San Francisco 49ers Super Bowl 2020 sweatshirt and matching cap that he had purchased from the airport when he arrived from Park City. He still hadn't shaved in the past two days and was sporting a pair of black-rimmed aviator sunglasses, denim jeans, and a well-worn pair of Timberland boots. With his six-foot-four frame, he had challenges blending in. As he rode the escalator down to the main floor, Myk punched numbers on his phone and waited for the connection.

"Director Adelberg, it's Myk. The suspect just picked up a package, and he's on his way out of the store."

"Okay, thanks for the update."

Myk stepped off the escalator and stayed a comfortable distance behind Jamal. "Why did the FBI pass him along to us?" Usually the FBI only called Myk's organization when they didn't want to get their hands dirty.

"They received an anonymous call that Jamal is going to use a biological weapon, so they got a warrant and took him in. They searched his apartment but didn't find anything. The FBI director called me and said they were short on manpower this weekend and he didn't want to take any chances on a biological threat. So we need to keep a watch on him for a few days."

"He looks Middle Eastern. Where's he from?"

"He was born here . . . the guy is a loner. His father bolted back to Pakistan when he was two years old and left his mother to raise him. He attends the Masjid Darussalam Mosque in downtown San Francisco. Apparently, he got his panties in a wad a few years ago when the mosque decided to knock down the eight-foot wall that separates the men from the women."

Myk chuckled. "How sad, a mosque actually makes an effort to get women on equal ground, and he takes offense."

"Call me if anything develops. If he has a biological weapon, then we need find out where he's hiding it."

"Will do."

Myk pressed the end button and zipped up his jacket as the chilling San Francisco breeze picked up. Myk followed Jamal out of the store and down Polk Street. He took a deep breath as the smells from Fisherman's Wharf filled his lungs. He waited across the street as Jamal turned down McAllister Street toward the Superior Courthouse. While Jamal pulled the camera out of his pack and began to attach the large zoom lens, Myk purchased a coffee from the corner café and kept Jamal under tight surveillance. He leaned against the marble-clad wall of the café and took his first sip. The smooth taste of the slow-roasted Chilean coffee beans warmed his insides and revived his senses.

A woman crossing the street and staring directly at Myk caught his attention. She had fluorescent-orange dyed streaks in her hair and a spiked collar around her neck with matching spiked bracelets. Other than dressing like she had walked directly off the stage of a punk rock band, she was attractive. Her tall-heeled leather boots made her already curvy hips sway even more as she continued to walk in a direct path toward Myk. Her dark blue eyes were accentuated with heavy blue eyeliner. Myk peered back to check on Jamal as the woman approached.

He gave her a puzzled look and said, "Excuse me." Myk looked at her as she raised her hand to give him an envelope. He asked,

"How can I help you?"

The girl stopped chewing her mouthful of gum long enough to reply. "Some guy just came up to me and gave me five hundred dollars to give this envelope to you."

Myk grabbed the manila envelope and scanned up and down the street. "Who was it? Where is he?" he asked.

The girl turned and looked back. She paused her precipitous chewing and said, "He's gone."

Myk ripped open the envelope as he asked, "What did he look like? What was he wearing?"

She replied, "Some Arab dude in his twenties, I think. He had a heavy accent. His car looked like the Batmobile. He pulled alongside the curb, rolled down his window, and said he would give me five hundred cash just to hand this to you."

"Can you spot his car anywhere?"

She looked around and replied, "Nope."

Myk unfolded the letter from inside the envelope and read:

MY NAME IS YASSER. I AM THE ANONYMOUS CALLER WHO TIPPED OFF THE FBI. I KNOW YOU HAVE JAMAL UNDER SURVEILLANCE. IF YOU WANT TO PREVENT HIM FROM UNLEASHING A DEADLY VIRUS ON YOUR CITY, MEET ME IN TWO HOURS AT UNION SQUARE. LOSE THE GUYS THAT ARE FOLLOWING YOU, AND COME ALONE.

Myk immediately looked up from the letter and scanned the area for anyone following him. He folded the letter and put it in his pocket. Myk's eyes narrowed as he stared at Jamal across the street. *What are you up to Jamal?*

# CHAPTER 3

---

# TEHRAN, IRAN

Jaafar had given his pound of flesh for his beliefs. In his case, several pounds of flesh—literally. The old man's right ear had been blown off along with half of his right leg in an assassination attempt on him when he was younger. Had he not run for the safety of the parking garage stairwell, he would have perished too. Jaafar wore a prosthetic leg that was attached above where his right knee would have been. He had no hearing in his mangled ear, but it was his hands and eyesight that were critical to Jaafar's occupation. And for the past three decades, Jaafar Venzi's eyesight and hands had worked with the precision of a Swiss watchmaker. It was his child's small fingers that had allowed him to make his bombs substantially smaller—and that brought him to notoriety. His meticulous methods made his bombs the most sought-after explosives on the planet. One look at his disfigured face gave him instant credibility in the world of death and murder. His bombs and techniques had found their way to Indonesia, India, Iraq, Jerusalem, and Syria.

But his days of bomb making were over. He had moved on to something entirely new. Jaafar had secretly been given access to biological weapons from the Communist Chinese Regime, who blamed the US for turning the world against them because of the COVID-19 pandemic. The tide was changing in Iran. With the US sanctions putting a stranglehold on their economy and the groundswell of deep unrest in Iran—especially from the swelling population of the younger generation suffering from thirty percent unemployment— Iran's leadership was at a tipping point.

Jaafar walked along the water's edge of the massive pond of blue water on the grounds of the Mosque of Isfahan. High-powered water jets sprayed streams of water into the shallow pools of water. He sat down on a smooth marble bench and gazed up at the historic mosque while he waited for his son, Malcolm, to show up. The Mosque of Isfahan was considered a masterpiece of Persian architecture and was even pictured on the back of Iranian currency. Built in 1611, it had become famous for its beautiful calligraphic inscriptions and seven-color mosaic tiles. The ancient Persians were looking to create a unique identity to Iranian architecture when they designed the four-iwan format. Four tall towers stood at the entrance to the mosque and could be seen for miles. Jaafar looked down from the mosque and spotted his son Malcolm walking resolutely toward him.

Malcolm was a professor of history at the University of Tehran. Like many of the students that he taught, Malcolm did not subscribe to the same policies of his father and the religious fanatics that ran the country, but self-preservation kept him from being outspoken, so he rarely communicated with his father. Jaafar stood to greet him.

Malcolm shook a stiff index finger at him. "Sit down, you old fool!"

Jaafar took a step back and furrowed his eyebrows as the palms of his hands turned upward in an attempt to embrace him. "Malcolm, is that any way to greet your father?"

Malcolm swiped his father's hands aside and glared back. "What have you done with him?"

"What are you talking about?"

"You know damn well what I am talking about. Raji said she received a text message from Yasser. He said he is in San Francisco. Why is he in the US?"

"Your sister knows nothing. If he is in the US, then it is by his own choice."

Malcolm sneered as he shook his head, "You really are a fool aren't you! Raji is not a little girl who you can use anymore. Frankly, I'm surprised she hasn't used her bomb-making skills on you for brainwashing her son! Raji knows full well that it was you who sent Yasser to the United States."

"That's nonsense, Malcolm."

Malcolm shook his head again. This time more noticeably. His brows furrowed as he replied, "Her husband is the commander in chief of our entire military—I think her info is good!"

Jaafar interrupted, "Ali would never divulge top secrets to her. I am sure Yasser is perfectly safe wherever he is."

Malcolm snapped back, "It's your will that brought him to the US. You know that Yasser is a very impressionable young man. Raji and I have told you to stay away from him. Use someone else to do your bidding."

Jaafar gave a forced smile and sat. "You know not of what you speak, Malcolm."

The wrinkles in Malcolm's forehead came screaming to the surface as he gave his father a questioning look. "You think I'm stupid? Yasser looks up to you . . . feels sorry for you, with your peg leg and disfigured face."

Jaafar sternly replied, "The explosion that maimed me was a sign."

"That's right, you fool. A warning sign to quit spewing out your hateful dogma before another member of our family gets killed. Please, I implore you, Father." Malcolm took a deep breath. "Contact Yasser and tell him to come home. He will listen to you."

"I'll do no such thing."

Malcom shifted his balance and shrugged his shoulders slightly. "Then tell me how I can contact him so I can reason with him."

Jaafar shook his head. "I have no way to contact him. It is out of my hands now. Perhaps this will finally bring you to your knees to exercise a little more faith."

Malcolm's eyes narrowed as he glared at his father. He slowly shook his head and lowered his tone. "The only person who's going to be on his knees is you, begging for Raji's forgiveness if Yasser does not return. But no forgiveness will be granted . . . ever. Do you understand me?" Malcolm paused and stared. "What you do is not out of some sense of faith—it is revenge for that metal leg of yours and my mother's death! But that was your fault—they were there to kill *you*! Thank God that bomber saved Raji and me. If you won't help, then maybe Ali will!"

Malcolm was surprised to see his sister Raji walking toward him. He had told her about his meeting with their father, but he hadn't expected her to show up. Raji had not spoken to Jaafar in over four years. Since the day after she and Yasser had gotten into a tearful argument. She tried by all her powers of persuasion to convince her son that his grandfather was evil, that he was being manipulated by him—just like she had been manipulated by him when she was a child. That was the day she realized she had lost her son to violent extremists because of her father. Raji stood in front of her brother. Her face was completely expressionless. She appeared as calm as a crystal mountain lake on a windless, sunny day. Malcolm gave her a brotherly hug while he spoke softly, "I tried Raji. Apparently, blood isn't thicker than blind faith. Perhaps you'll have better luck." He walked away as Raji approached her father.

Jaafar stood again and outstretched his hands. "Malcom didn't tell me you would be coming."

It took every ounce of self-control to keep her rage tamped down. Other than her dilated pupils, there was no physical sign of the unadulterated hate that pulsed through her veins. If there was any chance of her convincing Jaafar to contact her son Yasser, she would have to exercise extreme control of her emotions. She sat calmly next to her father even though her insides recoiled when her leg brushed against his. She cleared her throat and spoke. "Mother died when I was so young that my real memories have faded and I have nothing but her photographs. My husband is only a shadow in my life. You abandoned me when I became a young woman, when my fingers grew too big to assemble your bombs and you no longer needed me. It made me feel so insignificant. When I was finally allowed to attend public school and made a friend, she and her family were snatched up by the Iranian regime. Yasser is all that I have left, Father."

Now came the hard part. If she thought of the love she had for Yasser instead of the hate for her father, she could pull it off. If she put her hand on his leg, perhaps Jaafar could feel her love for Yasser. Raji summed up the courage and placed her hand on his thigh, just above the joint where his prosthetic was attached. "Please help me contact Yasser. I have a very strong sense that something bad is going to happen. You know, I have never asked anything of you, and I will never ask for anything again. Please, Father, tell me where he is?"

She brushed her long thick brown hair away from her face which put her almost-effervescent gold eyes on full display. Raji was one of the most prominent female figures in Iran. Her face was what most Iranians saw when they turned on the evening news. Her network proudly displayed her face on billboards throughout the country. Raji's features were stunning. Her glowing eyes had the effect of magnetic poles—once you looked at them, you couldn't turn away; they seemed to pull you in. Her smile was genuine, and her sparkling white teeth were a perfect contrast to her olive skin. A perfect face with one exception: a small scar that ran across the upper corner of her left eye. She had received the scar in the same explosion that had left her mother dead. As flawless as Raji was on the outside, inside, her soul was a ferocious caged tiger.

Her life was a mask. A perpetual lie. A decade of pent-up rage was ripping her apart. But it wasn't her loveless marriage to a husband she rarely saw that was the source of her tumult. She was ferociously independent and a free thinker. Not exactly safe for a woman living in Iran. Tragically, she lived in a society that taught that those attributes in women were a vice, not a virtue. She was a puppet. A puppet to her father that had used her tiny fingers as a child to help assemble his bombs. A puppet to a husband that used her as window dressing for the illusion of a happy family. And Raji was a puppet to the Iranian regime that put her on display every night on the national news in order to make their lies credible. The gorgeous, smiling puppet peddled the regime's lies and their censorship to a public that was growing more skeptical of its leaders by the day. Her beauty was surpassed only by her intellect and tenaciousness. It was a weekly occurrence for her to veer off script and slip in a few nuggets of truth during her newscasts. It was the only thing that kept her sane. It had become her secret life's ambition—to get the truth to the Iranian people. Iran had once been the envy of the Middle East, with a highly educated and sophisticated population. Iranians were heirs to a long and rich history steeped in the arts and literature, something they were very proud of. Now, the country was dominated by religious zealots, and women in Iran had few of the rights that women in the West enjoyed.

Raji dreamed of the day her people would take their country back from the religious rulers. Whenever possible, she would try to create doubt about the regime. Raji had known several in the media who had tried to do the same, but they were immediately "jailed" by the Iranian regime, never to be heard from again by family or friends. The fanatics that ruled Iran were not to be taken lightly. Dissidents were met with torture and death. Were it not for Raji's husband, who ran Iran's military, and her father's close ties to the ayatollah, she would have been permanently silenced long ago. But her popularity skyrocketed overnight from her very first broadcast. She was different than any broadcaster the Iranian public had ever seen. She was an overnight sensation. Somehow, Raji had developed such a rapport with the Iranian people that there was a general consensus among the public that she was one of them. Fearing a revolution of the masses, the regime tightened the reins on her and put her under constant surveillance.

It had been four years since she aborted her plans to flee the country with her son Yasser. It was her "aha" moment. She chose to forgo a life of freedom away from Iran to try and achieve freedom for her country from the tight grip of a hate-filled theocracy. Who else but her would ever be in the unique position to get the truth to the Iranian people without getting killed? So she made it her calling in life, and her fame skyrocketed even more. The regime had someone loved by the people to peddle their lies, and she had a platform, albeit a tiny and tenuous one, to help a people ruled by religious zealots. It was an unspoken understanding.

Raji cleared her throat and said in as soft and compassionate a voice as she could muster to a man she despised, "Father, please, please speak to Yasser, and tell him to come home." Her gold eyes stared unflinchingly at his until she noticed him look away. Jaafar grabbed her hand and was about to speak. Raji interrupted him. "Wait," she said. "Let me add one thing before you respond. I would like to make a deal. If you get Yasser back home, I will end my silence with you."

Jaafar breathed in deeply while he sat in silence. He hadn't heard her voice or seen her for years. He refused to look her in the eyes, which glowed even brighter when she was as passionate as she was now. Had it really been four years since he had seen her magical eyes in person? Her offer caught him off guard. Jaafar continued to look away. He gripped the bench so tight that his knuckles began to turn white. After another minute of silence, he said, "I can't help you, Raji." He waited for her to say something, but there was only silence. He avoided looking her in the eyes. Instead, he kept his gaze downward, staring at her perfectly manicured feet and her flawless, glossy red nails. He could feel her penetrating glare on the back of his head. *Why hasn't she moved? Why doesn't she say something?* The red-glossed toes remained motionless. Then, the awkward silence ended with the sound of sand grinding against the concrete as Raji's feet turned gracefully and walked away. Only then did Jaafar look up. He watched her long, thick, dark hair and red silk hijab blow in the wind as she floated away like a ghost hovering through the dense fog. Raji was resolute. The only question that remained for her was whether it would be a bomb or a bullet. For the first time in weeks, she laughed—she shook her head as she thought about the irony of using a bomb to kill him.

As Raji descended down the steps to the parking lot, she saw Malcom leaning against the bus stop shelter with a cigarette drooping from his bottom lip. Malcolm's cigarette lit up bright auburn as he inhaled. Raji quickly strode down the concrete stairs and ran her open fingers through her long hair. She reached out for his cigarette and yanked it out of his hands. Raji's chest expanded as she inhaled deeply. She shook her head disappointedly and let out a thick cloud of smoke.

Malcolm asked, "I assume it didn't go well?"

Raji shot back, "Didn't go well?" Her eyes narrowed on her older brother. "It went smashingly! He has really simplified things for me now. It's quite easy, really. If Yasser dies, Father dies. I just can't decide if it'll be a bomb or a bullet."

Malcom's brows furrowed when he questioned, "Raji, he's our father. You can't really—"

Raji interrupted, "Father? Are you serious? You of all people should know, Malcolm. That beast with a metal leg sitting back on that bench is no father! Real fathers spend time with their children. Real fathers don't pay servants to dole out love and attention to their children. Real fathers don't teach their children how to murder inno-cent men, women, and children. Real fathers don't brainwash their grandchildren against their parent's wishes. No Malcolm, it didn't go well. Yasser is in the United States because of him." Raji paused as she slowly shook her head back and forth.

She took another hit on the cigarette and then exhaled resolutely. "Because of him, we had no mother, and a loveless childhood. Ali isn't much of a husband, and now the one thing that brought so much meaning to my life might be gone." Raji's eyes met Malcolm's. Their bond formed in childhood was stronger than ever. "If Yasser loses his life, then I'll take Jaafar's.

# CHAPTER 4

# SAN FRANCISCO, CALIFORNIA

Myk heard the familiar sound of a cable car and glanced down the street to see the iconic San Francisco trolley climbing up the steep hill toward him. He scanned over the handwritten note from Yasser one last time and slid it into his pocket. He carefully scrutinized the two other passengers who were waiting to board and wondered if Yasser was right—was someone actually following him? It had only been two days since the attempt on Myk's life. When the newly painted red cable car came to a stop, Myk stepped aboard and grabbed onto the stainless-steel overhead bar. The cable car operator torqued back on the gears extending through the middle of the floor, and the cable car, packed mostly with tourists clinging to both sides of the trolley, lurched forward and continued its ascent up toward Union Square in the heart of San Francisco. Myk looked back at the operator who tugged down on a thin rope as the metallic sound of the trolley bell clanged twice. Other than a young couple who clung to each other like honeymooners, Myk was the only one who had entered the cable car at the stop. While the trolley clacked noisily and methodically across the steel tracks, Myk glanced through the corridor of tall skyscrapers and caught a glimpse of Alcatraz off in the distance through a thin haze of fog as it sat perched above the water. Myk's short prison experience was a walk in the park compared to those who had served time in Alcatraz.

At Powell Street, the lumbering trolley squealed to a stop on its well-worn metal tracks. Myk stepped off and squeezed his way through the flock of people waiting to board. As evidenced by the crowds, San Francisco had clearly moved past the social distancing days of the pandemic. He walked across the street and looked up at the ninety-seven-foot-tall monument that stood in the middle of Union Square.

Myk continued up the concrete steps toward the monument, which had been dedicated to Admiral George Dewey and the United States Navy sailors for their victory at the Battle of Manila Bay during the Spanish-American War. Prior to that, Union Square had inherited its name from the pro-Union rallies that were held there on the eve of the Civil War. The mostly flat concrete plaza of Union Square was bordered with planters, bench seats, long rectangular grassy areas, and trees with thriving foliage along each side of its two-block plaza. The area surrounding Union Square was considered one of the premier shopping districts in the world and was constantly bustling with shoppers. Myk walked deliberately toward the designated meeting place at the monument. His eyes squinted as he slowly examined the multitude of people. He noticed that about a third of the plaza was occupied by some sort of art festival and estimated there were over seventy artists with their paintings propped up on easels and sculptors who had their work on display.

As Myk rounded the monument he spotted a man with his back to him wearing a baseball cap, a San Francisco Giants jacket, and a pair of brand-new white Adidas shoes. He briefly entertained the thought that he could be walking into a trap, but dismissed the idea.

Myk walked around to face the man leaning against the monument and instantly knew he was the source of the note in his pocket. He was a Middle Eastern-looking man in his early twenties, just under six feet tall with an athletic build, distinguished cheek bones, and two weeks' growth of facial hair. The giveaway was his sunglasses. His cap and jacket were obviously bought at a local store to blend in. Myk had noticed the creases still in the shirt from having recently been folded on the store shelf, but the expensive sunglasses didn't match the rest of his ensemble and were showing signs of wear. The man had on a pair of two-thousand-dollar Chrome Hearts Kufannaw sunglasses with their distinct floral dagger cross in between the two lenses. Myk pulled the note out of his pocket, held it in front of him, and confidently said, "I assume this is yours?"

The Middle Eastern man seemed somewhat surprised by Myk's bluntness. He stood up straight and looked away from Myk as he replied in a heavy Persian accent, "Thank you for coming." He turned and scanned across the crowd. "Were you followed?"

"No. How did you know I was watching Jamal?"

"Because I was watching him too."

Myk's head tilted to the side as his eyebrows furrowed. "What do you mean, 'watching' him?"

"I knew your government would follow Jamal, and I needed to warn someone about what he has planned."

Myk said tersely, "You could have just picked up the phone and called the FBI and avoided all this unnecessary cloak-and-dagger bullshit."

"I'm sorry Mr. . . ." Yasser hesitated, waiting for Myk to fill in the blank.

"You can call me Agent Miles."

Yasser nodded. "I arrived here from Iran two weeks ago, and I know very little about how your country operates. I was fairly certain that someone would be following Jamal since the FBI has already taken him into custody once."

Myk folded his arms and squinted his eyes. "I see. I assume you're the author of the note?"

"Yes."

"Your note said that Jamal has a biological weapon."

Yasser's eyes darted nervously back and forth from one end of Union Square to the other. "Jamal and I were sent here to start another pandemic with a mutated version of the COVID-19 strain, except this one is much more deadly."

Myk ran his fingers through his hair as he shook his head. "Two weeks ago you were on a plane to the US, presumably to kill innocent people, and now you've become a traitor to those who sent you. Why the change of heart?"

Yasser nodded as he put his shades back on. "If I was in your shoes, I would have my doubts too. I'm sure you heard how hard Iran was hit with the coronavirus. I personally witnessed the mass graves that very few people outside of Iran know about. Two of my best friends were buried in those graves. Iran grossly underreported the deaths—probably twenty times what they reported to the world. Hundreds of thousands of Iranians were killed by the pandemic last year. My grandfather as well as other leaders in Iran convinced me that the Americans were responsible for the virus in Iran. My mother tried to convince me otherwise, but when you've buried your two best friends—reason tends to fly out the window."

"Who is your grandfather?"

Yasser hesitated. There was an awkward silence before he responded, "Jaafar Venzi."

Myk cringed at the mention of his name. "Well, that erases any doubts about the seriousness of your operation. Your grandfather is a vile killer that has slaughtered innocent people for decades! How in the hell did you get mixed up in this Yasser? You don't strike me as a person who wants to bring calamity to this world. Would you be willing to help us locate the biological weapon that Jamal has?"

Yasser nodded. "Of course! That's why I reached out. I'll do what I can, but when I told Jamal that I was calling off the operation, he hid the two containers of the virus somewhere and said he was still going to release it. I honestly don't know where he's keeping it."

Myk folded his arms and said, "It'll be a hell of a lot easier with your help. You still haven't told me, why the change of heart?"

Yasser looked to the ground and put his hands in his pockets as if in deep thought. "My mother is the polar opposite of my grandfather. She's somewhat of a celebrity in Iran because of her nightly newscast. I suppose that being heavily influenced by my grandfather was my way of rebelling against my mother. But on the flight from Tehran, a man sat next to me—it was a defining moment. Perhaps he could sense I was weighted down by the thoughts of what I was about to embark on. What I had originally taken as the ignorant words of an uncompromising mother now came screaming back to me as I sat and listened to this man. I still wonder if it was chance that he happened to sit next to me."

"So what was it that he said that got you to see the light?"

"He told me that, like many in the radical Islam community, he had been taught that the only mistake Hitler made was that he didn't kill enough Jews and that the Jews were murderers and usurpers. Pretty much the same thing my grandfather taught me, and much to the contrary of my mother's personal beliefs. You have no idea what it's like growing up in Iran. The Iranian regime bludgeons into everyone's minds hate for Israel and the US. People like my mother and uncle have to go underground to inform people what's really happening in the world. All social media and news are controlled by the regime. The man told me about his trip to Jerusalem when he was my age and how his eyes were opened. He showed me pictures of his trip and talked about how the Koran had been twisted to meet the designs of malicious men." Yasser gazed off in the direction of the crowd gathered at the art festival and then turned back to Myk. "I boarded that flight as a jihadist but disembarked with my free will restored, wanting to know the truth. He told me not to take his word for it but to find out the truth for myself. He gave me his contact information and the address of the library. I never believed what my mother told me about how distorted the truth was by the Iranian regime until I stepped into the library in San Francisco."

Myk's face softened with a slight smile. "Okay, Yasser, you have my undivided attention. You do realize you'll never be able to return to Iran?"

Yasser nodded. "I know."

"Okay, tell me what Jamal's plan is."

Yasser shuffled his feet slightly. "Agent Miles, I wish I knew. Ever since I told him I was pulling the plug, he's gone off on his own."

Myk shook his head. "Damn. Alright then, what was the original plan?"

"The plan was to be executed two weeks from today. The first container was to be sprayed in the boarding areas in the San Francisco airport. He was given specific instructions to release the virus at the boarding areas of the flights to Jerusalem, New York, and Los Angeles in order to quickly spread the virus. The other container was to be used on the subway. Jamal knows he's being watched, so I'm sure he's made different plans for the virus. Here's a zip drive of all the information I have. I hope it will help."

Myk took the drive from Yasser—and that's when he saw it. Before a conscious thought even entered his mind, Myk's body reacted to the reflection of a laser light that he saw on the left lens of Yasser's sunglasses. For most people, a hand on a burning surface causes an involuntary reaction; an impulse moves through the neurons and sends a message to the brain. Myk Miles had an entirely different set of impulses.

Most people refer to it as "being in the zone." Hall of Fame legend Michael Jordan said when he was in the zone, the basket appeared bigger and everything seemed to slow down. For Myk Miles, the moment he caught a glimpse of the red laser in Yasser's sunglasses, he went into the zone; everything slowed down for him, as if he were the only one moving and everyone else stood as frozen spectators. Myk instantly leaned to his left, dropped to one knee, and drew his weapon in one sinuous flow. He squeezed off three rapid rounds before he heard the sound of Yasser's body crashing to the concrete.

The advantage of a laser scope on a rifle is the pinpoint accuracy it provides the marksman. The disadvantage is that any chance of camouflage is forfeited. Myk's eyes immediately followed the red laser right back to its source—a gunman perched on the rooftop. Even the best of marksman would have had difficulty hitting the target with a handgun at this distance with perfect wind conditions. Fortunately, one of Myk's three bullets hit something. His first round barely caught the assassin on the right side of his face, partially severing his ear.

The crowd at Union Square went into an instantaneous frenzy at the sounds of shots being fired. Many dropped to the ground, while others ran in all directions like a dazed herd of gazelles not knowing what part of the tall grass their predator would attack from. Myk sprang up from his position and quickly glanced at Yasser's body lying behind him. He holstered his weapon and called Director Adelberg as he sprinted toward the building the shots were fired from. Myk ran across the street and almost got hit by a taxi. He effortlessly hurdled a trash can and burst into the building where the shooter was located and ran to the back of the store for the stairwell. Trails of blood were on the stairs, and a handprint of blood was on the push bar of the metal exit door. Myk kicked the door open and stepped into the alley with his weapon drawn. He spotted the assassin running away, clutching the right side of his head. Myk yelled out, "Freeze, you stupid fuck!"

The man kept running. Myk needed information, so he couldn't kill him. He shot the fleeing man in the back of his left leg, causing him to immediately topple to the ground. The assassin began crawling on his hands and knees and attempted to reach for a weapon strapped to his left pant leg. Myk shook his head in disbelief and then shot the hand of the assassin. A cloud of red blood erupted in the air like a popped water balloon. The man turned on his back and put his hands above his head while he groaned in pain. Myk continued to aim his weapon as he approached. The assassin was panting and out of breath. Myk noticed the assassin attempt to press his dangling ear back to the side of his head. His thick brown hair was matted and drenched with blood. Myk stood over the bleeding mess of a man who had his eyes closed. Myk nudged him with his foot. "Look at my face or I'll put a bullet in your groin."

The man groaned.

"Stop your whimpering or your life ends right here!"

The man opened his eyes and looked up at Myk who had his arm extended and a gun pointing directly at his forehead.

"This is what defeat looks like, you moron! Now tell me, how did you know about Yasser?"

The assassin mumbled, "What? Who's Yasser?"

Myk barked back, "Don't play games with me! That's the guy you just shot and killed, dumbass!"

The bloodied man looked at him, puzzled, and replied, "That bullet was meant for you."

Myk paused and redirected his train of thought. "Who hired you?" he demanded.

"He was older and taller than you. I have no idea who you pissed off or what dirty information you've got on them, but somebody with deep pockets really wants you dead."

Myk's eyes narrowed and his teeth clenched as he shook his head. He picked up his right foot and stepped down hard onto the wounded leg of the gunman. He dug his heel into the leg and twisted. The man screamed in agony. Myk yelled at him as he waved his gun back and forth like an index finger. "You picked the wrong guy to play games with, asshole! Give me a name or I'll introduce a source of pain you never knew existed." Myk put all of his weight on his right foot. The man gasped for breath.

"I don't know. I swear to God he's a spook like you."

Myk tilted his head and furrowed his eyebrows. "He's an agent?"

"Someone in your government put a hit on you, man. I don't know which agency he's with, but he paid me a lot of money to see you dead."

"How do you know this?"

"I can spot a government agent when I see one."

Myk leaned down and searched the man's pockets and retrieved a cell phone. He placed the barrel of his gun on the assassin's temple and calmly demanded, "Give me the bank and account they wired the money to." After recording the information, he said, "Consider this your lucky day. If you don't bleed out first, I'm going to let you live." Myk put zip ties around the man's hands and ankles and then secured him to a steel pipe so he couldn't escape. He called in the location to his agency and then left to check on Yasser.

As he walked with a slow, resolute pace, Myk took in a deep breath and began to think about what transpired—someone knew his position at Union Square. There was one person he knew he could trust. Whether or not she would actually be forthcoming on any information was an entirely different matter. Myk's entire life consisted of his mother concealing deep secrets of their family history. He didn't learn that his mother had been a Mossad agent until he was in high school. That was when he learned the real truth about how his father was killed. His mother told him when he was younger that his father died in a car accident—a partial truth at best. It was true that his father died in a car. But he was killed by an assassin's bullet in London, not by a car crash. Myk continued to uncover more and more as he grew older. He pulled his cell phone out and dialed the number. After seven rings the tired voice of a female answered, "Hello."

"Mom—it's Myk."

She quickly asked, "Is everything okay? Did you meet your uncle Levi yet?"

"Not yet. Director Adelberg needed me in San Francisco because the FBI was shorthanded for a few days. I rescheduled my flight for tomorrow. Did you say that Uncle Levi worked for Mossad?"

There was a long pause before she answered. "Yes, why do you ask?"

"Something came up with this investigation in San Francisco that I'd like to pick his brain on."

"I don't think Levi will be any help, Myk. He hasn't been involved in espionage in about thirty years. Something got to him."

Myk asked, "What was it?"

Myk's mother, Hannah, paused again. "You know it's difficult for me to talk about these things. Our family has suffered a lot. Levi and I left about the same time—after your father was murdered in London. Both Levi's brothers were violently murdered right in front of him. If I didn't show up when I did, Levi would have been killed alongside your father. Tell me, what's behind the questions, Myk?"

"An assassin tried to kill me when I was in Park City a few days ago, and moments ago, a sniper tried to kill me."

"Oh my God! Are you okay?"

"I'm fine. Very few people know I'm in San Francisco, so this has to be someone that's well connected."

"I don't like this one bit, Myk. You need to talk to Director Adelberg about getting out of the limelight for a while. Did anyone get hurt?"

"Sadly, a young Iranian man got killed with the bullet that was meant for me. I've got to run now, Mom."

"Okay, be safe. Give my regards to Levi for me."

# CHAPTER 5

## TEHRAN, IRAN

When Raji arrived at her news station that day, she felt something was off. Everyone at the station went through their same routines, discussing lead stories, listening to what perspective the producer wanted pushed, and discussing the usual small talk about the happenings in Iran and the world. But she sensed her producer was more courteous than normal, less edgy.

Fifteen minutes before going on air, her intuitions were confirmed. Her producer informed Raji that they were going with a different lead story. The American media was in a frenzy over an Iranian that was shot and killed in San Francisco. He feigned sorrow as he informed her that it was her son, Yasser. As if it was any consolation, he said that Yasser would be a national hero to Iran and that his death would be further evidence that the West was indeed the Great Satan. Stunned, Raji sat stoic. She watched her producer's mouth move, but she heard no words—her mind was elsewhere. Raji didn't know how long her mind had wandered or that she had been staring blankly into space, but when she felt his hand on her shoulder and heard him say, "Raji, are you listening?" she finally snapped back to the present and questioned, "My son, Yasser, is dead?"

"Yes," her producer replied.

"How did he die?"

"It's all right here in the story. They are loading it on the prompters as we speak."

Raji stood and clenched her fists. She gritted her teeth and said, "Over the years, you have asked me to go on the air and tell our people so many lies that I have lost count. You've asked me to paint a picture of the world that is blatantly false. You cannot deny it. I am no fool, I know I am just a puppet, but this story will be told by pulling someone else's strings—not mine, not today!" Her thoughts instantly turned to her father as she strode past her producer who tried half-heartedly to stop her.

From behind her, she heard him say, "They told me they would pay you five years' salary if you ran with the story."

Raji just kept walking. *Of course they did*, she thought. Raji drove home with a frenzied and sorrowful mind.

It was tempting: the irony of the bomb maker suffering the same fate he had inflicted on thousands of innocent people. Except Jaafar was far from innocent. It was incomparable—the satisfaction she would feel in blowing him to pieces, as opposed to ending his life with a single bullet through his evil skull. Raji set her pride aside and decided that it would be a bullet rather than a bomb that would end her father's existence. As expert as Raji was at bomb making, she wouldn't take the risk if there were even the remotest of possibilities that there would be any collateral damage. Besides, it had been decades since she used her adolescent fingers to wire bombs for her father. He simply wasn't worth the risk. Her father's last moment would be seeing his daughter raise her arm and squeeze a trigger, and feeling the "ping" of pain as a bullet passed through his skull.

Raji pulled into the garage of her contemporary, posh custom home and immediately walked to her master suite. The gun safe was located in a secret room attached to her husband's closet. Any Iranian citizen caught with a weapon would receive instant jail time without a trial. Being married to the regime's top commander had a few perks—not many. Raji slid her husband's clothes across the rack to access the door to his secret room. She gazed at the sky-blue colored suit that was still swaying on its hanger and reflected. It was the suit he wore for their wedding. He never wore it again. Nothing could have prepared Raji for what she had encountered the night of her wedding.

Technically speaking, it wasn't an arranged marriage. But in Raji's mind, it was. Her husband, Ali Isma, came from a highly religious family that had strong ties to the Iranian Revolution. Ali's family began coming to the house after Raji's mother was killed. Ali's father and Raji's father spent hours together behind closed doors every time they came to the house. Ali's mother took an immediate liking to Raji. It was the first time that Raji had felt any semblance of affection since the passing of her mother. Ali and Malcom, Raji's brother, would always run off and play together, which left her alone with Ali's mother, an event that Raji had always wished was more than just four times a year. It was through these infrequent visits from Ali's mother that Raji gained the permission speak her mind and the courage to grow and find her potential.

Because of her family's high status, she was allowed much more freedom than the average Iranian woman. As her intellect and heart grew, so did her beauty. Because of her intellect and stunning looks, she intimidated most of the boys, so she rarely snuck off on a date as her friends frequently did. Dating was still not allowed in Iran, so young people found creative ways to meet. When Raji heard the horror stories from her friends of how they were groped and mistreated, she concluded that she hadn't been missing much. Unfortunately, as sharp as her intellect was, when it came to understanding men, she was left quite naïve. Which is why when Ali and his family began spending an inordinate amount of time at the house during her final years in college, a union between her and Ali seemed so natural. His mother would subtly insert admirable qualities of her son in her discussions with Raji. On one particular night, Ali's mother switched from subtlety to a hard sell. By that time, Raji had become outspoken and was consistently questioning the Iranian government. Ali's family were hard-liners. Raji seriously questioned why Ali's mother seemed to be pushing a union between the two of them when it was clear that Raji had rebellion running through her veins. Ali could have had any woman in Iran. His family was wealthy and well-connected. He had a tall, athletic build, with dark hair that was thick and wavy. During his years on the Iranian national soccer team, he'd kept it long.

Ali was always respectful to Raji, but never showed the least amount of interest until her last years of college. During her senior year in college, they ran into each in a bakery close to campus. They sat down and began talking. Ali was bright and a great conversationalist. It was a rare occurrence that Raji was ever impressed by another Iranian's world view. Too often, the men she met would just regurgitate what they were told by the Iranian government. But Ali had traveled the world and had his own opinions. They talked for hours, which Raji loved. Their secret relationship continued for another year and a half until Ali proposed. She looked forward to her wedding night with great anticipation. Inside, she yearned to be held and feel his flesh against hers. Her only fear, which made her giggle when she thought of it, was that she wouldn't be able to control herself and might scare him off.

Raji slid Ali's sky-blue wedding suit to the side and opened the door to the hidden room. The room was as dark as a volcanic tunnel on a moonless night. She felt for the switch just inside the door with her right hand. As her fingers skimmed across the light switch, she flipped it on. The LED lights illuminated Ali's bunker of weaponry. It was a long rectangular room at least twenty feet deep and eight feet wide. The long sides of the room were lined with floor-to-ceiling racks and cabinets that were all filled with every sort of armament. She scanned the room for the pistols. Ali had enough weapons in the room to arm a formidable army. She walked past the racks of AK-47s sitting next to open cabinets filled with an assortment of RPGs. She knew the pistol she was looking for. It was the exact same one her father had trained her on. She smiled as she noticed the shelves of IEDs—she had wired hundreds of them as a child. On the back wall, the surface-to-air missiles were lined up. Located under them were eight drawers filled with pistols and ammunition. Raji knew exactly where it was, the second drawer from the left. She slid the door open and pulled out the SIG Sauer P226 semiautomatic handgun. Raji lifted the gun to her face and looked down the scope. Instantly a memory flashed through her mind of her and her brother at the firing range, both with soundproof headphones on, firing round after round at their father's instructions. It seemed so harmless at the time; while she got to fire real rounds into a target, most children had to suffice with the pretend world of video games. If only she had known what a monster her father was at the time—he made everything fun for a child, like a game.

Growing up, Raji had every amenity that most little girls could only dream of: a servant at her beck and call. Her own bedroom suite complete with a Cinderella-esque canopy bed and every wall covered by hand-painted murals. A closet full of clothing and shoes along with a bathroom suite that surpassed most five-star resorts. She had her own doll room and art room. But what she didn't have was a mother or any form of love and affection from her father. The only time Jaafar spent with her was in his work room outside the house. He told her that the work they did together assembling the explosives was for their beloved country, Iran.

"In order to keep other little girls safe from losing their mommies, like the bad men who killed your mommy, you can help by wiring these devices," he told her. It was the only time she could count on spending any time with him. It was a rare occasion that her father joined Malcolm and Raji for a meal. They were fed and bathed by servants, instructed and taught by tutors, and left to explore and grow on their father's estate. Surrounded by everything and yet she had nothing—love was absent from her life. Raji grew up as a lonely little girl. When she grew older, her fingers became too big to wire her father's bombs, and he no longer needed her. She began to feel insignificant—a feeling that was later reinforced by her marriage to Ali.

In the picturesque backdrop of the city of Tehran lay the beautiful Alborz Mountain Range, which spanned the entire southern coast of the Caspian Sea. Located within the Alborz Mountains were two large ski resorts. Jaafar's estate was nestled along the hillsides of the Alborz Mountains and looked out at Tehran, a city with more than twice the population of Los Angeles. Raji's only chance of getting through her father's heavily guarded estate fell on the lap of one person—her former servant, Habiba. She knew that Habiba was still employed by her father, but Raji wanted to be sure that Habiba would keep her visit a secret. The good news was that she still had the same phone number. She didn't answer on Raji's first attempt, so she got in her car with her concealed weapon and began the nine-ty-minute journey to her father's estate in hopes that Habiba would eventually answer. If not, Raji would improvise. The tiger was out of her cage and on the prowl. Her only cub, Yasser, was shot dead in San Francisco. Vengeance-infused blood pumped furiously through Raji's veins. She could not get to Jaafar's estate fast enough.

Thirty minutes into the drive, the screen on her phone lit up and began to vibrate in the cup holder. Raji briefly glanced at the screen and focused back on the black pavement in front of her. She stared blankly at the methodic dash of yellow lines whipping by. It was Habiba, the only woman to treat Raji like her own child. Raji took three deep breaths in an attempt to appear calm as she answered the call. She had no forethought of what she would say. It had been years since she had spoken with Habiba. Raji reached out and touched the answer button. "This is Raji."

She heard the unmistakable voice of Habiba. "Raji, I am sorry I didn't call sooner, my dear. I wanted to wait until we could talk in private."

In relief, Raji said, "It's so good to hear your voice, Habiba. I'm sorry I haven't kept in touch."

"Oh goodness no, child! I see you every night on the news. We are all so very proud of you!"

Raji laughed. "Well, thank you. I have a sensitive question to ask, but I need you to be completely honest because I really want to avoid putting you in an awkward position."

"Yes, what is it, Raji?"

Raji paused in thought momentarily and then said, "I need to talk to my father in private without anyone knowing that I am there. Would you be willing to sneak me onto the estate in your car?"

Without hesitation, Habiba quickly replied, "Of course I will. My Audi is a four-door with dark tinted windows. The guards wave me through every morning. When and where shall we meet?"

"Can you meet me now?" Raji asked.

"Of course. Where do you want me to pick you up?"

"At the bakery we always shopped at."

"I'm on my way."

"Thank you, Habiba." Before she disconnected the call Raji asked, "Habiba, are you still there?"

"Yes, what is it?"

In a puzzled tone, Raji asked, "Aren't you going to ask me why?"

Habiba answered, "If you wanted me to know, you would have told me. If anyone asks, I will say I never saw you."

Raji smiled as she disconnected the call. She pulled into the bakery parking lot and waited for her Trojan horse to arrive.

# CHAPTER 6

## ASTORIA, OREGON

Myk drove along the Oregon coast on Highway 101, doubling back several times to make sure he wasn't followed. He glanced out the window at the raging Pacific Ocean pounding against the shoreline, the aftereffects of a storm that had just passed. He had been kept in the dark about his family history for so long, a past that was shielded by a mother, scarred by death and tragedy from a world that had its moments of indescribable cruelty toward humanity. His unknown father had been assassinated in the streets of London before Myk was born. Now, he drove to meet an unknown uncle, Levi, whose name had been mentioned by his mother for the first time just one month ago. Myk had exposed a defector that was hiding in the United States. Ever since exposing the defector, Myk had become a target.

Nine miles outside of Astoria, Myk spotted the dented and rusted mile marker on the side of the road and turned off Highway 101 onto an undistinguished dirt road covered in an overgrowth of vegetation. Myk's vehicle slowed to a crawl and he wondered if the rental car was getting scratched as it squeezed its way down the dense forest road. Branches and huge ferns swayed and dropped their moist leaves as his car passed by. After a quarter mile, the dirt road, which was muddied by the recent storm, took a sharp turn and began to descend toward the beach. Myk noticed the bright blue turbulent ocean and the explosion of white clouds of mist as they dashed against the cliff through a clearing in the lush trees. He spotted a beautiful Victorian-style home, modest in size, located close to the beach and perched on a knoll. The steep-pitched clay tile roof house with auburn-painted eves looked like it had been plucked from the Swiss Alps and transplanted onto the hill on which it sat. A few minutes later, he pulled into the gravel driveway of the house and parked. He saw an elderly man sitting on the porch staring out at the Pacific.

Myk got out of the car and walked up the steps of the porch. Levi was sitting on a worn wooden bench on the front deck. He stood and turned toward Myk. He was tall, like Myk, and had a full head of wavy silver-white hair that covered half his ears. He wore a blue-and-black checkered flannel shirt, a light rain jacket, and a new pair of Adidas walking shoes. As he stood in front of him, Myk noticed the man's eyes were moist. He embraced Myk. As he hugged Myk, he said, "I am sorry this has taken so long, Myk. You have no idea how happy I am to finally see you. Your mother was wrong to keep you away from me."

They broke the embrace, and Myk replied, "It's great to finally meet you, Levi."

Levi stepped back and scanned him up and down. "My God— look at you—your father would be so proud. Your mother named you after him you know—Mykel."

Myk felt his emotions swell but held them in check. He wanted desperately to know more about his father. A man whose identity wasn't revealed to him until he began high school. "I wish I knew more about him. I have so many things to ask, but I'm not sure where to begin."

Levi smiled, then grabbed Myk by the arm, just above his elbow, and said in a soothing voice, "Come, let's go for a walk. The storm has passed, and I would like to go down to the beach before the next system moves in."

Levi moved slowly but resolutely as they stepped off the front porch and strode down an elevated wooden walkway that extended half the length of a football field and ended at the top of the beach. He clung to Myk's arm as they walked. Myk glanced up from the boardwalk and took in the majestic trees rooted steadfastly into the rocky cliffs that were being pounded by the massive after-storm waves.

"Your father was a great man and a terrific brother, Myk."

Myk felt the urge to feel the wet sand beneath his feet and stooped down and began to unlace his shoes. He looked up at Levi and replied, "That's what I am finding out—I just wish I would have been told the truth growing up."

Levi shook his head. "Believe me, after your father was killed, I pleaded with your mother not to shut everyone out, but she was haunted by the past and chose to isolate you while she reared you. Her quest to shield you from her violent world has had the opposite effect—you are now fully engulfed in it."

Myk said, "Yeah, she definitely had some ghosts of the past that haunted her." He shook his head and then added, "I think the fifteen years of vodka slayed them all!"

"I'm sorry to hear that. She's been through a lot," Levi said.

Myk stepped onto the beach in his bare feet. "I didn't know any better—I just assumed all five-year-olds were taught how to use a gun."

Levi shook his head and smiled. "She is something else."

Myk dug his toes into the cold sand as the forceful gusts of wind whipped through his thick brown hair. Unable to recall ever seeing the Pacific so violent, he stood peacefully, inspired by the wonder of nature in commotion. The sound of the forceful wind and thunderous clap of waves slamming against the mammoth boulders along the shore made it tenuous to converse.

Levi put his hand on Myk's shoulder. "I was there, Myk—I was with him when he died. Did your mother tell you that?"

Myk turned and looked at Levi with a puzzled face. "I just learned a month ago that he was assassinated. For years, she told me he died in a car accident."

Levi put his hands in his pockets and looked down as he brushed the sand with the side of his foot. "I am convinced it was an inside job, Myk. We never should have collaborated with the FBI. Our suspect got tipped off that we were onto him. Our backup got distracted, and your father took the brunt of the shots fired that day in the streets of London. If your mother hadn't wounded the attacker, I would have been killed too."

Myk nodded and listened to the seagulls squalling while there was a moment of silence between the two. He said, "I'm still getting over the initial shock of some of these things in her past. She told me that if she wasn't so far away, she would have killed the assassin. She said she did her best on the long-range shot and got him in the left knee. She was seven months pregnant with me at the time. I knew she was a tough lady—but she's got ice in her veins."

"We were quite the team. A day doesn't go by that I don't think about your father."

"Mom has too many secrets. I just wish I could get inside her head."

Levi grabbed Myk by the elbow and squeezed hard. "No, Myk—trust me, you don't want to go there. No one should ever have deal with what she's experienced."

Myk gazed up and fixed his eyes on a flock of seagulls that seemed to be frozen in midair, like kites being held by an invisible string. He looked Levi in the eyes. "I've seen my share of evil men."

"I'm sure you have. So tell me, what brings you here, Myk? You were very cryptic on the phone."

Myk answered, "Well, my original intent was to meet you during the last week of my vacation, but I got called to San Francisco because of a threat. The Iranians have developed an extremely deadly version of the COVID-19 virus that they plan on releasing. His partner decided to reach out to me. Turns out he had a change of heart. Unfortunately, he was shot by a bullet meant for me before I could get much information from him."

"What—how'd that happen?" Levi asked.

Myk humbly replied, "The dumbass used a laser scope, and I caught the reflection just in time. There is no possible way he could have known my location unless someone in our government tipped him off."

Levi frowned and shook his head. "Déjà vu—similar to your father's experience except he wasn't so lucky. Who was the Iranian that reached out to you?"

"He told me his name was Yasser. His mother has some notoriety in Tehran. She tried to keep him on the straight and narrow. He had to bury his two best friends because the Iranians botched how they handled the pandemic last year. His grandfather got into his head and sold him on the same old anti-American garbage."

"Did he give you a name?"

Myk cringed at the thought of the bomb maker's name. "Jaafar Venzi."

Levi's right knee gave out at the mention of Jaafar's name. Instantly, his mind flashed back to the parking garage in Beirut. The little girl in the yellow dress. He remembered her iridescent eyes and the bandana he tied around the deep cut above her eye.

"Are you okay?" Myk asked.

Levi turned and grabbed the wooden rail on the boardwalk. "Bad knee. We should go back up to the house. It's cooling down quickly."

Myk knelt down and swiped the sand off his feet as he put his socks and shoes back on. He cursed as one of his laces snapped. He looked up, and a chill came over him as he noticed Levi gawping down at his broken lace. It looked as if Levi had seen a ghost.

Myk tilted his head and paused before he asked, "Are you sure you're okay?"

Levi stared a few seconds longer and then shook his head. "I'm fine—let's go up to the house—there are some things you need to know, Myk."

Levi locked his arm around Myk's like a proud father escorting his only daughter to the altar. The two gracefully strode back to the house while the sounds of the ocean became muted under the heavier thoughts of unsaid words. Why hadn't his mother told him more about his uncle, Myk wondered. Now he was walking arm in arm with the man who was at his father's side as he drew his last breath. Myk's stomach tightened. He inhaled the crisp air and drew a deep breath as he imagined his father next to him instead of Levi. They neared the front door, and Levi released his arm and pushed the massive hand-carved ten-foot mesquite wooden door open. Myk looked up at the twenty-foot vaulted ceiling with massive hand-hewn exposed timber trusses and wood-planked tongue and groove ceiling. As Levi pushed the door shut, the sound of the thunderous waves and wind-blown trees deadened as if they had entered the vault of a bank. Myk looked out through the floor-to-ceiling windows and watched the thick spray of ocean waves being broken by the solid anchored boulders on the shore—the tumult of the noise was gone inside the peaceful confines of Levi's sturdy home. Levi removed his jacket and draped it over the side of the couch. He motioned with his hand for Myk to sit as Levi took a seat in a well-worn brown leather recliner.

# CHAPTER 7

L evi leaned forward with his elbows on top of his knees, his fingers interlocked together, and his unshaven chin of gray whiskers resting on his hands. He squinted and asked, "What has your mother told you about your father and I?"

Myk shook his head slightly as his eyes narrowed. "Very little, especially during my pre-high school years, she was checked out. She opened up a little after that, but not much. I have spent most of my spare time digging deeper into her past in order to find out the truth. I feel compelled to find out more."

Levi nodded. "Good for you, Myk—you should know. There are some extraordinary events that happened to your parents that should never be forgotten."

Myk looked away from his uncle through the large expanse of glass windows facing the Pacific. The wind had begun to calm as Myk watched the vast billows of clouds break into smaller wafts, like white wisps of cotton candy slowly floating across the bright blue sky. "Mom had told me that her family was killed in the Ravensbrook concentration camp, but I learned otherwise. She told me that she was born during the last days of the war and was raised by a Catholic family when the Germans came for her parents. I was in the Holocaust Museum in DC several years ago and stumbled across a display about Lidice—Mom's hometown in Czechoslovakia. That's where I discovered that her parents never even made it to a concentration camp. Her father and mother and the entire town of Lidice were massacred against the side of a barn. It took the Nazis two days from sunup to sundown to do it. Stories like that keep me searching for more history that she might be keeping from me."

Levi replied, "Thank God they found someone to hide your mother and her twin sister from the Nazis. I'm sorry she hasn't been more forthcoming about her past, but that's her decision."

Myk looked back at Levi. "It's frustrating. I didn't even know you existed until recently. It's not right." Myk paused as his eyes widened. "Tell me more about my father."

Levi smiled and let out a small chuckle as he shook his head. "He looked a lot like you, Myk—strong and athletic. He was tenacious."

"How'd he and Mom meet?"

"Through Mossad. The Israelis began a search to ferret out a special group of people that could track down the hundreds of Nazis who had escaped the justice that was due them. Your mother and father were eager to be a part of the program. It was their belief that the hand of Providence had spared them from the grips of the Nazis."

Myk shook his head. "These are the things I should have learned from my mother when I was growing up—she has too many secrets." He paused and tilted his head. "I noticed you weren't limping when we came back up from the beach. I don't think it was your knee that caused you to fall when I mentioned the name Jaafar Venzi."

Levi's lips quivered as he nodded his head. Levi's chest swelled as he inhaled deeply. Myk sat silently while he watched his uncle gather his thoughts. Levi scanned around the room and then looked at Myk. "Did your mother tell you that I used to work for Mossad?"

Myk uncrossed his legs and slid to the back cushions on the sofa. "Like I said, I didn't know anything until recently. Mom told me that you got spooked by something decades ago—was it because my dad was murdered next to you in the car?"

"Yes, that was the beginning of the end for me with Mossad."

Myk nodded. "I thought so."

"I lost both of my brothers at the hands of evil men. We were very close during childhood, Myk. Like your mother and her twin sister, we were orphaned during the war, as were many Jewish children back then. My other brother, Micah, died when his bus was blown up a block from the stop I was standing at." Levi looked down at his shoelaces. "I should have been on the bus with Micah that day—it was one of Jaafar's bombs that blew Micah's bus to pieces."

Myk tried to read Levi's facial expression. It was a mix between anger and sadness. "Mom never mentioned anything about another brother. One more secret locked up in her vault," he said sarcastically.

Levi continued, "Micah was the middle brother. He was an amazing Israeli boxer—and may have been the first Israeli to win a gold medal in the '76 Olympics. Your father and I had posters of him all over our bedroom walls. Jaafar's ignorant minions couldn't read a damn compass, so they landed their boats forty miles from their intended target, on a beach outside Tel Aviv. They improvised—and my beloved brother was slaughtered right in front of me. I should have been on that bus, but . . ."

Myk didn't speak a word. He looked back at Levi with a sorrowful and puzzled glare. He was about to say something when Levi held his hand up and said, "If I close my eyes." Myk watched as his uncle slowly shut his eyelids as he spoke. "I can still feel the heat from the blast on my skin and the reverberations of the bomb like the sound waves from a huge concert speaker. I can still smell the smoke and the scent of human flesh being singed." He opened his eyes and looked at Myk. "Micah was a fighter. As I wiped the soot off my face and stared at the smoking wreckage, I realized that he would never lace up his gloves again. I went home and your father and I stared at the poster of Micah and decided from that time forward, we would be fighters. But our fight would not take place in a boxing ring—we would never fight *against* someone, but rather *for* someone—the innocent people going about their normal lives who become the targets of evil men. We would fight for them—much like you do now."

Myk could never understand why it made a difference, but it did. It wasn't hatred for murderers that motivated him—it was his love for the innocent victims of those killers. He knew exactly what Levi was talking about. He and his uncle spent the next four hours snacking on finger food, talking about Micah, and answering questions about Myk's father. But there was one last nagging question that had not been answered during their conversation. There was a short pause. Myk asked, "I feel like there's more about Jaafar that you haven't told me."

"You're right." Levi nodded. "It was actually something that stuck with me from one of my first operations. My partner blew his assignment, and I almost killed two young children." He paused as his face tensed up. "They were Jaafar's children. Many years later when your father was killed next to me—that was the end for me. My two brothers were killed by radical anti-Semites. I left Mossad and moved to the United States."

Myk's stomach sank. It was the one thing, the only thing, that Myk feared—kids getting in the way of an operation. He asked, "What happened on the operation that you almost killed Jaafar's kids?"

Levi shrugged his shoulders and replied, "I had to make a choice, Myk. We had already tripped the timer when Jaafar's wife and children showed up on the scene. Jaafar's bombs had killed hundreds, and would continue to kill innocent people. Was it worth sacrificing his wife and children too? My mind flashed back to the bombing of Micah's bus. That's all it took, Myk—he would not have wanted me to let those kids die. So, I jumped out of the car, grabbed the kids, and leapt behind the cover of the other vehicles before the bomb detonated. I saved the kids. We were less than a mile from the scene when I completely shut down. That was a very sobering moment for me, Myk—I don't kill children. In my decades of work with Mossad, not one child ever perished."

Levi offered Myk a beer, and the two of them took their conversation to the kitchen island and sat on the barstools. Myk told him about the two recent assassination attempts.

Levi said, "Obviously, the defector you came across last month must have damaging information on whoever it is that's trying to kill you. Have you been able to get anything out of him?"

Myk shook his head. "No. He was assassinated while in transport."

"Any idea who did it?"

"It has to be someone in our government. The first assassin that tried to kill me spoke the name Heinrich Mueller right before he passed. Isn't he supposed to be the highest-ranking Nazi to escape?"

A serious look came over Levi's face as he nodded. "When I was with Mossad, we received a tip that someone recognized a former Nazi, Heinrich Mueller. They weren't sure because it had been almost thirty years since he had last been seen. Mueller was the last living survivor who was in the bunker before Adolf killed himself. Mossad had evidence that Mueller began to stockpile Nazi gold, jewels, and valuable artwork at various hiding spots in the last weeks of the war before the Russians arrived. Your father and I followed the man we thought to be Heinrich Mueller to a lake in Switzerland. He was much older of course, and we only had a visual on him through the binoculars. We were across the lake and well concealed. We watched for hours as Mueller and the FBI met. They used heavy machinery and scuba divers to pull fifteen massive metal crates out of that lake. They popped the top off of one of them, and it was full of Nazi gold bars. Mueller stood by as someone came from one of the vehicles and inspected the gold bars. He was the agent in charge. He was very tall, and he had blond hair. As soon as he set the gold bar back in the crate, he nodded to someone standing behind Mueller, and they cracked him over the head with a club. Mueller collapsed, and they dragged his body to the back of one of the vehicles. That's the last I saw of Heinrich Mueller. Within thirty minutes, they had loaded everything up. And that's when it happened."

"What happened?"

"It was brutal, Myk. The agent in charge and one other agent got back out of the vehicles with machine guns and slaughtered every agent and worker on site. Fortunately, the scuba divers and most of the workers had already left. One of the operators of the forklifts escaped into the woods. They worked with precision as they gunned down nine people, most of who were their fellow agents!"

Myk shook his head and asked, "Are you sure they were FBI?"

"Without a doubt."

Myk spent two days with Levi sharing their espionage stories, bringing Myk up to speed on a lifetime of deep-rooted family history his mother had kept from him, and going on walks through the dense forest surrounding Levi's property. Myk finally felt a sense of family connection he had been yearning for his whole life. After hearing all of the stories that Levi shared, Myk developed a profound respect for his uncle. Most of all—Levi inspired him.

As they sat on the patio eating lunch, Myk received a phone call from a strange number. The screen on his phone filled up with zeros. Myk stared at the screen debating if he should take the anonymous call. He pressed the button and answered, "This is Myk."

He heard a lot of static before a voice with a heavy Persian accent said, "Agent Miles, this will come as a shock to you, this is Jaafar Venzi. I know I don't need to introduce myself. I have learned that you were with Yasser when he was killed. Yasser was my grandson. If you're willing, I would like to meet with you alone to discuss a deal."

The conversation between Myk and Jaafar was short and to the point. When he ended the call, Myk looked at Levi, bewildered. "Something strange is going on."

# CHAPTER 8

## TEHRAN, IRAN

The tiger lay perched behind the veil of tall grass, motionless, her muscles flexed and ready for the kill. Raji peered through the small crack of the closet door and waited. The SIG Sauer P226 pistol was gripped in her right hand with her finger poised on the trigger. Her breathing was effortless and easy. As she waited for Jaafar, her mind drifted back to tenth grade. Memories of her last day with Meera, her best friend. The look of terror on Meera's face that day was forever hardwired in Raji's synapses. Attached to the memory were the first words Meera whispered to Raji that morning: "We have to talk. Meet me in the bathroom stall at lunch." Raji didn't hear a word that came out of her teacher's mouth for the next three agonizing hours as she sat anxiously in her chair waiting for the lunch bell to ring. Her eyes were locked on the clock the entire time. When the bell rang, she was like a sprinter crouched in her starting blocks awaiting the sound of the starter's gun to fire. The bell rang, and she was out the classroom door and running down the hallway before any other student had even left their desk. Raji sat silently in the locked bathroom stall, seated atop the toilet seat with her knees pulled to her chest and her arms wrapped around her knees, waiting for Meera. It seemed like an eternity until she heard the soft rap of knuckles on the aluminum stall door.

"Raji, are you in there?" she heard Meera ask. Raji quickly unlocked the door and let Meera into the stall. Meera locked the door while Raji assumed her seated position on top of the bathroom seat.

Raji whispered, "What's going on?"

Meera nervously looked behind her through the small gap in the locked door and then turned to Raji. "Two black SUVs showed up at our house while I was at the bus stop and forced my parents into the back seat. I'm scared."

Raji felt her heart began to beat faster as she witnessed the panic on Meera's face. "Why don't you come to my house after school? I can have Habiba drive you home when we find out what's going on."

Meera snapped back, "What do you mean, what's going on? We know what's going on, Raji. We've talked about this. When black SUVs roll up in front of your house—it can only be one thing!"

"I thought your parents were being cautious?"

"Of course they were." Meera danced nervously back and forth on the balls of her feet while she flung hands up and down as if she was air drying them. "Oh my God—what am I going to do—what am I going to do?!"

Raji stood and embraced her best friend. "Don't worry, everything is going to be alright." Of course, she knew better, but what else could she say—the truth? *Meera, you'll never see your father again. And there's a pretty good chance you'll never see your mother either. I am so sorry, you may end up an orphan.* No, she did what good friends do, remained optimistic and encouraging.

But everything was not alright. Ten minutes after they returned to their class from lunch break, Raji sat in horror as the principal of the school entered her class with a behemoth man dressed in a dark suit and sunglasses who pointed at Meera and then motioned with his index finger to follow him. She watched Meera stand and walk sheepishly toward the door. Before she disappeared down the hall, Meera turned to make eye contact with Raji. Through watery eyes she stopped and stared at Raji. No words were needed. The look on Meera's scared face said it all—*I'm doomed.* It was the last time Raji ever heard from or saw her friend. Raji's stomach sank and tears began involuntarily streaming down her face. Raji had been isolated most of her life in her father's estate. She had occasional playmates, but it was only the children from those in the regime who visited her father.

Abruptly the sound from the echo of hard-soled shoes walking down the marble hallway at Jaafar's estate snapped Raji back to the present. Her grip on the handle of her pistol tightened as the steps got closer and closer. She heard the sound of the door handle turning while she squinted through one eye and peered through the sliver in the door opening. She saw Jaafar enter the bedroom. A second later he was out of her line of vision, so she listened to him make his way into the bathroom. Raji cracked the door open and watched her father stand as still as a statue in the bathroom.

The old man stared in the mirror at his disfigured face, his bloodshot and watery eyes, his gray hair, and his sunbaked, wrinkled skin. What stared back was a monster—a beast responsible for the heartache and death of thousands. He didn't blink but glowered at his reflection. Yasser, his last hope, his grandson was gone. And with his death, there was no doubt he would never see or hear from his son or daughter. It finally dawned on him that he would live his remaining life as a lonely man with no family to care for him. Jaafar had just come from his meeting with the ayatollah. The Americans had sent video footage from a camera across the street from where Yasser was killed. The Americans wanted to know what Yasser was doing in San Francisco. Jaafar had watched the recording of Yasser's death over and over. He shook his head and closed his eyes tightly. His life's journey down the roads of hate and revenge converged here—a solitary bathroom. Visions flooded his mind. A musky garage in Beirut—his young children bloodied by a bomb but saved by an Israeli. He had chosen the safety of the stairwell instead of trying to save his wife. Feelings of shame made him shudder. His recent conversation with his son, Malcolm, filled his mind. It was no veiled threat; he would never speak to him or see him again—ever.

He would never hear from Raji either. Images of the death and carnage he had caused bombarded his mind. Those same images that used to make him smile now tortured him. The last image of Raji's freshly manicured toes turning away from him—forever. He closed his eyes, but the pain wouldn't go away—the news stations showed images of Yasser's lifeless body surrounded by yellow caution tape lying motionless in the middle of Union Square. Why now? Was this his punishment—to live a lifetime in the dark, only to glimpse the smallest ray of light illuminated at the end of his life's journey? His son was right, death, pain, and destruction were not Allah's will. It was his own pride. Revenge and hate were cloaked in the false illusion of righteousness.

He gripped the sides of the sink as he lifted his head to look in the mirror at the soulless man glaring back at him. Thoughts of his handgun in the other room filled his mind. *I'll end it now*, he thought. He would stop the pain. He nodded his head and quietly whispered, "Yes." He turned and walked resolutely to the nightstand where a gun lying in the top drawer beckoned him. The vivid pictures of mangled dead children pounded his head like bricks thrown from the rooftop. Brick by brick the memories of his victims came uncontrollably crashing down on his skull. He wiped his nose and eyes as he slid his hand in the drawer and wrapped his fingers around the ultimate pain reliever—his Lionheart MKII 9mm pistol. He sat on the side of the bed and stuck the barrel of the gun underneath his chin, pointed heavenward. No need to check for empty chambers in the gun, they were always loaded. He clicked the safety switch off and eased his index finger on the trigger and then closed his eyes.

Suddenly, he put the gun back in the drawer and began to frantically look for his phone. His sources had given him the cell number of the man at Union Square where Yasser had been slain. Myk Miles, former Special Forces, a man who was both despised and feared by the Iranian regime. Jaafar ran back to the bathroom and grabbed his phone off the counter. He scrolled through his texts until he found it. He touched his index finger to the highlighted number on the screen, put the phone to his ear, and listened. After a long moment of silence, he heard the connection. On the sixth ring he heard an American voice answer, "This is Myk."

Jaafar inhaled deeply and replied, "Agent Miles, this will come as a shock to you; this is Jaafar Venzi." The conversation didn't last long; it didn't need to. Jaafar's name had been at the top of the most-wanted list for decades. His capture would be a grand prize for anyone. His next phone call was the one he feared the most: Raji.

Raji listened behind the closet door in utter confusion. When she had seen her father put the gun beneath his chin, she had screamed inside, *No! It can't happen this way. You won't deprive me of this!* And then just as she had placed her left hand on the door to push it open, and readied her right hand to shoot him through his earhole before he could end his own life, Jaafar had lowered his gun.

Why was her father meeting the American? *Could it be that Yasser is still alive?* She holstered her gun under her hijab while her mind raced. *Jaafar can lead me to Yasser's body.* She checked through the crack in the door and saw Jaafar dialing again. He put the phone to his ear as Raji listened to hear his conversation. She was startled by the sudden vibration on her side. Her phone, which was on silent mode, began to glow under her silky hajib. She quickly retrieved it and checked the caller ID. *What?!* she thought. The call was from Jaafar. She quickly checked to see if Jaafar had detected her. He was still standing in the bathroom with the phone to his ear. She listened closely as he left a brief voice message. "Raji, please give me a call. It's urgent." The next call Jaafar made was for flight arrangements out of Iran.

*This was not part of the plan.* She had intended to leave the estate either in handcuffs for killing her father or by escaping and making a run for the border and leaving Iran forever. Whichever happened, the evil beast that was her father would be dead. This was unexpected. She began to devise a way to sneak off the estate unnoticed. She retreated to the back of the massive walk-in closet and texted Habiba and wondered. *Could Yasser still be alive?*

# CHAPTER 9

## ASTORIA, OREGON

Myk was stunned by the call from Jaafar. He had long been on the top-ten most wanted list. Jaafar would give him all the information he wanted on Jamal, but only if Myk agreed to meet him in person. Myk told Levi about the call and asked him to join him on the flight to meet Jaafar. Without hesitation, Levi agreed. Myk discussed Jaafar's proposition with Director Adelberg, who wasn't keen on the idea. Adelberg warned him that it could cost him his life. Myk weighed the options and decided that he could not pass up the opportunity. Adelberg agreed to support him, but Myk would have to go off-grid and not use any company assets in case things went sideways. Adelberg made arrangements for the use of a private jet with a friend and former colleague of his.

Myk inhaled the scent of the new leather upholstery as he boarded the Bombardier Global 8000 jet. The $65 million Mach .85 speed jet with its hand-carved mahogany panels and gold-plated deco tile was the epitome of opulence. Myk and Levi were the only passengers. Levi looked around and asked Myk, "Is this how you always travel?"

"I wish. This is Rick Taft's jet. He and my director served together decades ago."

"*The* Rick Taft?" Levi asked. "The one that just filled the vacant US Senate seat for California?"

"Yep," Myk answered as they began to look for the best place to sit.

Levi reached out and lightly tapped Myk on the shoulder as he cleared his throat. "Who says money doesn't buy elections?!"

"I know. Can you believe Rick Taft used to be an agent?"

Levi replied with a smirk, "So maybe there's a jet in your future too!"

Myk laughed. "Not likely. I don't have wealthy parents leaving me a trust!"

Myk noticed the airline attendant trying to get his attention. She asked, "Would you gentlemen prefer to sit in our lounge recliners for our take-off or in the multimedia room with couches?"

Myk answered, "The media room. We have a lot of work to get done during the flight."

The flight attendant escorted them to a room near the wings of the plane that had two plush couches with a seventy-inch television mounted on the front wall that was richly clad in a dark-stained cherry wood. There was a wet bar and private bathroom located in the back of the room. Myk thanked the attendant and took a seat. Levi sat beside him and asked, "What do you think is Jaafar's real motive for wanting to meet?"

"He didn't say, but I think he knew that his grandson, Yasser, contacted me before he was killed."

"Jaafar is a heartless killer, Myk. He has murdered thousands, including women and children. He can't be trusted."

"I know—that's why I'm going to kill him after he gives me information on where Jamal is hiding the virus!"

Levi clasped his hands together. "So what do you need me to do?"

"For now, not much. We should land in Istanbul in about twelve hours."

"I'll do my best, Myk, but what are your plans with me once we get to Istanbul?"

"For now, I want you to stay on the plane. Although things may change when I get a better feel for what Jaafar is up to." Myk felt the jet lurch forward and heard the voice on the overhead speakers from the pilot announcing they had been cleared for takeoff. "As soon as we get to cruising altitude, I'll touch base with Director Adelberg. We'll have a clearer picture of how I am going to approach Jaafar after that." Myk felt the force of the engines' thrust push him back into the couch. A few moments later, he felt a dropping feeling in his stomach and knew the jet was now airborne. He looked out the window and saw the skyline of Portland get smaller and smaller as the Bombardier Global 8000 jet pushed upward.

After Myk felt the plane level out, he heard the captain's voice over the speakers. "Agent Miles, you and your guest are free to move about the craft. If we see any choppy weather out there, we'll be sure to let you know."

Myk pulled his phone from his pocket and dialed the director. After the first ring, Adelberg answered. "Myk, are you off the ground yet?"

"We sure are! This bird can really fly! I had no idea Rick Taft was worth this much."

Adelberg replied, "His campaign team did a fabulous job of deflecting his wealth back to his parents. The last thing he needed was to be painted by the opposition as being out of touch with the working class."

Myk chuckled. "Yeah . . . I'm sure Rick Taft feels their pain. This is one hell of a jet. How long did you work with him?"

"Almost three years."

"So—do you think I'm walking into a trap with Jaafar, or is it possible he really is reaching out? I can't imagine a man so drenched in evil for all his life coming clean at his age."

"It would be unparalleled, Myk. You need to be prepared to walk away if it doesn't feel right."

"Of course. I need details before I step one foot in Iran, if that's where we end up. What if it really is legit and this murderer wants to come over?"

"That depends on what he has to offer. Our first priority is stopping this biological attack. We'll listen and then make arrangements if needed. We're making preparations for him at a safe house on the outskirts of Istanbul."

"If he asks for protection and wants to come to the US, do you still want him killed?"

"Not until we have verifiable information on the biological weapon! Make whatever promises you need. Once we have the information, and we verify it, then put a bullet through his skull. That animal will never set foot on our soil!"

"Are you sure we can't use him as an influence peddler? We've never had a mullah switch sides."

"I know that, Myk, but he's got too much blood on his hands—rid the earth of that vermin!"

Myk nodded as he looked at his uncle who seemed to be turning pale and then replied, "Good, I was hoping you would say that."

He felt the phone vibrate in his hand and looked at the screen. "Hold on, Director, I have an anonymous call coming in on the other line."

"No problem, take the call, it could be Jaafar."

Myk switched lines and answered. "Agent Myk Miles speaking."

He heard the familiar voice that had warned Myk to stop the investigation he was pursuing. "It would appear that good fortune has smiled kindly on you, Agent Miles. I told you to leave things alone."

Myk recognized the voice and interrupted. "Good fortune, my ass! That first goon you sent gave me the name of Mueller." He paused for a few seconds and then continued. "Did you hear that? I'm getting closer. Listen close and tell me what you hear!"

After five seconds of silence, the caller responded, "I hear nothing."

"That's the sound of fear, asshole! I've got a name and it scares the hell out of you! Whatever nasty secret you're trying to hide, I'm going to expose it."

"I think not. You've been lucky, Agent Miles. But your luck is about to run out. I can call off the hounds if you agree to mothball your investigation."

Myk shot back, "Not a chance! And when I do find you, I'm going to—" The call went dead. Myk looked at his screen to see that the call had ended. He clicked back over to Director Adelberg. "Director, are you still there?"

"Yes. Who was the call from?"

"Unfortunately, it wasn't Jaafar. It was the same voice from the first call warning me to halt my investigation."

"That's pretty odd for a hit squad to call their potential victim. What did he say?"

"That I've been lucky."

"I can put a surveillance team at the house if you want, Myk."

"Completely unnecessary, Director. I already have private security watching my mom."

"I figured as such. I'll send you a briefing within the hour. Let's talk after that."

"Will do."

Myk disconnected the call and noticed the heavy breathing of his uncle. "Levi, are you okay?" he asked.

Levi raised his hand to his mouth in cupping shape and walked quickly across the room to the lavatory. Myk heard the sound of choking and then the splatter of vomit from the echo of the toilet. There was a pause and then the sound of more vomiting. "Are you alright, Levi?" Myk called out.

He heard running water from the sink, and then Levi replied, "I'm fine. My stomach is just really queasy."

Levi emerged from the bathroom, and Myk asked, "Have you ever flown hypersonic speeds before?"

"Never."

"That probably explains it. Motion sickness is quite common at these speeds. I'll see if the flight attendant has any Dramamine."

Levi wiped his face with a hand towel. "I'm not sure this was such a good idea, Myk. I don't want to be a burden."

"Nonsense. You were the closest person to my father. I want

to learn everything I can about him. Besides, you've got decades of experience in the clandestine world. You'll be a great help. When I get the file from the director, I'll share it with you."

Levi sat back down. "I'll follow your lead, Myk."

Myk flipped open his laptop and replied, "Give me a few minutes to see what we've got so far."

"Take your time—I'm not going anywhere."

Myk chuckled. "I have so many questions."

"Your father and I were very close, Myk. You have no idea how much this means to be here with you. It brings back memories of the operations we worked on together."

Myk looked at Levi's beaming and genuine smile and then nodded back in silent affirmation.

A few moments later, the flight attendant tapped Levi on the shoulder and held out her hand. "Here's the Dramamine you requested."

Myk smiled as he observed the insignia on the flight attendant's protective mask—Taft for Senate. He felt the vibration of his phone in his front pocket as it illuminated through his shirt. He looked at the screen full of zeros and answered. "This is Myk." It was Jaafar.

"Agent Miles there's been a change of plans."

Myk looked at his watch. "We just took off less than an hour ago."

"Good. Then I won't have to worry about a refueling problem for you."

"Are we still meeting?"

"Most definitely—but it won't be Istanbul."

"Why the change?"

"The Istanbul airport has become a problem."

"How so?"

"Too many agents and some unfriendly people that would like to see me in a body bag."

"You just called a few hours ago. There's no way you could know that this early."

Jaafar laughed. "I was killing infidels for Islam before you were even born. I know when trouble is brewing—and trust me when I say, there is definitely trouble waiting at the Istanbul airport. There's a reason I've never been touched, Agent Miles. Your government has never even been close to getting a shot at me."

Myk looked across at his uncle and smiled as he replied, "I see— so they weren't close to you in '78? You know—the musty garage in Beirut when you ran for safety instead of trying to save your wife from being blown to pieces?"

Complete silence followed Myk's comment. He knew what he said cut deep. The heartless gesture would send Jaafar a clear message about who the alpha male was.

The tone of Jaafar's reply changed dramatically and was more somber. "I'll text you the new coordinates for your pilot." There was more silence, and then Jaafar added, "Like I said, *your* government has never been close. I'll give you instructions in a few more hours."

The line went dead, and Myk put his phone back in his pocket. His uncle gave him a puzzled look. "Are you sure you want to agitate him before meeting?"

Myk pulled his computer back in front of him. "You mean before I kill him."

Levi's lips tightened as he stared back at Myk. "I have no regrets about saving Jaafar's children at the car bombing in Beirut. Do I wish I would have killed him? Absolutely. Thousands of lives would have been spared had I been successful. But it wouldn't bring back my brother, Micah. And it doesn't bring back the dead. Jaafar has had such a strong impact on the minds of those martyrs. He would be a huge influence in changing minds if that's the direction he wants to go. There's never been such a high-ranking defector from Islam before. It would be unprecedented. Perhaps keeping him alive could save thousands, Myk?"

"I don't think so."

"Why?"

"Director Adelberg wants him dead after we extract the information we need. And more importantly—I want him dead! He's a cold and heartless killer and justice is due to him."

Levi tilted his head. "Hmm."

"What?"

"It's nothing."

"C'mon. What is it?"

"Maybe you're not as much like your father as I thought."

Myk stared at him for a moment and then looked down at his computer and continued typing. "I wouldn't know."

# CHAPTER 10

# 41,000 FEET IN THE AIR

Myk tapped his fingers in synchronization across his laptop, like the four legs of a racehorse pounding the muddy ground as it sprints down the stretch. Too impatient to wait for details from Director Adelberg, he logged into the Triple Canopy database and tried to pull up the file on the name the assassin had given him before he died on the icy ground in Park City—Heinrich Mueller. Myk's computer flashed with a message, "FBI director's clearance only." He spent the next hour searching the internet for anything he could find on Heinrich Mueller. He felt there had to be a connection between Heinrich Mueller and whoever was trying to kill him. What his uncle had told him in Oregon was true—Heinrich Mueller was the highest-ranking Nazi that had neither been caught nor ever been confirmed dead. Myk learned it was Mueller's plan to fly Hitler to Barcelona as the Russian Red Army encroached on Berlin in the final days of the war. Mueller was last seen by Hitler's pilot, Hans Baur, on the evening of May 1, 1945, in Hitler's bunker. Hans quoted Mueller as saying, "We know the Russian methods exactly. I haven't the faintest intention of being taken prisoner by the Russians."

Myk looked up from his laptop at Levi and asked, "How did you and my dad know that Heinrich Mueller was still alive?"

Levi crossed his arms and then answered, "During Adolf Eichmann's trials, he told investigators that he had recently met Mueller.

After that, the Soviets, the Americans, and the Israelis put him at the top their manhunt list. Unfortunately, the FBI beat your father and I to the punch. After we saw him stuffed into the back of the FBI vehicle, Mueller was never sighted again."

"Did you try to follow the vehicles?"

"No. They were on the other side of the lake. We wouldn't have made it around the lake in time. We watched the efficiency of their operation. Within twenty minutes they had fifteen crates of Nazi gold bars loaded on the back of trucks and they were gone."

"Fifteen crates—wow! Any idea where it all went?"

Levi chuckled. "Your government has the gold locked up in Fort Knox."

"You're kidding!" Myk exclaimed.

"No, I'm not kidding."

"Why didn't we give it back to the Holocaust victims?"

Levi shrugged his shoulders as he turned his palms up in the air and shook his head in silence. Myk felt the vibration of his phone against his leg. He reached in his pocket and answered. "Director, what do you have for me?"

"We are sending files for you and Levi to review. Has Jaafar given you the new coordinates?"

"Nothing yet, but I'll forward them as soon as they come. I have a question for you. Do you have a second?"

"Sure, what do you need?"

"That first assassin in Park City gave me the name of Mueller. I looked in our database to see what we had on Heinrich Mueller, but I was denied access. Can you open up the file and send it to me?"

"No problem. Hold on, I'm in front of my computer right now."

Myk heard the sound of the director typing at his keyboard and then a long pause. "Hmm, that's odd."

Myk asked, "What's that?"

"Heinrich Mueller's file has been completely wiped."

Myk looked across at his uncle and shook his head in silence and replied, "I think there's someone in our government that's trying to hide their link to Heinrich Mueller. If they are willing to go to this extreme, then it must be pretty bad."

"Myk, the search for Mueller ended decades ago. I doubt if anything new will turn up, but I'll assign some of our agents to look into any possible connections."

"If they find anything, have them forward it to me."

"Will do. We put together a file on Jaafar that I'm sending over. Have Levi look at it as soon as you get it."

"We'll jump right on it," Myk replied.

Levi leaned forward as he rested his elbows on his knees. "You're right, Myk."

Myk furrowed his eyebrows and asked, "About what?"

"About Mueller. I think there's a connection between Mueller and whoever hired the assassins to kill you."

"I agree. I've got a question for you."

"Okay, shoot."

"When we spoke at your house you told me that the last time you saw Mueller was at the lake in Switzerland. Were you able to identify any of the FBI agents that were there?"

"I'm afraid not. The main agent, the one that killed everyone else, was tall and blond, I remember that. We were so captivated by the appearance of Mueller and crate after crate of the gold bars that they pulled from the lake that we didn't notice the rain clouds moving in behind us. By the time we rescued our electronic gear from the downpour, it was too late. All of our surveillance equipment was completely drenched. When we got the cameras back to Israel, our teams tried to salvage whatever film they could, but the rain ruined everything."

"Did you get a good look at them? Would you be able to recognize anyone at the lake that day?"

"Myk, that was such a long time ago. We were probably the last people to see Mueller alive. Your father was assassinated in London two weeks later, and then I left Mossad after that. Do you have any idea the deep connections the CIA had to the Nazis back then?"

Myk gave him a puzzled look. "No."

"When I joined Mossad, the Israelis hated the CIA almost as bad as the Nazis."

"Really?"

"Absolutely! In the postwar period, many of the CIA's recruits were stalwart Nazis. They include names such as Otto Skorzeny, Martin Bormann, Josef Mengele, and Klaus Barbie. Your CIA agency was born out of corruption." Levi squinted his eyes as he stared at Myk. "You've struck something that has your enemy extremely nervous. These people will go to any lengths to remain unknown. They will eat their own if they have to—including you!"

Myk shook his head. "I had no idea."

"Your CIA isn't the only US agency that the Nazis found refuge in. I doubt the Americans would have been the first to send a man to the moon and back were it not for Wernher von Braun. He was part of Project Paperclip—a program that saw your government bring hundreds of German scientists to the US in 1945. Von Braun was the inventor of the V-2 rocket, that launched Saturn V when it took the Apollo 11 crew to the moon."

Myk's phone vibrated and he glanced down at the screen. It was the coordinates of the new meeting place from Jaafar. Myk looked up at Levi and smiled as he said, "Have you ever been to Verona, Italy?"

# CHAPTER 11

# TEHRAN, IRAN

Typically, Raji removed her headscarf every opportunity she got. It was another of her many small acts of defiance to a regime she held in contempt. Prior to the Iranian Revolution, women wore the hijab as a symbol of defiance to the Shah, who they felt was too secular and not religious enough. But the wearing of the hijab in Iran had come full circle. Now, many Iranian women removed the hijab in protest of the regime that had become too religious. Women were required to wear a headscarf and manteau, enforced by the "morality police." If ever there was a time for her to don the full hijab and headscarf, it was now, on the same flight to Verona as her vile father. She set aside her defiance of what she considered an archaic culture and made sure she wore the required clothing. She even went as far as trying to camouflage her iridescent eyes. She had a pair of colored contacts that changed her eyes to a dark brown. She snickered at the irony—it was her natural iridescent eyes that always came into question. Raji made her way through the Tehran airport, blending in like an iguana clinging to a dewy rain forest tree, with one exception—her six oversized suitcases. On the slim chance that Yasser was somehow still alive, she was determined to find him and start a new life. If Yasser was indeed dead, she would kill Jaafar. Either way, Raji was not returning to Iran—ever.

She approached the counter to check in. The bagman rolled her six full-size suitcases up to the counter as Raji placed a large tip in the young man's hand. She turned and removed her passport from her burnt-orange colored Gucci bag that she had purchased on her last visit to Paris and handed it to the short, stout check-in clerk with a bushy mustache and untrimmed eyebrows. The clerk quickly scanned her passport and asked, "What is your destination and purpose of travel?"

Raji calmly answered, "I am traveling to Verona, Italy, on business."

After a flurry of finger strokes on his keyboard he replied, "Just one minute please."

Raji used the momentary pause to quickly scan her surroundings for any sign of her father. The clerk cleared his throat and said, "I'm sorry, it appears there is a hold on your passport." He looked at all the bags beside Raji and commented with a puzzled look, "That's a lot of luggage."

Raji politely asked, "Are you sure? Would you please run it again? I'm quite certain there's been some kind of mistake. I just left the country a few months ago without any restrictions."

"Of course. I'll run it through again." The clerk scanned her passport again. "Yes, I'm afraid you've been restricted from leaving the country."

Raji's heart sank. "Give me a few minutes. I need to call my husband." Raji stepped away from the counter and moved around to the other side of her six bags and retrieved her cell phone. She pushed the speed dial button for her husband and waited.

After three rings she heard the deep baritone voice of Ali. "Raji, where are you off to now, my dear?"

She fought back the urge to lash out and asked, "Why are there restrictions on my passport? Need I remind you of our agreement—"

Ali interrupted, "Now, now, no reason to let this turn into another one of our heated debates. You know I could never break that agreement. Have you forgotten that your unrestricted travel had one condition? You are supposed to tell me your travel plans. You've never failed to tell me your travel plans in the past, so why would you start now? I am just as upset as you are over the death of Yasser."

Raji shot back, "The hell you are!" She paused, becoming self-aware that she was practically yelling into the phone. She looked around to see if she had brought any attention to herself and then hunched over and spoke in a much quieter tone. "Yasser is nothing more than someone to pass your bloodline and name to. You have never had a connection with him. Take the restrictions off my passport immediately, or—"

"Calm down, Raji. Just tell me where you are going and why."

"Is this some kind of control thing for you, Ali? The minute after I check in, you'll know exactly where I am going. What a joke, you know the whereabouts of every Iranian who leaves the country. But I'll play your game. I am traveling to Verona, Italy."

"Why Verona? That seems random—and sudden."

"Why not? Besides, you've never inquired into my reasons for travel. Why start now?" she asked sarcastically.

Ali answered in a more somber tone. "To be completely frank, I am a little concerned that with the passing of Yasser, that you may have decided to leave Iran for good. However, what's most concerning to me is whether or not you'll stay true to our agreement."

Raji took a deep breath and spoke steadily "I am meeting my father in Verona."

Ali chuckled. "Do you really expect me to believe that? You haven't spoken to your father in over five years."

"Yes, Ali, I am telling the truth, and you can rest assured that I will keep up my end of our agreement. Now it's time for you to keep yours—I am giving you five minutes to lift the restrictions on my passport!" She was just about to disconnect the call before she quickly added, "And all my bags get a free pass through security. Do we have an understanding?" She listened for his reply but heard nothing but dead air.

After ten seconds of long silence, she heard him say, "Consider it done." Raji disconnected the call and turned her wrist to glance down at her watch.

Raji waited ten minutes and stood back in line. All restrictions were lifted from her passport and she was given her boarding pass. Her luggage was tagged with special security alerts that allowed all six bags to clear security. Inside one of her pieces of luggage, she had stowed several handguns and ammunition. Raji was still puzzled about the intentions of her father. She was perplexed as to why Jaafar was meeting the American named Myk Miles. *Who is he?* Perhaps he was an Iranian spy operating in the US. While the whole affair piqued Raji's interest, her only hope was that Yasser may still be alive. It was the only thing that had kept her from pulling the trigger back when she had preyed on her father from inside his closet. And it was that same hope that drove her to the airport to board a flight to Italy. Hope did not come easy for Raji. All her other hopes had been dashed to pieces like a massive ocean wave being eviscerated into a cloud of mist against an immovable rock cliff.

For Raji, her hopes had always ended in pain. She boarded the plane with her face veiled and took her seat in first class—both seats. She had purchased two first-class seats together just to be safe. She slid into the window seat, stared at the city skyline of Tehran, and began to wonder about what lie ahead for her. She felt a sense of guilt for abandoning her people of Iran, but there was nothing there for her anymore. She thought back to her first time in a first-class seat. She had been on her way to Paris for her honeymoon with Ali. She was filled with such hope that day. Raji had been a motherless child raised by a loveless father. Her wedding would fill the void of that lifelong pain. She would have a loving husband and pour out her love to her children—motherly love that she had craved all her life. She clung to her dashing husband as her pride inflated with each compliment of what a perfect couple they were.

Raji could never quite put her finger on why she hadn't slept with another man before she got married. It certainly wasn't for a lack of wanting or from some high moral standard. She shunned the theocratic domination of her culture. So much so that she had been openly rebellious, until the disappearance of her best friend, Meera, in high school. After that, she became much more discreet. If it wasn't her rebellious side, then it was either her keen intellect or her mesmerizing beauty that seemed to intimidate men. If someone would have just had the courage to ask if she wanted to have sex, she probably would have said yes, she thought. And then along came Ali. He seemed unfazed by what all the others had walked away from. Raji reasoned that it was because he had known her since childhood. But still, there was something that had puzzled her. She seemed to have a great intellectual and emotional connection with Ali, but the physical connection was a work in progress. She looked forward with great anticipation and hope of making that physical connection on her wedding night. She blushed and placed her hand over her mouth as her friends filled her head with advice on how to please Ali on her wedding night. She thanked them and then told them that she needed no such advice. Raji was very much attracted to Ali's mind, mannerisms, and physique. Nature would take its course, she told them.

Her wedding suite in Paris took her breath away. The master canopy poster bed was right in front of a huge quadruple sliding glass door that opened up to a massive balcony facing directly toward the Eiffel Tower. She held Ali's hand as they entered the room and walked to the large expanse of glass facing the Eiffel Tower. She embraced Ali and kissed him. Her stunning eyes looked directly at his, and she said, "It's beautiful, Ali. Thank you!"

Ali slid out of their embrace and held both of her hands in front of him. He scanned the room. "They were supposed to leave us wine. Why don't you slip into something comfortable, and I'll run downstairs real quick and grab a bottle of wine."

Raji raised up on her toes and gave him a gentle kiss. "That sounds great." As the door shut behind Ali, Raji's mind quickly changed gears. Since she had not yet been intimate with Ali, Raji had a difficult time deciding if she should slip into a negligee or simply crawl under the sheets bare naked and wait for him to return with the wine. She chose the negligee. Raji opened her suitcase and pulled out a red, silky, see-through negligee and slunk into it. She sprayed on a dash of perfume, quickly rinsed with some mouthwash, and then sat up on the bed and waited for Ali. Raji was giddy with anticipation. Thoughts flooded her mind. Would she be good in bed? Would he be good in bed? As thoughts of her lovemaking with Ali continued, her right hand, seemingly with a mind of its own, wandered slowly down between her legs. As her fingers began to curl and caress, her inner voice barked out, *Raji, not now!* She quickly moved her hand back to her side.

Raji eagerly waited on the bed for Ali. Every few minutes she would change positions or move her long thick hair from one shoulder to the other. After forty-five minutes of waiting, she picked up her cell phone and checked for any missed messages. After another thirty minutes of waiting, she began reading a magazine she had brought. Then, after ninety minutes, she got dressed and went down to the lobby to locate Ali. He was nowhere to be found. She inquired at the bar if the bartender had seen Ali or if he had purchased a bottle of wine. The bartender told her that there hadn't been anyone matching Ali's description that had been to the bar in the last two hours nor had anyone purchased a bottle of wine. Raji began to worry. She called his number, but it went straight to voicemail. She checked the front desk and one of the attendants said that she thought she had seen him leave the hotel a few hours ago, but she couldn't be completely sure it was him.

Raji went back up to the room and hoped that perhaps she had just missed him when she left. But Ali was not in the room. She noticed the red light flashing on the hotel phone and picked it up to retrieve the messages. There was one message waiting. It was from

Ali. "Raji, my love. An emergency has come up that requires my immediate attention. It is extremely sensitive information so I will have to fill you in later. I am so sorry." Raji's mind raced while her heart sank. She attempted several times to contact Ali during her two weeks in Paris, but he would only send short, cryptic text messages. Raji spent the two weeks of her honeymoon in Paris alone—well, not completely alone.

The jolt of the jet touching down in Verona brought Raji back to the present. She had made arrangements with the flight attendant to be the first off the plane by making up a story of needing to run to a connecting flight. She wanted to be the first off the plane so that she could track her father and find out what his meeting with the American was all about. As soon as she exited the plane, she looked for a seat among the passengers waiting to board and then chose an optimal seat to wait and watch for her father. After ten minutes, Raji spotted the familiar hobble of Jaafar and his cane behind a throng of people. She hadn't actually physically seen him, just the top of his head bobbing up and down behind the crowd. There was no disguising that limp. His familiar totter caused by his prosthetic leg had been forever imprinted on her mind. She waited for the wretched monster to limp past her. Jaafar and his entourage of bodyguards passed by Raji. Because of Jaafar's slow pace, Raji could keep a very safe distance behind him. Just as Raji was about to rise out of her seat, she stopped still at the sight of a large man in a dark suit and sunglasses. Raji was not the only one who was following Jaafar.

# CHAPTER 12

# VERONA, ITALY

I n their quest to feel the beauty and nostalgia portrayed in picturesque travel brochures of Venice, most world travelers scurry their way past Verona, oblivious to this hidden gem of romance and beauty, abounding in history. But ask any local Italian from Northern Italy, and they'll all tell you the same thing: Verona is dripping in the flavor of old, authentic Italy while Venice has been overrun by foreigners. Is it any wonder that Shakespeare chose Verona as his setting for *Romeo and Juliet*?

Myk felt the taxi slow down and looked up from his phone. He had been poring over every detail for the past hour, remembering every exit, manhole, and vantage point around the meeting place in Verona. Myk felt the vibrations of the tires as the street surface changed from pavement to cobblestone. He looked out the window and saw the Arena protruding above the rooftops off in the distance. Completed in the first century, this Roman amphitheater was considered the best-preserved ancient structure of its kind and the predecessor to and archetype for the Roman Colosseum. The driver stopped in front of an old bridge with six sweeping arches that spanned a large river and glanced at his rearview mirror. Myk handed him his credit card to pay the fare and then opened the door. He was still four blocks from the Arena, but he didn't want to be dropped off in the large open plaza that surrounded the Arena where he would easily be spotted. He would have time to gather his thoughts and loosen up from the long flight on his walk. He slung his backpack over his shoulder and turned to Levi.

"Are you sure you want to come along?"

Levi grinned. "I couldn't sit on that plane with my mind abuzz trying to guess what was happening with you!"

"I didn't think you would. I want to keep you close by me—your brothers are going to have to wait a long time before I let you join them."

Levi's eyes narrowed and he simply nodded. Myk and Levi began walking across the historic bridge. The Ponte Pietra Bridge, the oldest bridge in Verona, was completed in 100 BC. The timeworn brick bridge spanned the large and slow-moving Adige River. They reached the apex of the bridge and paused. They saw the top of the massive Arena and its stone arches as it stood out against the backdrop of the setting sun's burnt-orange sky—a perfect postcard picture for this ancient Roman masterpiece. They crossed the bridge and discreetly entered the large open plaza bustling with thousands of tourists and vendors. Other than a smattering of people wearing protective masks, there were no remnants of the pandemic that had been so destructive to northern Italy. He looked up at the Arena and the surrounding government buildings and thought of the hundreds of stories of plunder and deceit that were buried within the Roman stone walls. He walked under the massive stone arch of the Arena's entrance and wondered about the next story that he would soon unfold within these ancient walls. He slid his hand into his pocket and felt the cold metal of his Glock. Jaafar's bombs and his dogma of brainwashing gullible martyrs had caused thousands of innocents to die. He didn't know when, but he would kill Jaafar. Myk shook his head—as much as he despised Jaafar, it was decisions like this that had probably kept Jaafar above ground for so long. The Arena was a labyrinth with very limited means of ingress and egress. If ever there was a safety vault to hold a meeting at a public venue, this was it.

Myk scanned the throng of tourists, most of whom were leaving, since it was nearing closing time. His six-foot-four frame allowed him to see above most of the crowd. He spotted a young boy, probably eleven years old, holding a sign above his head with the name *Myk* written in black. The Italian boy's skinny frame could barely fill the oversized jersey drooping from his shoulders. The jersey had the name Del Piero on the back along with the Italian flag logo emblazoned on the front. It was the jersey of Alessandro Del Piero, considered one of Italy's greatest soccer players. Myk turned to his uncle and asked, "Are you sure you want to go through with this—I don't know what Jaafar has in store for us."

Levi nodded. "I'm quite sure, Myk."

"Alright then." Myk motioned his head toward the boy with the sign. "Looks like he's our escort." They approached the boy and Myk announced, "I'm Myk."

"Who's he?" the boy said in a heavy Italian accent as he pointed at Levi.

"He's with me," Myk answered.

The boy pulled his sign down. "I was told you would be alone."

Myk peered at him and replied, "Plans have changed. If you want to get paid the fee you were promised, you'll take me to Jaafar now."

The boy's eyes narrowed while he scratched his head and looked back and forth at Myk and Levi. After a long pause he said, "Okay, fine. Follow me." He turned and walked up the massive stone steps, which were worn smooth by thousands of years of foot traffic. Myk and Levi followed. The flight of steps led to a full view of the inside area of the entire Arena. A stage was being erected at the front of the Arena as work crews were busy setting up for the following night's orchestra performance. Unlike the world-famous Colosseum down south, the Arena was still in use and well-known for its concerts with a spectacular setting. The boy motioned to Myk and Levi to follow him as he turned toward a pedestrian pathway that circled around the entire Arena. As they walked the poorly lit pathway, Myk glanced down at the stone pavers adjacent to the wall. The ancient stones were rounded out and looked a lot like a modern street curb. Myk nodded to himself as he recalled what this design was used for in Roman times—raw sewage used to run down those curb-like stones in the ancient days.

They turned the corner and four men stepped forward—Jaafar's bodyguards. All four men had earpieces and guns holstered on their sides. One of them barked out to the boy, "I told you to only escort one person!"

The boy shook his head. "He refused to come. Besides, look at him, he's just an old man. Now pay me!" He held out his hand and one of Jaafar's men gave him a fistful of euros. The boy pulled up his oversized jersey and stuffed the money in his pocket. He turned and ran back the direction he had come.

The tallest of the four men demanded, "I'll need your weapons."

In that split second time stood still, and it seemed like there was an hour to debate the pros and cons of relinquishing control and surrendering his weapon to the enemy. Myk closely studied their faces and read the body language of Jaafar's four bodyguards. Once he handed over his weapon, it would most likely bring him to the point of no return. Myk asked, "Where's Jaafar?"

The taller guard quickly replied, "Around the next corner."

Myk continued to get a read on the four men as he reached into his pocket for his weapon. With his hand on his Glock, he could easily take out all the guards with little problem. It was obvious to Myk that they had not been trained in how to disarm a hostile. But there were lives at stake back at home. Jamal was in San Francisco with two containers of a highly contagious and deadly virus. If Myk took Jaafar's bodyguards out, Jaafar would, no doubt, be less cooperative. Myk trusted his gut instinct, pulled the Glock out of his pocket, and handed it to Jaafar's guard. The bodyguard gave them a pat down, took his Glock and said, "Follow me."

The group walked briskly about a hundred feet until they came to an alcove in the pathway. Myk saw two muscular, dark-haired, bearded men with their arms crossed. Behind them was an old man sitting on a stone bench. The two large men separated so that Myk could have a clear view of Jaafar. The other bodyguards that escorted them turned and took defensive positions while they checked the area for possible threats.

Myk glared at Jaafar as he took a few steps toward him. He looked down at Jaafar, who had his right leg stretched out. The clothing on his leg was pulled six inches above his shoes, exposing the metal of his prosthetic leg. Myk's eyes slowly moved up to the side of the old man's face to his missing ear. Old scar tissue had replaced the absent body part. Myk's spine stiffened and his body tensed when he looked at the grimace on Jaafar's face.

*I should snap his neck right now!* Myk thought.

Jaafar leaned on his cane as he slowly stood. "Agent Miles, I can only imagine the gamut of emotions that must be surging through you right now."

Myk relaxed as Levi stepped out from behind him.

Puzzled, Jaafar asked, "Who is this gentleman? I was very specific in my directions. Why would you jeopardize our momentous meeting with such an unimposing figure as this?" He pointed at Levi.

Myk calmly replied, "My partner is here for his wealth of wisdom since you said that I would not be allowed to communicate with my agency during our meeting." Myk knew the comment would have instant merit with Jaafar since a large amount of respect was given to elderly males in the Iranian culture.

Jaafar squinted while he looked at Levi. "Your face looks familiar."

Levi shook his head. "I am nobody that you would have ever known."

Jaafar examined him longer. "I see." He slowly sat and then spoke again, "No need to waste time on small talk. Agent Miles, I can see in your face that there's no love lost here, so I will cut to the chase." He put his walking cane in front of him and rested his two hands on the handle. "I would like to make an offer."

Myk tilted his head to the side and studied Jaafar for a few moments. "I am listening."

Jaafar reached inside his front pocket and pulled out a zip drive. He opened his palm toward Myk. "This drive contains all of the information you will need to stop the release of the biological weapon into the United States."

Myk interrupted as he took a quick step toward Jaafar, "What's the location where Jamal is hiding the virus?"

Jaafar's bodyguards quickly closed ranks on Myk and raised their weapons. Jaafar raised his hand in the air and gestured to his men. "Lower your weapons. The American is clearly agitated."

By the look on his face, Myk knew that Jaafar was surprised by his question. Jaafar turned to Myk and asked, "How did you know about Jamal, Agent Miles?"

"Your grandson was in the process of telling me everything about your plan just before he was killed. He had come to his senses and discovered all the lies you filled his head with. He was trying to do the right thing."

Jaafar grimaced. He ignored Myk's comment and said, "The release of the virus will result in fifty times the number of casualties from the COVID-19 pandemic. In exchange for the information, I want guaranteed protection in Britain for the remainder of my life."

Myk blurted back, "The UK? I can't make a deal on behalf of the British government. You should have reached out to someone in Britain if that's what you wanted. Here's what we're going to do. You are going to come back with me and board our jet back to the US, or there won't be any deal at all. We have enough drones and agents in the surrounding area that there's no place for you to hide now."

Jaafar chuckled. "I think not."

"What, you don't trust that we can give you protection?"

Jaafar stared at Myk and paused before replying, "No need to be coy, Agent Miles. I am like an old, deep-rooted, rigid tree that cannot be shook. Whether or not I trust you or your government is of no concern to me."

"True. You are an old and rigid tree—but you've been rooted in a lifetime of evil. My level of skepticism far exceeds my glimmer of hope that the information on that drive will actually save American lives."

Jaafar's eyebrows raised while the corners of his mouth curled. "What choice do you have?"

Myk ran his fingers through his hair and then gestured with his hands. "Why? This makes no sense. A man steeped so long in your beliefs would never turn his back on his faith."

Jaafar spoke softly and said, "For reasons I can't explain, I have come to a difficult realization. But we need not waste our time discussing my motives. My offer of information to you is my first step in the right direction."

Myk leaned toward Levi's ear and whispered, "Why should I believe him?"

Levi cupped his hand at Myk's ear and whispered back, "As much as I hate to admit it, I have a feeling that he's telling the truth. He could save a lot of lives if you play this right, Myk."

Myk remembered his conversation with Director Adelberg and then replied to Jaafar, "I didn't come all this way to hear about your 'aha' moment! We need to verify the information on the disk." He clenched his fist. *Then I'll snap your frail neck like an old, rigid tree branch.*

Jaafar reached in his pocket and pulled out a cell phone. He tossed it underhand to Myk. "Call your director and get confirmation of what we've talked about. Once I have assurances, the drive is yours."

Myk held the iPhone and turned it over. Attached to the bottom of the phone was a small digital device the size of a quarter. Most likely added by Jaafar's technicians to prevent calls from being tracked. Myk dialed Director Adelberg, which took so long to connect that Myk almost hung up in frustration. He assumed the call was rerouted through several sites to make it untraceable. Finally, the director answered, "Director Adelberg speaking."

Myk turned his back to Jaafar and replied, "It's Myk."

"Is everything okay?" Adelberg asked.

"So far, yes. I am with Jaafar now. He has a zip drive that he claims has all the information we need to stop the virus attack."

"What's that murderer want in exchange?"

"Asylum." Myk paused and then added, "In the UK."

"What the—"

Myk interrupted, "Director, this line isn't secure."

"I know, I know, Myk. Listen, there's not much we can discuss under these conditions. Tell him we'll have a deal once the information is verified."

"Got it. I'll ask him now." Myk turned to Jaafar and asked, "The director says we'll have a deal once the information is verified. So, what would you like me to tell him?"

"Tell the director we have a deal."

Myk pulled the phone back up to his ear. "Did you hear that?"

Adelberg replied, "I did. Good work, Myk. Get back to the jet as soon as you can so we can download the information on the zip drive."

"Will do."

Myk took a step forward, handed the phone back to Jaafar, and said, "We need to get back to the jet as soon as possible."

Suddenly, Myk heard the loud sounds of gunshots and instinctively coiled into a defensive position. One of Jaafar's bodyguards fell lifelessly to the hard cobblestone ground in front of him as blood poured like a faucet from the bodyguard's empty eye socket. Myk retrieved his weapon from the dead man. He took cover in the alcove where Jaafar was seated. Levi followed directly behind him. Jaafar's guards returned fire from both directions. The reverberation from the multitude of shots being fired within the solid stone walls was deafening. A second guard took several shots to his torso and then spun around like a novice ballet dancer, went limp, and fell to the hard surface. Myk quickly improvised a plan before they were overrun.

He barked out to Jaafar's remaining guards, "At my command, concentrate all your fire on the tunnel on the left." Myk looked back at Jaafar and Levi and pointed straight ahead, "There's scaffolding outside the archway that's—that's our escape! I'll create a diversion that should allow us enough time to make it to the archway. Are you ready?" Both Jaafar and Levi nodded. Myk yelled, "Now!" Jaafar's guards began shooting off repetitive rounds. Myk sprung from out of the alcove and immediately took aim at two fire extinguishers near them. He squeezed the trigger and shot both extinguishers. The fire extinguishers exploded with bursts of thick white powder clouds. Myk turned back to Jaafar and Levi. "Let's go!" The three of them quickly strode behind the cover of white smoke to the large Roman window archway that was open to the crowded square below. Jaafar and Levi crawled out of the large stone archway and stepped onto the scaffolding. Myk looked back and saw Jaafar's remaining guards receive fatal shots.

Myk's heart dropped when he saw three men with AK-47s emerge from the white clouds of fire extinguisher dust. With their weapons pointed directly at Myk, the man in the middle said, "Drop your weapon now!"

Myk's mind was already calculating every conceivable option. There were too many lives at stake back home. He needed Jaafar and the information. *Live to fight another day*, he thought. He placed his gun on the ground. "Now what?"

The gunmen pointed at Jaafar. "Step back off the scaffolding, you traitor. We're taking you back to Iran to hang you from a noose! All three of you turn around, get down on your knees, and put your hands behind your backs."

Jaafar said, "I am unable to kneel because of my prosthetic."

"Fine, then turn and put your hands behind your back!"

Myk and Levi turned and knelt. With their backs to the gunmen Myk heard them approach from behind. He felt his hands being bound with zip ties. Myk heard the familiar "zip" sound as the plastic tie constricted against his wrists.

99

"You two—rise to your feet and slowly start walking in front of me," the gunman said.

Myk rose, but his uncle needed assistance, so one of the other gunmen helped him to his feet. Myk's mind was racing to figure a way out. He'd have to wait until one of the gunmen got distracted or let his guard down—then he would make his move. The Arena was empty as they all walked slowly down the dark corridors. Between Jaafar's limp and his uncle's age, they were going slower than a bride walking down the aisle with a broken leg.

The gunman spoke to Jaafar, "How could you turn your back on your country? You turned your back on Allah!"

"I was gravely mistaken. Just as you are," Jaafar replied.

The gunman jabbed Jaafar in the back with the butt of his weapon and barked, "Silence, you conspirator!"

That's when Myk noticed it. An almost imperceptible movement ahead of him in the darkened alcove. As they walked closer, Myk could barely see the outline of a figure, completely veiled in black, standing perfectly still in the shadows. As the six of them slowly passed the alcove, Myk dared not turn around and draw any attention. They continued to walk but, surprisingly, nothing happened. Myk kept his ears keenly attuned to any sounds behind him but heard nothing more than the footsteps of their group. A minute passed and Myk kept listening for anything. He noticed they were approaching a section of the corridor in the Arena that was darkened because of a broken light. Myk slowed their already snail's pace to a crawl when they got to the dark section. He listened intently but kept looking straight ahead. Precipitously, he heard the inimitable sound of gunshots being fired with a suppressor on the gun. Three distinct sounds, "piff, piff, piff." All three gunmen fell lifelessly to the ground one after the other like synchronized Olympic swimmers falling in the water.

Myk thought, *Whoever the shooter is, he has to be a professional.* The shots occurred milliseconds apart with each shot directly in the center of each gunman's skull. Myk turned and saw a figure approach, completely veiled in black. He expected to see a taller, more daunting shape. The black-draped ghost-like figure was running toward them. Myk looked to make sure there was no movement from the gunmen on the ground. He could see the shimmer from the blood pouring out of the lifeless corpses. Myk heard the voice of a Middle Eastern woman.

The cloaked figure in the black hijab said, "Quickly, put your hands away from your back so I can cut the zip ties."

Myk complied and moved his hands. Levi and Jaafar followed suit. A woman's hand with perfectly manicured red nails gripping a sharp hunter's knife reached out from under the hijab and cut loose all the zip ties. The female voice said, "Follow me! We need to go back the way we just came. We can't exit at the main entrance; we'll have to go down the scaffolding. The Italian police will be here shortly."

They all began walking as quick as Jaafar could hobble. Myk heard the police sirens blaring off in the distance. *Who in the hell is this?* Myk thought. There was no way his agency could have put an asset in place so quickly. They stepped over the bodies of Jaafar's dead bodyguards and back onto the scaffolding outside the Arena. Jaafar went first, followed by Levi, then Myk, and then their rescue angel cloaked in black stepped onto the scaffolding. As they walked down the sloping planks, Myk sarcastically said, "Jaafar, I thought you were untouchable?!"

"True, but I've never had to worry about being killed by my own people."

Myk pointed at Jaafar's thobe and turned to the mysterious figure in black and said, "We've got to get him out of that, as well as you out of your hijab if we're going to have any chance of getting out of here undetected. I have an idea, follow me."

"Okay," said the female voice.

The four of them quickly moved from the scaffolding to the gift shop attached to the Arena. Myk scanned the store that was filled with paraphernalia to make tourists feel like a part of ancient Rome. He snatched three hats off the rack, a few shirts, and tourist maps, and threw them on the counter. An unknown woman, an ex-FBI agent, an ex-Mossad agent, and a renowned terrorist had entered into the gift shop; what emerged five minutes later were three men and a woman looking like typical tourists. Levi, with his newly donned t-shirt and cap, held a gift bag, while Jaafar had discarded the Iranian thobe that covered him from his head down to his ankles for a white shirt with a picture of the Arena emblazoned on the front. Myk wore a "Verona" baseball cap and held the tourist map. The woman pulled the veil from her face to disrobe from the hijab and smiled at Myk. He couldn't look away. Her eyes seemed to be from another realm. He was drawn in by an unseen force. Myk thought she could see right through him.

Jaafar saw her and started to speak, "Raji, I never knew—"

Raji cut him off mid-sentence. "Shut up, you babbling fool! You're lucky I didn't shoot you dead with the rest of your lot!"

Once out of the gift shop, they quickly merged in with the thousands of people in the open plaza surrounding the Arena. There were over thirty quaint Italian restaurants, with all of the seating outdoors under the large colorful canopy of umbrellas. Each table was filled as the throng of people enjoyed the food, wine, and ambiance of the spectacular night life of Verona. The plaza was filled with the sounds of conversations, laughter, and Italian music. But off in the distance, Myk heard the screeching of the Italian police sirens and then saw the glow of the red and blue lights against the darkening Verona night. He turned to Jaafar and asked, "What the hell was that? Who's after you?"

As they continued to walk briskly through the crowd, Jaafar answered, "I don't know. I only made one call before I left for Verona."

Raji spoke up, "It was probably Ali. I couldn't get through security at the airport, so I had to call him. I told him I was meeting you in Verona. I think I saw one of them following you at the airport."

Myk motioned to a street ahead that was too narrow for cars. "This way." Many of the ancient streets of Verona were too narrow for automobiles but served as a beautiful setting filled with thousands of stores and shops. The four of them hastily walked down the narrow cobblestone streets crowded with people. As they turned onto a wider street, Myk looked back to make sure they hadn't been followed and quickly hailed a cab. A fluorescent-green cab, barely large enough to hold the four of them, rounded the corner and stopped. Levi and Raji crawled in the back seat while Myk stared at Jaafar, who hesitated. "What are you waiting for?!"

Jaafar answered, "How do I know I can trust you?"

Irritated, Myk shot back, "What choice do you have?"

Jaafar's eyebrows raised. "Does that mean we have a deal?"

"Nothing has changed. Assuming your intel can be verified, then we have a deal." Jaafar ducked his head and slid into the cab. Myk gave the driver directions and the cab sped off in the opposite direction of the oncoming Italian police vehicles.

# CHAPTER 13

---

# IN THE SKY OVER EUROPE

M yk felt the force of the engines press him into his seat as Rick Taft's jet lifted into the air. Jaafar, Myk, and Levi sat in the plush leather chairs that faced each other. Raji turned her chair away from the others to look out through the windows. She hadn't said a word since they got in the taxi. Jaafar had attempted to make small talk with her on the ride, but she had immediately cut him off and said, "You've lost the right to ever converse with me. Don't you ever utter another word!"

After the jet finished its rapid climb to its cruising altitude, Jaafar cleared his throat and told Myk, "I would like to speak to your director about what assurances he's going to extend to me."

Myk laughed. "When we have assurances that we've stopped Jamal from releasing your virus, then we'll talk."

Jaafar closed his eyes momentarily. "I can't change the past, Agent Miles, but I believe that I can be an asset for the future."

Myk exhaled sharply through his nose as he shook his head. "Is that so? A common saying comes to mind right about now."

"And what is that?" Jaafar asked.

"That it's hard to teach an old dog new tricks! I don't believe you, and I have no reason to trust you. So what's your reasoning for turning your back on your lifelong beliefs anyway? Pardon my cynicism, but it doesn't make sense. At your age, you could simply quit and spend the rest of your life in Iran. Was it because someone in your family was killed?" Myk noticed the question seemed to pique an interest from Raji, who half-turned her chair toward the conversation.

Jaafar replied, "If that was the case, I would have stopped decades ago when my wife was killed by a car bomb that was meant for me."

"Then what was it?" Myk asked.

Jaafar briefly paused. "An awakening of my soul—that's the only way I can describe it. And, if I'm being honest, seeing the video footage of my grandson being shot."

Raji thought back to watching her father through the crack in the closet door. He had just been standing and staring at himself in the mirror. She looked at Myk and then back out the jet window.

Jaafar continued, "If I was in your shoes, I would have serious doubts too. Agent Miles, two minutes before I contacted you, I had a gun to my head and was going to end my life as the remorse tormented my soul and consumed me. That's when the light turned on for me."

Myk stood up and stared at Jaafar in silence for a moment. Then he said, "I don't give a damn about your guilt, you worthless piece of shit! I can't even sit in the same space as you. I have to restrain myself from ending your life right now." He motioned to Levi and said, "Come with me, Levi; I can't be in the same space as him. Let's go sit in the lounge." Levi stood slowly, and the two began to walk away.

Jaafar cleared his throat and said, "Before you leave, I'd like to share one thought."

Myk paused and turned back around to face Jaafar. "What's your thought?" he asked snidely.

Jaafar said, "I can't fix the lives I've broken, but because of my position, maybe I can make a difference going forward."

Myk shrugged.

Jaafar continued, "Radical Islam is an idea, and you can't eradicate an idea with bombs and drones as the West vainly continues to do.

Islam can be beautiful and exist peacefully in this world when it's not misinterpreted to justify killing. Knowledge is the key. Knowledge and truth are the only way to stop an idea. We must start changing minds—and my influence can do exactly that."

Levi turned toward Myk and whispered, "He might be on to something, Myk."

Myk folded his arms together. "That's a utopian dream from the lips of a mass murderer. The ideology of the Islamic extremists is too far gone to ever be reined in."

Jaafar replied, "Your country went through something similar to what Islam will have to go through."

Myk chuckled. "I think not! American ideology doesn't influence our people to strap bombs to themselves and blow up unsuspecting citizens! American ideology doesn't weaponize viruses to kill off populations. We don't bomb people in planes or trains, and we don't behead people because their beliefs differ from ours! That's your twisted belief, not ours. That ideology is a disease that has grown tentacles in every country."

Jaafar's shoulders drooped as he took a deep breath and clasped his hands. "Yes, there is still a gap that separates the radical side of Islam from a peaceful side of Islam. But you know the statistics as well as I do—ninety percent of the Muslim world is peaceful."

Myk snapped back, "That's a pretty wide gap."

"It's time for an awakening, and I can be that voice. Your country went through its own awakening. There was a time when your country strung up its own citizens and hanged them from trees because of something so insignificant as the color of their skin. Luckily, your President Lincoln wasn't as pessimistic as you. He didn't believe that slavery was too far gone to be reined in."

Myk shot back defensively, "That was a very small fraction of the country that were hateful bigots—"

Jaafar interjected, "And it is a very small fraction of Islam that are jihadists."

"You are comparing apples to oranges!"

"True, but they are both fruits."

Myk's eyebrows raised. "Point taken."

Levi joined the conversation. "Perhaps he is on the right track, Myk. The jihadists justify their actions based on a set of false beliefs that are fueled by hatred. Their ideology could be corrected through education. But only if their own people turn against them can they begin to eradicate their violent ideology. It would have to come from within. There are definitely similarities to the slavery, bigotry, and racism that the United States went through. The extent of hatred from racism in the United States is almost incomparable to what it once was. So perhaps there is hope for peace in this world if Islamist extremists can begin the journey to educate themselves."

Jaafar added, "I understand your country's stubborn philosophy behind my stick is bigger than yours. Your drones and bombs can only do so much. It's a temporary solution because it kills people but not the ideas that motivate them to kill others. The only way to stop an idea is to pull it up by the roots."

Myk ran his fingers up and down the back of his neck. "I see." He pointed at Jaafar. "And you're the one who's going to begin picking these weeds? I don't see it happening. You have yet to utter a word in public, and your own people have already gotten closer to killing you than anyone has in decades. They want to kill you, not listen to you!"

Jaafar added, "If I understand your history, there was a lot of death in your country before people began to listen. I believe that was your civil war. Perhaps, but hopefully not, Islam will have to go through its own civil war to rid itself of the perpetuation of extreme violence against nonbelievers."

Everyone turned to watch Raji as she gracefully rose from her chair and walked toward Myk and Levi. As she passed Jaafar, who was the only one still sitting, she paused and said to him in a soft voice devoid of any anger, "I can't listen to any more of your happy talk." She squinted her eyes. "Where were these thoughts when I was growing up? The thought that my childish fingers wired the bombs responsible for so much death continually haunts and torments me." She looked at Jaafar in silence and then continued. "None of this brings Yasser back." She turned and looked at Myk with her blazing eyes. "I can't bear to be in the same room as him either." With that, Raji turned and walked to the lounge in the back of the plane.

The lounge in the rear of the jet had a full wet bar that had a complete assortment of fine wine, beer, and hard liquor. As Raji entered the room, she eyed the wine glasses hanging from the rack. The wet bar had contemporary cantilevered cabinets with long chrome handles. Raji slowly swept her hand across the countertop that was made from a dark Italian limestone. The stone top had a leathery soft finish. She had never felt such a soft stone before. She removed one of the wine glasses that was hanging from its holder and opened the wine cellar. The wine cellar was glass on all four sides and stood about six feet tall and three feet wide. She scanned the fifty or so bottles of wine until her eyes landed on a red wine labeled "Vengeance." A smile calmly came across her face. *I'll definitely have a full pour,* she thought. Raji sat in the upholstered couch adjacent to the barstools. The couch was so supportive and soft it seemed to envelop her entire body and beckon her to close her eyes and drift away. She sipped the luscious wine from the glass in her left hand while her right hand patted the silenced pistol under her hijab. *Vengeance in both hands,* she thought. Once Myk got the information from her father that he needed to stop the biological attack, Raji was determined to kill him.

Myk walked behind the bar while Levi sat down on the couch opposite Raji. "Can I get you anything to drink, Levi?" Myk asked.

"Just some water please," Levi replied.

As he popped the cap off of his imported beer bottle, Myk asked Raji, "How's your wine?"

She gave him an inquisitive look with her iridescent eyes. "It's good."

"Your English is excellent; where did you learn?"

"I've had private tutors since I was four years old, so English has been my second language most of my life."

Myk took a sip of his beer and swung his barstool around to face Raji. The three of them formed a triangle: Raji and Levi sitting opposite each other on the couches and Myk seated up on the barstool. Myk's eyes narrowed, and then he said to Raji, "There's so much I want to ask you, I'm not sure where to begin."

Raji gave him a slight shrug. "Ask me anything you like. I have a few questions of my own . . ." She paused mid-sentence. "It's Agent Myk Miles, is that right?"

"Yes," Myk answered.

Raji and Myk looked directly at each other, neither of them saying anything. The momentary silence wouldn't qualify as an awkward silence because there was nothing awkward about it. Comfortable in the silence, her brilliant mind was racing, processing, and reading one Myk. She thought he might be simultaneously reading her. A serious look came across Myk's face. In a somber tone he said, "I am very sorry about Yasser." Myk shook his head. "He and I were talking when he got shot. Yasser had sought me out. He was in the middle of telling me the details of the Iranian regime's plan to release the virus when he died. He volunteered to help me find where Jamal hid the virus. I know it doesn't do much to comfort you, but I thought it important to let you know that Yasser realized his mistake and he was trying to correct it when tragedy took that opportunity away from him. He had good things to say about you and your brother."

"Thank you for sharing that with me." Raji's face was expressionless. "Would you take me to Yasser's body when we land?"

"Of course. It won't be first thing because we've got to stop Jamal; thanks, in part, to the beast sitting in the front of the plane. I haven't thanked you for getting us out of our predicament back at the Arena. Judging by what I've witnessed so far, your fortuitous presence at the Arena did not have anything to do with your father's plan, so . . ." Myk lingered and seemed to draw out the word. "Why were you at the Arena armed with a weapon?" Raji was about to answer, but Myk added, "By the way, your marksmanship and timing were impeccable."

"Thank you." Raji smiled. She eyed Myk up and down. There was something genuine about him. Should she tell him? *I was spying on my father in hopes that you would bring news that Yasser was still alive.* But the broken trust of her past made her thick walls of distrust rise up. People couldn't be trusted—not her father and not her husband and not her mother-in-law. She was raised in a culture where most women were viewed as property. A culture with too many misogynistic men that groped and mistreated women as if it was their right. Raji had become fiercely independent and devoid of any real connection with another man. It's how she survived. It's how she thrived.

Raji shook her head. "I'm sorry, I'm not at liberty to tell you what I was doing at the Arena." She wanted to share with Myk but couldn't.

Myk said, "Your husband is Ali Isma. I've only known you for a few hours, but it's quite clear you're not carrying any water for the Iranian regime. How does one of Iran's top leaders have a wife that is so anti-Iran? Agitators don't last long in your country—I know that for a fact."

What was it about the American that compelled her to divulge everything? His demeanor? His good looks? She stamped down whatever it was that he stirred up inside her.

"You are correct; agitators are unseen in Iran. I know this firsthand. My best friend in school had parents that tried to inform the public of the truth about our regime. Then, one day at school, men came and took her. That was the last I ever saw or heard from Meera. As for me . . ." Raji paused in thought and then continued. "How shall I put this—there is an understanding between those in the Iranian regime and myself. I am allowed a bit more freedom of speech on my network, which has resulted in a large following and a certain level of trust with the Iranian people. And in return, the regime gets to tap into that following so they have another platform on which to peddle their lies and propaganda. As for Ali, yes, I am married to one of Iran's top military leaders. Suffice it to say that I am allowed a great deal of freedom of speech and a tremendous amount of freedom in my movement. I have traveled all over the world."

Myk remembered his conversation with her son. "Yasser mentioned that he rarely saw his father."

Raji swallowed two deep drinks of her wine. She was unable to restrain from verbalizing her thoughts. "That makes two of us!" She immediately regretted letting the comment slip out. *Raji, bite your tongue. You hardly know this man.*

Myk stared at her with a puzzled look. Seeming to have no response to her comment, he turned to Levi and said, "This jet should get us to San Francisco in less than twelve hours. For commercial airlines it would have been close to seventeen hours. Once we land, I'm not sure when you'll have another chance to get some sleep."

Levi nodded. "Okay, Myk. I am fine for now, but I may try to get some shut-eye in a bit."

As the two continued to converse, Levi was glued to Raji. He couldn't take his eyes off her. He kept staring at the scar above her eye.

Raji reached into her beige Hermès Birkin handbag with gold hardware and asked Myk, "Since we're not on a commercial airline, is it okay if I smoke? It's a nasty habit—I know."

"That's fine with me," Myk replied. "Is it okay with you, Levi?"

Levi smirked and snapped out of his mesmerized stare at Raji. "No problem."

Myk said, "I'll inform the pilots, so you don't set off any alarms!" He smiled at Raji and then hopped out of the barstool and made his way to the front of the plane.

Raji took another sip of her wine while she set her pack of

cigarettes on her lap. *I can't believe you let that slip out,* she thought. But it was true. She rarely saw Ali. She wondered if she could trust the American. Every time she trusted a man she got hurt. Her independence allowed her to trust no one other than herself. And if she didn't have to trust anyone, then she wouldn't have to worry about getting hurt.

# CHAPTER 14

# SOMEWHERE OVER THE ATLANTIC

Raji heard the voice of the captain over the speaker. "We have disengaged the alarms. You are free to smoke now. However, smoking will need to be limited to no more than ten minutes every two hours."

Raji shook loose a cigarette from the pack and placed it between two fingers. She stroked the tiny wheel of the lighter backward, which ignited the flame. Raji calmly held the gold lighter up to her cigarette and inhaled deeply. The tip of the cigarette burned a bright amber color. Myk's questions had caused her to reflect. *Where did it all go wrong?* Thoughts of her wedding night came crashing to her forethought. She forced herself to think of something else, but it didn't work. The memory of her honeymoon was stubborn and wouldn't budge—so she obliged. Her chest swelled as she inhaled her elixir of cigarette smoke and then let her memory flow unimpeded.

Raji turned her body away from the wet bar and closed her eyes. The memory of the flashing red light from the hotel phone in Paris appeared in her mind's eye. It was as if she was back in the room, floating in the air and looking down on the sad, abandoned bride as she deliberately put the phone back on the receiver. Her feeling of loneliness after listening to Ali's message filled her soul. She already possessed complete contempt for her country of Iran before this, but now it turned into pure vitriol. She felt unimportant. *What Iranian business could possibly supplant your wedding night and consummating your relationship?* she had thought. Ali had chosen country over his marriage and it left Raji feeling unwanted. She sat on her bed, pulled her knees up to her chest, wrapped her arms around her knees in a tight ball, and wept. She shook her head back and forth as the tears poured out of her beautiful eyes and fell like soft droplets from a solitary cloud of rain. As she crept closer to despair, the strength of her deep-rooted inner character rose up. Raji filled her lungs with three huge breaths. She wiped her eyes and forced a smile. *I am responsible for my own happiness. Paris is one of the most beautiful cities in the world,* she thought. Raji looked up through the large expanse of glass and out to the distance. The Eiffel Tower was all aglow.

She scooted off the bed in search of her luggage. She spent the next thirty minutes unpacking her clothes and placing them in the dresser drawers. She hung her dresses and blouses up and organized the twelve pairs of shoes she'd brought. She unzipped her makeup bag and touched up her mascara, then reapplied her lipstick, gave herself an appraisal in the mirror, and said to herself, *Let's go explore Paris!* She forced a smile at the mirror and then spun on her heals and walked out of her suite.

Raji exited the elevator and entered the ornate hotel lobby. She saw a couple that was seated and speaking with the concierge. Her eyes scanned across the lobby and she saw a group of three couples with drinks in their hands engaged in what appeared to be a lively and humorous conversation. Her eyes moved to the plush lounges adjacent to the fireplace, which were full of people nibbling on assorted hors d'oeuvres and engaged in conversation. Raji continued walking through the lobby until the doorman pushed open the massive glass door framed in shiny brass. He smiled and bowed his head. "Enjoy your evening, miss." She followed the walkway around the extravagant porte cochere. The thirty-foot-tall porte cochere was held up at each corner by mammoth columns. The columns were clad in a matte-finished hand-carved marble. An enormous crystal chandelier that was at least ten feet in diameter hung from the tall ceiling. Some of the finest cars she'd ever seen were parked in the valet slots. Taxis came and went while dropping off or picking up their passengers. Raji continued walking out from under the porte cochere until she turned and began to walk up a street named La Huchette. The street was bustling with people. She heard the sounds from rock bands and jazz bands playing up the street. She immediately felt more energized by getting out and being completely surrounded by the sights, sounds, and smells of Paris's vibrant nightlife.

Raji felt her stomach growl with hunger pains. She tried to recall the last time she had eaten. *Had it really been seven hours?* she thought. Her plans changed. Rather than explore and see the sites, she would find a place to eat. She began reading the signs of all the trendy restaurants and cafés, looking for a place she could get something to eat while listening to some live music over a good drink while drowning out her sorrows. She could explore Paris later—she did have two more weeks after all. Raji wanted to think. Being abandoned on her honeymoon was never on the radar screen. She construed that Ali's exodus from their honeymoon validated her lifelong belief not to trust others. She had learned as a child that others couldn't be counted on. She had no mother, Malcolm was always off on his own, and her father used her, so she learned to only rely on herself. Her belief system was consistently reinforced by events in her life. It was this fiercely independent mind that was strolling the lively streets of Paris looking for a place to sit down and analyze and weigh her options. Raji may have lacked the love of caring parents during her life, but she filled that void with an abundance of confidence and intellect.

Raji heard the thumping bass sound of blues music that seemed to draw her in. She looked up and read the sign: Rayon D'espoir Café. She smiled when she translated the name—it meant Ray of Hope Café. *Perfect*, she thought. She entered and approached the hostess. Raji asked, "Do you have an open table by chance?"

The young hostess looked like she was barely eighteen. She was thin and had more of an athletic build, unlike Raji's curvy figure. Her dark, thin hair was pulled back in a ponytail so tight that it seemed to cause her eyes to squint. She asked Raji in a heavy French accent, "How many in your party, miss?"

Raji replied somewhat ruefully, "Just one—it's only me tonight."

The hostess turned and looked at the bar. "We have open seating at the bar."

"The bar won't work," Raji replied. "Would you see if you have any tables?"

The hostess looked down at her laminated seating chart and scanned back and forth. With her index finger, she pointed at a section on her chart and said, "I have a small table here. You can't see the band from there, but it's open."

Raji smiled. "Yes, that would be great."

The hostess grabbed the drink menu and food menu. "Right this way, please."

The hostess used her palm-size flashlight to help seat Raji. Rayon D'espoir Café was extremely dark inside—like a cavern. The building itself dated back to the sixteenth century. They began playing jazz in the café in the 1950s. Legends the likes of Count Basie and Louis Armstrong had played numerous times at Rayon D'espoir Café. In their pre-fame years, The Beatles had begun to find their legs at the café. Raji took her seat and opened up the drink menu, which came equipped with its own built-in light in order to see the selections. She looked up and scanned the dark café. It looked like a mysterious labyrinth with large gothic groin-vault ceilings twisting at odd angles. Raji settled on a red wine and pasta selection and put her menu aside. After placing her order, she began to think. Her first thought was to figure out those things she had control over and those that she didn't. She wouldn't waste her time and emotions on those things she had no control over. In her mind she began to take inventory. *I have a good job at the network. I am financially secure. I am healthy.* The mental inventory went on several minutes until "I am married" came to mind. She paused just in time for the waiter to appear and pour her wine.

Raji took a sip of her wine and tried to relax and soak in the ambiance and rhythmic blues music. The waiter placed the plate of pasta with buttery wine sauce in front of her and asked, "May I get anything else for you?"

"No, thank you. This is perfect." She ate her meal slowly and thoughtfully, completely unaware that she had finished her second glass of wine. The crowded café had thinned out. Raji remained and continued to drink her wine. After seriously contemplating starting over outside of the stifling Iranian regime, she decided that she would go back to Iran. But she ultimately decided to give Ali a chance. She would never again trust Ali—or any other man. She would devote herself to her career and her people of Iran. So she sat in the café trying to think (and drink) her way through the pain while shielding her heart. But her feelings kept crowding out her logic and her emotions flowed through. She listened to the soothing and rhythmic music, sipped some wine, and shed another tear. *It's my wedding night and I am in Paris alone.* She clenched her fists trying to fight back feeling lonely and betrayed. Raji heard a voice, but the words passed through her like the wind through a fishing net. She heard the voice again and looked up, but saw nothing but a blur. She heard the voice again for the third time, but her eyes wouldn't focus. Then she felt a hand on her shoulder. The blurry figure seemed to be bending down and moving closer.

Raji's eyes came into focus. A female face came into her view. A beautiful face. She heard her voice, "Miss, are you okay?"

Raji's mind started scrambling. She looked around the restaurant and realized it was half empty and wondered how long she had been staring into space, lost in her thoughts. She glanced at her watch. *Where did two hours go?* she thought. Raji replied to the blonde-haired, blue-eyed stranger sitting in front of her, "Yes, I guess I just got lost in the music." She paused and saw the two empty bottles of wine on the table. She smiled and said, "I guess I got lost in the wine too."

The stranger shook her head dramatically. "I don't think so, darlin'. Unless you're telling me that you were so lost in the music that it's caused all those tears?"

Raji's sharp intellect was dulled by the wine, she was off-kilter and couldn't make sense of this foreigner with an American southern drawl talking to her. "It's been a rough night. Who are you, anyway?" Raji asked.

The blonde stranger squeezed her shoulder affectionately one more time and then removed her hand. She answered, "Rebecca Bell. The Rayon D'espoir Café is like a second home when I'm in Paris. I've known the owners for more than twenty years. I'm usually in the café a few nights a week. I've had my eye on you since you first arrived. Don't worry, I just enjoy people watching when I'm at my café. When you entered, I wondered to myself what type of man could be worthy of a catch like you! But no one came. And then I saw your tears that you tried to chase away with the wine. But they still kept coming." She put her hand on Raji's knee and lowered her voice. "I know pain when I see it, my dear." She nodded her head. "Because I've been in that very same chair, crying and staring into space many years ago. I sat down because I wish someone would've sat down with me. I'm here to listen. If you'd like me to leave, just say the word."

Raji nodded, smiled genuinely, and said, "Thank you. That is very sweet, Rebecca."

"Call me Becca. And what is your name, sweetheart?"

"Raji. I'm from Iran. How about you?"

"I'm from the US. I'm not sure if you've heard of Texas, but I'm from Austin, Texas."

"Yes, I've heard of Texas. I don't know the cities though."

Becca said, "I lost an adult child five years ago, that's what put me in your chair drinking my tears away. I don't know what pain you're going through, but I've had my fair share. What's troubling your heart, dear?"

Unsure where to begin or what to even say, she tried to gather her thoughts. Raji heard the band go on break behind her and then watched Becca as she broke eye contact with her and began watching one of the band members walk by. Becca swung her head around to continue gawking at the lead guitar player. When he was out of sight, Becca turned back to Raji and said, "Good Lord—I'd like to ride that one! I've had my eye on him for a month!"

Raji sat shocked with no response. She squinted and thought, *Who is this? Who talks like this to total strangers?* She reasoned that maybe a listening ear, as strange as this one might be, might do her some good. "I was supposed to spend two weeks in Paris with a man, but something happened, and it's just going to be me, alone."

Becca looked at the diamond ring on Raji's hand. "And was this man that you were supposed to spend two weeks with your husband?"

"Yes."

Becca shook her head, then said, "Men are selfish. I've had three husbands and only one of them wasn't! Where's your husband anyway?"

"He's away on an emergency."

Becca asked, "What's he do?"

"He's pretty high up in our government."

"I see." Becca paused. "How long have you been married?"

Raji took a sip of wine and stared blankly—contemplating whether or not to go further down the rabbit hole. Her lips pursed. "Not even a day. I was married this morning and arrived in Paris about four hours ago. Minutes after we entered our honeymoon suite, he went out for a bottle of wine and never returned. He left a message on the hotel phone apologizing and said he had to leave for something urgent."

Becca placed her fingertips over her lips. Her eyes widened as she placed her other hand over her heart. "Oh my! You poor thing.

I've experienced a lot in my life, and I've heard many stories in my decade of coming to this café, but nothing like this." She paused and shook her head expressively. "Wow!"

Raji added, "I've known him since we were children. It just doesn't make sense to me. I thought we had a good connection on an intellectual and emotional level." She paused, then added, "I was looking forward to the start of our physical connection tonight, but he's gone."

"What do you mean, the start of your physical connection? Are you saying that the two of you have never had sex?"

"No, but we kiss."

A questioning look came across Becca's face. "Has he ever touched you in a sexual way—your breasts, between your legs?"

Raji shook her head. "He grabbed my butt a few times. I asked him once why he hadn't made any sexual advances. He said that he was raised by his mother to save himself until the night of his marriage. Also, we come from a culture where premarital sex is forbidden."

"Hmm. Well, maybe there really was some sort of emergency. But just between you and I—that must be one hell of an emergency to leave you alone in the bed, because you are pure eye candy, my dear!"

Raji smiled. "Thank you. I've never had a conversation like this. Do all Western women talk without a filter?"

Becca laughed. "Heavens, no, you sweet thing. I'm afraid I'm one of a kind. I was raised a cowgirl in Texas. I was the US Roping Champion five years straight—unbeatable until that fucking steer broke three ribs and punctured my lung."

Inquisitively Raji asked, "Roping Champion? What's that?"

Becca shot back, "A waste of time! That's what that is." She laughed and then continued, "Not sure if you've ever seen any old American western cowboy movies, but a roping competition is to see which competitor can be the fastest to rope a small cow. Basically, I'm in one corral on my horse, Dolly, and there's a young steer in the corral next to me. The clock starts when the gates open. When that happens, Dolly and I tear after that steer like a hungry cheetah chasing down a gazelle. It's my job to throw my rope around the steer's neck and then flip him over and tie him up faster than anyone else."

Just as Becca finished, the guitar player she'd been eyeing passed by. Becca motioned her head in his direction and said with a smile, "Speaking of roping, he'd be fun!"

Raji felt the release of some of her pent-up anger. *There's something disarming about her.* "That's absolutely fascinating. I've never heard of roping. I assume that's quite an accomplishment to be a US champion—let alone five times."

Becca deflected the compliment. "Well, thank you. But it was all Dolly. That girl could run like the wind! My ropin' skills were good, but Dolly was the real champ."

Raji felt herself being drawn in, forgetting about her loneliness. "Did you ever go back to roping after your injury?"

"Nah. Made the mistake of gettin' married instead!" Becca shook her head. "I had become somewhat of a celebrity in the rodeo world and got starry-eyed over a charismatic hunk of a cowboy. How about your husband—is he handsome?"

Raji nodded. "Oh yes! He played on the Iranian national soccer team. I was really looking forward to that part of our relationship, but it'll have to wait until I get back to Iran."

"I hope that works out for the two of you. My first one only lasted three months."

"Wow, what happened—if you don't mind me asking?"

"Of course not. I should've paid more attention before we got married—but damn did that cowboy know how to curl my toes! He had a drinking problem, which then turned him into an angry drunk. I saw the signs but ignored them. Call it optimistic youth. More like stupid youth now that I look back. Anyway, he got drunk and hit me a month after we got married. I blamed it on the booze and gave him a pass. A few weeks later he came after me again."

"What did you do?"

Becca moved the right side of her hair over with her hand, exposing her right ear. There was a large scar from her temple down across her ear. She said, "He smashed a bottle against my face. Boy did he light me up. He's awfully lucky I didn't kill him that night! He could hardly walk he was so drunk. I shoved him and he tipped over like a toddler first learning to walk. That only added fuel to the raging fire. He wobbled his way back to his feet. I ran over to the fireplace and grabbed the iron fireplace shovel and swung it at his melon head like I was Babe Ruth swinging for the fences! His legs turned to Jell-O and he swayed and spun to the floor like a bounce house getting the plug pulled out."

Raji listened, mesmerized, unaware that the troubles in her mind had been replaced by a charismatic cowgirl. Raji and Becca talked through the night and closed the Rayon D'espoir Café down. Becca walked her back to the hotel at two a.m. As they approached the lobby, Becca asked, "Are you close with your mom? You should call her."

"She died in an explosion when I was a little girl. I would have died too, but a man saved my brother and me. It left this scar above my eye." She pointed to her scar.

"I'm so sorry to hear that. Since your husband is away on urgent matters, would you like me to show you around Paris?"

Raji looked at her, puzzled. "I'm sure you have better things to do."

Becca laughed. "Ever since we discovered oil on my ranch, I've got more money and more time than I know what to do with! It would be my pleasure to see you discover Paris for the first time. And you can educate me about Iranian culture too."

"That would be great! I look forward to it."

Becca smiled and said, "I'll meet you tomorrow morning in the lobby. What time?"

Raji looked at her watch. It was almost two-thirty in the morning. "How about eleven?"

"Deal. But don't eat breakfast. I've got a place you'll love."

"Great, I'll see you tomorrow morning."

Before she had even completed her sentence, Becca was already moving in for a hug. She wrapped her arms around Raji, giving her a warm embrace. When they broke, Becca winked and said, "Don't you fret. Things are gonna work out just fine for you, Raji." With that, she spun and walked up the dark street.

The two weeks in Paris with Becca were the happiest of Raji's life. She had never experienced so much freedom and joy. She had tasted the best wine, eaten the best food, listened to the best music, and learned so much about the world outside of Iran that it frightened her. For the first time, she gained real perspective and context about Iran. A country where women were almost a century behind Western civilization. Raji and Becca formed an inseparable bond. After Raji was back in Iran, they communicated on a weekly basis, but it was cryptic. They couldn't be completely open in their communication because someone was always watching or listening in Iran. Letters weren't private. Almost all her mail was screened. But the two of them figured out a way to keep their friendship alive. Becca learned how to decipher Raji's ambiguous wording. She learned that Raji's physical connection with Ali never did blossom. Not only did it not blossom, it never even grew roots. Ali was a different person when Raji got back to Iran.

They eventually did consummate their marriage—a month after Raji returned. Becca learned that Ali would only have sex with Raji when he thought that she was ovulating. So Raji lied to him about her menstrual cycle. When Raji got home from Paris, she frequently reflected on what a life-changing two weeks the trip had been. It changed her entire view of the world and her outlook on life. Yes, she was a caged tiger. She felt trapped in Iran. If she hadn't experienced what true freedom was, her feelings wouldn't have been as intense. Her hatred toward her country's leadership grew. Two months before the one-year anniversary of her marriage, she received a mysterious letter from Becca—more cryptic than usual; perhaps because of its importance. From what Raji was able to decipher, Becca had devised a plan. Raji's part in the plan was clear—she and Ali had to return to Paris for their one-year anniversary. Becca's part in the plan, well, that wasn't clear at all. But Raji trusted her roping cowgirl friend. Which wasn't something that came easy. Raji was pleasantly surprised at how easily Ali had acquiesced around the idea of going back to Paris. Perhaps it could provide the much-needed spark in their new marriage. If Raji thought her first trip to Paris was life-changing, then her second trip to Paris—that would redefine her understanding of the term *life-changing* forever.

# CHAPTER 15

Raji's body jolted up off the chair from the hard turbulence. She heard the pilot over the speaker, "We've run into a patch of rough air. We've located some smoother air out there, but it will take a few minutes to get out of this, so you may want to buckle up." Raji felt the thrust of the jet banking right as the three of them continued to shake in their seats like they were in an old-school wooden roller coaster. When they cleared the turbulence and made their way to smooth air, Raji unbuckled from her seat and poured herself another glass of wine. The memories of her first trip to Paris got tucked safely back into the hippocampus of her brain.

Myk was still sitting nearby, watching a fidgety Levi. Myk asked him, "Are you okay?"

Levi forced a smile. "I'm fine."

"You don't look fine. You're quivering. What's wrong?"

Levi stared down at the laces in his shoes as moisture filled his eyes. "It's too much, Myk. I shouldn't have come." He raised his finger slightly, pointing at Raji, and said, "That's her, Myk."

They both looked at Raji. She felt a puzzled look spread over her face.

Levi asked, "She doesn't know—does she?"

Myk's reply was slow and deliberate. He shrugged, "How could she?"

Raji piped up, "Know what?"

Just then, Jaafar walked in the room and grabbed a bottle of water from the mini fridge.

Raji raised her tone. "Know what?"

Levi adjusted himself on the couch and faced her directly. His eyes were moist, his hands were quivering. Levi raised his trembling hand and pointed directly at her face. "I am the one responsible for that scar over your eye."

The world stood still for Raji. She stopped breathing and her stomach sank. She sat speechless staring at Levi. Memories of the parking garage in Beirut tried to wiggle their way from her memory, but they were faded and unclear. She tried to pry them loose. Raji stared at Levi's eyes. Those eyes she questioned. And then it came—a picture in her mind's eye of her rescuer's face—that memory would never fade. He was older now, much older. But it was him. The last memory of her mother looking back at her in the parking garage came to mind. An involuntary tear rolled out of the corner of Raji's eye. *What's happening?* she thought. She felt a strange mix of emotions.

She knew the answer, but she didn't know what to say so she asked, "That was you?"

Levi nodded slowly. He wiped the tears from his eyes with the back of his hand. "I am so sorry. I wish I could have saved her!"

Raji whispered, "Me too."

Levi went on, "I'll never forget that look of fear in her face. And her eyes—she had iridescent eyes that glowed just like yours. She was wearing a long red dress with matching shoes and scarf in her hair that day. She wasn't supposed to be there, Raji! You weren't supposed to be there." Levi's fists clinched as he continued. "Your mother stood frozen in place while I sprinted to pull you and your brother out of harm's way—she knew she was about to die. The minute I hit the pavement with you two kids, the explosion went off and she was gone."

Jaafar stood tall and leaned on his cane from behind the wet bar. He looked quizzically at Levi. "You're the Jew who killed my wife?! I knew there was something familiar about your face."

Levi looked at Jaafar and grimaced. His lips tightened and then he rebutted, "And you're the man who killed my brother! *My* bomb was meant for *you* and not her mother. It was meant for you! I saved your children that day and would have saved your wife if I could." Levi paused and shook his head. "What was your excuse? Why didn't you at least try? I've never seen such a coward. You ran for the stairs instead of for your wife!"

Few things impressed Myk. What he was about to witness he would never forget. The instant the last syllable left Levi's mouth, Raji's arm was reaching for her weapon under her hijab. Myk would later recount that he saw Raji find her gun under her hijab, flip the safety switch, stand, and take two large steps forward, then point the loaded weapon with a stiff arm that was as perfectly still as a statue, in what seemed like less than one second. Few people would appreciate such a thing. To Myk it was like fluid art—a thing of beauty.

Raji stood unflinching with her weapon pointed directly at Jaafar, daggers in her eyes. "You pathetic coward! Is that true, did you run for the stairwell instead of my mother?!"

Jaafar stood frozen. "I would do anything to relive that moment. I am so sorry, Raji."

Myk watched. A part of him wanted Raji to squeeze the trigger. They could figure things out without Jaafar now that they had the zip drive, he reasoned. Raji's iridescent eyes were raging. She was livid.

Raji took three deep breaths. Her eyes were fixed on Jaafar. Through her gritted teeth she said, "You filled my head with lies! You used me! You convinced me to wire your bombs and told me I was protecting other little girls from getting their mommies killed by men like him." Raji motioned with her head toward Levi, all the time her pistol remained fixed on Jaafar.

Her rage continued, "What this world needs is *more* men like him." She pointed to Levi. "And fewer men like you!" With her thumb, she pulled the hammer back on the gun. Everyone heard the click of the metal and waited for the sound of the shot. As they all stood still and stared at Raji in anticipation of a gunshot, Levi's peaceful voice said, "Please don't."

"Why not?" Raji barked back.

"Because it won't stop your bad dreams."

"He's a monster!" Raji shouted out.

"True, but you're not. Please put the gun down. He may have deceived you into wiring his bombs, but you didn't kill anyone."

"Yes I did. I wired the bombs that killed thousands. The dead visit me in my dreams!"

Levi's voice was calming. "You didn't kill anyone. Let go of your unjustified guilt. You were an innocent little girl. Somebody else set those bombs off, not you."

"He needs to pay!"

"He will, but not you. He's not worth it, Raji. I have seen too much death and tragedy in my lifetime. No more. Please lower your gun."

Raji walked resolutely toward Jaafar. She stood on one side of the bar while he stood perfectly still on the other side. Her arm was still raised, and the gun was six inches from his skull.

Raji whispered so low that only Jaafar could hear, "I wish you would have pulled the trigger last week when you sat on the side of your bed with the pistol pointed under your chin." She lowered her gun, turned, and slowly walked back to the couch and sat.

Jaafar stood, eyes wide, with his mouth gaping open and per- spiration rolling down the sides of his temples. Everyone let out a sigh of relief while Raji coolly slid another cigarette from her pack and began smoking.

Levi smiled at her and said, "You did the right thing."

Jaafar broke the five-minute silence, telling Levi in a subdued voice, "I should thank you for saving my children. My people would've never done such a thing as you did—that tells me something about you. I can't change the past, but perhaps I can influence minds and change hearts." Jaafar walked around the wet bar and sat in the stool.

Myk sarcastically replied, "From the look of things back in Verona, you need to be more concerned about saving your own life if you're ever going to have a chance of saving anyone else's!"

Levi turned to Myk. "It's worth a shot. We may never get another chance like this. Someone as high profile as Jaafar could change minds. Even if he only manages to change one, it would be worth it."

"Let's not get ahead of ourselves. Jaafar's information has yet to be corroborated."

As Levi sat, he studied Jaafar's face. His eyes scanned down to Jaafar's leg. The metal from his prosthetic was exposed above his sock. Levi stared at Jaafar's contorted ear, then lifted his index finger and asked, "Was that from the bomb in Beirut?"

Jaafar nodded. "Yes." He lifted his pant leg further up and rubbed his titanium leg like a trusted dog lying beside him. "I almost bled to death because of this."

Levi blurted, "If I could have saved her, I would have. I am just glad I was able to get to the kids."

Jaafar looked at Raji. "Me too."

Levi asked, "Do you really think they'll listen to you?"

"Without a doubt! Unfortunately, there are those in Iran that know this too. That's why they've already put a price on my head."

"So where do you begin?" Levi asked.

"First I have to find a place of refuge in which to operate before I can reach out."

Myk's phone rang. He looked at the screen and then stood and walked away from Levi and Jaafar. He answered, "Director, what's the news?" He listened but had difficulty hearing, so he increased the volume on his phone. "We have a weak connection. What did you say?"

Adelberg said, "He's telling the truth, Myk. There's a lot of useful information on the zip drive. We've have Jamal under surveillance but we can't take him until he leads us to the containers of the virus."

"That's great news. We had an incident on the plane, but it's all ironed out." As Myk's thumb was poised to end the call he quickly put the phone back to his ear. "Director are you still there?"

"Yes, Myk, what's up?"

"Did you find out anything on the missing Heinrich Mueller file?"

"Nothing yet. I went as high as I could up the chain of command to see who authorized it, and the trail went cold. I reached out to a few retirees that were tracking Mueller. One of them knew about the eleven crates of Nazi gold that are in Fort Knox that're connected to Mueller."

"Are you sure he said eleven crates?"

"Yes, quite sure. Why?"

"It's nothing. Do you think Heinrich Mueller escaped to live out his life?"

"From what I have heard, I highly doubt it."

"Okay, please find out who authorized his file to be purged. There's someone out there that's extremely nervous about me making the connection to Mueller."

"I know, Myk. We'll turn our attention to it as soon as we find the virus containers. I've got a call coming in on the other line."

In light of the previous assassination attempts on Myk, Adelberg suggested changing airports from San Francisco to Oakland. If they could locate Myk as quickly as they did at Union Square, then surely he'd be easy prey now. Myk's head was spinning as he walked back to the room. He sat down, crossed his legs, and made eye contact with Levi. He knew the answer to the question but asked it anyway. "How many crates of gold did you see them pull out of the lake in Switzerland?"

"Fifteen. Why?"

"Just wanted to make sure I heard you right." He looked at Jaafar. "The director said the intel you provided was accurate. You can talk to him about a deal when we land in Oakland."

Jaafar asked, "I thought we were landing in San Francisco?"

Myk leaned forward on his knees. "Our pilot flew several

missions for me in Afghanistan. I asked him to change airports as a favor. Oakland is only ten minutes further from downtown San Francisco." He slowly shook his head at Jaafar. "I have a mandate to end your life. That was the plan after we verified your information. To let a high-profile murderer such as you step foot in our country, let alone make a deal of immunity and protection, is unconscionable! But if there's any ray of hope of starting a real movement that will actually rupture the foundation of radical Islam—it's going to have to come from within their community—from the voice of one of their own leaders. There's no other way."

Jaafar nodded and then asked, "Why the last-minute change from landing at San Francisco, if you don't mind me asking?"

Myk thought for a minute about the wisdom of sharing any information with Jaafar. Both Jaafar and Myk had assassins trying to kill them. "I'm on the verge of uncovering information that has some very powerful people extremely nervous. I want to avoid Raji or Levi getting caught in the crossfire. I have no idea what may have been waiting for me at the San Francisco airport, but I have no doubt that someone in my government is trying to kill me. I made the change as an extra precaution."

Raji asked, "So what's the plan when we land?"

Myk motioned toward Jaafar and then looked back at Raji. The look in her eyes seemed to glow and draw him in, causing him to have a momentary loss of thought. He shook off her mesmerizing eyes and replied, "Jaafar is at the top of every US and international most-wanted list. I'm going take him and Levi to a personal safe house of mine that's off the grid. If I would have landed in San Francisco, they would have immediately taken Jaafar into custody. There are those in my government that would use his capture to score political points, but I'm not relinquishing him so easily. I might need him for leverage later on."

Raji gave him a puzzled look. "What about me?"

Myk smiled. "You were one squeeze of the trigger away from

killing him—a little distance between the two of you might be best. Besides, I told you that I'd bring you to see Yasser's body after we locate the containers of the virus. If it's okay with you, I'd like to have you come with me."

Raji smiled. "The less time I have to spend with him, the better."

# CHAPTER 16

## SAN FRANCISCO, CALIFORNIA

Myk's safe house looked like millions of other production homes that had been built across the United States by a national home builder. It had clay-colored concrete tile on the roof with a stucco exterior that was painted gray-beige. The small front yard had a solitary tree and a few hedges. The two-car garage door had arched clear plastic windows to let light in. It was exactly what Myk wanted when he purchased the home for a safe house—to blend in. In stark contrast, the interior of the house was professionally decorated with furnishings and appointments that could be found in a multimillion-dollar luxury home. Myk parked the rental car in the garage and shut the door. Myk, Levi, and Jaafar all entered the house while Raji waited in the car. After getting Levi and Jaafar situated, Myk got back in the car with Raji. Before starting the engine, he asked, "Are you sure you don't want to stay here?"

"Yes, quite sure."

"Okay. Surveillance can be a bit tedious and boring."

Raji replied sarcastically, "I've done a bit of surveillance myself." She smiled and continued, "Before the network made me the lead broadcaster, my camera crew and I chased down countless stories that required long stakeouts."

Myk nodded and started the car. "Of course. It will be nice to have your company."

As they drove the rental car out of the neighborhood, Myk called Director Adelberg to check in. "Director, what's the latest developments with Jamal?"

"He's behaving like a model citizen. We have a team that follows him wherever he goes."

"Any leads on where he's hiding the virus containers?"

"None at all. What's your ETA to his apartment?"

"We're about twenty minutes out right now."

"We?" Adelberg asked by dragging *we* out in a long, exaggerated tone.

"Yes. Raji and I. She's quite capable of handling herself, as you probably read in my email. Also, the relationship between her and Jaafar is . . ." Myk paused as he thought of the right word, "a bit toxic. She was more than happy to ride along. Whenever we get a break, I told her I would take her to see the body of Yasser."

"No problem, Myk. The FBI has two agents following Jamal right now."


Jamal glanced up at the Walnut Creek Station sign that was illuminated in red letters. The distant sounds of the approaching subway train echoed out of the tunnel. He felt the vibrations from the coming train under his well-worn suede shoes. The lead car whooshed by him and wafted his dark hair across his face. The US had fully recovered from the lasting effects of social distancing. The vaccine was the final hurdle that quelled all fears and filled the restaurants, sports stadiums, theatres, and music venues. Jamal stood aside while a group of women with shaved heads and piercings in their lips, noses, and ears stepped into the half-empty train car. Two muscular men holding hands entered the train next. They were covered in colorful tattoos and wearing denim jeans and tight t-shirts exposing their ripped physiques. One man had long hair in a ponytail and a groomed goatee, while the other wore a Las Vegas Raiders beanie cap and sleek tortoise-framed glasses. An unknown being with orange spiked hair, black eyeliner, a dangling nose ring, and black combat boots boarded. Jamal stared self-righteously at the squalid group of people surrounding him and cringed. He looked down at his feet, held his arms close to his body, and skirted onto the train, trying his hardest to avoid any contact. He quickly sat in the first available seat. The train doors closed, and it lunged forward.

As the clacking of the metal subway wheels across the steel tracks increased its rhythmic sounds, Jamal closed his eyes and leaned back in his seat. It would be another ten stops before he would exit at the Civic Center Station where his apartment was located. If things went according to plan, he would release the new virus and cripple the US economy with a second pandemic. One of the female riders that had been holding on to the center pole sat down beside him. Jamal opened his eyes and looked at the girl. His face impulsively scrunched up like he had just seen a dog run over by a car. The gaping purple gauges in her ears made them droop down like an elephant. Her tongue and eyebrows were pierced. Her jet-black, straight hair hung over her threadbare Imagine Dragons concert t-shirt. She wore a pair of faded denim designer jeans that had several rips. Indignant, Jamal immediately stood and walked to an empty seat away from the girl, back to the comfort of his isolated island. It's where he resided most hours of the day; it's where he was comfortable. Just Jamal and his pious thoughts.

All through high school and college, he had been a loner on his island of one, until the day he was discovered by Jaafar—someone who finally understood him. For the last year, he had communicated with his online friend, Jaafar, several times a week through the internet. He met his operation partner, Yasser, just a month ago, but when Yasser tried to convince him to stop their operation, Jamal was livid, so he reached out to Jaafar. He was never told that Yasser was Jaafar's grandson. Jaafar told him not to worry about Yasser and that he should continue with the plans without him.

A voice came over the loudspeaker of the BART train. "Next stop, Embarcadero Station."

Jamal looked at the station list. *Two more stops before this Zionist country is brought to its knees*, he thought.

The train slowed and then stopped at Embarcadero. The girl who had sat next to him stood and held the overhead bar with both hands as she waited for the train doors to slide open. With her hands above her, it became obvious to Jamal that she was braless and that her ears, lips, and nose weren't the only body parts that had piercings. She turned back to Jamal and caught him ogling. She chuckled and then smiled directly at him and winked. Jamal became flustered and immediately gazed at the floor until he heard the swishing sounds of the doors closing. The train moved forward, so Jamal slowly peered out the window.

There she was again!

She raised her arm and wiggled her fingers back and forth in a polite good-bye motion as the train moved on. Jamal stared at the two women toward the front of the train. They were clasping the vertical pole and being affectionate in front of the passengers. He shook his head and thought, *Reprobates.*

A voice piped in overhead, "Next stop, Civic Center Station."

Jamal slipped his arm through the strap on his backpack and grabbed onto the overhead bar as he stood. He watched through the window at those who were gathered on the platform waiting for the train. Most of them were businessmen dressed in dark suits and ties, while many of the women wore skirts and professional blouses. He entered the bustling and crowded station and began his ascent up the stairs. As he exited the station and walked to Polk Street, the smell of the salty ocean air filled his lungs. A chilling breeze whisked across his body and he instantly quickened his pace to get back to the warmth of his apartment for the final time.


Myk and Raji parked outside of Jamal's apartment building and watched as he entered the front door. Every street surrounding the building had been barricaded off by police. After a week, the residents of the building had grown accustomed to showing their identification in order to access the parking structure. Myk stepped out of the car and walked to the vehicle parked in front of him. Agent Jodee Black had been waiting in her car for Myk to give her a short dinner break from her surveillance of Jamal. As Myk approached the driver's side of Agent Black's vehicle, she rolled down the window.

"Agent Black, it has been a few years. How have you been?" Myk asked.

She smiled. "Still above ground. Can't ask for more than that!"

"So true!" Myk put both hands on the door and asked, "So what's the situation?"

"I'm bored out of my mind, that's the situation!"

Myk laughed. "So I've heard."

"He hasn't done shit since we've been watching him."

Myk nodded. "He will."

Black shrugged her shoulders. "We'll see. We've stopped him randomly several times, and he's always clean. His apartment has been searched twice, and they won't grant any more warrants. Every exit from the building is covered by four agents. His apartment is that one up there with the blue dots on the curtains." Agent Black pointed up to the window of Jamal's apartment.

"I see."

"He has yet to open the curtains, though. He's been following the same routine every day. Now that he's in his apartment, he won't leave. How was your trip—were you able to gather any useful information?"

Myk nodded. "I think so, but it's still being verified by Adelberg."

"I appreciate you giving me a break. I should be back in a couple hours."

"No problem."

"Do you want me to bring you anything back?"

"I'm fine, thanks for asking."

Agent Black slowly pulled her vehicle away. Myk walked back

to his car and then slid into the front seat. He asked Raji, "Would you mind grabbing the binoculars out of the glove box for me? We shouldn't be here any longer than two hours. After that, I should be able to take you to see Yasser's body."

Raji handed him the binoculars and said, "Thank you. So, what's going on, if you don't mind me asking?"

"They have been following Jamal for several weeks. Every exit is being watched and they have agents follow him everywhere he goes."

"Why don't you just arrest him?"

"They have! They took him in and interrogated him, but he hasn't broken any laws, so there's not a whole lot the authorities are allowed to do at this point."

Raji nodded. "Interesting." She smirked and then said, "Things would be handled much differently if this were Iran."

Myk smiled. "I know!" He brought the binoculars to his eyes to get a closer look at Jamal's window, but nothing was happening.

Raji spoke up. "You seem to know quite a bit about my dysfunctional family, but I know very little about yours—other than your sweet uncle Levi. I thought I overheard Levi talking to you about your father. What happened to him, if you don't mind me asking?"

Myk continued to closely watch the apartment building as he answered, "He was murdered in London. Levi was in the front seat of the car with him and saw the whole thing. Sadly, I just found out about it a few months ago."

One of Raji's eyebrows raised above the other. "I'm sorry to hear about your father. Why so long for you to find out about him?"

Myk shook his head. "My mother is unlike any other. Unfortunately, she's seen humanity at its worst."

Raji's nodded. "Then she's seen some awful things."

Myk continued, "She and her twin sister were orphaned as newborns because of the Nazis. They were born a month before the Nazis arrived in Lidice, Czechoslovakia, toward the end of the war. When word got out that the Nazis were on their way to her town, my grandmother brought her babies—twins—to a Catholic friend in a neighboring farming town to watch over them. Lidice was obliterated by the Nazis. The town was flattened by bulldozers, farms were leveled, and rivers were filled in and diverted. Lidice was removed from all German maps as if it never existed. My grandparents were lined up on the side of a barn and shot along with the rest of the town. It took the Nazis two days to massacre the entire town."

Raji slowly moved her hand over her mouth. "That's awful. What happened to your mother and her twin sister?"

"When they were adults, my mother—Hannah—and her sister joined Mossad and eventually became part of an elite team. Because of her passion over her career, she put off marriage until she was forty-five. At the age forty-nine, miraculously, she gave birth to me."

"She sounds like an extraordinary woman."

Myk shrugged. "I was definitely a whoops baby at her age. Anyway, she moved to the US to start a new life with a new identity after my father was murdered. When I met with Levi for the first time last week, he told me that she was never the same person."

Raji shook her head. "That's so sad."

Myk nodded. "Yeah, the assassination of my father and her decades as a Mossad agent left her with bouts of anxiety and depression. To cope, vodka was her remedy of choice. On the days she was sober, the guilt for her neglect of me drove her to be the Mother of the Year. It was a difficult cycle for her. The vodka made the pain go away, but then she was absent or in bed for days, which basically left me abandoned. When she would sober up, she would over-parent because of her guilt over the neglect. The vicious cycle of neglect followed by overcompensation continued for almost twelve years, until I started high school."

"Did she ever share anything about her past when you were growing up? I imagine that would really spark the interest of a little boy."

"Not a thing. She never spoke a word to me about her days as a Mossad agent. Since she was almost always on pills or the drink, I learned at a very young age how to dress myself, make my own lunch, and put myself to bed. Most mothers would have their kids all cleaned up and looking good for picture day at school." Myk laughed. "I have bedhead and wrinkled shirts in all of my school pictures. I felt unimportant at home, so that's why I put all my time and energy into sports."

"Did your mother ever get any help?"

"Not that I'm aware of. She's not the type that would ever ask for help anyway. Her anxiety caused by the murder of her parents, my father's murder, and her decades as a spy, spilled over into how she raised me. By age seven, she had taught me to be an excellent marksman with handguns. By age ten, I was a blackbelt and a National Karate Champion. In junior high, she made me attend three different wilderness survival camps."

"Makes sense. So, what's your sport?"

"Well, if I knew you a little better, I'd try and be funny and say a better question would be what's not my sport. But I really don't want you to think I'm arrogant or anything. I guess sports were my security blanket, so to speak. I did really well at most sports. Wrestling, however, is what I excelled at. I became an all-American wrestler at the University of Southern California and won three national championship matches."

"Ali was an excellent soccer player and played on the Iranian national team. Did you ever play soccer?"

Myk laughed. "Of course the first sport you'd ask me about would be the one I'm terrible at. I never got into soccer."

"Hmm. I can't say that I'm much of wrestler." She smiled and then continued, "But my brother Malcolm and I were in karate and learned to shoot on our father's gun range."

"If I was a betting man, I'd say you've got better marksmanship than ninety percent of all the agents surrounding this building right now!"

# CHAPTER 17

As Raji and Myk filled in the time conversing outside the apartment building, Jamal was making his final preparations to unleash another pandemic on the United States—with a much more deadly virus.

Jamal stood up from his prayer rug, determined. He resolutely walked to his closet and put on his San Francisco Giants shirt and cap. For the first time since leasing his apartment, he opened the heavy curtains and stood at the window. He remained in front of the window for over three minutes and looked in all directions. He left the curtains open, turned away, and found his backpack on the couch.

Myk was looking through his binoculars when Jamal opened the curtains.

"That's odd."

Raji asked, "What's that?"

"Jodee told me that Jamal has never opened the curtains to his window the entire time they've had him under surveillance. And there he is, standing in front of his window with his curtains open."

Raji peered up at Jamal's window. "Hmm. Why do you think that is?"

"I don't know." Myk tapped his earpiece to communicate over a secure line to the rest of the team. "This is Agent Myk Miles. Is anyone else seeing this? Jamal just opened the curtains to his window, and he's just standing there."

A scratchy voice chimed in, "This is Agent Glover. Yeah, I'm seeing the same thing as you, Myk. All agents, keep a tight watch on the exits. Jamal has a Giants shirt and hat on."

Myk pushed the button. "Roger that." He turned to Raji and said, "That's too obvious."

"What's that?" she asked.

"Jamal knows we're watching him."

"I'm with you, Myk, I think he's definitely up to something. Why don't you go up to his apartment and check things out?"

"I can't. They've come up empty on their two previous search warrants."

Raji's eyes narrowed as if in deep thought. "What's his apartment number?"

"He's in number 3042, why?"

Raji reached for the door handle. "I am going to knock on his door! I have no affiliation with your agencies." Before Myk could stop her, she opened the door and walked across the street.


Inside his apartment, Jamal quickly made his way to his closet and sat down next to the large dresser situated along the back wall. He placed both feet on the bottom of the dresser, braced his back against the wall and pushed hard against the heavy furniture piece. After shoving it out of the way, he crawled over and tugged up on the carpet. The carpet flapped back, exposing a hidden door in the floor. Jamal pulled the door open and stepped down the ladder that dropped into the closet of the lower apartment.

Jamal quickly set his backpack on the ground and grabbed the bald-man disguise sitting on the shelf. He tugged the plastic disguise over his head and adjusted the eye holes. Next, he pulled the skin-colored shirt full of tattoos off the hanger and stretched the tight fitting, long-sleeve nylon shirt over his head and walked to the bathroom mirror to make an appraisal of his disguise. Jamal was immediately repulsed by the image staring back at him: a bald white man covered in tattoos from his neck down to his wrists. He walked back to the closet where a small refrigerator was located. He took the two spray bottles containing the deadly virus and put them in his pockets. He grabbed a light jacket from the closet, zipped it up, and then slung his backpack over his shoulder and headed for the door. As Jamal approached the exit door of the apartment building to go to his car, he passed one of the most beautiful Middle Eastern women he had ever laid eyes on.

Raji entered the apartment building and walked past a creepy bald man that was ogling her. She ran up the stairwell to the third floor and quickly located apartment number 3042. She knocked on the door several times and then listened. She heard nothing, so she tried the door handle. It was unlocked. Raji discreetly entered the apartment and called out, "Jamal, are you here? I am Yasser's mother." She stood still and waited for a response—nothing but silence. Raji slowly walked down the hall and called out his name again, nothing. She entered Jamal's closet and gasped. She stared at the huge hole in the closet floor with a ladder leading to the apartment below and shook her head. *Damn*, she thought. Raji turned and ran to the window. She opened the window and began frantically waving her arms and then motioned a "come here" gesture to Myk. Raji watched as nine agents immediately appeared from nowhere, as if a magician had waved a magic wand, and began to storm the building.

Myk was the first to arrive. Raji showed him to the hole in the master closet. Myk slid down the ladder like a seasoned fireman being alerted to an inferno. He opened the mini-fridge and exclaimed, "Shit!"

"What is it, Myk?" Raji asked.

"He was hiding the virus right under our noses—quite literally!" Myk made his way back up the ladder as Agent Jodee Black came running into the closet along with six other agents.

She asked, "What did you find?"

Dejectedly, Myk replied, "An empty mini fridge." He then turned to Raji. "Did you see Jamal?"

She shook her head. "No."

Chaos immediately ensued as all the agents began talking over each other about how Jamal had slipped through their net. Myk's phone lit up and began to vibrate. The caller ID indicated the call was from Director Adelberg.

Myk answered. "Director, Jamal is gone!"

"I know. I've been watching everything that's happened from our webcams here. We've scoured the area's CCTV cameras and may have picked him up at a coffee shop a mile away. The video footage is a bit grainy, but I think it's him. How quickly can you get there?"

"Five minutes! I'm on my way now."

Jamal parked his car across the street from his designated meeting place. He waited for a gap in the traffic and then crossed the street and ducked into the Daily Grind Coffee House. He pulled up a chair and sat down across the table from a Middle Eastern man who was staring down at his cell phone. Jamal flung his backpack onto the tabletop and slid it across the smooth wooden surface.

The man placed his phone in his pocket as he glanced around the coffee shop and then pulled the backpack toward him. He unzipped the pack and reached in. He grabbed the items, stood, and then looked at Jamal. "I verified the money was wired to my account half an hour ago. My family and I cannot thank you enough."

Jamal nodded. The wooden legs of the chair made a loud grating sound as the man pushed his chair back under the table and then walked out of the coffee shop. Jamal looked down as he turned his wrist toward him and looked at the time on his watch. After waiting a few minutes for his coffee, he exited the coffee shop and walked down the stairs leading to the subway station.

Five minutes later, Myk's rental car came to a screeching halt at the Daily Grind Coffee Shop. As he was getting out of his car, he heard his phone ring and answered, "This is Myk."

The deep baritone voice of Director David Adelberg replied, "Myk, we just flagged a picture from a traffic camera of Jamal leaving the coffee shop. He left about five minutes ago. He was wearing the same San Francisco Giants cap and shirt that he had on when they identified him at his apartment window. The NSA traced an email and wire transfer from Jamal's IP address half an hour ago."

"Where is he?"

"We're working on it. Unfortunately, there's a lag time on CCTV cameras. Sit tight, I'll be back with you shortly."

Myk stood and leaned against the car. Raji got out and asked, "What's happening?"

"They spotted Jamal leaving the coffee shop, and they're trying to locate him."

Myk felt the vibration of the phone in his pocket and quickly answered the call, "Did you find his location?"

"He boarded the subway at the Glen Park station. He's still five minutes ahead of the tracking team monitoring all of the cameras."

"I hope we're not too late. If his target is the subway there's nothing we can do now."

Myk looked ahead, up at the backlit rectangular Balboa Park Station sign. "We'll grab the next train. Let me know where he pops up."

"We notified all security personnel along the subway routes. Hopefully, we can detain him before any disaster occurs."

Myk turned to Raji. "Are you up for a chase, or do you want to wait for me at the coffee shop?"

Raji grinned. "Let's go! If Jamal knows I'm Yasser's mother, perhaps I can negotiate with him."

Myk and Raji dashed down the stairs. He flashed his ID to the cashier and barely made it on the train before the doors closed. They both clung to the overhead grab bar as the train sped forward. Myk's eyes narrowed as he spoke. "I don't think the subways are his target."

"Why is that?" Raji asked.

"He would have done something on the platform before he got on the train." Myk's pocket vibrated again. He pulled his phone out and looked at the text message that flashed across his screen: **Jamal got off at the Powell station. Our tracking team is closing in on him.** Raji stared at Myk and gave him a quick head nod.

"Jamal exited on Powell."

"You were right, then, it's not the subway he's after."

Myk tapped his fingers and looked up at the flashing sign on the train: Next Stop—Powell Station. He glanced out the window as the train buzzed along the tracks and then back up at the sign. His eyes shifted back and forth from the sign to the train barreling its way through the tunnel outside. Finally, the train began to brake, and he instinctively gripped the rail tighter. The doors slid open, and they bolted out the doors and up the stairs to the street above. Myk snatched the phone from his pocket and called Director Adelberg. "Director—we're on Powell Street now. Where to?!"

Myk heard Adelberg breathe in deeply before replying, "We lost him, Myk. Our team is replaying all the camera locations again."

"Damn! If his target wasn't the subway, then it's either Fisherman's Wharf or the Giants game. I'll grab a cab and head to the stadium."

"Good call, Myk."

Raji hesitated and then asked, "Are you sure about the stadium? Mostly locals will be going to the game. Fisherman's Wharf will be filled with tourists that will be getting on planes and heading back to their homes all over the country. The virus would spread across the US much faster that way."

"Valid point. But from what Yasser told me about Jamal, he's the type that wants to make a big headline."

Raji nodded.

As they neared the stadium for the Giants game, traffic came to a standstill. Myk was shocked to see that authorities had not begun to shut the stadium down.

He immediately called Adelberg. "What the fuck! Why are people still pouring into the stadium? They need to lock it down!"

"I know, Myk. We're doing everything we can. We're meeting a shitload of resistance. Apparently, those in charge of this stadium used to be leaders of that damn 'defund the police' movement. They think we're the enemy."

Myk stopped running and looked heavenward and shouted, "Jesus!" He put the phone back up to his ear and said, "I'm going in. Call me if you find anything."

Myk and Raji entered the stadium and began closely scanning the throng of spectators walking through the crowded concourse. Myk shook his head and laughed—every other person seemed to be wearing a San Francisco Giants shirt.

They continued to walk at a fast pace while trying to spot Jamal among the crowd. As they neared the third-base side of the stadium, he noticed a commotion near the men's bathroom and saw an officer. Myk flashed his credentials and glanced at the man's badge. "What's going on, Officer Strauss?"

"I've been following some nut job as he walked around spraying an aerosol all over the crowd. When I confronted him and asked him what he hell he was doing, he sprayed that shit in my face and ducked into the bathroom. That son of a bitch is holding two kids at gunpoint in there."

"Good work, officer. Contact your dispatch and get a hazmat unit here immediately. Tell your officers that no one leaves this stadium. The man in the bathroom most likely sprayed a deadly virus on you."

"Shit!" the officer exclaimed.

Myk asked, "Is there anyone else in the bathroom?"

"I don't think so. Those poor girls are terrified." Myk shook his head as he crossed to the other side of Officer Strauss, who said, "Agent Miles, that man has a gun pointed directly at their heads! If you go in there, you'll be putting their lives at risk."

"Maybe—but I don't think he's going to shoot anyone."

"What makes you so sure?"

"Terrorists don't make veiled threats. They just fire off their guns or detonate their bombs without hesitation." Myk turned and walked into the bathroom. As he turned the corner into the women's bathroom, he saw a dark-haired man with a San Francisco Giants cap bending down, trying to console the two children he was grasping.

As Myk approached, the man stood straight and yelled, "Come no further or I'll shoot them!" He stiffened his arm holding the pistol against one of the girl's head.

Myk quickened his pace toward him. The man yelled, "Come no further or you will be responsible for the death of these children!" The two girls began to cry uncontrollably.

Myk finally got close enough to see his face. He gritted his teeth. Under his breath he exclaimed, "Shit!" Angrily, he asked the man, "Where's Jamal?"

"I am Jamal, and if you take one more step, it will be your last."

"I don't think so." Myk walked directly in front of the man and snatched the gun from his hand, clenched the man's throat, and squeezed. "Tell me where Jamal is before I rip your throat out!"

"Go ahead, I am going to die anyway."

Myk released him and quickly patted him down to check for explosives and turned to the kids. "Are you girls okay?" They both shook their heads as they sobbed with tears streaming down their faces. "There is an officer waiting for you outside the bathroom. He'll help you locate your parents." As the kids ran out of the bathroom, Myk turned to the man. "You don't strike me as a violent man. Jamal is going to hurt a lot of innocent people if we don't find him."

"I told you, I have no idea where he is. I met him for the first time an hour ago in the coffee shop."

Myk squinted at him and tilted his head. "What?"

"Jamal found me two months ago through the Palo Alto Cancer Center. I was diagnosed with terminal brain cancer. Jamal gave me his hat and shirt to wear up here, and the only thing I had to do was spray this air freshener in the air. He wired the money to my account just before I met him. He paid me five hundred thousand dollars for this silliness."

Myk jabbed his stiff index finger violently into the man's chest. "This isn't 'silliness,' you stupid fuck! You've diverted valuable resources up here for your little escapade while Jamal is on the loose getting ready to kill innocent people." Myk cuffed the man to the bathroom pipes and quickly exited. He pulled his phone out and dialed Adelberg. "Director, it was a ruse!"

"What?"

"This wasn't Jamal, just a decoy with terminal cancer."

"Son of a bitch!"

"You better have your team go back to the cameras across the street from the coffee shop and find the real Jamal."

The aerosol was nothing more than air freshener with the labels peeled off the can. Jamal's decoy was a man with terminal cancer who had a wife and three young children. He was the third patient from the Palo Alto Cancer Center that Jamal had interviewed. The previous two were quick to reject Jamal's proposal, but the man in handcuffs at the Giants game received half of a million dollars to play in Jamal's game of deception. The arrest was another embarrassment to the FBI that still hadn't recovered from its prior years of improprieties. Meanwhile, Jamal had done his homework and mapped out a transportation path to his first target that would be almost impossible to track by tapping into all the city cameras. The only way Jamal could be found was if he was followed. And with his bald-man disguise, he had made sure that he wasn't—or so he thought.

# CHAPTER 18

It was after ten that night when Jamal approached an elderly clerk at Walmart who was stocking items on the shelf and asked, "Do you sell any masks other than these?" He held up a package of disposable safety masks and said, "Like the tighter fitting masks that painters use?" Jamal had forgotten to remove his personal protection mask from the backpack that he gave to his decoy at the Daily Grind Coffee House.

The silver-haired Walmart employee peered over his reading glasses, glanced at the box Jamal was holding, and replied, "I'm afraid not."

As fate would have it, Jack Elderberry happened to be standing behind Jamal in the hardware section and heard the conversation. Jack said to Jamal, "If you want anything other than the disposable masks, you'll need to go to a paint store. There's a Sherwin-Williams paint store five miles from here."

Jamal hesitated and stammered as the large man in his sixties began to glare at him. He looked away. "Thanks, but I'm in a bit of a hurry."

Jack continued to assess Jamal as he walked away.

Had anyone ever asked Jack Elderberry if he considered himself to be extraordinary, he would have genuinely laughed and then flashed his big smile and humbly answered, "Heavens, no." But this day would prove otherwise. The sixty-seven-year-old Jack Elderberry could easily pass for a man in his early fifties, and often did. His physical and mental abilities far surpassed most men twenty years younger, but it didn't come from a routine of diet and exercise or daily visits to the gym. It was simply who Jack was. He owned a sawmill with his two older brothers in the small town of Cazadero, California. His family owned twenty-one-thousand acres of red-woods in northern California that Jack's grandfather had purchased in the 1880s. Jack's family had been running the timber company ever since. His image would best fit the rugged cowboy on a GMC truck commercial throwing hay bales on the back of his truck and fixing a barbed wire fence on his ranch. When Jack made eye contact with Jamal at Walmart, he knew something was off. Jamal was nervous and sweating even though it was cool outside. What struck Jack as peculiar were the fake tattoos and what appeared to be a bald-man disguise. He noticed lumps of dark hair underneath Jamal's plastic disguise. Jack had spent three years of hardcore combat in Iraq and had lived his whole life near San Francisco, so he knew a real tattoo from one that was printed on a tight-fitting shirt like Jamal was wearing. When he was eighteen, Jack had *Semper Fidelis* tattooed on his right arm the day after he joined the Marines. When he returned home from the war, he put an iron cross tattoo on his left chest pectoral as a sign of his faith and gratitude.

Psychologists had performed studies of soldiers in the Vietnam War to see if they could identify why some soldiers would stay and fight while others would flee. They termed it "fight or flight." Those in the flight category tested markedly lower in the values/principals/ beliefs category. The study didn't uncover any heroic quality or a lack of fear from the fighters. The fighters came from a stable home environment, which is exactly the kind of home Jack grew up in. His mother was raised by missionaries in Tibet. His grandfather founded the Home of Peace for missionaries in 1885, which was where Jack and his two brothers were raised. It was a large Victorian-style home, like many in the surrounding San Francisco hillsides. The home had survived every earthquake since then, but the historic Home of Peace was not without its constant maintenance problems, and that's precisely what had brought Jack to Walmart.

He followed Jamal outside and watched him locate his car. Jamal looked back and Jack immediately ducked behind a brick-clad support pillar in front of the store and then peered around the corner at Jamal. He observed Jamal, who stood erect and turned in every direction before he got into his car. Jack slipped his hand into his pocket and felt around for his keys and phone while keeping an eye on Jamal. He retrieved the phone and glanced down quickly to hit the speed dial button for his older brother Bruce. He watched Jamal start his car as he heard the phone continue to ring for his brother. He began a fast-paced walk toward his truck and then heard his brother's voice as the call connected. "What's up, Jack?"

"I'm not sure—that's why I called you." He opened the door to his crew cab F-350 Ford truck, jumped in, and started the engine. "I've got a real bad feeling about a guy I was next to in Walmart, and I decided to follow him."

"What? I thought you were getting supplies for the Home."

"I was, but a man standing in front of me was acting really fidgety. I took a closer look and noticed he was wearing one of those bald-guy disguises with a fake tattoo shirt. The tops of his hands and shirt were dripping with sweat." He paused as he flipped on his blinker and turned out of the parking lot two cars behind Jamal. "Something's not right with this guy, Bruce. What do you think I should do?"

"Keep following him. All the local TV stations were just broadcasting video footage of a Middle Eastern guy who they thought was carrying a biological weapon at the Giants game. Remember, a few days ago, there was a Middle Eastern man that was shot in the middle of Union Square? Maybe there's a connection. You should call the authorities."

Jack's heart sank. "Okay, I'll call the cops as soon as I hang up."

Bruce quickly added, "Call me back if he does anything strange." There was a pause and Jack's brother said in a more somber tone.

"Don't do anything stupid, Jack."

"Of course not." Jack noticed Jamal's car veer into the left-hand turn lane, so he pulled in behind him. His large truck sat high above Jamal's sedan. "Don't worry. I better make that call." He was about to disconnect and then put the phone back to his ear. "Hey—you still there?"

"Yep."

"I love you, bro."

"I love you too, Jack. Are sure you're okay?"

Jack followed Jamal's car as he turned. "I'm fine." He looked down at his phone, disconnected the call, hit the "voice command" button, and spoke into the phone. "Dial the San Francisco Police Department." A soothing female voice from the phone repeated the command, and then Jack heard the dialing of numbers.

After a few rings someone answered. "San Francisco Police Department, is this an emergency?"

"Yes. I am following a man that I believe is connected to the threat at the San Francisco Giants game."

"What is your location?"

"I'm on Lombard Street."

"Why do you think there is a connection, sir?"

"He was acting really nervous, and I think he's wearing a bomb."

"Did you see a bomb?"

"Well—no. But he is running around in a fake disguise, and I've got a feeling this guy is up to no good."

"Sir, most of our officers have been deployed to the Giants game. We cannot divert officers because you have a bad feeling."

Jack said, "He just parked in front of the Krave on Lombard."

"I'll see if we can send an officer to your location to check on things."

Jack disconnected the call and watched Jamal pull on the top of his head and remove the mask he was wearing, exposing his longer black hair underneath. Jamal exited his car and looked in all directions. He waited for a clearing in the traffic before crossing. Jack jumped out of his truck and ran toward Jamal, trying to get his attention. He yelled, "Excuse me!" Jamal continued to look straight ahead, so Jack yelled again, "Hey—I need to ask you a few questions!"

Jamal bolted across the street toward the club while Jack followed suit. Jamal reached out to grab the handle to the entrance of the club, but Jack smacked his hand off the handle.

"Are you deaf?! You're not going in there until the police arrive."

Jamal shoved Jack out of the way. As Jack staggered back, Jamal pulled the door halfway open. Jack regained his balance and gave the door a swift kick with his boot. He pulled hard at Jamal's jacket and tried to yank it open. Jamal surprised him with a quick punch to his midsection. Jack countered with a hard punch to Jamal's torso. He had to act fast. His only choice was to knock him out to prevent him from doing anything. Instinctively, Jack clenched his fist and recoiled with a hard blow to Jamal's jaw, spinning him around and causing him to fall to the sidewalk against the wall of the club. Jack was poised to pounce when Jamal looked up at him with a sinister smile. Jamal slid his right hand into his jacket while Jack attempted to jump at him. As Jack was in midair, Jamal pulled the trigger of his handgun and fired two shots. Jamal scrambled up and quickly entered the dark and crowded club. Loud music was thumping, which made it impossible for anyone inside the club to have heard the shots outside. Jamal paid the cover fee and squeezed his way into the jam-packed nightclub.

Shortly after Jack's call to the police, Director Adelberg was alerted to the suspicious call and contacted Myk. As he pulled into the parking lot and parked, he asked Raji to stay in the car. Myk saw the fight between Jamal and the stranger. Before he could pull his gun out, he watched in horror as Jamal shot the stranger and then entered the club. Myk immediately called Director Adelberg and sprinted across the street to the club.

Adelberg answered, "What is it, Myk?"

"We've got him! Jamal just entered the Krave. He shot someone just outside the club before I could stop him. Send an ambulance and get a hazmat team here! I'm going in."

Myk pushed through the club door and immediately turned around and locked the door. The muscular security guard grabbed Myk firmly by the arm. He had to yell at Myk in order to be heard over the loud thumping music. "What the fuck are you doing man?!"

Myk flashed his badge and yelled over the top of the music, "Nobody goes in or out of here. Do you understand?!"

The security guard released his tight grip on Myk and nodded. "Absolutely. What's going on?"

"The man who just entered has a biological weapon. If shots are fired, then there may be a stampede for this door. Guard it with your life! If he's already started to spread the virus, then we can't let it get outside this club."

"Damn! Okay, you got it. One thing though . . ."

"What's that?"

"I wouldn't be flashing that badge of yours in the club. There ain't a whole lot of respect around here for authority—just thought you should know."

"I appreciate the heads up." Myk switched the safety off of his Glock and entered the dark, crowded club. *Jesus*, Myk thought. The Krave was unlike any nightclub Myk had ever seen. It was like an uncontrollable celebration in a locker room after winning the Super Bowl—only the locker room was a fifty-thousand-square-foot nightclub with laser lights and music so loud it was deafening! People were packed shoulder to shoulder in the colorful and lively club—elbow room was a commodity. On the tall ceiling were massive ten-foot balloon-like balls that glowed with every color in the rainbow. Bright blue, yellow, and orange lasers created a moving grid-like pattern throughout the frenzied club. Myk looked for a place to gain higher ground so he could locate Jamal.

At full capacity, the Krave could hold six thousand people. Myk estimated they had surpassed that number. He stepped up to a lounge area that looked over the club and began to scan for Jamal. Among the crowd of uninhibited partiers, Myk stood out like a fly in a punch bowl because of his conservative attire—but so did Jamal. It didn't take long for Myk to locate him. He watched Jamal raise his arm and spray the virus into the crowd. He saw Jamal move another ten feet and spray it again. Myk quickly wedged his way through the crowds, never taking his eyes off Jamal. Progress toward Jamal was slow, so Myk began pushing people out of the way while at the same time trying not to alarm Jamal. Myk positioned himself to take Jamal down from behind so that he wouldn't have time to get his gun. When he was within arm's reach, Myk reached out through the throng of people and grabbed Jamal by the back of his shirt collar and yanked him backward to the ground. He had taken Jamal completely by surprise. Before Jamal had a chance to react, Myk took the spray cans of the virus from him. Jamal reached in his pocket for his gun, but Myk landed a violent punch to Jamal's jaw before he could get a grip. The hard blow stunned Jamal. Myk quickly disarmed him.

A six-foot radius in the mass of partiers formed around Myk and Jamal. Myk was ready to put zip ties around Jamal when someone shoved him hard in the back. The loud music in the club stopped. Myk briefly lost his balance from the shove, then turned and saw four large men standing between him and Jamal. Instinctively, he pulled out his badge, forgetting the warning from the bouncer, and held it above him for the four men to see. As he was about to speak and tell everyone that they may have come in contact with the virus from Jamal, Myk got tackled by two men from his side. Myk threw one of the men off and stood. Another attacker lunged at him. Myk spun and kicked the man in the head with a roundhouse kick. Gangs of men went on the offense and came at him from all directions. He knocked two men out, one with a kick and the other with a hard punch to the head. There were too many. As the group subdued Myk, all the laser lights and disco lights turned off and the dark club lit up as fluorescent lights throughout were turned on. Myk saw seven people in hazmat suits enter the club.

The DJ announced, "Attention! I need your attention. For your safety, anyone standing needs to immediately sit down exactly where you are. If you are seated, remain so. You gentlemen that are in the skirmish need to release the man you are holding. He is here for our safety." The seven men who had a tight grip on Myk let go of him.

Myk immediately turned to cuff Jamal, but he was gone. "Shit!" Myk exclaimed. He turned to the men that just released him. "Did you see where the man that I disarmed went?!"

The group looked around and shrugged their shoulders. Myk barked out, "You fucking dumbasses!" He pulled one of the virus cans from his pocket and displayed it. "That piece of shit you heroes were trying to protect is here to kill you! This is a biological weapon, you morons!" Myk shook his head, pointed, and said, "Now go and find him!" Myk quickly made his way to the DJ and told him to ask everyone in the club to help locate Jamal. After five minutes, two women approached the DJ's booth and told him they had seen Jamal leave the club out the back door emergency exit.

Myk immediately called Director Adelberg. "What is it, Myk?"

"Jamal escaped out the back of the club."

"I know. Our agents tapped into the cameras, but they've already lost him. Did you get the cannisters of the virus?"

"Yes."

"That's great news! Any idea how much of the virus Jamal sprayed?"

"He had barely started releasing one of the cans before I detained him."

"Got it. The hazmat team will get everyone in the club to a quarantine facility. There's a special van outside with a medical group that can diagnose if you've been exposed to the virus. I've given them instructions to escort you to the van."

A woman in a hazmat suit followed Myk outside of the Krave

nightclub. As he exited, Raji was waiting outside for him. She approached, but Myk quickly raised his hands up and said, "Don't come any closer, Raji. I may have been infected." He noticed Raji's hands and blouse were drenched in blood. "What happened? Are you okay?"

Raji stepped back several paces and replied, "I'm fine. I tried to help the man that got shot."

The woman escorting Myk to the medical van spoke up. "When we arrived, your friend was performing CPR on him. She probably saved his life!"

Myk's phone rang as he stepped into the medical van. "Yes, Director?"

"Our team just uncovered something from the zip drive Jaafar gave us."

"What is it?"

"Jaafar lied. We have a bigger problem than we thought."

"What did you find?"

"This mutated virus didn't come out of Tehran. It was developed in China! All of the genome and mapping sequences of the virus on the zip drive are in Chinese. Communist China is behind this. Their fingerprints are all over it!"

# PART II

# CHAPTER 19

Two hours after being thoroughly tested for the virus, Myk was cleared. The Krave was locked down and the spread of the virus was completely contained. By the time Myk was allowed to leave, ten positive cases had been confirmed. Those that were infected were already receiving plasma transfusions with the antibodies. It was getting late, so Myk asked Raji if she wanted to wait until the next day to visit the body of Yasser. She told Myk that even though they were bruised, battered, and covered in blood, she still wanted to see Yasser as soon as possible. When Raji learned the hotel Yasser had stayed at was on the way to the morgue, she asked if they could stop there first. Director Adelberg cleared the way with the FBI for Myk and Raji to enter Yasser's hotel room. Myk was allowed access to the room so that Raji could gather any of Yasser's personal belongings that investigators deemed nonessential.

Raji timidly ducked under the yellow caution tape and entered Yasser's room. His hotel room was filled with dozens of books and stacks of printed articles lying around—she was puzzled.

She asked Myk, "Am I allowed to touch anything?"

"Yeah, you're fine. They've processed everything. I just need to document anything that's removed from the room."

Raji began rummaging through the multitude of print material. Bewildered, she asked, "What was he doing?"

"Yasser told me that he sat next to someone on his flight from Tehran that he made a deep connection with. The man told Yasser that when he was his age, he had also been indoctrinated to hate the Jews and the West."

Raji set the book she was holding back on the couch. She shook her head. "Why didn't he listen to me? I told him the truth."

"He heard you," Myk replied, "but he just didn't believe you. How could he? He was surrounded by a culture that droned their propaganda nonstop into his head. He was at a vulnerable and influential age when he had to bury two of his friends. What you taught him did make a difference and influenced Yasser's decision to change."

Raji continued to walk about the room and slowly browse a grieving mother trying to feel the presence of her lost son. She held a favorite necklace of Yasser's she found on the dresser in front of her and asked, "May I have this?"

"Of course," Myk said.

Raji stepped into the bathroom and stood completely still. She gazed at the picture taped to the mirror and then covered her mouth with her hand. Her emotions overwhelmed her. It was a picture of Raji and Yasser together. She gently removed the picture, slowly moved to the couch, and then sat down. Raji shielded the picture from the drops of tears falling from her eyes.

"I am sorry for your loss," Myk said sorrowfully.

Raji's nod was almost imperceptible.

Myk tried to console her. He said softly, "Yasser told me that many of the things you taught him flooded his mind when he got off the flight. He said that he spent all his time here educating himself and validating what you taught him all his life—as you can clearly see from what he was reading."

Raji was nonresponsive.

"Take whatever time you need. I'll give you time alone," Myk said. He left the room and waited for Raji in the hallway. After fifteen minutes, she approached Myk. "Would you take me to his body now?" she asked with watery, gloomy eyes.

On the drive to the morgue, Raji was oblivious to the sights and sounds around her—from the loud, tinny clanging sound of the trolley bell to the squawking sounds of the large seagulls to Myk's conversation with Director Adelberg on his cell phone as he drove the rental car. She wiped the tears from her eyes with the back of her hand and stared at the picture she had taken from the hotel between her thumb and index finger. It was a picture of Yasser at Azadi Stadium in Tehran after he had won the championship soccer game. He had his arm wrapped tightly around Raji, and the two of them were smiling from ear to ear. She had a vivid memory of when the picture was taken. She remembered that it took forever for Habiba to take the picture. She kept fussing about people in the background of the picture. Raji glanced down at the picture again—she grimaced, shook her head, and wiped more tears. In the picture, Yasser had long hair that almost touched his shoulders. His headband, drenched in sweat, held his hair out of his face. Raji reflected that soccer was the only good thing that Ali had passed on to his son. Yasser had three assists that game and was the top recruit to the Iranian national team. Raji begged him to accept an offer from one of the Italian teams. It would have been their ticket out of Iran for good. But that's when his grandfather got into his head. Yasser began to spend more and more time with Jaafar.

Myk pulled into the FBI parking lot on the outskirts of San Francisco. Raji asked, "Why are we stopping here? I thought you were taking me to see Yasser."

"His body is here. The FBI performed an autopsy on him. They were looking for any clues from the bullet that killed him." Myk paused then said somberly, "The bullet that was meant for me."

"Yes, you already told me. I'd like to make a call before we go in."

"Okay, I'll wait for you at the entrance."

Raji hadn't communicated with Becca for several weeks. Becca had left Raji a message when she learned of Yasser's death, but Raji had yet to speak with her. She dialed the number and waited for the connection. The call immediately went to voicemail. Feelings of loneliness began to envelop her. But underneath the loneliness, pure rage began to stir.

"That was quick," Myk said, surprised, as Raji walked through the entrance door.

"The call went to voicemail," she said curtly.

Raji and Myk emptied their pockets and placed their items in the containers at the security station. Myk put his gun on the conveyer belt and held up his badge. The officer on duty scanned his ID and said, "We were expecting you a little earlier."

"We made an unexpected stop on the way," Myk replied.

"No problem."

Myk asked, "Where's the body located?"

The officer pointed. "Take the elevators to the sixth floor and turn right when you exit. Keep walking all the way to the end of the hall. The morgue is at the other end of the building."

Myk nodded. "Okay, thank you."

He and Raji gathered their things on the other side of the security screening and walked soberly to the elevators. The silent walk to the morgue seemed like an eternity for Raji. Questions filled her mind along with feelings of hopelessness. There was nothing for her in Iran. With Yasser gone, she would no longer propagate the public image of a happy marriage for Ali—it was sham. She was lonely and yearned to talk to the only person that truly knew her—Becca.

Myk slowly pulled the sheet back from Yasser's face. Raji stood by his side. Her lips tightened. She clenched the cold stainless-steel table and gazed at the lifeless body of her son. The pale form stared straight up at the ceiling.

Myk asked, "When do you want his body flown back to Iran?"

"I don't," Raji replied tersely.

"I'm confused, why not?"

She shook her head. "I don't want his body flown to Iran. The soil of my country isn't worthy to hold my son."

"What would you like me to do with him?"

"That's why I made the phone call before we came in. I consider Paris my second home. That's where I'll bury Yasser. I will never step foot in Iran again."

Myk nodded. "I guess that explains the six full-size pieces of luggage you've been toting around."

Raji smiled. "Yeah, I guess so." She walked away from the table. "You can cover his face now, I've seen enough. I did my reflecting back on the couch at Yasser's hotel—this place is just too stoic to think about him."

"So is that where you're planning on going after this—Paris?"

Thoughtfully Raji said, "Yes, I have a good friend there. It's where I got my real education."

Myk stared at her. He knew he should ask, but he paused and tried to answer the question himself. He came up blank. "If you don't mind me asking, what do you mean 'real education'?"

"No problem. Iranians are not taught the truth about much of world history and most current events. I spent my honeymoon, if you can call it that, in Paris and then returned the following year. I've been back there several times a year for the last twenty years, along with traveling all over the world. Traveling all over the world these past twenty years has been my real education."

"Makes sense." A puzzled look came over Myk's face. "That's quite unusual for an Iranian, let alone an Iranian woman, to have such freedom to travel abroad. Is it because your husband is so high up in the military?"

*Husband? That's a joke*, Raji thought. She contemplated explaining why she had so much freedom, but then settled on the short answer. "Yes."

Myk gazed at her. His head tilted to the right as he asked, "Why do I have a feeling that there's something more behind that?"

"Because there is," she said bluntly. "I might share more later. But not here. Not now."

Myk covered the body and slid the corpse back into the large refrigerated wall unit. As they stood and waited for the elevator, Raji said, "It's customary in Iran for men to step into the grave of the deceased and turn the body on its side, so that it faces qibla, the direction of Mecca." She paused momentarily and then continued, "I think I'll do the exact opposite—I'll have Yasser's body turned so that he has his back to Mecca. Islam turned its back to Yasser, now I'll turn his back to Islam."

The elevator opened and they walked in. Alone in the elevator, Raji asked, "Will you turn my father over to your government when you're done with him or actually convince the Brits to give him diplomatic immunity?"

"Hopefully we can work a deal with Britain, because I sure as hell don't want him in our country."

Raji shook her head. "Levi was wrong."

"How so?" Myk replied with a bewildered look.

"I really regret not pulling the trigger when we were in the jet."

Myk nodded. "I see. Perhaps that may change. Let things play out. Just between you and I, I would hate to see one minute of my government's time or one dollar of my government's money spent on him. We were days away from another pandemic because of him. He sickens me. To be frank—if you tried to kill him again, I wouldn't stop you."

Raji grinned. "Perhaps I should oblige."

The elevator opened and the two exited to the corridor and back to the car. Myk slid into his seat, started the engine, and then put his arm behind Raji's seat as he turned his body and head halfway around to see behind him as he reversed out of the parking stall. As he put the car in drive, he said in a lighthearted tone, "You're a bit of a walking oxymoron."

"A what?" she asked.

"Oh, sorry. That may sound awful to someone with English as a second language. Probably a poor choice of words. Let me clarify. You're a living paradox to the stereotypical view of women in Iran—if that even makes any sense."

Raji looked at Myk and smiled. "It does. And I'll take that as a compliment."

Myk smiled. "Good, because it was. I've been trying to get a read on you ever since you came out of the shadows at the Arena in Verona. You are . . ." Myk hesitated on the right word and then said, "Unique."

Raji looked at the picture of Yasser with his arm around her again. She stared blankly at the road ahead. "All of the tragedy has made me this way, Agent Miles. I chose not to be a victim."

Myk nodded. "That's evident. Call me Myk, please."

"So what's next, Myk?"

"Once I'm confident we're not being followed, we need to go back to the safe house and talk to Jaafar. After I have things situated, I can take you to the airport whenever you're ready to go to Paris."

Raji thoughtfully replied, "I've become interested in seeing things play out, as you say. I decided I am going to stay."

"It's not safe. I've got someone trying to assassinate me, and your father has people that would love to kill him—"

Raji interrupted, "I am quite adept Agent Mil—" she stopped herself before finishing and then said, "I mean, Myk. On the other hand, I am pretty sure you were the one that was walking with your hands cuffed behind your back and being taken hostage back in Verona—was it not?" She looked at him with a sarcastic smile.

Myk half laughed. "Point taken! So how is it that Paris became your second home?"

Raji thought about the question. "Two reasons I suppose. My friend, Becca, who is very special to me, lives in Paris. And it's where Yasser was conceived, so it's only fitting that I bury him there."

Myk stared ahead at the city lights of San Francisco all aglow against the backdrop of the dark moonless night. Few cars were on the road in the early morning hour as he drove on. He asked, "Honeymoon baby, eh?"

"Ha!" Raji burst out. "I don't think so! Ali abandoned me on our wedding night. Yasser was conceived the following year in Paris." She instantly bit her lip and thought, *Raji, what are you saying? You hardly know this man.*

"I see. So, Ali tried to make it up to you by taking you back there the following year?"

*It wasn't even Ali's idea*, Raji thought. Just then, Myk's cell phone began to ring. He answered the call from Levi. Raji tuned out the phone call while her mind began to wander back to her second trip to Paris.

# CHAPTER 20

As Myk spoke to Levi, Raji closed her eyes and let her mind freely wander. On her second trip to Paris, Raji stayed in the exact same suite as her honeymoon the year before. Nothing had changed—it was the same duvet on the canopy bed, the same curtains on the side of the windows, and all of the same décor. What wasn't the same was Ali. He actually made love to Raji their first night and didn't leave her alone in Paris—at least, not at first. The following morning as Raji began to wake, she slid her hand across the silky-soft sheets to feel for Ali, to check if he was still there. She felt the bare skin of his back and felt a sense of relief. She began to softly caress his back. Raji yearned for Ali to make love with her again. Her fingers ran gently back and forth over his buttocks. She stroked her hand across his thigh while he lay with his back to her. Raji's fingertips moved slowly up his leg. She reached around to put her hand on his manhood, but when Raji touched him, Ali turned and hung his legs over the side of the bed and stood up.

"Sorry, love, I need to pee," Ali said as he walked to the bathroom.

Raji watched his backside as he disappeared behind the bathroom door. She heard the door lock and then the shower turn on. Dejected, she let out a large breath of air and rolled on her back. *If he won't take care of me, then I will*, Raji thought. She reached down between her legs and began to feel herself. The sound of the running shower had a calming effect. Raji closed her eyes and let her mind wander to the previous night. As her fingers continued to move back and forth, Raji thought, *What if he's done with his shower before I finish?*

With that in mind, she made quick work of her pleasure time and finished well before Ali. Ten minutes later, Ali stepped out of the bathroom and announced, "I'm starved. Let's go grab breakfast at one of the cafés down the street."

"I'd like that," Raji replied. "I'll throw something on and be ready in ten minutes."

A dangerous thing happened after spending the day with Ali in Paris—Raji began to hope. The first twenty-four hours of Raji's return trip to Paris were the polar opposite from her honeymoon. For the past year, they had been more like roommates than newlyweds. On the first night, Ali had stayed and made love with Raji. The next morning he took her out for a lovely breakfast in which they talked like they had when they were dating, about hopes and dreams—and they even dabbled in talking about a few fears they had. Ali took her shopping after breakfast and was a perfect gentleman. They made an impulsive stop in a trendy café for lunch. Throughout the day, Ali stopped several random strangers and asked them to take a picture of the two of them. After shopping in the afternoon, Ali suggested they visit the Eiffel Tower, which was walking distance away. She couldn't explain it, but that's when she got the faint feeling that Ali seemed to be just going through the motions. She tried to drive the thought from her mind, but it kept surfacing. So Raji went along with everything, hoping that Ali's behaviors were genuine. Still, this was not normal behavior for Ali she thought. At the Eiffel Tower he wanted even more pictures. Ali held her hand on the stroll back to the hotel. It was a magical day for her. In their first year of marriage, he had never paid so much attention to her as he had on this day. He told her that he had a special evening planned for the two of them. That he wanted her to get dressed up in her best dress. He was able to negotiate a reservation at the exclusive Benoit restaurant in Paris. Normally, it took eight months to get a reservation at the elite restaurant, but Ali somehow got a table for the two of them.

When they got back to the hotel, Raji showered first. Ali told her that would allow her more time to get ready. It was such an invigorating shower; she was full of anticipation of an evening that would follow such a perfect day. She was beaming when she showered. Thoughts of an exciting evening in Paris's exclusive restaurant and then the invigorating nightlife of Paris filled her mind. Something she had not yet experienced with Ali, only Becca. She toweled off after her hot, steamy shower. She checked in the mirror, wrapped a towel around herself, and then ran her fingers through her hair. She opened the bathroom door and then froze like an ice-sculpted statue in the snow—she called out, "Ali?" But there was no answer. There was a white piece of paper folded in half on the dresser. Raji slowly walked and stood in front of the dresser. She saw her reflection, wrapped in the bath towel, and the white piece of paper that seemed to be whispering the words "I told you so." Raji picked up the piece of paper and read, "I just got called to Cairo on an emergency. I can't believe this happened again. I'll try to make it back to Paris in a few days; I just don't know what awaits me in Cairo." Raji sat on the edge of the bed and shook her head as she looked down at Ali's handwritten note. *It was all a ruse*, she thought. *All the pictures were just for show.*

Resolutely, Raji found her phone and called Becca. "Sorry for not calling you earlier," she said meekly. "I have a reservation at Benoit tonight. Would you be able to join me?"

"It's so nice to hear your voice, darlin'," Becca replied in her southern Texas drawl. "I thought you were supposed to arrive in Paris yesterday?"

"We did. I'm sorry I didn't reach out when I landed. Can you make it tonight?"

"Of course I can. I've been waiting to see you since I sent my message last month. How in the hell did you get a reservation at Benoit anyway? It usually takes six months to get in there," Becca asked.

"I didn't, Ali did. I'm not sure how he finagled the reservation. Can you meet me at seven thirty?"

"Count on it. Are you okay, Raji?"

There was a long pause, and then she answered, "Yeah, we can talk about it tonight."

"Alright, see you in a bit."

Raji ended the call. She stood and looked at the reflection of herself in the mirror. The image of a girl, wrapped in a towel, abandoned by her husband stared back. Feelings of insignificance marched their way to her forethought. Raji looked back at the reflection and whispered, "Never again."

The round, well-polished mahogany table for two rested against a large expanse of glass on the second floor of the Benoit restaurant. Raji stared out at the iconic tower that was aglow. *Why go to all of this trouble for a reservation if he had preconceived plans to leave again?* Raji thought. But then again, the day had seemed scripted. As much as she loved the day, this was not the Ali she had come to know her first year of marriage. It was Becca who put the whole "honeymoon redo" in motion. What was the plan that Becca was being so cryptic about, Raji wondered.

She reached into her purse to feel for the arcane receipt. Ali's reasonings for his disappearance during their first "honeymoon" made sense—except for a receipt that Raji found in the back pocket of Ali's pants when she returned from Paris. It was the wall that stood in the way of Raji fully believing Ali's reasonings for his disappearance. For twelve months it had been her dearest possession. The solitary piece of paper kept her sane amidst all the gibberish that foamed out of Ali's mouth for a year. It was a receipt from a restaurant in Paris five days after Ali had supposedly headed back to Iran the night of their honeymoon. All of the weight of her marriage hung on the balance of that faded receipt, safely tucked away in the secret corners of her purse. Did he really leave Paris for an emergency, or did he stay for some mysterious reason? A trusting wife would have just asked why he had a receipt in his pocket that dated five days after he said he had left—but she didn't trust Ali.

Raji faintly heard Becca's voice with its familiar southern accent. She turned and saw her standing with the hostess and pointing toward her.

"That's her right there." Raji heard her say. Raji stood and gave her a clandestine wave of her hand, trying not to draw too much attention. Becca quickly made her way over to Raji and gave her a warm hug. Raji gazed out at the well-dressed restaurant patrons and sheepishly hugged her back and then quickly took her seat.

"It's so great to see you. I am so glad you could make it on such short notice," Raji said.

"No problem. I blocked out most of this week knowing that you were coming. So where's Ali this time?" Becca asked sternly.

"I don't know. I got out of the shower, and there was a note on the dresser saying he had an emergency in Cairo. He spent a day with me in Paris this time—as if that's any kind of consolation."

"Do you believe him?"

Raji shook her head fervently. "Not one bit! I don't know what to do."

"You should toss him to the curb, that's what you should do!"

"That's easy for you to say. Women in Iran have very few rights. Part of me is really angry, and I want to do something about it. And then there's a small part of me that wonders what I did wrong or what's wrong with me."

Becca reached across the table and put her hand on Raji's. "I swear, God must have put something in women's DNA, because you'd never hear about a man getting mistreated and then asking himself what he'd done wrong! Just us women." She smiled and then continued, "This has nothing to do with you my dear, absolutely nothing. So you wipe that thought from your mind. We're going to get to the bottom of this—trust me, I've got a plan."

Raji said, "It was hard to tell from your last text, but I got the impression you had an idea. I was a little surprised that Ali agreed to come. He's already left, so now what?"

"I assumed he would, that's why I asked you to convince him to come back to Paris. Except this time—I've got you covered." Becca winked at Raji with a sly smile.

Raji's eyebrows furrowed. "How so?"

Becca leaned over the table and whispered, "I have a good friend in the security business. He used to be on the prime minister's security detail. I hired him and his team to follow Ali from the minute you two landed at the airport." She leaned back in her chair. "No more guesswork, my dear. Your husband is under surveillance by a team of professionals."

Raji's eyes widened. "Oh my goodness. Thank you! How could I ever repay you?"

Becca chuckled. "Repay me? Never! I wouldn't think of it. This will give me something fun to spend my money on. Hell, I had more money than I knew what to do with before they opened another oil well on my property last month. Besides, I've always wanted to play detective!"

"But what if he actually does go to Cairo?"

Becca shook her head while her bottom lip curled up. "Doesn't matter. That security team has enough clearance that they could follow him to the moon and back if Ali chose to go there."

"So, what do I do in the meantime?" Raji asked.

Becca grabbed her hand. "You enjoy Paris with me—that's what you do!" she said enthusiastically. "Don't worry about a thing. Let the professionals do their work and enjoy your time outside Iran. Before you go back home, they will share their findings with us."

Raji and Becca continued to chat and catch up in between placing their orders for drinks and food. Raji went silent for a moment and stared blankly out of the glass.

Becca noticed the look of concern from Raji. "What's on your mind? All of a sudden you've got a serious look on your face."

Raji's head shook slightly. "I think I may have made a serious mistake, but I don't know what else I could have done."

"Go on," Becca said.

"You know that Ali only has sex with me when he thinks I'm ovulating—right?"

"Yes. You said that you don't tell him your real dates. So what's the problem?"

Raji answered slowly. "I assumed, since he thought I wouldn't be ovulating for another two weeks, that he wouldn't make love to me while we were here. Surprisingly, he made love with me last night—and I'm ovulating right now."

"Oh my. That would make things much more complicated if you were to get pregnant. There are ways to fix that you know. I had an abortion once."

Thoughtfully, Raji said, "Yes, I know that is a choice many women make, but that's not an option for me. As much as I disagree with most of the policies of the theocracy that runs my country, that's still not something I can do."

"I understand. I hope you don't think worse of me for doing it," Becca questioned.

"No, no, Becca. I respect your choice. I'm sure your circumstances must have warranted your decision."

"They did indeed. I'll let you know the story behind it another time if you want."

Raji reached into her purse and pulled out Ali's receipt from the previous year. "I found this in one of Ali's pockets when I got back from Paris last year. It's a receipt from a café around the corner. I'm not sure he ever left Paris. If so, how can he explain the date on this receipt? I don't know if it will help, but give it to your security team." Raji handed the receipt to Becca.

Becca looked at the receipt and then folded it and placed it in her purse. "I've got a few ideas about what's going on with Ali, but I could be wrong, so I don't want to speculate. I'll let the security team do their job and hopefully that will shine some light on what's happening."

The two of them then turned their conversation to what they

would be doing while Raji was in Paris. Becca rattled off an entire list of activities to see which things piqued the most interest. For the next two hours, while they chatted over their wine and enjoyed the ambiance, they put together a rough itinerary for the week that Raji was excited about. It gave her something to look forward to and perhaps take her mind off things while Becca's security team did their work.

A serious look came across Raji's face again. "Why are you doing this for me?" she asked. It was something she wasn't used to. People had never gone out of their way for her. That was how she had grown so independent. She learned to do things on her own because there was rarely anyone there for her.

Becca smiled and answered, "I've had many people cross my path, Raji, but none quite as special as you. If you lived in the US or Europe, I have no doubt that you'd be the CEO of some corporation or have attained a high political office or owned some amazing company you started up. You can blossom into a beautiful rose with the right soil, water, and light, but the Iranian regime criticizes and discourages those admirable qualities. So I'm going to do everything I can to provide whatever soil, water, and sunshine that I can for you."

Raji sat speechless. Never before had she heard such words of praise—it was like a foreign language to her. She didn't know how to process it. She never had a mother or father in her corner rooting for her. Her caregivers were polite, but nothing even close to this. Her eyes darted back and forth, thinking of the right response. Finally, she uttered, "I don't know what to say. You are such a nice person. Thank you."

Becca smiled. "There's a place I want to show you tomorrow. It's a three-hour drive, so why don't you get a good night's rest?"

Raji was still taken back by Becca's response. She looked at her watch and said, "That's a good idea."

The next morning, Becca was waiting for Raji in the lobby. She handed Raji a knapsack and said, "Let's do breakfast on the road since we've got a long drive this morning."

180

Raji took the knapsack and looked inside. There was an assortment of fresh fruits, yogurt, croissants, and granola. "Where are we off to?"

"You'll see. I know you'll like it." Becca smiled and then asked, "Any word from Ali?"

Raji shook her head. "Not a peep. Why do you ask?"

"I was thinking that we might stay the night to avoid the long drive back to Paris if you're okay with it," Becca replied.

"I don't think I'll see Ali until I get back to Iran. I would love to experience a new place."

"Oh good. We can take our time then and really enjoy the day."

After two and a half hours of driving along the beautiful French countryside, they pulled into the Acres of Sun Vineyard in Normandy. When they parked and got out of the car, they both stretched their legs and then walked to the entrance. Becca paid for the wine tasting tour, and then the hostess escorted them to their seats on the outdoor patio. The large open-air patio was covered with a weathered terracotta tile roof that had vines with beautiful white blossoms growing up the columns. Their table had a spectacular view of the entire coast of Normandy. There was a slight breeze that was cool and crisp. Raji looked out at the vast blue ocean and the white-capped waves crashing into the bluffs.

"It's gorgeous," Raji said.

"Yes. This is my favorite winery in all of France."

Raji smiled. "I can see why."

The two of them sampled wines for an hour and then went for a walk along the bluffs overlooking the ocean. Becca cleared her throat. "I have a great-uncle that died here."

Raji asked, "What happened?"

"World War II happened. He was twenty-five."

Raji shook her head. "That's too young to die," Raji said sorrowfully.

As they continued to walk, Becca asked, "I'm curious. I've been told that Iranians aren't taught much about World War II or the Holocaust. Is that true?"

Raji replied, "Unfortunately, yes. Censorship is rampant in Iran so it's almost impossible to decipher what's true or not without outside sources—which are illegal in Iran."

"Do you know who Adolf Hitler was?"

Raji tilted her head. "Of course. He was the leader of the Germans. I've heard that he committed crimes against humanity, but there are many in Iran who don't think he was as evil as others depict him to be."

"Do you know the details of the Holocaust?" Becca asked.

"I'm sorry. I really don't know what the facts are. I can tell you that there are definitely a few people in Iran that say it's just a myth made up by the Jews."

Becca showed her where her great-uncle had perished and gave her a brief synopsis of D-Day as they overlooked the bluffs of Normandy. Then she told Raji there was a place not too far from where they were that she wanted to show her. She drove her to the Normandy American Cemetery and Memorial in Colleville-sur-Mer. The parking lot was completely full. Reservations were required prior to entrance since over one-million visitors went to the site each year. Fortunately, Becca was good friends with one of the guides, so she was able to get in without notice. The crystal-clear day that they had enjoyed while sipping wine at the cafe had turned overcast. A fog descended on the cemetery that, somehow, added an air of reverence to a place that was dripping in an overabundance of it already. Becca walked and talked with Raji about historical truths—as evidenced by the sea of white crosses. Raji contemplated the endless rows of white crosses standing in contrast to the bright-green grass. The crosses seemed to go on forever until they disappeared into the fog. From the outside looking in, Raji began to understand Iran's place in the world. She had always been a rebel toward much of the dogma that was forced on Iranians—which made it that much easier for her to grasp the truths that Becca was telling her.

Every day, Raji went to bed with her head swimming in thoughts.

She anticipated the next day with such excitement that it made it hard to sleep. It seemed like each day outdid the previous one. They attended concerts, museums, and historical sites. Some of Raji's favorite moments were just sitting with Becca over a glass of wine and talking philosophy. The stories that Becca shared with her made her gasp. Her stories were full of men, parties, tragedies, and successes. With such a colorful life, Raji was surprised at Becca's sharp intellect. She was the smartest and wisest person Raji had ever met. There was no doubt in Raji's mind that Becca enjoyed life to the fullest and viewed each day as a blessing. Raji's week in Paris seemed to vanish in an instant. On the night before her flight back to Iran, Becca called Raji to tell her that her security team discovered what was going on with Ali. She wanted to visit with her the next morning and talk before she left.

On the day of her flight back to Iran, Raji heard the anticipated knock on her door. She knew it was Becca. Her bags were packed and sitting next to the door. When she entered, the expression on Becca's face was noticeably different—it was as serious as Raji had ever seen her.

Becca was holding a laptop under her left arm. She said, "Let's sit down, Raji."

The two of them sat on the couch. Becca placed the laptop on the coffee table in front of them and opened it up. She typed in her password and a picture of Ali popped up. Raji looked at Becca and asked, "What's going on?"

Becca sat back in the couch. "My security team uncovered some very shocking things about your husband, Raji. I need you to take a few breaths and prepare yourself. You might find what you are about to see as extremely disturbing. You were probably right about your honeymoon trip here—Ali never left Paris. I can tell you unequivocally that he has been in Paris this whole week. He just boarded a plane this morning for Iran."

Raji asked, "How long have you known this?"

"I've known since your second day here. I didn't want to say anything because I didn't want to ruin your time in Paris."

"So, what's on the computer?" she asked.

"You'll see," Becca replied. Then she reached out with her index finger and pushed the play button.

Raji leaned forward with her elbows on her knees and watched closely. Three minutes into the surveillance video, Raji leaned back against the couch and gasped. She covered her mouth with her hand, looked directly at Becca, and exclaimed, "Oh my God!"

# CHAPTER 21

# SAN FRANCISCO, CALIFORNIA

"Are you okay?" Myk asked as they drove to the safe house. Somewhat startled, it took Raji a moment to gather her thoughts. She replied, "Yes, I'm fine. Why do you ask?"

"I've been observing you since I ended my phone call, and you seem to be really tense."

"Hmm. I was just daydreaming. I got lost in some old memories." Raji looked at Myk as if sizing him up. She snickered and thought, *This guy is pretty astute.*

Myk heard Raji's snicker. "What's so funny?"

"It's nothing." Wanting to change subjects, Raji quickly asked, "How long before we arrive?"

"Probably thirty minutes or so." Myk began to steer the car with his knees while he turned off his phone's location. "I need you to turn your location off on your phone. I am the only one who knows the location of this safe house, Director Adelberg doesn't even know where it is. I don't want to take any chances of getting tracked."

Raji began to turn the location off on her phone. "No problem."

After several minutes of silence Raji said, "Iranians are nothing like what your American media portray us to be, you know. The vast majority of my country don't run around burning American flags and chanting 'death to America.'"

Myk smiled. "Yes, I am well aware of that. I've worked in the intelligence world all my adult life. From what I've seen, most Iranians are intelligent, caring people who love their families. I'm pretty sure that most Iranians feel suffocated by your government. Unfortunately, both of our governments have an agenda they try to push."

With a more passionate tone, Raji said, "It sickens me when I think of the perceptions the world has about the people of Iran. I have been an adversary to the Iranian regime my entire life. I can tell you with absolute certainty that the good people of Iran are being held hostage by a small minority. Unfortunately, it is that small minority of zealots that have all the power. Sadly, the world has forgotten what Iran was like before the overthrow of the Shah. Our beautiful Persian heritage has been supplanted by a theocracy with tunnel vision."

"I have a good friend whose parents fled Iran after the revolution. I can see the pain in their eyes when they talk about the country they once loved." Myk glanced at Raji and then asked, "On the flight from Verona, when I asked how it was that you have been allowed so much freedom, I wondered why an agitator such as yourself is left alone by the regime. You said that you had an understanding. That's pretty vague. Did your husband divulge some dirty secrets to you about the regime or something?"

Raji peered at Myk and squinted. There was only one other person that knew—Becca. Unbeknownst to Myk, Raji had been taking inventory of him since she followed him in the tunnels at the Arena in Verona. She logged every gesture. Studied every facial expression. Read between the lines of everything he said. Two words came prominently to her mind: he's safe. Raji adjusted herself in the seat and replied, "Yes, you're on the right track. I am in possession of some secretive information—damaging information. That's what has allowed me so much freedom."

"What do you have on them?" Myk asked.

Raji hesitated and then said, "I've never used the information I possess for any personal gain. I could never ask for money or any assets. That would make me just as bad as them. No, I wanted something much more valuable—freedom. The freedom to travel and the freedom of speech. The latter has its limitations though. Still, I have been allowed to inform the Iranian people on my nightly broadcasts of a tremendous amount of truth that they would otherwise not have known." Raji paused and waited to have eye contact before she continued. "Myk, Iran is so ripe for an overthrow of our theocratic government right now. You have no idea how close we are."

Myk glanced over at Raji. One eyebrow was raised higher than the other. "You're serious, aren't you?"

"Yes, I am."

"There's no way that happens without blood being spilt. Likely a lot of blood."

Raji nodded. "I know."

"So what makes you think Iran is at a tipping point?"

Raji folded one leg up on her seat and turned toward Myk. "The ratings of my hour of news broadcast are triple the competitor. My career at the station has been a constant fight. They have the talking points they try to push to the public, and I debate them on everything. I fight for as much truth as they'll allow. Every battle, I try to take new ground. This past year has been horrific. The arguments with my producer have never been worse. I was on the verge of quitting at one point."

"Why is that?"

"The regime kept the Iranian people in the dark about the coronavirus, and I wouldn't stand for it!" Raji said passionately. "The virus decimated the Iranian leadership. They've never been at a weaker point. The Iranian leaders cozied up to the Chinese, and they paid a very heavy price for it. Ali called me one night. We rarely talk or see each other, but I think he was scared. He said almost everyone around him had died from the virus. Very few people know how bad it was."

"So that's why you think they're ripe for an overthrow?"

"No, no," Raji answered. "That's only part of it. My producer was relentless in trying to push the narrative that the regime had things under control. They wanted me to underreport the cases and the death toll, but I wouldn't do it. We settled on a middle ground, but the people of Iran aren't so gullible and stupid. I saw the mass graves, Myk. Death and sickness were rampant. They tried to blame it on the US sanctions, and they actually tried to tell the country that the virus was from the US. Do you know why Iran was hit so hard with the coronavirus?"

Myk answered, "I've heard there were a lot of variables."

Raji shook her head. "Well, I can tell you the biggest variable—greed! Our leadership got what they deserved if you ask me. They were all in the pockets of the Chinese. The US tightened their sanctions against Iran and our leadership turned to the Chinese. They got our oil, and our leadership got their money and their virus. The Iranian people have never been so ready to take back their country. They see right through the regime's cover-ups, and they want to fight."

Myk replied, "Well, if that's true, and I think there's a lot of validity to what you've said, then the two biggest parts of the equation for an overthrow are in place: leadership is weakened, and the people are at a boiling point."

In a more somber tone Raji said, "I've never seen my country like this. Nothing even close. I was too young to remember the revolution in '79, but I've been told that the groundswell on this is much more broad. The greed of the Iranian leadership let the Chinese come in here and perform multi-billion-dollar contracts that our people were perfectly capable of doing. That did not go over well with the public. Our leaders got into bed with Beijing. The Chinese wanted to build a two-thousand-mile high-speed rail from western China through Turkey and then to Europe, but they needed to go through Tehran. Our unemployment and inflation are astronomical, and yet it was the Chinese companies who got all the contracts while our leaders got rich. Thousands of Chinese workers flew back and forth from Iran and China, which caused Iran to be one of the hardest hit countries by COVID-19. The Iranian people have not forgotten. I would not be surprised in the least if there was an attempt by the Iranian people to take their country back in the next few years."

"They'll need help," Myk commented.

Raji laughed and shook her head.

Myk asked, "What?"

"The last two times an uprising started in Iran, you Americans were nowhere to be found. They've learned their lesson—don't rely on the Americans for help. The Iranian people will do it themselves. If the US gets involved, it will never take hold."

"I don't disagree. I think we missed an opportunity to help the Iranian people years ago, but perhaps that was for the best."

Raji and Myk pulled into the safe house at 2:30 a.m. The house was dark. Levi and Jaafar had long since gone to bed. Raji and Myk tried to be as quiet as they could when they entered the house to get some much-needed sleep.

# CHAPTER 22

The next morning, Myk woke up and entered the kitchen for a cup of coffee. Jaafar was seated on a barstool at the kitchen island writing feverishly on a pad of paper. Levi was outside smoking a Gurkha Black Dragon cigar. Myk watched as Levi tilted his head up and blew a dense haze of smoke to the sky. From the expression on his face, Levi was clearly enjoying the pricey cigar. Myk walked past Jaafar and glanced at his notes. He counted at least five pages scattered on the granite counter, written in perfect Persian penmanship.

Myk peered over Jaafar's shoulder. "What's that?"

Jaafar spun his barstool halfway around. "This is how I make a difference."

Myk asked snidely, "Meaning what?"

"Meaning I've written some ideas down on how I can make a difference. How to educate hearts and minds. I have a contact that works for the Al-Jazeera network. He can read my letter to the Islamic world explaining my defection from radical Islam."

Myk's eyes narrowed. "That's your plan? You're going to write a letter, and all the jihadists are going to throw down their weapons and join you?"

"I need to start somewhere." Jaafar spun his stool back around and continued writing. Then he asked, "When can I speak to your director?"

"If you want my honest opinion, I think you're going to lose credibility with those you're trying to convert if you turn yourself in right now."

"How so?" asked Jaafar.

"If your followers think you're being held against your will, then whatever message you put out there is going to come across as coerced. However, if you stay underground and you've got both your government and my government actively looking for you, then your message will come off as being genuine. Then, you might actually be able to convince someone."

"You've got a point," Jaafar said.

Raji was sitting by herself on a sleek, contemporary Italian leather couch that was stained a bright orange color, brooding. She was staring at the profile of her father as he spoke. Her fists were clenched. She was in a quandary. The old man on the barstool was responsible for her son's death, but the Iranian people were suffering under an oppressive regime. She decided to speak up. "I have a better idea. I am in no way trying to help you either! I want to help the Iranian people—not you!"

Myk said, "Let's hear it."

Raji elaborated, "Rather than a letter, let's do an interview-style format. I've done hundreds of interviews throughout my career. If done correctly, it will have a lot more credibility than a letter."

"Who will do the interview? It can't be you. That would put your life in danger and probably come off as less believable since you're his daughter," Myk added.

"I agree. It can't be me. I can set up the format and questions, but I can't be the one asking the questions. Honestly, I think it would be best if the interviewer remains anonymous. Nobody in their right mind would ever want to show their face interviewing a defector from radical Islam. That would be an instant death warrant. If the interviewer is anonymous, it makes it more authentic."

Myk smiled. "That's a great idea, Raji. Give some more thought to how you want to set it up and let me know what you'll need."

Raji nodded affirmatively. Myk opened up the French door and joined Levi on the patio couch. Myk's safe house sat at the top of the cul-de-sac and had the largest backyard in the neighborhood. There was a long and narrow pool designed for swimming laps. At the head of the pool was an elevated putting green and a small sand pit to practice chipping on the green. The patio furniture was made of a brushed-nickel metal frame with designer fabric in bright striped colors of yellow, blue, and orange. Opposite Levi was a large-screen TV mounted on the covered patio wall. Underneath the TV was a long, rectangular fireplace that stretched seven feet wide. Levi stretched out his hand and offered his cigar.

Myk took the cigar and inhaled. After letting out a cloud of smoke he asked, "Ooh, that's nice. It's complex—a hint of sour combined with sweet. What is it?"

Levi smiled. "My favorite. They're made in Connecticut. They come in a box carved out of camel bone. A bit exotic, I know. But damn good!"

Myk took another puff and handed the cigar back to Levi. "Best cigar I've had, that's for sure. How are you holding up?"

"I'm doing just fine. I was just sitting out here reminiscing and appreciating my stogie. Last week I was enjoying life in my secluded Oregon retreat and the next thing I know, I'm back in the thick of things in international affairs. Things seem to have come full circle for me. The murderer I tried to kill decades ago is sitting on a barstool forty feet in front of me. And the girl that I risked my life to save has turned out to be quite an exceptional human being."

Myk looked through the glass toward Raji. "She's something else, isn't she?"

"She sure is. I thought for sure we were going to have to clean Jaafar's brains off of all those nice wine bottles in the jet. I saw her index finger tightening up and thought that was the end of Jaafar. That's when I spoke up."

Myk laughed. "I would hate to waste any of that good wine on his empty soul. Raji has a good idea on getting a message out to Jaafar's followers."

Levi asked, "Do you know who Raji reminds me of, Myk?"

"No idea."

"Your mother, back when she was a Mossad agent. They both have the same tenaciousness."

"Really?"

"Yes. It's uncanny how much Raji reminds me of her."

Myk smiled and nodded. "That's interesting."

Levi asked, "So, when are you going to hand Jaafar off?"

"I'm hoping to buy some time. I might need him as leverage."

"That's smart, Myk. I'd hold on to him as long as you can. So where do we go from here?"

"I want to see what Raji needs for the interview that we'll send to the Al-Jazeera network. I need to check my laptop for any messages, since our phones aren't safe. Can I get you anything?"

Levi let out another puff of smoke. "No, I'm just fine, Myk. You do what you need to do, and I'll stay out of the way. I've been mulling over a few ideas of my own, but they involve Raji. I'm just not sure it's worth the risk."

"What is it?" Myk asked inquisitively.

Levi stared at Myk as if in thought and then said, "I need to process some ideas on Raji a bit more. I'll share it with you later. However, I spoke with my former boss at Mossad, Mordechai, about the assassination attempts on you, and he said he was going to work on a few things for me."

One of Myk's brows furrowed. "Wow—thank you! Let me know if he comes up with anything."

Myk walked back into the house. Raji was still on the couch and seemed to be deep in thought.

Myk asked, "Are you sure you don't need anything?"

"Not right now. Where is the bathroom?"

Myk pointed. "It's the first door on the left. I've got a secure laptop in the office. I need to check for messages. After that, we can figure out where to start."

Raji nodded. "Okay."

Myk entered the home office and logged on to his computer. He impatiently tapped his foot as he waited for the computer to boot up. He typed in his password and watched as two days of messages scrolled across the screen. He scanned the messages and then stopped when he came across a message from Poe's Raven. It had been over a year since he'd received anything from the Raven. It could only mean one thing—trouble. He clicked on the message and opened it up. It was cryptic, but he knew exactly what it meant. The message read, "Poe's Raven flies south when dark clouds from the east approach."

"Shit!" Myk mumbled under his breath. There were a few prearranged messages that were scripted by Director Adelberg for Myk if security had been breached. This particular message meant they needed to meet in person. Myk knew the exact location. He typed in the clandestine reply and hit send.

In the early evening hours, Myk told everyone at the safe house that something urgent had come up and that he would be gone for a few hours. On his drive, he continued to consider the possibilities of what Adelberg deemed so urgent. He decided the most likely reason would involve Jaafar. If he had to turn him over, his plans on how he wanted to use Jaafar would be compromised—justice would have been better served by a bullet from Raji's gun. Myk flipped his blinker on and turned onto Embarcadero Street. When he passed Pier 9, he began to look for a place to park. Four blocks from the designated meeting place, Myk began to survey his surroundings to verify it was secure before he sat down with Director Adelberg.

After observing Director Adelberg and the surrounding area for twenty minutes, Myk pulled his hoodie over his head and rounded the corner to the Fog City Diner. The diner was long and rectangular and somewhat resembled a railroad car, except much larger. The décor was from the post–Roaring Twenties with black-and-white checkerboard tile cladding on the outside and shiny chrome trim throughout. When you entered the nostalgic restaurant, it was like stepping back in the 1920s and its sense of post-war optimism and booming economic growth. The energetic, brassy music of the twenties played, and all the adornments of the era were everywhere. Myk crossed the street and approached the diner. The large circular Fog City Diner sign appeared to glow even brighter as it began to get dark and a layer of thick marine fog rolled in. Adelberg was seated on the outdoor patio adjacent to the entrance under large, mature Ficus trees that surrounded the diner. He did not stand to greet Myk.

The second Myk sat, Adelberg discreetly asked, "How is Jaafar?"

"He's already working on what he wants to say to his followers. It's hard. Every time I look at him, I have the urge to snap his neck."

Adelberg's eyes darted back and forth, trying to detect anything out of the ordinary. "There's been a lot of chatter about Jaafar. The Iranians already have a team in the US looking for him, so be vigilant. We just don't know their location."

Myk gave him a puzzled look and asked, "We assumed there might be several teams. That can't be the reason for your signal flare to me is it?"

Adelberg put his elbows on the table and leaned in. "No, of course not. I did some digging when you questioned me about the number of crates of gold that were recovered by the FBI operation in Switzerland. Eleven crates of gold are accounted for."

"Who in the hell was in charge of that operation?"

Adelberg became even more fidgety. "Every file on that operation has been purged, so I reached out to an old contact from Mossad. Apparently, they had two of their agents at the lake when the extraction of the crates of gold took place."

Myk wondered if he should tell Adelberg Levi's story about what he and Myk's father had witnessed.

Adelberg continued, "The agents at the lake took pictures of the operation. Their equipment and film got damaged in a storm that blew in while they were there—they didn't have the technology back then to restore the pictures, but now we do. They found the old film and took it to their forensics lab. They restored just enough of the film to identify who the FBI agent was."

Myk gave him a puzzled look.

Adelberg leaned closer while Myk did the same. Their faces were about a foot apart. Adelberg whispered, "There was a very young FBI agent who is pictured at the lake that day—Rick Taft."

They both sat back in their chairs. Myk shook his head and mumbled, "Jesus!"

Adelberg said, "He's got a lot of close ties with people in high places. Everyone assumed that he got his billions from his parents, but I did the math. The valuation of their company and their assets are only a fraction of Taft's net worth."

Myk shook his head. "What do we do?"

"We lie low until I know who I can trust," Adelberg answered. "They've flipped the agency upside down since they booted me out. You couldn't be touched while you were in prison, I made sure of that. Now we know why they came after you two weeks after you got out."

Myk whispered, "I know the Mossad agents who took the pictures." He was on the verge of telling Adelberg that it was his uncle and his father that were the Mossad agents at the lake when Myk instantly caught the look on Adelberg's face. There was no mistaking Adelberg's expression of horror. There was someone behind Myk, and Adelberg's face said it all—he was a dead man. In the nanosecond that it took Myk's brain to process it, Adelberg was shot in the head, and Myk was shot in his left shoulder. Had he not impulsively spun out of his seat, Myk would have been shot in the head too. The gunman fired again and hit Myk in the leg as he rolled out of his chair. With his other leg, Myk swiftly kicked the assassin in the back of the leg, causing it to buckle and sending him along with the table crashing to the pavement. The glass table shattered as the silverware noisily clanged against the hard ground. The assassin lunged for his gun, which had fallen from his hand. Just before he could turn and shoot, Myk violently planted a sharp steak knife in the back of his neck right next to his spinal cord. Blood shot out of his neck like water from a high-pressure hose. Immediately, the gunman started to convulse.

Onlookers inside the restaurant immediately took cover. Myk stood, but the shooting pain prevented him from putting any weight on his wounded leg. Blood pulsed out from the bullet hole in his thigh. He grabbed the metal container full of napkins and began to hobble across the street, leaving the pandemonium behind. He rounded the corner and checked behind him to see if he was followed. Myk yanked out a handful of napkins and pressed hard against the hole in his leg. The pain was excruciating and almost toppled him to the ground. He kept moving, dragging his leg behind like an overweight suitcase with broken wheels. He heard sirens off in the distance. He hoped the dense fog would provide him the cover he needed to make it back to his car.

Myk got to his car and was driving up Embarcadero Street when the first responder flew past him. He reached for another fistful of napkins and pressed it against the gunshot wound in his shoulder. *Not enough hands*, he thought. He only had one free arm available, but there were two critical wounds that needed pressure. He improvised. Myk pulled his shirt over his head and ripped it in half. He looked up just in time to swerve out of the way of a car attempting to back into a parking spot. He stuffed a fresh pile of napkins on his bleeding leg and then cinched his shirt, now a tourniquet, tightly around the wound. He checked his rearview mirror—nothing. He drove on, trying to process everything, but he couldn't. He was beginning to feel light-headed from the loss of blood. If he could make it back to the house, he had medical supplies and Levi could patch him up.

Myk was barely conscious when he pulled into the garage of the safe house. He turned the ignition off and opened the car door, but the room was spinning, and he couldn't keep his balance when he stood. Everything went black, and he couldn't see, so he stepped toward the location that he last remembered the door to the house being and tried to feel for the door handle. It was locked. Myk pounded on the door. Then he felt himself falling.

Before he hit the ground, the door opened and he heard the voice of Raji say, "Oh my God!"


Myk blacked out and fell through the doorway like a gunnysack of sand used to shore up a flooded dike. Levi saw Myk's limp body fall through the door, and Raji tried her best to catch him. But the only thing she could do was prevent his head from smacking against the hard travertine stone floor. As she eased his head to the ground, she asked Levi, "Should we move him to the couch?"

Levi quickly replied, "No. We need to stabilize him. Every safe house has medical supplies. Search the house and see if you can locate them and tell me what you find." He turned to Jaafar. "Toss me that pillow from the couch, and bring me as many towels as you can find."

Despite Levi's quest to leave the brutality and death of the espionage world behind him, violence had now found its way back to him. His nephew lay unconscious and bleeding to death in front of him. Decades before, Levi's brother, the man who Myk was named after, had been gunned down in front of him. He said a silent and solemn prayer about how the family had experienced too much pain and tragedy. Tears rolled down Levi's cheeks. He couldn't have both the father and his son die on his watch. "Please. Spare him," he pleaded.

Raji ran back to Levi from the far bedroom and told him, "The far closet is like a mini triage unit. There's even a small refrigerator with several pints of his type O blood."

"Great!" said Levi. "Bring it out here. Once we get him stabilized, we can move him."

Levi worked quickly. He acted with such precision it was as if he was back in his thirties. He had seen more than his fair share of death, and he had performed dozens of medical procedures in the field. Most were gunshot wounds mixed with a few knife wounds he had stitched up, including one on his own lower leg. The bullet in Myk's shoulder went clean through. Unfortunately, the bullet in his leg was buried deep. Levi would have to extract it later. He had enough supplies to keep it from getting infected for now.

Raji asked, "Shouldn't we call for an ambulance?"

Levi shook his head. "I'm afraid not. He would have driven himself to a hospital if it was safe, but he didn't. He was meeting with his director. Anyone who knew about his secret meeting could certainly find him and finish him off at any hospital. That's why he drove back here."

# CHAPTER 23

T wo days had passed since Myk had collapsed on the floor from his gunshot wounds. Once Levi got him stabilized, he had to figure out how to get Myk's six-foot-four, two-hundred-and-twenty-pound frame of muscle transferred onto a bed. They improvised by sliding a doubled-up bedsheet underneath his body, and then the three of them grabbed corners of the sheet and slowly moved him onto a bed. As they nursed Myk back to health, Levi did the interview of Jaafar while Raji directed and recorded it. They kept it short in hopes that Al-Jazeera would air the interview in its entirety. The sole purpose was to somehow start a grassroots movement of educating followers of radical Islam. In the interview, Jaafar explained that he had awoken to the truth. He made an emotional appeal to his followers and fellow mullahs to choose a path of peace instead of violence. He told the world that Iran had developed an extremely deadly mutated form of the COVID-19 virus and that they had attempted to release it in the United States. The interview detailed the lies that the Iranian regime had propagated on its people. Jaafar named all the leaders in Iran who were paid off by the Chinese government and gave a detailed account of the exact amount each leader had received. The fifteen-minute interview exposed the Iranian leadership's lies, corruption, and evil plans. Because of Jaafar's high ranking status within the Iranian regime, the interview had instant credibility—one of their own had turned against them.

Raji stepped out to the back patio where Levi was enjoying another of his expensive cigars. "Mind if I join you?"

Levi exhaled and answered, "Of course not, I'd enjoy your company."

"Mind if I smoke too?" she asked.

Levi chuckled and motioned to his cigar as if to say, isn't it obvious?

"Sorry, I've been told Americans are a little sensitive on the whole smoking thing," she said apologetically. Raji took a seat and lit up her cigarette. "Is he going to be okay?" Myk had only said a few words and needed assistance to go to the bathroom.

"The first twenty-four hours were the most critical. He'll be just fine."

"That's good. It's all over the news we've been watching. There's a manhunt for Myk, and they're saying he killed Director David Adelberg. That's not true—right?"

Levi shook his head and laughed. "There are some extremely powerful people in the US government that don't want to be exposed by Myk. They've been discreet in trying to eliminate him up until now. The fact that they've put him on a wanted list and killed his boss means he's getting close."

"So, your government is no different than Iran's?" Raji asked sarcastically.

Levi gave her a puzzled look. "It's quite different."

"Not from my perspective—powerful men in both governments getting bought for a price," she quickly retorted.

Levi rubbed his chin as if in thought. "A valid point, but that doesn't make our governments the same. Iran has a theocratic totalitarian government that oppresses its people, the US government is a democratic republic that values individual freedom and lifts people up. But both of our governments employ men who have succumbed to their human natures of greed and selfishness. Those type of men have a price at which they can be bought. But not everyone has a price."

Raji blew a cloud of smoke upward. "I suppose." She inhaled from her cigarette again. "So what happened to him? What's he going to do?"

"He hasn't said anything yet. Hopefully, he'll be able to talk more today. He's only got one option—he has to expose his killers before they get to him." Levi looked at his watch and asked, "Would you mind bringing Myk some soup?"

Raji stood. "Sure. I'll take it to him now."

Before Raji entered the house, Levi said, "I'll join you in a minute."

Raji entered Myk's room balancing a large bowl of soup with a saucer underneath it in one hand and a tall glass of water in the other. When she entered the room, Myk was lying on his side with his back to her. The bedsheet was pulled down to his waist, exposing his muscular bare back and his wounded shoulder. She slowly entered the room, admiring the tattoo on his back. She had never seen anything like it. She didn't even care for tattoos, but this one was artwork—a beautiful, curvaceous woman with flowing long hair. She was half woman, half tree. Her rounded figure made up the tree truck of an old, majestic tree. Her long, wavy hair was the tree branches, which were being blown by a strong wind with leaves floating in the air. The profile face of a stunning goddess-like woman was embedded in the top of the tree trunk. It was serene to look at. The large tattoo ran from his waist to the top of his shoulder.

Raji rounded the foot of the bed and approached the nightstand to place the soup down.

Myk opened his eyes and said, "Thank you."

Raji smiled politely but said nothing. As she turned toward the door, she heard Myk say, "Stay."

She looked back at him and asked, "Are you sure?"

"Yes." She sat in a chair against the wall that was facing Myk. "I am sorry about Yasser. How are you doing?" Myk asked.

Raji's eyes narrowed. A look of question came over her face. *He's lying in a bed almost shot to death, and he asks* me *how I'm doing?* she thought. "I'd been preparing myself for almost a year that I might lose Yasser, so that may have cushioned the blow. Truthfully, it just hasn't sunk in yet."

Myk said, "He was on his way back to you. You lost him for

a little bit, but he found his way back. It's a tragedy that he didn't quite make it."

"That's very kind. Thank you." Raji tried to lighten the mood. "It looks like your tree-lady survived the shots too!"

Myk laughed and then stiffened in pain. "Don't make me laugh, it hurts."

Raji smiled. "I'm sorry. Is the tattoo someone you know?"

Myk shook his head. "A creation of my mind when I was young and dumb. No one in particular."

Raji's iridescent eyes widened. "I've done my fair share of dumb things, that's for sure. Do you regret the tattoo?"

Myk quickly replied, "No, not at all. How about you, do you have any?"

"I thought about it. My friend Becca almost had me in a chair at a tattoo parlor in Paris, but I backed out." Raji shifted in her seat and crossed one leg over the other. "So, who did this to you? It's all over the news. They're saying you killed Director Adelberg."

Myk gently shook his head as he admired her stunning eyes. "Director Adelberg found out who put the hit on me. The assassin chose to kill him first, or else I'd be dead. He came from behind me. I was able to move just enough so that I didn't get hit with any fatal shots. How'd the interview go with your father?"

"He got what he wanted," Raji said tersely.

"Meaning what?" Myk asked.

"My father got to tell the Islamic world about his change. It was done well enough that I think it was effective. I think he'll change some minds."

Myk looked at her and squinted. "But . . ."

"He's murdered thousands! Where's the justice in it all? Where's my justice? He took my mother. He took my childhood, and he took my son. It's so damn hard to watch! I can't even look at him. I can't believe I'm going to say this, but . . ." Raji shook her head and then said, "It's just not fair. I taught Yasser his whole life that the phrase

'It's not fair' is a swear word. It's what I believe. Life isn't fair. It's not supposed to be. But sometimes, it just feels good to say it."

"It's a small world—my mother said the same thing to me: 'Life isn't fair.' David Adelberg was like a father figure to me. He took me under his wing when I first joined the FBI after serving in the Special Forces, and we've been extremely close ever since."

Raji said, "I'm sorry he's gone. I'm sure you must be sad."

Myk slowly tried to sit up in bed so he could eat the soup. "There will be a time for me to grieve. But right now, I am a lot more angry than I am sad. I hardly recognize my country anymore. There is so much petty politics. That's why Adelberg ultimately left the FBI. He was tired of the politics."

Raji watched Myk struggle to sit up. "Can I help?"

Myk continued to work his way into a sitting position. Once he was sitting up with his back leaning against the headboard he asked, "Would you mind putting the soup and tray on my lap? I'm trying to not use my wounded arm."

Raji stood. "Of course."

After she put the tray and soup on his lap, Myk asked, "How'd you get mixed up in all this? Don't get me wrong, if it wasn't for you, I'd be back in Iran getting tortured. But why in the world were you even at the Arena in Verona in the first place?"

Raji sat back in her chair and replied, "When I found out that Yasser had been killed, I snuck into my father's estate. I went there to kill him. My brother and I had previously pleaded with him for information so that we could try to talk some sense into Yasser. But my father was too stubborn. We both warned him that he would have a price to pay if Yasser was harmed. So I went to my father's house to collect payment on his debt—his life for Yasser's."

Myk sarcastically said, "Not exactly an equitable payment."

Raji smiled. "Hardly, considering his life is worthless to me."

"So, what happened?" Myk asked.

Raji continued, "I was hiding in his closet, gun in hand, when he arrived home. I saw him enter his room and then go into his bathroom. He seemed to be shaken up because he was crying in the mirror—I've never seen him cry. He went to his nightstand and pulled a pistol out and placed it under his chin. I was shocked. But mostly, I was upset. I didn't want him to take this last satisfaction away from me by killing himself. So, I was ready to burst from his closet and put a bullet through his skull, but he didn't pull trigger. He put the gun down. I was a little surprised, so I watched and waited."

"What did he do?"

"He got his cell phone out and made a call. That was to you. I had no idea why he would reach out to an American. Part of me wanted to believe that Yasser was still alive. I had seen the pictures, so there was little doubt in my mind. But, you never know with the Iranian regime. They could have manipulated the pictures. It wouldn't be the first time. I heard him book his flight to Verona, so I decided to postpone his execution until then. And then I saw you and your uncle Levi show up and get ambushed, so I stepped in."

"Does anyone know you're here?" Myk asked.

"Not a soul."

Myk took a few spoonfuls of soup and then asked, "How did you explain your absence to your boss?"

"Like I said, they know I travel extensively, so it's not out of the ordinary for me to leave the country for a few weeks at a time. I had a bit of a run in with my producer before I left. They wanted me to peddle lies about Yasser's death." Raji laughed and shook her head. "Can you believe that? They wanted me to lie about my own son. Anyway, I called and told him I was in mourning and that I'd let him know if and when I'm ready to come back. I packed all my valuables, that's why the six large suitcases. I have no intention of ever returning."

"Wow! They really expected you to spin a story about the death of Yasser?"

"My producer was just following directions from above. He knew what I would do without even asking."

Myk shifted his weight and then said, "There's nothing left for you to do here. Maybe it's a good time for you to meet your friend in Paris, before things get ugly. I can call an Uber if you want."

Raji stared directly at Myk as if she didn't hear what he asked. "I have another question," she said.

"What is it?"

"Do you need my father for anything else?" she asked sternly.

"I think I know the answer, but why do you ask?"

"If you think he's of any use to you, then get everything out of him that you can. But the minute you're done with him, then I need to end his life."

Myk set his spoon down beside the bowl and asked in a very serious tone, "There's no love lost between you two is there?"

A memory instantly flashed into Raji's mind. It was more than a memory, it was a feeling attached to a memory. The memory was from her third year of wiring bombs for her father. She was getting older and beginning to question things. It was one of the only times she could count on seeing her father. She craved any kind of attention from him or acknowledgment that she was important—that she even existed. She had finished wiring three devices, and she walked them over and placed them at the workstation Jaafar was seated at. He was reading.

Raji had placed the explosive devices beside her father and asked, "Are these okay?"

It was in moments like this that Raji received any validation that she might have some importance to her father. But on this occasion, Jaafar was busy reading and never even bothered to look up at her work.

Without as much as a glance, Jaafar said, "They are fine." Raji stared and waited for him to either look up at what she had done or look up and acknowledge that she was even in the room. He didn't. He just continued to read. *I don't matter, I am insignificant*, she thought. Feelings of loneliness flooded Raji and her eyes began to water. The little girl stood beside her father aching for the smallest of gestures from him. *Just look at me*, she remembered thinking. Jaafar's head remained down.

She told Jaafar, "I'd like to go to a public school."

Jaafar replied, "That's enough. I told you to never bother me again with questions about going to a public school. Leave me now."

Jaafar kept reading without ever looking at Raji. He even shifted positions in his chair so as to turn away from her. Raji's work had become so impeccable that inspecting it had become rote for Jaafar. Raji realized that it didn't matter how perfect her work was, nothing she could do would ever garner the attention of her father. Resentment was born that day.

Raji's eyes were aglow and fixed on Myk. She repeated his question, "No love lost between us?" She shook her head. "There was never any love to be lost in the first place."

Myk nodded. "Yeah, I can see that. I think it would be a good idea to send two more interviews to the Al-Jazeera network. After that, he's all yours."

Raji smiled. "That's good. Can I get anything for you?"

"I'm fine. Thank you," Myk said.

Raji stood. "I need a smoke, and there's something I want to ask Levi."

"Anything I can help with?" Myk asked.

"Not yet, but I'll let you know after I talk to Levi."

Raji left the room and walked back toward the kitchen. After getting herself a glass of water, she looked across the room at Jaafar. At this point, even looking at her father was something she avoided doing. He was sitting on the couch fidgeting with his cell phone.

Raji exploded and screamed at him from across the room. "You stupid fool! What are you doing?"

Raji left her glass of water, ran over to the couch where Jaafar was sitting and snatched the phone out of his hand. She threw his phone on the ground in front of her and then smashed it with the heel of her foot. She stomped on it three more times and then said, "The Iranian regime wants you dead. What were you thinking?"

"I received an important message," he replied.

"I hope your stupidity didn't put us in danger!" Raji was visibly upset. She shook her head and then went outside to have a smoke and talk to Levi.

# CHAPTER 24

Raji wrote the script for the follow-up interview between Levi and Jaafar. Once she edited it, she sent it off to the Al-Jazeera network as well as two other national networks. Myk was no longer bedridden but out and walking around, albeit with a limp. He had the use of his wounded arm, but it was only at 60 percent. He was no longer the lead story in the local news but was still getting some coverage. Myk figured that within a few days the news media would forget about him and move on to the next big story. Most of the day, Jaafar sat alone. Raji, Myk, and Levi ate together and conversed frequently, but they left Jaafar to himself.

Since they both had an affinity for smoking, Raji spent most of her time talking with Levi on the back patio. Levi shared with her some of his experiences with Mossad and talked about his family. He told her about his wife who had passed away and his only daughter who lived in New York. She asked him about the day her mother was killed, and Levi shared everything he could remember. Raji grew fond of Levi and instantly bonded with him. When she began asking questions about Myk, Levi concluded that perhaps she was growing fond of him too.

During the early morning hours around 2:30 a.m., Myk was lying awake in bed with his eyes closed, lost in thought. With the third and final interview of Jaafar completed and emailed to the networks, he tried to think of what else he would need him for. Myk's sixth sense automatically kicked in when the red glow of the alarm clock vanished from his closed eyelids. Instinctively, Myk opened his eyes and looked at the dark alarm clock. There was no storm, so a power outage was unlikely. It could only mean one thing—someone had turned their power off. He quietly rolled to his side and pulled his Glock from the nightstand. He slowly tiptoed to his bedroom door and listened. If there was someone in the house, they weren't making any noise. Myk turned the door handle in slow motion. Without a sound, he cracked the door open and peered through the sliver in the door with one eye. He saw the shadows of two figures entering through the garage service door. Myk slowly closed the door and pulled his cell phone out of his pocket. He had the safe house wired with a security system controlled by a backup battery. He quickly scrolled to the security system app and hesitated. Once he pushed the button, a few select lights would turn on and the screeching sound of the smoke detectors would go off.

Myk crouched down on one knee behind the door and got his gun ready. In his other hand he held his cell phone and had his thumb waiting just above the security system app. He took a deep breath and then pushed the button on the app. There was a momentary delay in the signal, but after two seconds, half of the lights in the house turned on and the smoke detectors began blaring loudly in a high-pitched tone. Simultaneously, Myk burst through his door with his arm extended and his gun in the ready position. The first person Myk saw was an armed man in the kitchen who was completely surprised by the lights being turned on and the screeching sound of the smoke detectors. Myk squeezed his trigger and the man dropped to the floor. Myk noticed movement in his peripheral vision to the right. He swung his extended arm to the right, and a Middle Eastern man came bursting through the garage service door. Myk stayed in his crouched position on one knee and shot two rounds into the gunman, a headshot and a heart shot.

Myk heard female screams of terror from down the hall—Raji's room. He stood up and limped as fast as his leg would allow to

Raji's room. Myk heard screams and then loud yelling in Persian. He reached for the handle and heard four bursts of gunshots in the room. Myk shoved the door open and swung his outstretched arm with his Glock in the room looking for the target. Raji was standing above a bloodied corpse with an unrecognizable face from two gunshots. The gun in Raji's hand was still smoking, and she was yelling uncontrollably in Persian at the motionless body underneath her left foot. Myk exhaled a huge gasp.

"Are you okay?" The words had slipped out before he realized what a stupid question it was. He left it alone and then said, "There are two more that are dead in the front room. I'll check on Levi and Jaafar. I don't know if there's any more. Please stay in the room."

Myk closed the door and slowly worked his way up the hallway to the great room. The home was a split floor plan and the other two rooms that Levi and Jaafar slept in were on the opposite side of the house. Myk cleared the hallway without resistance and was beginning to cross to the other side of the house when he heard a noise behind him. He turned and saw Raji, gun in hand, exiting her room. He shook his head at her and mumbled, "Of course she wouldn't stay," under his breath. Myk turned back just in time to see the gunman pop up from where he was crouched behind the kitchen counter. Myk instantly pulled the trigger twice, but he heard three gunshots not two. He turned to see if Raji was hit. When he looked at her face, she was smiling at Myk. The residue of smoke was still lingering from the tip of her gun. She had shot the gunman just before he did. Myk walked over to the dead man sprawled out and bleeding on the kitchen floor. He had two bullet holes near his heart and one through his left cheek bone.

Myk yelled out, "Levi, are you okay?"

He heard Levi's muted voice yell back, "I'm fine, Myk."

Myk yelled again to Levi, "Are you alone?"

Levi responded, "Yes, I am alone."

He yelled, "Jaafar, are you okay?"

Jaafar yelled back, "I am fine."

Myk walked to Levi's room and knocked on the locked door. "Levi, it's Myk. Open the door, please."

Levi opened the door and Myk scanned the inside of his room. Other than Levi, the room was empty. Myk moved on to Jaafar's door and knocked. "It's Myk, open up. We're all safe."

Jaafar opened the door. "What happened?"

Myk shook his head. "This is a secure location, I am the only one who knows about it. I don't have any idea how they could have found us."

Myk, Levi, and Jaafar headed down the hall, rounded the corner to the kitchen, and froze. Another gunman had Raji in a headlock in one arm and a gun pointed at her head with the other.

When they came into eyesight the gunman said in Persian, "Not one step closer or she dies."

Jaafar spoke to the gunman in Persian calling him by name, "Jamal, it's over. Please lower your gun."

Jamal barked back, "You are a coward and a traitor, Jaafar. How could you turn your back on us and conspire with that Jew!"

Myk and Levi made eye contact. Levi looked at Myk who was slowly inching his hand closer to his gun.

Jaafar implored, "I was wrong, Jamal. Everything I taught you was wrong."

Jamal gripped Raji's neck tighter. Jaafar was only making him angrier. Jamal yelled at Jaafar, "Step forward right now, traitor, or she dies! It's time for you to answer to Allah!"

"Okay, just don't harm her," Jaafar said.

Jaafar began to step toward Jamal. Levi observed that Myk's hand was inches away from gripping his gun. When Myk and Levi made eye contact again, Levi smiled at Myk and then winked. It was a *Twilight Zone* moment for Myk. His mind couldn't process why Levi would wink and smile at him in this moment. It was like a round peg in a square hole—it didn't fit. Later, it would make sense. But in the moment, there was but one choice for Myk. When Jaafar took his first step with his gimpy prosthetic leg, Myk watched Jamal remove his gun pointed at Raji's temple and take aim directly at Jaafar. What Myk didn't see in that exact same moment was Levi lunging in front of Jaafar. Two loud gunshots went off simultaneously—*pop pop!* Myk watched as Jamal's body fell lifeless to the floor like a limp noodle. But he also saw the look of horror on Raji's face, and he turned to see if Jaafar was shot. Myk's heart sank to his stomach. Levi was propped against the wall with his two hands drenched in blood covering his heart. Levi had jumped in front of Jamal's bullet and sacrificed himself for Jaafar.

"No! Goddamn it, no!" Myk yelled. Tears burst uncontrollably from Myk's eyes. He put his arms around Levi and helped ease him down to a sitting position against the wall. A huge swath of blood streaked against the wall as Levi slid down.

Crying, Myk held Levi, looking at him with his tearful eyes. He pleaded, "Why? Why would you do this?!"

With his hands drenched in blood, Levi raised his arm toward Myk. Clenched between his thumb and index finger was a zip drive that he handed to Myk. An unexplainable smile appeared again on Levi's face. It was a smile of peace. It was a smile of confidence. Levi reached out and touched Myk on the cheek. His eyes seemed to sparkle as he whispered his last words: "This had to be, Myk. I'm sorry. Your father would be so proud of you."

Myk felt Levi's body go lifeless in his arms as he embraced his uncle. He held Levi's body tight. Myk's mind went numb. He shook his head slowly back and forth and just cried. He had barely known the man, and yet he felt an overwhelming sense of sadness. Levi was gone, and with him, his memories were gone too. Memories of Myk's father. Through Levi, Myk had begun to know his father. Now they were both gone. The last of the three orphaned brothers would now join his other two brothers in death.

# CHAPTER 25

Myk gently laid Levi's body on the floor. Raji walked over and knelt beside him. With her open palm, she pulled Levi's eyelids shut. Then she reached out and gently touched the *kippah* on his head just as she had done decades earlier when Levi had saved her life in the parking garage of Beirut. She whispered, "You were an angel in our midst." Myk looked at Raji and then at Jaafar and said, "I am the only one who knows the location of my safe house. How in the hell did they find your location, Jaafar?"

Jaafar was about to speak but Raji cut him off. Her eyes narrowed, and she glared at him with her eyes on fire. "You waste of flesh! How could you have been so stupid? This is your fault!"

"What did he do?" Myk demanded.

Raji answered, "When I left your room a few days ago, I found him sitting on the couch on his phone."

Myk stood and asked Jaafar, "Is this true? You've been in this business all your life; how could you make such a careless mistake?"

Jaafar replied, "The Chinese contacted my nuclear engineer in Tehran again, and he sent me a message. I should have known better."

Myk was infuriated. His adrenaline kicked in, and the pain in his wounds momentarily disappeared. He picked up Jaafar by his collar with both hands and slammed him violently against the wall. Jaafar's foot was dangling six inches above the ground. "You fucking idiot! Levi was my only lifeline to my past, and he stepped in front of a bullet for your sorry ass!" Myk slammed Jaafar to the ground so hard he heard Jaafar's breath explode out of his lungs. The sound of his metal prosthetic clacking on the hard floor reverberated. Myk kneeled on top of him and held his clenched fist suspended above Jaafar's face ready to unleash his fury.

Raji spoke up, "Myk. You can't do it! Not now."

He looked at Raji with an angry and puzzled face. "Of course I can. Especially now!"

Raji shook her head. "No, Myk, you can't."

He tilted his head and asked, "Why not?"

"Because, if you do, then Levi's sacrifice will be in vain."

Myk closed his eyes. He took a deep breath and then lowered his fists. He stood with his eyes closed inhaling deep breaths. He had grown to love Levi, but at this moment, he hated him. Levi's sacrifice handcuffed Myk. Raji was right. He couldn't kill Jaafar, not now—maybe not ever. He could feel the anger growing inside him like thick black clouds on the horizon.

His eyes opened and he screamed uncontrollably at the top of his lungs, "Fuck!"

Jaafar looked back at him. He was visibly shaken. He did not utter a word. Myk walked to the barstools at the counter and sat. He rested his elbows on the counter and folded his arms. He and Raji looked directly at each other without saying a word.

They continued to stare until Raji broke the silence. "I am so sorry, Myk. Levi was such a good man," she said sadly. The dichotomy between Levi and her father was as bright as staring at the noonday sun with her eyes wide open.

She asked Myk, "What kind of man takes a bullet for his enemy?" She broke eye contact with Myk, put her head down on her folded arms and rocked her head back and forth. Levi had been such a stark contrast to the men in her life: her father, her husband, her lovers. All selfish. *Why does the good man have to die?* she thought. Anger began to build within her again. Another memory was trying to dislodge itself from her cortex, but she stuffed it back in. No use.

The memory was more stubborn than she was. *Not now,* she thought. *Not this one,* she pleaded.

Raji's thoughts brought her back to another time that she had become so angry that she could kill. Her mind wandered back to her second trip to Paris—when she truly wanted to kill Ali. Becca had come to her hotel the morning that Raji was scheduled to fly back to Tehran. She told Raji that her security team had uncovered something about Ali that would be shocking to her. She remembered Becca opening up her laptop and pushing the play button. The video began with Ali sitting on a couch in a hotel. The video was partially screened because of the sheer see-through curtain that was drawn. There was a knock at the door and Ali got up from the couch to answer it, but the door was out of view from the window that the video was being recorded from, so it was just video of an empty hotel room until Ali and his guest came back into the picture. The guest was a younger man that was dressed nicely. The two of them took a seat on the couch and conversed for several minutes. She couldn't hear any conversation, but she saw the younger man reach over and grab Ali's hand. A few moments later Ali moved the man's hand to his crotch.

At first, Raji was confused at what she was watching. Her confusion turned to shock and then anger. She continued to watch the secret surveillance video. The younger man unbuckled Ali's pants and began to fondle him. It was clear that Ali was enjoying himself. Three minutes into the video the younger man began to perform oral sex on Ali. Raji looked up from the video and met Becca's eyes. Raji didn't say a word; she couldn't. She let her iridescent eyes do it for her. She stared at Becca while her eyes asked, *What's going on?*

Becca's lips tightened. She reached out and put her hand on top of Raji's. "Your husband is gay, Raji," Becca said.

Raji watched the video as Ali and his lover undressed and moved from the couch to the bed. She watched another five minutes and then shook her head and told Becca to turn it off. Becca pushed the stop button and then folded her laptop shut.

Raji asked, "How much longer does the video go on?"

"This one goes on for another hour. It gets a lot more graphic toward the end."

"What do you mean, this one?" she asked.

"My security team has video of Ali having sex with three different male prostitutes."

Raji interjected, "Prostitutes? Ali paid for these boys?"

"I'm afraid so," Becca replied.

Raji was in shock. She had never seen a pornographic video in her life, and she had just witnessed her husband having sex with another man. She was lost.

Becca said, "I understand that this is frowned upon in your culture. I can tell that you are shocked by all this. I was just trying to help. I am sorry, Raji."

Anger began to build up in Raji. She sarcastically said, "Frowned upon in my culture? Ali would be a disgrace to his family and country if they found out. He used me! He thinks he can prop me up as window dressing to hide who he really is. What if I'm pregnant? I'm trapped! He caught me in his snare like wild prey. I'm so angry I could just shoot him dead right now."

Becca tried to calm her in a reassuring voice, "You're not trapped, Raji. You have some options—maybe more than you realize."

"What do you mean *options*? I am a woman living in Iran, we have no options. Now I've become Ali's puppet wife!"

Becca snapped her fingers sternly. "Hey! Snap out of it. Stop feeling sorry for yourself. Take a step back and look at the big picture. Yes, you've got some challenges, perhaps yours are more severe, but we all have them." Becca picked up her laptop, held it in front of her, and asked, "But who's the puppet and who's pulling the strings now, Raji?"

It took a moment but then the light clicked on for Raji. Her eyes widened and she tucked her hair behind her ears. She looked at the laptop held in front of her and then back at Becca. Raji gently took the computer from Becca with both hands. "I pull the strings now."

Becca grinned at Raji. "That's right. If that's how you want to play this, and I hope by God you do, then you need to be patient. You need to protect yourself first. Don't let your anger show. I can help you set up all the safeguards you'll need. Once you've completely covered yourself, then you can go to Ali and make him do whatever you want. You're the puppet master, and he's the puppet now."

Raji called Ali and left a message. She knew he was on his flight back to Iran. She told him that she had become sick and couldn't make it on her scheduled flight home. She stayed another five days in Paris with Becca. She spent most of her time enjoying Paris and the beautiful culture, so unlike the stifling Iranian regime. They talked a little, but not much about the deal Raji would broker with Ali. There was one very large variable to the equation that she didn't know yet—whether or not she was pregnant.

A month later, it was no longer an unknown variable. Raji was pregnant. The night she conceived was the last time she ever made love with Ali, a fact that neither party ever complained about. On Yasser's first birthday, Raji made Ali an offer that he could not refuse. By that time, Raji had gathered even more evidence of Ali's activities. The higher Ali rose in the rankings of the Iranian regime, the more valuable the deal became for her. Eventually, Ali settled down with one partner, a soccer teammate who had played on the Iranian national team with him who also rose in the rankings of the Iranian military.

Raji began to hear the faint sounds of a familiar voice. It was as if she was in the bottom of a pit and someone was calling her name from the top.

She heard it again. "Raji? Raji, are you okay?"

Raji lifted her head off her folded arms on the countertop and opened her eyes. Myk was calling her name. She looked around and saw the dead bodies everywhere. She looked over at Levi's lifeless form and shook her head.

Myk said, "We can't stay here tonight, it's not safe. We've been compromised. We need to get going."

"Okay." Raji stood from the stool and turned to Myk. A determined look came over her face. "I'm not going to Paris." She hesitated and then said, "I need to go back to Iran."

# CHAPTER 26

# YOSEMITE NATIONAL PARK

A tsunami was at Myk's heels. There was no time to think and no time to assess the oncoming threat. There was only enough time to run for higher ground. With a national manhunt underway in the US for Myk—and the Iranians and the FBI on the hunt for Jaafar—higher ground would not be found in the United States. Safe haven from the tsunami, which Myk was already ankle-deep in, would come in the form of Paris. He only had time to grab his belongings, which included fake identification, passports, and matching disguises, and then eliminate any evidence of his existence at the safe house. On the drive to Yosemite National Park, Myk contacted Levi's daughter to inform her of Levi's death. He spoke to her for almost half of the three-hour drive from San Francisco to Yosemite.

They had to avoid all major airports. Myk did not have the chance to find out what was behind Raji's sudden change of mind to go back to Tehran instead of Paris. Myk didn't choose to go to Yosemite to wait things out in some secluded rustic cabin in the woods while surviving on rabbits and fish. No, there was a very small airport in Yosemite that was a direct pipeline to Los Angeles International Airport. Myk had been through the small airport on his dozens of visits to Yosemite, and every time, he couldn't help but chuckle when he went through security. On one rare occasion, he brought a girlfriend to Yosemite, and she couldn't find her ID when it was time to leave. After a few stories, lots of smiles, and some handshakes, the one-man security crew let her through. The two most wanted people in the US would board their flight in Yosemite with ease, allowing them to completely bypass the extremely stringent security at LAX.

Having had many conversations with the Yosemite airport security personnel over the years, Myk knew exactly which topics to strike up that would gain instant credibility and pass them through with ease. Had Myk not been donning his graying wig and goatee disguise, Sergeant Todd Kerr would have surely recognized him from past years—especially since Myk had informed Sergeant Kerr of the location he had spotted a nineteen-point bull elk just prior to hunting season. The security check at the Yosemite airport was jovial and uneventful. The three fugitives had a few hours to kill before they would board American Airlines's smallest plane, the Embraer 190, which only had ninety-nine seats. Pictures of Yosemite National Park adorned the walls of the of the tiny waiting area. The most impressive pictures were those taken during spring and early summer, when all the waterfalls throughout the park were flowing at maximum capacity from the winter snow melt-off. Yosemite National Park was first protected by President Abraham Lincoln's signing of the Yosemite Grant in 1864 and later gained international recognition. The majestic and tranquil park had been a favorite destination of world-renown artists, photographers, and authors for centuries. The airport was too small for any restaurant chains, so there were two vending machines—one for snacks, the other for beverages. Raji, Myk, and Jaafar sat, eating their prizes that dropped from the vending machine chutes.

Finally, with a moment to think and breathe, Myk asked Raji, "You previously said that you would never be returning to Iran. Why the change of heart?"

Raji placed her water bottle in the cup holder on her seat. "I was fortunate enough to spend most of my time talking with Levi these past few days. When I learned of Yasser's death, I was done. I was done with Iran and its stone-age government. I was done fighting for change. I just wanted out and to start a new life. When you took me to see Yasser's body and you told me the change that Yasser had gone through, it gave me hope. I floated a few ideas past Levi, and he and I talked about them quite a bit. When he sacrificed himself for those ideas, it sealed the deal for me—I had no choice."

When Raji told Myk that Levi sacrificed himself for her ideas, he leaned in to Raji with laser focus and said, "I'm listening."

Raji leaned in as well. She lowered her voice and continued, "At first, Levi said it was too dangerous. But the more details I gave him, the more he encouraged me that it just might work. I have been an antagonist to the Iranian regime most of my life. These past six years, I've had a high-profile platform on which to reach even more Iranians, even if it is somewhat limited. My bags were packed, and I was ready to live out my life seeing the world and enjoying whatever crossed my path. But I have an opportunity because I have a voice."

Impatiently, Myk asked, "You can't be talking about picking up where you left off are you? That would take years, if not decades, to create change by parceling out what little information they allow you."

Raji smiled. "Let me finish. I believe you have a saying here, 'Go big or go home.' Right?"

Looking puzzled, Myk answered, "Yes."

Raji continued, "On our drive after seeing Yasser, I told you that Iran is ripe for a revolution. The coronavirus crippled our leadership, the Iranian people have lost all trust in the regime, and I believe Iran is at a tipping point—it just needs a nudge."

"And you're going to give it the nudge it needs?" Myk asked.

Raji nodded slightly and looked at Myk with her mesmerizing eyes and whispered, "I am going to start a revolution, Myk."

Myk's stomach experienced the sensation of a high-speed roller-coaster when it goes over a massive drop. He did not break eye contact. "Damn. You're actually serious!" He whispered, "What's your plan?"

"I can't take full credit, Levi had some very critical input. When the coronavirus decimated Iran, my network set up a studio at my home that is an exact replica of our national studio in Tehran. My plan is to tell my producer that I'm ready to get back to work and that I am done mourning. I have no doubt they are extremely anxious to get me back on the air. I think after a few days, my network studio will fall back into their routines. I plan to record a message that looks as if it is a live feed of the news. Becca and I have people that can hack into the network and play my message on a continual feed. They told me with the technology they possess, it will take at least six hours before the Iranian government will figure out how to cut off the transmission. In my recorded broadcast, I will detail the lies and corruption of our government and then I will call for Iranians to rise up and take their beloved country back. Ali has a cache of weapons for a small army at my home. My father has weapons at his estate. There has been an underground movement that has been swelling for years. The revolution bomb is ready to explode. I just need to light the fuse. I am telling you—the Iranians are ready to take the country back from those who hijacked it."

Myk sat back and ran his fingers through his hair—thinking. He put his elbows on his knees, leaned back in, and whispered, "And you ran all of this by Levi?"

"Yes. That and much more." She couldn't figure out why she did it at the time. It wasn't a conscious decision. By the time her hand was on top of Myk's, it was too late. And better yet, Myk didn't flinch—not even an eye twitch. In the nanosecond that it took place, it was as if her entire body did a relaxing exhale. Her involuntary affection was welcomed. Raji continued in a whisper while trying not to think of her hand that seemed to have a mind of its own when it gently squeezed Myk's hand.

"Your sweet uncle sealed his belief in the idea with his life. This is what he spent his life fighting for—peace. Did you know that doctors did not know how Levi was going to live with his third pacemaker?

They wanted to replace it. Levi told them no. His daughter fought with him, but he told her that he was ready to be back with his wife. He wasn't sure how much longer his heart would keep pumping, but he told me he was at perfect peace."

Myk was captivated. "I had no idea."

"I know it's none of my business, but it was a tragedy that your mother kept Levi out of your life. That man was an angel." Raji's hand was still holding Myk's. With her other hand, she pointed to the scar above her eye. "He was my angel, Myk."

He shook his head. "I was really looking forward to spending some time with him and getting to know him better. I have no idea what Levi shared with you about my mom. Ironically, I think that everything she tried to shield me from is exactly what I've landed right smack in the middle of."

A half-smile came across Raji's face. *He told me more about you and your mom than you know*, she thought. "Nobody knows how much time Levi had left. His doctors told him six months. Maybe it was less, or perhaps it was more. I believe you got to know more about who Levi truly was six hours ago than you ever would have gotten to know in six months."

"How so?"

Raji put both hands on top of Myk's. "Sure, you would have learned about his experiences and more about your family history, but you wouldn't see who the man truly was. There are few people walking this blue orb that we live on that would take a bullet for someone. But there are far fewer that would forfeit their life for an enemy. Your uncle was the rarest of good men." She paused. Tears began to gather but didn't drop. She wasn't expecting the emotion and tried to hold it in check. She squeezed his hands—this time it was a conscious decision. "He did it twice—once for me and then once for one of the vilest of men." She glanced at Jaafar, let go of Myk's hands, and sat back in her chair.

Myk sat up and gave her a warm smile. Then he put his elbows on his knees again and whispered, "I can help with your revolution."

Raji looked at him with a puzzled face, measuring him up. There was no doubt; she knew he was genuine. "Every agency in the US is on a serious manhunt for you. Don't you have your own problems to tend to first?"

Myk grinned. The tsunami had come, and he had created enough distance from the rising water. When they landed in Paris he would be on higher ground, safe. Myk shrugged confidently. "I've got no worries."

There was an added shimmer in Raji's naturally sparkly eyes. She smiled and put her hand on his knee. "I think the time has come for the Iranian people to take their country back."

# CHAPTER 27

# FORTY-ONE THOUSAND FEET
# IN THE AIR

R aji sat in the window seat on the flight from Yosemite to LAX, soaking in all of the visual beauty of the Sierra Nevada Mountains from her bird's-eye view. In her years of world travel, she had never visited the United States, but had met many Americans who were very proud to share stories of their favorite places in the US. Not traveling to the US was one of the few conditions Ali requested when he and Raji struck their deal. It was the only one she actually honored, until now.

At LAX, they had just enough time to grab something to eat before their eight-hour flight to Paris. With no place safe to stay in the US or Iran, Raji contacted Becca, who was thrilled to have her stay. Because of the last-minute reservations for the flight to Paris, the seating selection was sparse. Myk was still nursing his wounds and needed more leg room. He found two seats for himself and Raji in first class and handicapped seating for Jaafar in coach.

Raji gazed out the window and thought, *What if things go horribly wrong? Thousands would die in vain.* When Raji conversed with Levi on the back patio, he enjoying his expensive cigar and she her cigarette, she remembered how candid and solemn his tone was when he said, "You do understand that there is a high probability that you won't survive this? And even if the Iranian people are successful in their attempt to overthrow the regime, which has a good chance, then there will be many who will look to take their revenge out on the ones that took the power from them—and that will be you! Whatever the outcome, Raji, you will have to look over your shoulder for the remainder of your days. Is that something you can live with?" She told Levi that his perspective was invaluable and that she was willing to live with the risk.

Raji leaned back in her first-class seat. She had a window seat and Myk had the window seat directly behind her. She was beginning to feel the weight of what would happen if she were to light the fuse of revolution. If not now, then when, she reasoned. Her head was spinning with questions: who could she trust, what if they couldn't hack the newsfeed, what if she got caught, should she tell Ali? The flight attendant came by with a tray of white wine. Much to the amusement of the attendant, Raji took three. Forty minutes into the flight, and with five empty clear plastic cups on her tray, she began to relax, and her mind began to slow down.

Raji tucked one leg up under the other and shifted her body toward the window. Her mind drifted back to Yasser's first birthday, which they celebrated at Jaafar's estate. Her brother, Malcolm, was there with his wife and two young daughters. Ali's parents brought an elaborate birthday cake. After a delicious meal of spicy stew over jasmine rice and flatbreads, Raji helped Yasser open his birthday presents and blow out his first candle. Her one-year-old was wiped out by the middle of the day, so Raji put him down for a nap while the others retired to the expansive hillside back patio that overlooked the city of Tehran. The only thing that would have made the day perfect would have been a bottle of wine and Becca's company. But that was an irrational thought—alcohol was forbidden in her culture. Raji was on her way to join the others outside when she saw Ali's mother alone in the kitchen nibbling on the spread of food. Raji decided to join her. Ali's mother said, "What a lovely day this has been. I am so proud of you."

Raji deliberated for a moment on whether or not this was the right time to share something that had been gnawing at her. She knew the answer to the question but asked anyway—just so she could witness her mother-in-law's reaction. Raji asked, "So how long have you known?"

Ali's mother continued picking at the different dishes, pretending that she hadn't heard the question. So Raji asked again. This time in a louder tone. "How long have you known?"

"Known what, Raji?"

Raji glared. She put both palms flat on the granite top of the kitchen island. She shook her head at Ali's mother and sternly said, "Don't pretend you don't know what I'm talking about. How long have you known that Ali was gay?!"

Ali's mother quickly scanned the room and bent over to look and see if there was anyone in the adjacent room. Then she briskly walked around the island and grabbed Raji by the elbow and said, "Come with me." They walked to the far side of the house and entered Raji's old room with the dollhouses. She closed the door and locked it. In a hushed voice, she said, "How dare you speak of that in public. You could cost Ali his career or life."

Unfazed, Raji said, "I have lost all respect for you. When I was a little girl growing up without a mother, I looked forward to every time you came to visit. Ali always ran off with Malcolm, and I got you all to myself. You knew!"

"Of course I knew. I was his mother."

Raji's rage began to swell. "You still haven't answered my question. How long have you known?"

Ali's mother waved her hands back and forth frivolously as if she was shooing away gnats. "I had my suspicions when he was growing up. He never had any interest in girls. Then one day, when he was sixteen, I came home unexpectedly, through the side door, which was next to Ali's room. I heard some unusual sounds as I passed his door. Surprisingly, it was unlocked, so I entered his room. I was completely shocked by what I saw. Ali and another boy were naked on the bed. The other boy was performing oral sex on Ali. I've never told his father or anyone. As far as I know, you are the only other person that knows."

It took every ounce of self-control for Raji not to unleash her anger. She fought the urge to slap her face with all her might. Raji took three deep breaths while she scowled at Ali's mother. "I trusted you! I feel so betrayed! You knew Ali was gay, but you still promoted our marriage without saying a word to me. You used me, like everyone else in my life. You even encouraged my independence. You disgust me!" Raji shook her head and gritted her teeth. "You have grossly underestimated me—you assumed that since I was an independent, free-thinking, confident woman that I would be okay with a marriage that's a façade?" Raji's eyes narrowed. She pointed her index finger at her mother-in-law. "I'm not okay with it. I'm not okay with a loveless life without a partner to hold and be affectionate with. I'm not okay being unwanted by my husband. And I am not okay with a mother-in-law who pimps her son out to an innocent and unsuspecting motherless girl who trusted her. You are pathetic!"

Ali's mother replied unempathetically, "You haven't told anyone have you? Promise me you will keep this a secret."

Raji's fists clenched so tight that her knuckles turned white. She walked within a foot of her and said, "Take your things and leave immediately. You are a disgrace to motherhood. Your son needed grace and compassion, and you gave him shame instead!" Raji raised her stiff arm and pointed. "Get out now!"

Ali's parents left abruptly, which broke the rest of the party up. Her brother and his family took the cue and left shortly thereafter. Raji said to Ali, "It's time for us to go too. I'll get Yasser if you'll gather his things and put them in the car."

"Is everything okay?" Ali asked.

Raji smiled and said, "We have some things to talk about on the way home."

Raji had been preparing for the conversation with Ali for nine months. She would dictate the terms of the agreement. There would be no negotiating or compromise. Raji had the final word on everything. After they exited the palatial gates of her father's estate and reached the bottom of the hill, Raji pulled out a thumb drive and put it in the cupholder on the center console of their Mercedes-Benz S-Class. Ali heard the clanging sound as she dropped it in the plastic holder and looked down.

He asked, "What's that?"

"It's a thumb drive."

"That's new technology. Right? I heard those are supposed to replace discs someday," Ali said.

"I've heard that too."

Ali asked, "Why did my mother leave so suddenly?"

"I'll get to that in a minute. But first there's something I need to discuss with you. Specifically, what's on the drive I just put in the cupholder."

Ali hesitated and kept his eyes forward on the illuminated road in front of him. "So what's on the thumb drive?"

Raji turned and looked at Ali, who was looking ahead. "I have had you followed and under surveillance for the last nine months. What's on the drive is video footage of you having sex with other men." She paused as if in thought and then continued, "Twenty-one different lovers if my count is right. I don't know, it's hard for me to watch."

Ali interrupted, "You're crazy, Raji! I would never do such a thing. Is someone blackmailing you for money because I guarantee that's not me."

Raji sat in silence and shook her head back and forth in the dark car. Suddenly, both of her hands came crashing down on the front dash with such force she thought she fractured a bone. "You left me on my wedding night, you piece of shit!"

Ali snapped back, "I told you that I had an emergency that I had to fly back to Iran for. I tried to make it up to you the next year. That's when you conceived Yasser."

Raji held her hands up. "Stop lying, Ali. Stop. You're only making a fool of yourself. I have receipts that show you were in Paris a few days after our wedding night. You were probably fucking some male prostitute, I don't know. But I do know the next year we came back that's exactly what you did, because that's the first video you'll see on the drive. And, just to be clear, I'm the one who suggested we go back to Paris the next year, not you. Do you know why I wanted to go back? Because I wanted to find out why the man who had befriended me and the man I fell in love with treated me like I didn't exist after we got married. Was it all fake, Ali? The late nights we talked openly about our dreams, our country?" She turned and stared at Ali waiting for a reply.

They drove another mile in silence until Ali spoke in such a faint voice that Raji had to lean over to hear him. He said, "I respected your intellect and that you didn't let what others thought about you change how you acted or talked. So—no, it wasn't all fake."

"You're more of an idiot than I thought. You knew I was smart and determined, and yet you still went through with the marriage? Maybe you didn't know me after all. Because if you did, you would have known there's no way I would have just rolled over on this. I guess you didn't think this through, did you?"

Ali shook his head. The only reply he could come up with was, "I don't know."

Raji continued, "You know as well as I do, I have almost no rights as a woman in Iran if I divorce you. I would have no legal rights over Yasser. That's how screwed up this misogynistic country is. I would have to give up my son if I divorced you, and then I would be treated even worse as a divorced woman. Unlike this stone-age culture and theocratic government, I could care less what your sexual preference is. I don't judge you for that. Do you understand that, Ali? But you manipulated and deceived me! What you did is awful.

You purposely deceived me so that you could prop up a fake image of a normal Iranian family and advance your career. You used me, Ali. If you would have just come to me and told me, at least I would have had some respect for you. I sure as hell hope you don't treat the men you have relationships with the way you've treated me. If so, you are going to have a very lonely and miserable life."

A tear appeared in Ali's eye and rolled down the side of his cheek that was facing Raji. He shook his head but said nothing.

Raji adjusted herself in her seat and then said, "Fine. If you've got nothing to say, then I'll tell you how this is going to go down. First of all, no more lies—ever. Next, treat me with respect. Those are the most important. Do you think you can treat me with respect and never lie to me again?"

Ali turned and answered in a serious tone, "Yes."

Raji nodded and then continued, "Okay, there are a few things I want that will cost you nothing—I actually don't want your money, I can take care of myself. What I want is my freedom. I want to be able to travel when I want and where I want. I will have the freedom to say whatever I want. I need your unquestionable approval every time. As your daddy moves you further up in the regime, you must always have my back. Do we have an understanding?"

He made eye contact and then looked ahead and said, "I would like to add a few conditions."

"You're in no position to add conditions, Ali!"

"Just hear me out," he replied.

"I'm listening."

"You're right, I have no right to ask for conditions. Let's call them requests then. Just two actually. I'd like to know where you are, that's all. If I'm ever questioned, I'll look like an idiot if I don't know where my wife is. The other, I would prefer if you'd not travel to the US, I don't trust them."

"That's fair."

Ali asked, "And in exchange, no one ever sees the footage on the thumb drive and you never speak a word of it to anyone. Is that right?"

"Actually, I'll do more than just keep your secret. Even though it goes against everything I believe, I will propagate the façade of a normal, happy family as well. You live your life, and I'll live mine. And when occasion necessitates it, we will don our happy husband and wife masks."

Ali responded, "Deal."

They drove the rest of the way home in silence until they pulled in the driveway of their house. After Ali parked and turned the ignition off, he turned to Raji. "I am sorry, Raji."

Raji nodded and simply said, "Yep." Six months later, Ali moved out of the house. He visited Yasser on occasion. They continued the façade of a happily married couple and attended all family and public functions together. When people asked about their second home, they explained it was a place for Ali to sleep on the occasional long nights he had to work late, and it prevented the hour-long drive home late at night followed by an hour-long drive the very next morning.

# CHAPTER 28

## PARIS, FRANCE

The first-class section of the plane was dark. Raji was startled by a tap on her shoulder from behind her. She turned and Myk was leaning forward wanting to ask a question.

"What is it?" she asked.

"I'll need a visa from one of Iran's diplomatic missions in order to get into Iran. Do you have someone that can take care of that?"

"Yes." Then she lowered her voice so that it was barely perceptible. "I need to know what name you'll be using."

Myk smiled. He knew that Raji had seen all his fake passports. The two continued to talk through the small gap in the seats until the woman sitting next to Myk nudged him and asked, "Excuse me. Are you two together? I'd be happy to switch seats with her if you'd like."

Before Myk even had a chance to answer, Raji had stood up and was on her way back. The woman sitting next to Myk snickered. "I guess that means yes."

Raji thanked her as the two women passed. When she sat, Raji turned to Myk and said, "I am getting nervous. So many things could go wrong. A lot of people will lose their lives. Possibly me." She grabbed his hand again.

Myk looked her directly in the eyes. "Sure. But a lot of things could go right. Focus on that instead. When we get to Paris, we'll go over the details, but with everything you've shared with me so far, it's a brilliant plan, Raji. It's going to work."

Myk's hand traded places with Raji's. He put his hand on top of hers for the first time. He gently squeezed it and smiled.

A few small butterflies fluttered in Raji's stomach. *Oh my. Why do I feel so safe with him?* she thought. His face was so close that she could smell the wintergreen gum flavor of his breath. Her eyes were locked on his. *I want to kiss his mouth. No, Raji. No,* she thought. This was new. She had never felt this way before. She didn't know how to process it. It was like learning how to ride a bike the first time—there was no prior experience to draw on. Since her agreement with Ali, she had been with many men over the years—and even one woman. But she had never felt anything like this—safe and trusting.

Myk whispered, "You've been wanting this all your life. Opportunities like this rarely come along. You're doing the right thing." He reached over with both hands, slid his fingers in her hair on the sides of her head, and gently kissed her forehead above her right eye.

*No, no. Put your hands back in my hair and kiss me on the lips. Stop it, Raji!* she mused. Her eyes narrowed slightly. She said, "You're right. I have been wanting this all my life. This is a rare opportunity." *And I'm not just talking about my plan for Iran,* she thought. "It's pretty scary, but it's also very exciting," she added.

The flight attendant had been making her rounds. She stood in front of Myk and Raji and asked, "Is there anything I can get the two of you on this final three-hour leg of the flight?"

"I'll have a glass of that white wine please," Myk said.

"Ma'am, anything for you?" she asked Raji.

"No thank you. I'm fine."

Myk asked Raji, "So who is this friend of yours that we're staying with in Paris?"

"Her name is Becca. And, actually, she lives just outside of Paris in southern Normandy."

"How well do you trust her?" Myk asked.

"Completely."

"Really?"

Raji shifted in her seat and answered, "Yeah. She is the only person I trust completely. She knows all of my secrets, and I know all of hers."

Myk nodded approvingly. "Becca sounds like a great friend. There was only one person that I trusted completely, David Adelberg. I'm going to miss him." Raji put her hand on Myk's.

"So how does a bomb-maker's daughter become best friends with a French girl?" Myk asked.

Raji laughed and said, "Actually, she's an American—all-American I suppose."

"What's so funny?"

"I was just remembering the first time I met her. She told me she was the National Roping Champion five years straight, and I didn't have a clue what a roping champ was. I don't know where I'd be without her. She's tough—mentally and physically. Her first husband beat her—she almost killed him."

Myk commented, "If she grew up in that world of riding and roping, then I would imagine she's had her bumps and bruises. I'm looking forward to meeting her."

"You'll love her." Raji grinned and then said, "Just don't find yourself alone in the horse stables with her."

"Why's that?"

"Because I know her. She'll want to ride you instead of her horse."

Myk laughed and shook his head. "She sounds like quite the character. I'm sure she must do well if she's got a property with horse stables."

"She's a rodeo girl turned oil tycoon. Her property in Texas has been pumping out oil ever since I've known her." Raji paused and then asked, "How about you? How did you get involved in espionage? I would imagine that my father would be quite the big fish for you."

He nodded. "It wasn't that long ago that your father would have been a big fish. But things have really changed. China's Communist

Party is by far the world's biggest threat. For decades they've gone almost unnoticed as they slowly reached their tentacles into almost every nation. The COVID-19 pandemic changed everything. People have begun to wake up. As far as how I got involved in this line of work, it was 9/11 that did it for me. I wanted to make a difference."

Raji said, "I remember the news of that day. They showed Iranians celebrating and burning American flags, but that was all a front. Most Iranians didn't feel that way, but that's not what the regime wants to depict to the world. That's why I got involved in the news—I guess I wanted to make a difference too."

"It sounds like you have. There's a reason your segment of the news kills it in the ratings—people trust you."

The comment made Raji smile. "Thank you. I need to ask you a question, because I shouldn't assume things." She paused and then leaned in closer. "Do you have a girlfriend?"

Myk smiled. "No, I wouldn't be sitting here holding your hand if I did. I scared the last one off."

Emojis of a girl doing cartwheels flashed in Raji's mind. *Her loss*, Raji thought. "You don't strike me as very scary—unless I were a criminal of course. What am I missing? If you don't mind me asking."

Myk tilted his head and replied, "She knew the line of work I was in and she said she was fine with it. We were skiing, and there was an assassin that tried to kill me. Unfortunately, she was there, and it scared the hell out of her. I guess it's one thing knowing what someone does for work, but it takes on a whole new meaning when you actually experience it. The other thing that seems to scare them off is my walls, I'm always trying to protect myself from getting hurt. Something I'm still working on."

She gave Myk a puzzled look. "Why the walls?"

"I was raised by a single mom. She had me when she was close to fifty years old. She wasn't around much in my childhood—actually, she was there physically, but just checked out most of the time. A large portion of my childhood memories of my mother is of her lying unconscious in bed. So I learned to do things for myself. As far as I can remember, starting in kindergarten, I got myself dressed, put myself to bed, made my own meals. It was pretty obvious I got myself ready for school."

She asked again, "So why the walls?"

"My mom is a pretty tough lady, but I think the assassination of my dad finally broke her. The vodka and the pills helped her forget. Unfortunately, it helped her forget about me too. On her sober days, it was great. But those days didn't happen often enough. No one was there for me, so I had to be there for myself. Hence, I learned to put walls up and take care of myself so it wouldn't hurt so bad when she wasn't there. My building of walls scared off most of my earlier relationships."

Raji squeezed Myk's hand. *Oh my God, he was lonely just like me,* she thought. Raji questioned, "But your walls are down with me."

"You're different. And I've learned how to recognize it."

Raji paused and then said, "Thank you—I think?"

Myk smiled. "Yes, it was meant as a compliment."

"What happened with your mom?" she asked.

"She's better now. I had the misfortune of being born two months after my father was killed in London. Levi was sitting right beside my dad when he was killed. It was my mom who saved Levi's life before the gunman would have killed him too. My mom and dad had worked together with Mossad for over twenty years. She assumed she couldn't get pregnant because they had tried for years. I was a bit of a surprise for them. I think Dad's death along with everything else she went through was just too much. Then, when I was in high school, she got sober for good, and she's been back ever since."

Raji's eyes narrowed. "Hmm?"

"What?" Myk asked.

"Just wondering if it would have been worse to have a mom who wasn't really there, like you had, or have no mother at all like me."

"No, Raji. The occasional mom is better than having no mom—hands down."

She shook her head. "I suppose."

"You never did answer my question. How'd you meet Becca?"

Raji chuckled. "Oh, right! I met her on my first trip to Paris. Ali took me there for our honeymoon. Our wedding night we stayed at a beautiful luxury hotel in Paris. My engines were roaring and ready to go that night and he bounced."

Myk laughed unexpectedly. "What?! Oh—sorry, I didn't mean to laugh. He just left you?"

Raji smiled. "Oh, that's fine, I laugh about it now too. Anyway, he said he had some emergency back in Iran. He left a phone message to tell me he left, instead of letting me know in person. I sat there crying on my bed and then decided I had enough of crying and I was going to figure out a way to enjoy Paris without him. I was wallowing in my second bottle of wine at a café near the hotel when a cowgirl with a big Texas drawl stood over me and asked, 'Are you okay?'"

"Becca?"

"Yes. She rode into my life that day and she's been a part of it ever since."

Myk asked, "Did Ali really have an emergency?"

"Nope." Raji had never broken her agreement with Ali. She had kept his secret. But Yasser was dead. Iran would be in chaos soon. And the nature of the agreement was to protect Ali, so, telling Myk wouldn't violate that—Ali's secret would still be protected. Raji was ready to move on. She leaned closer to Myk and whispered, "I'll tell you why Ali abandoned me on our wedding night only if you promise to keep it secret—especially if the overthrow of the Iranian regime goes badly."

Myk whispered back, "Of course."

"Ali is a gay man. Always has been. His marriage to me was a façade. It provided cover for him to rise in the ranks of the Iranian regime."

Myk sat back in his chair in silence for a moment. He leaned back into Raji and whispered, "That is stunning! You've held his career, his life, in the palm of your hand this whole time. No wonder you have so much freedom. How did you find out?"

"I owe everything to Becca. She had a security team put him under surveillance when we returned the next year, and they got him on video tape having sex with a male prostitute."

Myk shook his head and replied, "I understand now. But where did you get the shooting skills? The way you handled yourself in Verona and at my safe house was impressive. You were better than many agents I've crossed paths with. Your timing was impeccable."

Raji smiled at the compliment and replied, "We had a shooting range on my father's estate growing up. I had a lot of time to kill since he wouldn't allow me to go to a real school until I was thirteen. I loved shooting though. I'd stay out on that range for hours. We had nannies that homeschooled us. At some point, I grew to hate wiring his bombs and detested him. I was his little bomb maker and never his daughter. He used me and so did Ali."

Myk shook his head. "What a shame. So how often did you travel after you struck a deal with Ali?"

Raji thought for a minute and then answered, "At least four times a year. I took Yasser with me half of the time until he was sixteen. After that, he rarely came with me. The first four or five years I always traveled with Becca. After that, I didn't have a problem traveling on my own."

Raji stopped and shook her head. Myk asked, "What?"

She shook her head again. "It's nothing."

Myk put his hand just above her knee and said, "C'mon?"

Chills went up her spine at his touch. *Calm yourself, Raji, pretend his hand isn't there*, she thought. "You know, I have been fortunate to have traveled to some of the most beautiful destinations in the world, except Yosemite of course." Raji winked and then continued, "But I have no doubt it would take it to a whole new level to have someone to enjoy it with. I am free, but not really free. That's why I packed six full suitcases and planned to never go back to Iran after Yasser died."

"Why didn't you find a man you liked to take with you on some of the trips?" He moved closer and looked her directly in the eyes. "You're beautiful. You have no problem attracting men."

She looked at his eyes. Hungered for his lips. She felt something pulling her in. *Control, Raji. Control,* she told herself. "I did. It was enjoyable, but it was temporary. It's just not the same when you know you won't see each other again because you have to jump on a plane in a week and go back home. Besides, I never had a connection with any of the men I've been with. I knew that I'd leave in a week or two, so it was just physical encounters with men. I am a woman with needs too. I came to the conclusion that those are just the cards I was dealt."

"Just curious. Did you meet someone every time you left Iran?"

"No. Only on the trips Yasser didn't join me. I've met my share of men—and a woman too," Raji said with a smile.

Myk chuckled. "You never cease to surprise me. If you don't mind me prying, was your experience with another woman, Becca?"

"As a matter of fact, it was."

"And?"

"In a word—awkward." Raji laughed. "I had grown very close to Becca. She had become like some soul mate sister or something. After five years, we began to wonder if the relationship was something more. She had been with other women, but I hadn't. After talking about it, we both agreed to give it a try one night." She laughed again. "It was disastrous and so awkward. Let me put it this way—we are best friends, but definitely not lovers!"

Myk smiled.

"My turn," Raji said.

"Shoot."

Raji inched closer and asked in a whisper, "How about you? Have you ever been with another man? Fair game, seeing as my 'husband' failed to share that tidbit of information with me."

Myk's replied, "Nah. That's not my thing."

They went silent for a moment. Myk stared at Raji's iridescent eyes that seemed to be glowing. Raji looked at Myk's blue eyes and wondered if he was feeling anything that she was.

"I'd like to ask you something," he said.

Raji said, "Okay," with her voice and with her eyes.

Myk moved the hair away from the side of her face and placed his lips next to her ear. She could feel his soft breath on the back of her neck. It sent chills down her spine. He whispered in a tone so low she could barely hear him say, "I would like to kiss you."

*I'm melting*, she thought to herself. Raji then put her lips next to his ear and whispered in the same barely audible tone as Myk's, "Then what are you waiting for?" Before she pulled away for her much anticipated and welcomed kiss, she had some fun. She nibbled softly on the bottom tip of his earlobe and then ran her tongue softly on the perimeter of his same lobe. Then she backed off and looked at him with a playful smile.

Myk grinned and tilted his head. "That's not fair."

It brought a big smile to her face. Myk put one hand at the back of her neck, with Raji's thick hair intertwined between his fingers. His other hand was still on her knee, but he moved it up ever so slightly as he pulled her mouth to his. Their lips met. Raji became lost in the moment. The seven-second kiss seemed like an eternity for her. He broke off the kiss and gently brushed his lips back and forth across the top corner of her upper lip. He slid his lips to her jawbone and kissed it. Raji sighed audibly. His lips never left her skin as he continued to move to her ear. *Don't go there, or I swear I'll be on your lap before you know it*, she thought. Myk moved to her earlobe and performed the same torturous kiss on her, except half the speed. He gently bit the bottom of her lobe with his front teeth. Then he traced the outside of her lobe with the tip of his tongue. Her body stiffened, and she took a deep breath. She gripped his hand that was on her leg. He whispered, "I told you—it's not fair, is it?"

Myk pulled away and was grinning ear to ear—almost laughing.

Raji's eyes burst wide open and she slapped him playfully on the shoulder and exclaimed, "You're bad!"

"Ahh!" Myk moaned. "That's my wounded shoulder!"

Raji's jaw dropped, and she put both her hands on the sides of his face. She looked like she was going to cry. "I am *so* sorry, Myk! I forgot. Are you okay?"

He started laughing uncontrollably. "It's the other shoulder!"

She smacked him again, except harder. "You're not bad—you're terrible!"

Raji leaned back in her chair. A minute later, she was startled by a figure standing in the aisle. Jaafar leaned over on his walking cane and whispered to Myk, "Agent Miles, I haven't been totally honest with you. I need to share some things with you after we land."

Myk replied simply, "Okay."

After he hobbled back to his seat, both Raji and Myk gave each other a puzzled look. Myk asked, "Any idea what that's all about?"

Raji shook her head. "No idea."

# CHAPTER 29

# NORMANDY, FRANCE

It took a little over an hour to make the drive from the Caen-Carpiquet Airport outside Paris to Becca's equestrian estate in northern Normandy. The driver turned off the paved street onto a well-maintained crushed gravel road. The mile-long road leading to Becca's sixteenth-century farmhouse was lined with ancient sessile oak trees on both sides of the road, which formed a shaded tunnel-like canopy along the entire drive. The trees no doubt dated back to the days before King Louis XIV. Raji heard the sound of the gravel crackling under the tires of the slow-moving van. The tranquil blue lake on her left was undisturbed and glass-like until a flock of Normandy geese floated down from the cloudless sky and skimmed across the lake on their landing. Both sides of the road had an old stone and mortar wall that looked to be at least two feet thick. Raji smiled as, on the right, a muscular mare and her young filly were stooped over and feeding on the tall grass. The mare, Penny, was an American quarter horse, the breed most commonly used for roping and barrel racing. She was Raji's favorite horse to ride. She couldn't wait to meet her new filly. The rolling hills of grass and mature oak trees seemed to go on forever until they disappeared on the horizon. In dark contrast to the surrounding beauty, an embodiment of hate had sat parked on the side of the road for seventy-seven years—a bombed out German panzer tank.

Myk noticed it but didn't say anything. He pointed at it and looked to Raji with a puzzled face.

Raji said, "There's a story behind it, but I'll let Becca tell it to you."

The van cleared the end of the mile-long canopy of trees and emerged onto a large, curved cobblestone driveway that circled to the farmhouse. The home was large but unpretentious. The exterior of the home was covered in old limestone bricks of different sizes. Most of the stones and mortar were blonde in color with a smattering of darker contrasting stones throughout. The home was surrounded in lush vegetation with large trees and shrubs. An entire side of the home was covered in vines that grew to the top of the clay roof and had white blossoming flowers. The van rolled to a stop at the front door of the house. The unassuming front door opened, and out stepped Becca, wearing a pair of wranglers, a cowgirl hat, boots, and a white blouse and smiling from ear to ear.

Raji stepped out of the van first. She hurried over to Becca's outstretched arms and was greeted with a warm embrace. Myk stepped out of the van and stretched. He walked toward Raji and Becca with a slight limp from his injured leg.

Raji introduced him. "Becca, this is Agent Myk Miles."

Myk gave her a friendly hug and said, "Raji had a lot of nice things to say about you. It's good to meet you."

Becca hugged him. She was a full foot shorter than him and seemed to disappear when he wrapped his arms around her. Becca stepped back and eyed him up and down. She turned to Raji and said with a smirk, "Have the driver put his bags in my room. He can stay with me."

Myk grinned and said, "I don't know. With my injuries, I may not be ready for getting roped and tied up tonight."

Everyone laughed and Becca shot back a snarky reply. "I'll be gentle on your first rodeo, darlin.'" She winked at Myk. "The guest bedrooms are on the right. Pick whichever one you like," Becca said with a smile.

Jaafar hobbled out of the van and waved courteously toward Becca.

Becca froze and looked at Raji in bewilderment. She asked, "What's he doing here? I thought you were going to . . ." Becca formed the shape of a handgun with her right hand and then pantomimed as if shooting a gun.

Raji said, "Things have changed. I'll fill you in later."

Becca wrapped her arm through Raji's arm. "You three have to be tired and hungry. Come in, and make yourselves at home. I've prepared something for us to eat."

Myk entered and felt instantly at home. There was nothing ostentatious about the billionaire cowgirl's home. The ceilings had hand-hewn wooden beams. A rustic bookcase that was home to Becca's five National Roping Champion solid-silver plaques stood in the hallway. On the same bookcase was a picture of Becca with her arm around Dallas Cowboys owner, Jerry Jones. On the opposite side of the room was a picture on the wall with Becca and a much younger Clint Eastwood. All of the furnishings and adornments seemed to say, *You are welcome here, sit and enjoy.*

After they all freshened up, the four of them gathered at Becca's dining room table, which sat just outside the kitchen of the restored French farmhouse. The kitchen, dining room, and great room were all open to each other. With oven mitts covering her two hands, Becca pulled the dinner dish out of the oven and placed it on the counter next to the rest of the food.

Becca announced, "We're informal around here. Y'all grab a plate from the table, come up and serve yourself."

The main dish was chicken breast covered in a mushroom, onion, and wine sauce that was coated with melted swiss cheese. The smell was rich and zesty and caused Raji's stomach to growl in hunger. There was a bottle of white wine and red wine on the table. Outside, the sun had just lowered beneath the horizon and left the sky with a glowing swath of auburn and dark lilac colors. After dinner,

Becca slid open the expansive glass doors that separated the dining room from the huge back patio. They took their wine glasses and bottles of wine outside, except Jaafar, who didn't drink. The four of them reclined onto the plush, comfortable couches on the back patio, which was raised six steps above a large, grassy area. At the edge of the grassy area stood a solid two-foot stone and mortar wall that looked centuries old. On the other side of the stone wall, a sheer cliff dropped off to the icy waters of the English Channel below. Becca's farmhouse was located four miles west from where the D-Day Invasion occurred. As they sat, Raji was the first to light up a cigarette followed by Becca and then Jaafar.

Myk sprang up from the plush patio couch and said, "I'll be back in a second." He came back a minute later with a cigar in hand and said to Raji as he held out a cigar, "Would you give me a light?"

After taking a few puffs from the cigar to get it lit, he held his cigar in the air and said, "I found Levi's cigars before we left. I would like to dedicate a moment of silence and reflection to a man who touched our lives in different ways."

They all held their cigarettes in the air and touched the lit end to Levi's cigar. Myk somberly said, "To the memory of Levi."

After the moment of silence, Becca looked to Raji and said, "Levi sounds like a wonderful man, would you tell me more about him sometime?"

"I'd be happy to. I've never come across a better man in my life. He stepped in front of a bullet for him." Raji motioned with the point of her cigarette toward Jaafar. The smoke from the lit tip formed a lazy S shape as it wound its way upward until it disappeared.

"Oh my," Becca said.

Raji said, "I only knew him for a few weeks. Levi and his two brothers were orphaned by the same Nazi bastards that left their panzer tank parked along your roadside."

Becca asked Myk, "Is that true?"

Myk's mind seemed to be elsewhere—perhaps still reflecting on the memory of Levi. "I'm sorry. What did you ask?"

Becca repeated, "Is it true that your uncle and his brothers were orphaned by the Nazis?"

"Yeah. Levi, my dad, and his brother were rescued by an Englishman who sent trains full of kids from Prague to England for adoption. My mother and her twin sister were orphaned too. Their town of Lidice, Czechoslovakia, was wiped off the map, quite literally, by the Germans."

Everyone either took a drink of wine or took a puff of their cigarette. Myk continued, "While we're on the topic—why *is* there a German tank still sitting on your property?"

Becca exhaled cigarette smoke. "The owners I purchased the estate from left it there. It was the only request they had of me when I purchased the estate. When they shared their story, I told them I would be honored to leave that panzer tank parked there."

"Interesting. So what's the story?" Myk asked.

"In a nutshell, when the Nazis invaded France, they confiscated the property from the owners, Oscar and Josephine Le Fleur. The young married couple lived on the property with Oscar's parents. After the war, they came to take their property back. It had been lived in by some of the senior ranking members of the SS. Oscar's parents did not survive the war, so he and his wife inherited the entire estate. The place had been ransacked by the Germans. Oscar and Josephine burned or replaced anything that had been touched by the Nazis—except the tank. You probably noticed the crater-sized damage on the side of the tank?"

Myk nodded. "Yes, I saw it on the drive in."

"The huge dent on the side of the panzer is from an American troop that climbed up the cliffs of Normandy and liberated this estate from the Germans. According to Oscar, after the Americans disabled the tank's ability to move, the crew of five Germans inside still wouldn't surrender. One of those American soldiers was a famous Hollywood actor named Charles Durning. He climbed aboard the tank and dropped a grenade inside. The explosion killed all five Germans. When Oscar and Josephine wandered back up that road to take possession of their property, the corpses of the Germans were still in the tank, rotting. The tank has been untouched for seventy-seven years. Oscar kept it as a memorial to all who lost their lives on the sacred grounds of Normandy. The bones of the dead Germans are still entombed in the tank. Oscar was a religious and somewhat superstitious man, so he left it as a warning to fend off any future would-be invaders."

"What a great story," Myk said. "If it was my property, I'd keep the tank there too."

Jaafar cleared his throat, "Agent Miles, would it be an appropriate time now to talk about a few things?"

Myk shifted his body toward Jaafar. "I'm listening."

Jaafar hesitated and looked directly at Becca. Myk cocked his head and said, "Whatever you have to say around me you can say around her." Myk motioned with his head toward Becca. "Becca has turned out to be quite the guardian angel for Raji." He grinned and added, "Except instead of wings on her back, she's got spurs on her boots."

Becca raised her wine glass in a toast at Myk.

Jaafar's eyes narrowed as he said, "I lied about the source of the mutated coronavirus. There is no lab in Tehran."

"I know. Director Adelberg told me. I need to know who your source was in China."

# CHAPTER 30

Myk sat back in the couch, tilted his head back, and put both of his hands behind his head, interlocking his fingers. After thinking for a moment, he leaned forward and said, "Who initiated the plan to release the virus in the US—the Iranians or the Chinese?"

Jaafar replied, "The Chinese came to us."

"Do you know what this means?" Myk asked.

"Of course I do. I know exactly what it means," Jaafar said proudly.

"How in the hell did this come about?"

"The Communist Chinese leaders blame the US for completely embarrassing them on the world stage during the COVID-19 pandemic. The Chinese leadership is very prideful. They were publicly shamed, and their anger became vindictive. They used Iran get to the US covertly. When the US sanctions against Iran became too much to bear, the Chinese bailed us out by purchasing our oil. They tightened their grip even further on Iran when they loaned us billions in exchange for nuclear contracts and billion-dollar contracts for the light-rail system they want to build all the way to Europe. We couldn't pay the debt, so we became beholden to them."

Becca nodded her head. "Sounds like good ol'-fashioned extortion to me!"

Still unsure, Myk asked, "I just want to be perfectly clear on this. The Chinese came to you—right?"

"Yes. They came to us with the idea—or as Becca puts it, extortion."

Myk quickly asked, "Do you think they would risk doing it again since the first attempt failed?"

"Most definitely."

"How can you be so sure?"

"Because they've already reached out again. I'd hate to touch on a sensitive subject, but . . ." Jaafar's eyes darted back and forth between Myk and Raji, "that is why I was on my phone at the safe house. They contacted the same nuclear engineer in Tehran."

"Would the nuclear engineer still work with you?" Myk asked. "We need evidence for the world to see."

"Yes, that's why he reached out to me. But there's not much I can do. I am a wanted man in Iran now."

Myk nodded. "Okay. At least we have a place to start. I am still a little shocked. I just didn't think China would ever be this bold— or stupid."

Raji asked, "What do you mean?"

Myk sat back again. He took a sip of wine and then placed his wine glass down on the mahogany table in front of him. "The vision of the Communist Party of China has been to replace the US as the economic world leader. They've slowly been gaining a foothold in every nation. Businesses around the globe have switched to manu-facturing out of China. They are risking all of their economic gains over the last two decades by releasing a biological weapon in the US." Myk asked Jaafar, "Who else has direct knowledge that the Chinese gave Iran the biological weapon to use against the US?"

"Only three people. Myself, Ayatollah Khomeini, and a nuclear physicist who they first approached. The Chinese government has a billion-dollar contract with Iran to work on our nuclear facil-ities. That's where they first tested the water with the physicist, Amon Ellhon. He brought it directly to me, and then I met with our supreme leader."

Raji piped in, "You disgust me!" She stood and walked into the kitchen with her glass of wine. Becca followed her inside the house.

Jaafar sat uneasily and watched Raji and Becca leave the back patio. After they entered the house he said, "Apparently the Chinese are ready to do it again."

Myk grabbed his wine glass. "We'll need to talk more about this later."

Jaafar nodded and then stood. "I am going to get some sleep." He turned and tottered toward the house with the use of his cane.

Myk's body relaxed into the couch while his mind raced. He crossed his legs and sipped on his wine. Raji came back out to the patio with a fresh bottle of wine and a full glass. She gave Myk a half-hearted smile. He returned the gesture.

"What's wrong with this world?" she asked. "Is there any hope?"

"There's always hope, Raji."

She shook her head, "That hasn't been my experience. You're an optimist—aren't you?" she asked.

Myk thought for a moment and then replied, "Maybe. Perhaps more of a realist, I suppose."

"Nah. I think you're more of an optimist, Agent Miles."

Myk laughed. They both sat and conversed while they enjoyed their wine. After forty minutes, Raji asked, "How would you like to meet Penny?"

Myk gave her a questioning look. "Who's Penny?"

"One of Becca's horses I've grown close to. I ride her every time I come here. Hopefully, we can take her out tomorrow. She has a new filly."

"Okay," Myk answered. "Where is she?"

"She's in the stables next to the lake. C'mon." Raji waved her arm in a *follow me* motion.

On the slow walk down to the stables, Raji asked, "So what do you think of Becca?"

"She's everything you advertised and more! You are fortunate to have such a good friend. She seems very secure with herself."

"She is," Raji replied. "I hope we're here long enough for you to get to know her a little better." *And for her to get to know you*, she thought.

They approached the massive stable. The peak of the metal stable roof was twenty-five feet high. There were ten stalls on each side. The middle of the stable was open from end to end and was at least fifteen feet wide in the middle. Raji found a metal bucket and scooped a half-bucket of oats as if she were a regular hand around the ranch.

Raji pointed and said, "Penny is at the other end."

The two strolled to the down the dusty stable that smelled of hay and horses. The outskirts of the lake came within twenty feet of the edge of the stable. The opening closest to Penny led to a path that had an arched stone bridge that crossed over the narrow portion of the serene lake.

Raji whispered, "She's in here."

Myk was tall enough to look over the corral door, but Raji had to settle for looking through the large gaps in the gate slats. Raji put the bucket of oats down.

"Oh my goodness. She's sleeping with her baby. Isn't she beautiful?" Raji slipped her hand into Myk's.

"She sure is."

Something took control of Raji's hand. She was involuntarily pulling Myk toward her. Raji's other hand reached up behind Myk's neck and gently guided him down for a kiss. Her two mutinous hands were doing the bidding for Raji's unconscious desires. Their lips met and began a slow dance. Myk's fingers rested on the back of her neck. His other hand moved under her silky blouse onto the bare skin of her lower back. Raji moved her hand under the back of Myk's shirt, too, and pulled him in tighter. Raji broke off the kiss, turned her head onto his chest and hugged him. She looked up and kissed him passionately and placed both hands under his shirt. She nibbled softly on his upper lip—he nibbled back. Raji took the bottom of his shirt with both hands and began to pull it over his head.

"I want to see her," she said.

Raji held his shirt in her hand and rubbed her fingertips over his tattoo of the woman embedded in the stormy tree. She kissed it and then took Myk by the hand and led him to a stable across from Penny and her filly. Raji unlatched the gate, swung it open, and then latched the gate behind her. She took two of the blankets that were draped over the gate and unfolded them on to the ground. Myk sat down on the blanket. Raji could see part of his tattoo and Myk's muscular chest and lean torso in the dim light. Myk looked up at Raji who was still standing.

She stared at him. Her eyes spoke loudly, *I want you*. She slowly unbuttoned her blouse in front of him while never breaking eye contact. She draped her blouse over the latched gate and stepped purposefully out of her pants, still never breaking eye contact.

*He likes what he sees*, Raji thought. She smiled and posed for him a little longer before stepping closer.

Raji moved over him and gently nudged her foot against his. "Is your leg okay? Do you need help with your pants, Agent Miles?" she asked with a sarcastic smile.

He smiled back. "Sure."

Myk unbuttoned his pants while Raji knelt down at his feet. She held the end of one pant leg and then the other as Myk pulled his legs out. After removing his pants, she knelt over him, straddling his good leg. She put her elbow down on the side of him and then slid in next to him. Myk wrapped his arms around her.

Their lips touched and Myk murmured, "I didn't envision this happening in a horse stable on a dusty blanket."

Raji put her index finger up to his lips. Her eyes told him, *Sshh*. Raji leaned in and their lips met again. His right hand caressed her face while his thumb brushed over her eyebrow. She locked her legs around his thigh and began to kiss him passionately. His hand slid from her face to the back of her head, his fingers tangled in her thick hair. He gently tugged a handful of her hair. It sent shivers up her spine, causing her to squeeze her legs tightly around him. He turned her over so that he was on top of her leg. He was propped up on his good elbow, fixed on her goddess-like eyes. Myk reached around his back and found Raji's hand. He began slowly removing her hand from his back. *No, I want to embrace you,* she thought. He placed her hand above her head and then did the same thing with her other arm. With her hands above her head, she felt completely vulnerable, but safe with him. Myk slowly traced her skin with his index and middle finger. He started with the palm of her hand and inched his fingers across the soft skin of her wrist slowly down to her elbow. His sensual touch continued down to the tender skin under her arm where it stayed momentarily.

Raji closed her eyes and melted into his touch. She was oblivious to the sounds of the horses shifting about their stalls or the flickering sounds of the leaves outside from the light breeze. She was oblivious to the scent of the outdoors or the aroma of the stable. She was conscious of one thing only: his touch. Myk's fingers continued from under her arm across the side of her breast and down to her pelvic bone where he paused. Myk pushed himself up on his knees while still straddling her leg and admired her.

"You're beautiful," he said softly.

Raji smiled and tried to mentally fight off the compliment. *Men don't care,* she thought. Any man of importance to her had used her. Her father used her for his bombs. Ali used her for his fake marriage to hide his sexuality. Even Raji's mother-in-law used her. Her network used her to peddle their lies. *He genuinely cares.* The desire she saw in Myk's eyes seared right through her. His fingers picked up where they left off at her hip bone and crept across her leg and down to the velvet skin under the arch of her foot. She kept her eyes open and observed. *He's drinking me in with his eyes and with his touch.* On his sensual journey back up her body's same path, Myk leaned back down on his elbow, and he tucked his head under Raji's chin. His mouth drank in the skin of her collar bone. *Devour me.* His mouth left no skin untouched.

Raji's hips began to gently rock. *Closer, I want you closer.* Her body yearned. She wrapped her legs around his, skin on skin. "Closer," she mumbled under her breath. Her hands reached around and pulled him in. Their breathing was slow and synchronized. The rhythms of their movements matched each other. Slow breaths turned to panting. Myk moaned under his breath while Raji groaned audibly. From a bird's-eye view, they looked like one entangled body with too many limbs.

In one motion, he rolled to his side and lifted Raji on top of him without ever breaking rhythm. "I want to see all of you," he said. Raji put her palms on his chest. Her movements were in perfect unison with his. Something about the way he looked at her brought on feelings and sensations she had never felt before. Her body began to convulse as her head tilted back involuntarily. Raji groaned and she fell on top of Myk and began kissing his mouth. Their sensual dance continued amidst the crisp air of the Normandy cliffs in the confines of a private horse stall on top of a bed of straw that was covered by riding blankets. Myk continued to explore her—slowly, purposefully, knowingly.

Three hours later, they walked back into the house. The lights were on, but they didn't need to be. Both Raji and Myk were glowing. Raji's body was still thrumming. As the sound of the closing door echoed behind them, Raji was startled by movements in the front great room. She saw the back of Becca's head as she turned toward them from the couch. Becca stood and grinned from ear to ear while she shook her head back and forth. Raji's hair was strewn about, and there were pieces of hay hanging loosely from her head. Myk's hair was disheveled, and his shirt was inside out.

"Good Lord—you just couldn't wait until tomorrow to go for a ride, could you?!"

Raji bowed her head sheepishly like a teenager who had just been caught sneaking out. Myk chuckled. He leaned down and kissed Raji above her eye. "I'll see you in the morning." He strode down the hallway and into his room.

Raji sat down at the dining room table as Becca pulled out a chair and joined her. "Well?" Becca asked in eager anticipation.

Raji smirked. "A girl doesn't kiss and tell, Becca."

"Oh, really?" she questioned. "That didn't stop you before."

Raji shook her head and smiled. "There's never been much to tell."

Becca grabbed Raji's hand and squeezed and stared directly at her. "I've never seen you like this. You're absolutely radiant."

The insecurities in Raji began to surface. "We didn't talk much. It was just so wonderful. I hope I was okay?"

Becca slapped the top of her hand playfully. "Okay?" she questioned. "From what I saw on Myk's face, it was way beyond 'okay,' my dear!"

Raji looked at her friend and nodded. "Thank you."

Becca looked inquisitively at her and asked, "Now, throw this fifty-year-old single girl a bone."

Raji stood and said, "I'm tired. I need some sleep." She patted Becca on the back and walked toward her bedroom.

She heard Becca plead from behind her, "C'mon, give me something, girl?"

Raji grinned at her and then turned to open the door to her room. She stopped herself halfway and changed her mind. Instead, she went to Myk's room. She thought of knocking before she entered but decided to walk right into the unlocked room. She entered and locked the door behind her. The light on the nightstand was on, and Myk was sitting up in bed. He smiled warmly as she walked toward him and sat next to him in the bed.

"I can't just lie down and go to sleep after what just happened. My mind and heart are still racing," she said.

"Mine too," Myk said affectionately.

"Oh good." Raji grabbed Myk's hand. "Hey, this is new for me. I understand this is very early, but still, I've never had a connection like this."

"I've never felt this close or at ease so early with someone, Raji. It's easy to open up with you. And for me—that's saying a lot."

Myk smiled.

Raji turned to face Myk. "When we were in the car last week, you shared with me that you sometimes put your walls up. You said the reason for it was because you were neglected by your mom, so you learned to be independent and distrustful."

Myk gave her a questioning look. "Yes?"

"I'd like to know if you are putting any walls up now?"

Myk sat in silence pondering the question. After several minutes, he thoughtfully replied, "It's hard. It's still a struggle within."

"What?" Raji asked.

"Please understand, I don't want to put any walls up. I have to consciously work at it. I've been told by therapists that the hurt little boy from my childhood was lonely for so long that he wired my brain with the thought, *You're not wanted, so you have to take care of yourself*. I'm an ex-convict wanted by my own government. I'm a mess. Part of me says, 'Why would she want this, she'll leave too.' There have been other women that I've wanted, but I failed. My unconscious mind, that I have no control over, tries to protect me from the feeling of being unwanted because of my childhood."

Raji tenderly grabbed his hand, but Myk pulled it away. "No," he said emphatically. "You see, that's exactly what happens with the others. Did you notice? I struck a chord in you, and you instinctively reached out. That's what the others have done. They wanted to fix me."

Raji confidently grabbed his hand and didn't let go. "I'm not like the others, Myk. I don't want to fix you. There's nothing to fix. Your past pain makes you who you are: genuine and caring. Why would I ever want to fix that?!"

Myk relaxed. "I'm an American former Special Forces agent with deep Jewish lineage, and my government wants me dead. You're an Iranian daughter of a notorious bomb maker with Muslim lineage. Any dating site would not rate us as a good match! This is the unlikeliest of relationships." Myk smirked.

Raji laughed audibly. "This isn't a dating app. This is real, you silly man!" She laughed again. "Stop trying to convince yourself otherwise. There is something very tangible and real here, and you know it."

Myk slid down from his sitting position and rested his head on her lap. She affectionately combed her fingers through his thick brown hair. She felt him agree with the shake of his head as he said, "Yeah. I know."

# CHAPTER 31

Raji woke to the sounds of voices in the distance. She reached over to feel for Myk. *Cold sheets*, she thought. She heard the talking continue but couldn't distinguish the words. She rolled out of bed and slipped an oversized shirt of Myk's on and walked out to the kitchen. Becca and Myk were seated at the barstools deep in conversation.

"Good morning," Becca said with a chipper smile.

Myk winked at her and said, "Morning." He brought his coffee mug to his mouth and sipped. The aroma of the freshly brewed Costa Rican coffee filled Raji's senses, and she began looking for a mug.

Becca said, "I offered to take Myk out for a ride this morning and show him the property, but he turned me down. He said that you warned him he wasn't allowed to be in the stable alone with me." She grinned at Raji.

Raji shook her head and laughed. "Smart man!"

Myk asked Becca, "Do you have a computer I could use? It's not safe yet for me to turn any of my devices on, and I'd like to check up on a few things."

"Absolutely. Just use mine in the front den."

Myk eased off of the barstool and turned toward the den with his coffee mug in hand. Before he disappeared around the corner, Raji spoke up. "Hey, Myk?"

He turned and asked, "Yeah?"

"I might have an idea about your dilemma with the Chinese."

"That's great," Myk said with a smile. "Fill me in when I'm finished getting an update."

Raji nodded as Myk turned and rounded the corner.

Becca chimed in, "I'm not gonna lie—I'm impressed."

Raji whispered almost apologetically, "Me too!"

"How in the heck did this happen? There's something palpable between you two."

Raji shook her head. "I don't know, it just did. I was focused on ending my father's miserable excuse of a life and seeing Yasser's body, and Myk was frantically trying to stop a biological attack and assassins trying to kill him. Who knows, mutual hatred of my father maybe!" She laughed and then continued, "I closely observed Myk from the shadows the minute he and his uncle showed up at the Arena in Verona. He's unlike anyone I've ever met. He's just so real."

"I've been in more rodeos than I can remember. Cowboys like him don't come along very often. Now what?"

Raji shook her head. Her lips tensed. "I don't know. I'm having second thoughts about my plan for Iran though. Maybe I should put those plans on hold."

"I agree. That's awfully risky and dangerous, Raji."

Raji leaned back and glanced up looking reflective. "You know, after I found out about Ali and then decided it wasn't right to stay married to Ali and be celibate, my experiences with men were somewhat out of spite for what Ali had done. It was exciting at first, to feel so wanted, since I had been shunned by my own husband. But whenever I got around to having sex, it's like I wasn't even present and somewhat numb. There was just no feeling. It was like I had Ali in the back of my mind, and I was still having sex out of spite for him. But last night . . ." Raji closed her eyes and shook her head.

Becca asked, "What?"

Raji squinted at Becca. "I was *present* last night—completely. I could feel last night. And it felt amazing, physically and emotionally. I wasn't numb like I had been before, but I had new sensations of feeling wanted for who I am as a person."

Becca smiled and put her hand on top of Raji's. "I'm happy for you. I feel for you though, it's not exactly convenient."

Raji nodded. "Definitely not convenient."

Becca stood and asked, "How about a ride and some fresh air?"

Raji hopped off the barstool. "Great idea!"

While Raji and Becca rode the horses, Myk sat on the back patio contemplating the phone call he would make. He flipped his burner phone back and forth between his hands, thinking of what he wanted to say before he powered the phone on. He would have to be brief so the call couldn't be traced. Myk spent the first fifteen minutes vacillating on why he would even bother to call Rick Taft. He couldn't figure out what was driving him to reach out to Taft when he knew what his answer would be in the first place. *Give a man a chance before you destroy him*, he thought.

Myk held the burner phone in the open palm of his left hand and pressed the power button with his thumb. A constant, cool, salty breeze blew in from the Normandy coast. He looked up from his phone beyond the ancient stone and mortar wall that separated Becca's estate from the drop-off of the sheer cliff and the vast horizon of the blue waters of the English Channel. The only thing missing from the perfect, picturesque setting was an artist with his easel and paints. He reflected on the sudden and purposeful murder of his longtime friend and director, David Adelberg. Emotions began to swell within Myk. A strong gust wafted his hair. He cast his gaze down from the endless coastal waters to his phone. Myk dialed the number.

It took a while before Myk finally heard the ringing begin. After the fifth ring, he heard a secretary say, "Senator Rick Taft, how can I help you?"

"Give the phone to Rick. Tell him it's Myk Miles. Don't delay, or I'll hang up."

Myk heard shuffling and the sound of someone covering the speaker on the phone as they spoke. He heard the faint mumbles of Rick Taft telling people around him that he needed privacy for the call. A few moments later, Rick Taft said, "Agent Miles, this is quite unexpected. To what do I owe your call?"

Myk leaned back in the couch, his eyes focused on the outer edges of the azure horizon. "The game is over, Rick. I know it was you."

"I haven't the foggiest idea what you are referring to, Agent Miles. Last I checked, you are wanted for the murder of former FBI Director, and personal friend of mine, David Adelberg."

"Spare me the bullshit, Rick. I was there. I saw your goon that shot Director Adelberg. Before you had him gunned down, he told me that it was you that murdered your entire team for the crates of gold in Switzerland, so don't refer to yourself as a friend of David Adelberg."

The comment clearly caught Taft off guard as evidenced by his momentary silence. He replied, "You've got nothing. You're bluffing, and I'm holding a royal flush."

"My uncle was a spy for Mossad and was at the lake. He described you in detail and told me how you systematically slaughtered every FBI agent on that operation. Give it up, or I'll devote the rest of my life to hunting you down. I'm a patient man, Rick—I'll wait for the moment you least expect, and I'll end your life. You'll spend the rest of your life looking over your shoulder."

Myk heard Taft's boisterous laugh before he said, "Does that tough talk actually work with others? And to think you were Adelberg's ace. You don't have anything, Myk. Your uncle is dead, and along with him, so are his delusional memories."

Myk shook his head. He pictured in his mind's eye when Levi described what he saw—a young Rick Taft with his machine gun in his grasp, spraying bullets on his entire team. The pallets of gold loaded on the huge truck. *If I told him, he'd lie awake at night the rest of his life*, Myk thought. He held back. Instead, he said, "No, it's not tough talk, just the truth. It's like Babe Ruth pointing at the fence and then smacking the ball out of the park. It's the same thing as Mike Tyson telling his opponent what round and what time he's going to knock him out. I am coming for you, Rick. Fifteen crates were pulled from the lake but only eleven are accounted for at Fort

Knox. How'd you pull it off—pay someone to look the other way and then murder them too?"

"Ahh, I see. You're going to take down the senator of California on an accounting error? I think not. I'm untouchable, Myk. I'll be surrounded by secret service agents for the rest of my life, and every agency, including Interpol, is casting a broad net out for you. It's only a matter of time. You were lucky yet again. I would have had you at the San Francisco airport if you hadn't called an audible."

Myk turned his wrist and looked down at his watch. He had to end the call soon. "You're right, it is only a matter of time. Enjoy it while you have it!"

Myk heard the unmistakable sound of horse hooves clacking on the hard cobblestone. He looked toward the stables and saw Raji and Becca leading the horses by the reins to the oversized watering trough. Raji glanced up and saw Myk looking and waved. After putting the horses back in their corrals, Raji walked up the paved pathway to the back patio where Myk was seated.

He asked, "How was the ride?"

"Not as good as my ride last night!" Raji laughed.

Myk couldn't contain the huge smile that instantly appeared as he shook his head.

"It's beautiful." She looked out over the English Channel. "I've missed this. I could never get enough of it. I'll grab an iced tea and join you."

"Okay, I could use a cold drink."

Moments later Raji walked out to the patio holding two large, overflowing glasses full of ice and tea.

Myk said, "I don't know if you want to talk about it now. I've got a lot of questions. I started to put a plan together this morning, but I need to know what kind of assets we can rely on in Tehran. Until I hear some details, I've got serious questions about the viability of your idea. Also, you said something about the Chinese."

Raji put her cold drink down in front of her and said, "I need to make a call and inquire, but I am confident the Chinese would talk to Ali. I just don't know if I can trust him. I will call and get a feel for what position he'd take without having to divulge what we're after."

Myk's eyebrows raised. He was surprised he hadn't considered Ali. "What do you think the chances are?"

"Pretty high, actually."

"Why's that?" Myk questioned.

"Ali is not the hardliner he once used to be. He has witnessed, firsthand, the hypocrisy and selfishness of the regime. He knows there is a huge disconnect between the leadership and the desires of the Iranian people. I've been fooled by him before, so I'll test the waters first."

"When do you want to call him?"

Raji grabbed her cool drink. Condensation engulfed the glass and dripped off as she took a sip. "I'll call him today. I need to follow up on the guest visa for you anyway."

"Okay, great! I left my notes in the den. Can we talk in there and map a few things out?"

Raji stood and said, "Let's do it."

Myk and Raji took their drinks to the front den and began to go over the five pages of Myk's initial questions about Raji's plan for the coup d'état. After four hours, they decided that they would pace themselves and take as many days, weeks, or even months to get all of the details in place. On their third day of discussing the plan, it became evident that they had to consider and plan for two scenarios for the coup d'état. One scenario involved the use of weapons and force while the other did not. Which plan they used hinged completely on Ali. Raji planned to meet with Ali when they arrived in Iran. After her meeting with Ali, they would know which direction to take.

Meanwhile, the excess baggage, in the form of Jaafar, was getting heavier and heavier by the day. By the morning of the third day of their stay on Becca's estate, Raji told Jaafar he was not allowed to be in the same room with her. The next day, they moved him to the detached guest house. A day didn't go by that either Raji or Myk didn't seriously contemplate killing Jaafar. The only reason they kept him around longer was just in case they needed him for anything while they were in Tehran. Raji told Myk that she would kill Jaafar when they got back. If things didn't go as planned in Iran and Myk and Raji didn't make it back to the estate, they told Becca to turn Jaafar over to the authorities. Raji and Myk spent three weeks at Becca's estate planning the uprising and potential coup in Iran. All of the final planning for the revolution needed to take place in Tehran. When Myk and Raji left for Tehran, Becca flew back to her ranch in Austin. They stocked Jaafar's guest house with food and left him to fend for himself until they got back.

# CHAPTER 32

# TEHRAN, IRAN

R aji's stunning home was nestled in the base of the foothills of Lavasan, a town just on the outskirts of Tehran. Lavasan was home to many of the prominent figures of Tehran, Raji being one of them. The architectural design of the exterior of her home was modern and looked like a collection of rectangular masses assembled in a seamless symmetry of linear shapes. Each mass consisted of a different color or material. One portion of the home was clad entirely in flat alabaster stone from a nearby stone quarry, while another section appeared to be mostly large spans of glass and metal. The inside of the home had high, soaring ceilings with floor-to-ceiling glass. At the front entry, she had a water feature that would normally be seen in a luxury resort. A sheer descent of water flowed over clear glass that was fourteen feet tall and ten feet wide. The floors were a combination of smooth marble with rectangular sections of wood flooring inserted. The modern kitchen had rift-sawn oak veneer cabinets with a coffee-color stain. The entire kitchen was angled toward the back of the house, which was mostly glass and situated so that Raji could see the city views of Tehran from almost every room in the house. The backyard had a sixty-foot-long rectangular pool that dropped off to an infinity edge on the end.

On Raji's second day back at her network, she received a text from Ali asking if she could talk. She replied that she was at the studio and would need to wait until she got home to make sure the call was secure. When she arrived home, Myk was there waiting. She went to a secure line and called Ali.

When he answered, the first thing he asked was, "Are you on a secure line, Raji?"

"Yes. It's safe."

"Okay, good. I met with the Chinese leader earlier and the meeting went well. During our discussions, he said it was sheer luck that the Americans were successful in containing the first biological attack, and he wants us to try again."

"Did you get the meeting recorded?"

"Yes, I had hidden cameras and a microphone. I'll review it later. If everything is good, I'll send it to you tonight on a safe network."

"Okay. Thank you again."

She was just about to disconnect the call when she heard Ali say, "Raji, are you still there?"

"Yes, still here."

Ali asked, "Hey, how are you doing? Since we haven't spoken about it yet, I wanted to tell you that I am really, really sorry about Yasser. I hope you know I had nothing to do with that. As you know, we rarely talked. That was all of your father's doing."

Raji sat down in the couch and looked at the city lights of Tehran off in the distance. She said, "I am doing okay. Thank you for asking. I wish you knew him better; he would have been a good man."

"Me too," Ali said somberly.

"Hey, can I ask you something?" Raji had an impulse and wanted to explore it.

"Sure, what's on your mind?"

"It's just a feeling, but I am sensing more unrest among the Iranian people than I've ever felt. I don't know if it's because the emotion of Yasser's passing is so close to the surface, but I was curious if you're seeing the same thing too?"

Without hesitation, Ali replied, "Absolutely. The ayatollah brings up the topic every meeting. They are sensing a groundswell, and they're a little nervous."

Raji didn't know if she could trust her own instincts when it came to getting a true read on Ali. She set her internal debate aside and asked the question that was gnawing at her anyway. "What side of the coin are you on, Ali—the people's side or the regime's side?"

"I'm curious why you ask, but I'll give you my answer anyway." Ali's tone lowered to a whisper. "I'm on the people's side, but as you are intimately aware, I am trapped. Hakeem and I talk frequently of how wonderful life would be if we lived in a society that accepted us. If we could be ourselves in public like most gay men in the West, that would feel so liberating. I can't ever see that day happening in Iran. Where is that question coming from anyway?"

Raji hesitated and thought, *No, not yet. I just can't trust you.* She replied, "It's just a story my producer has been working on. I'm seeing the same thing. Well, thank you again. Have a good evening, Ali."

"You too."

She disconnected the call. Myk was sitting on the couch listening to her half of the conversation and asked, "What did Ali have to say?"

Raji's mind instantly switched gears from the man who was a fake to the man who was very real. She closed one eye slightly and bewitched him with her gaze. She stood and said, "Let's talk about it later. Why don't you join me in the bedroom?"

Myk rose and smiled as he followed her into her bedroom.

# CHAPTER 33

R aji closed and locked the door after Myk entered. She stood at the door and said seductively, "I'd much rather share something else with you instead of my conversation with Ali."

Myk stepped closer and slowly undressed her. He kissed her softly and led her to the bed. After making love, Raji ran the tips of her fingers softly over the lady in the tree, contemplating. Myk lay on his side, his back to Raji. Her legs were tangled in his. Her breasts were lightly pressed against the bare skin of his back as she traced the exotic tattoo from the roots of the tree to the wind-blown leaves floating in the air. The room was dark and still with only dim lighting coming from the landscape lights outside the window, which illuminated Raji and Myk's bare bodies. She put her arm around him and pulled him in closer. Her gaze was drawn outside to the dark and windless night. Beyond the reflection of the glass-like water on the pool, beyond the city lights of Tehran, flashes of lightning were barely perceptible in the distance. At her network that day, the meteorologist couldn't stop talking about the impending storm. Record rainfall, flooding, and strong winds were forecast. In the far distance, she saw signs of the approaching storm. The air outside her window was so calm that leaves on the trees didn't flicker—there wasn't even a ripple on the tranquil pool.

Raji's mind wouldn't rest. She rolled over and reached in the nightstand drawer and grasped her elixir cure for worries. With the pack of cigarettes in hand, she wrapped a thin blanket around her and stepped out to the patio. Raji and Myk had been in Tehran for three weeks. Everything was in place for the coup d'état, except the most important piece—Ali. For security reasons, they had to wait until the very last moment to find out who he would side with. Raji was scheduled to meet him later. The unknown was what had her nervously smoking a cigarette in the still darkness of her back patio. She sat with legs crossed on the couch and lit a cigarette that she held between her index and middle finger. With the first deep inhale, she felt her mind begin relaxing. Before she could exhale, she heard the metal latch of the door handle clink. She turned to see Myk, who had slid his colorful boxer shorts back on.

He slithered onto the couch next to her and placed his hand affectionately on her knee. "Are you okay?" he asked in a soft tone.

Raji took another drag and held her cigarette out in an offer to Myk. "I've thought about this since grade school. Tell me I'm doing the right thing."

Myk took the cigarette from her and inhaled. The tip glowed bright orange against the darkness of the cool pre-dawn sky. "I think the time is right, Raji. There's no question that a majority of Iranians are extremely unhappy. Perhaps the only thing they need is their Kaveh to show them the way."

Somewhat surprised, Raji purposefully turned her focus to Myk. "You've heard of Kaveh?" Kaveh was from a tenth-century Persian myth, who led the Iranian people in a successful rebellion against a ruthless dictator.

"Yeah, Kaveh the Blacksmith. Kaveh is you, Raji."

"How did you—"

Myk cut her off mid-sentence. "I ran across Kaveh the Black-smith on the internet when I was trying to learn more about you and the Iranian culture."

Raji placed her hand on top of his. She was stunned by the unexpected emotion that filled her. *Why am I so affected by such a simple gesture?* "Myk, I don't want to be overdramatic, but I really wasn't expecting to be so touched by learning that you would take an interest." She looked at him with a sincere smile.

"Well, it's worth repeating: you're an enigma, Raji." He smiled back, leaned over, and pressed his lips to hers. He sat back up and said, "Tell me what's on your mind."

"It's the calm before the storm, and I'm worried. Fear of the unknown, I suppose. Is this going to fail like Tiananmen Square and the Iranian Green Movement where hundreds of people lost their lives and nothing changed? Or will it succeed like the Iranian Revolution of '79 when the movement successfully, and somewhat peacefully, took over the government? I'm the one who's going to strike the match, and if I'm being honest, I'm scared."

Myk moved his fingertips over his lips as if in deep thought. There was silence between the two for several minutes as they watched the encroaching storm and lightning strikes inch closer to Tehran. Myk put his hand back down and said, "The big difference between what's happening now and what happened in '79 is in the leadership that's running Iran. Back then, the Shah, for the most part, refused to use violence in order to crush the rebellion. You and I both know that your theocratic government will not hesitate to put any rebellions down. The real question is whether or not the military will follow their orders."

"I know. It's just hard," she said solemnly.

"What about Ali? Would his ranks follow him if he revolted?"

Raji shook her head. "That's another thing that's adding to my anxiety. I don't know for sure if I can trust him. When you've been burned once, it's hard to go back. But he could prove to be the one thing that makes the difference."

"What do your instincts tell you?"

"To bring him in—but I'm fighting with it internally."

Myk scooted closer, put his arm around her, and held her tight. "Stop fighting yourself. Follow your instincts, Raji. Never let fear dictate your choices."

Raji twisted the cigarette out in the ash tray in front of her and then rested her head on Myk's shoulder. She whispered, "I'll call Ali in the morning."

Myk combed his fingers through her hair. The touch of his fingers began at her forehead and slowly glided across her scalp to the back of her ear. Each soft stroke brought her closer and closer to him. Each time his hand arrived behind her ear, he gently tugged on the fistful of her thick hair. She moved her head from his shoulder down to his lap and stretched her legs across the sofa. Myk caressed her shoulder and arm as she lay on her side. She reveled in the moment and got lost in his gentle touch. She felt his hand move back and forth from her curvy hips to the top of her shoulder. Raji reached up and ran her fingers across his bare chest and firm torso. She sat up and cuddled up next to him, one leg across his lap and her other leg behind him. She put her hand behind his neck and pulled him in for a kiss. Raji put his upper lip between her front teeth and gently nibbled. She released her soft bite, moved to his lower lip, and nibbled again. Myk held her by the hips and moved Raji's body with such ease it was like moving a pillow from one side to the other. She sat on his lap, her face in front of his. They put their arms around each other in a tight embrace and kissed. Raji gently placed her hands on his face and began to caress her forehead across his. She kissed him again, then began to brush her nose against his. Raji felt desires building inside her. She traced his cheek bone with her nose and then ran her nose along his jawline and back to the lobe of his ear.

She gently kissed his ear and whispered, "Agent Miles, how do you expect to tame this Persian tigress with those silly boxer shorts on?"

Myk held Raji firmly on his lap with one hand while sliding his boxer shorts off with his other hand. Raji's hips began rocking back and forth involuntarily. She felt Myk's awakened state beneath her.

She continued moving her hips across his lap and playfully said,

"You're not going to leave your friend out in this cool air, are you?"

Myk grinned directly at her. Raji's iridescent eyes were ablaze again. He placed his hand under her butt and raised her body up slightly. As he eased her body back on to his lap, he entered her.

With her hands on the sides of his face, she said with a smirk, "I think your friend is much happier now!"

Myk chuckled.

There were no thoughts of impending storms. There were no worries of failures and things that could go wrong. Raji was present, and she lost herself in the here and now.

She awoke on the back patio couch to the sound of clattering raindrops on the wide leaves of the lush trees. She felt the warmth of Myk's body spooning beside her. She opened her eyes to see the confluence of thick gray, charcoal, and white clouds moving across the colorful dawn sky. The mature trees bent back and forth by the force of the wind. Three of the cushions from the sofa, where they had made love hours ago, were blowing across the patio. Her first instinct was to walk over and secure the loose cushions, but she stayed and relished an experience that had escaped her for over twenty years. *He makes me feel like I'm important to him. He cares*, Raji thought. Myk's arms were wrapped around her as she stared blankly at the tumult of the storm. She squeezed his hands and nestled as close as she could against Myk. *So this is what it's like.* The thought brought a smile to her face. She felt Myk's body shift. His strong arms began to hug her tightly.

"Good morning," he whispered with his breath on the back on her neck.

Raji turned to face him. She slid one of her legs between his. "Yes, it is a good morning. Thank you for coming out on the back patio with me."

He smiled. "The pleasure was all mine!"

After one last good morning kiss, Raji stood up and stretched, then put away the loose cushions. They moved inside and after closing the porch door, Myk asked, "What time are they expecting you at the studio?"

"I have plenty of time. I need to call Ali before I leave. He could really tilt things in our favor. If he could get his men to stay neutral, it would still be a victory."

Myk nodded. "Without a doubt."

Raji's phone lit up and began to vibrate. She spun around and picked up her phone that was charging on the nightstand.

"I should probably get this, Myk."

"No problem."

Raji took the call from her news studio. She stood and walked out of the room as she spoke. Myk sat on the edge of the bed and looked outside at the blowing storm. He leaned forward with his elbows on his knees and gathered his thoughts. Myk reached for his binder that was full of his notes as well as several maps and skimmed through them. As he thought about the possibility of Ali joining their side, he began to formulate the adjustments that would need to be made as he walked out to the kitchen to check on Raji.

"I've got some coffee started. Would you like some?" she asked.

"That would be great. Is everything okay at work?"

"Yes. Slow news day, so they'll spend most of the time on the storm. I'll call Ali as soon as I get a cup of coffee in me."

"Good idea," Myk said. "I'm going to take a quick shower."

Raji's eyes widened and she gave him a sensual and playful smile.

Myk grinned. "Hey, you're welcome to join me!"

"Perhaps I will after my call with Ali."

Myk turned back to the bedroom while Raji poured herself some coffee. She brought her cup of coffee and her head full of uncertainties to the sofa and sat down. Halfway through her coffee, she thought, *Trust my instincts. Don't let fear dictate my decisions.* She dialed Ali's number and waited for him to answer.

"Hello," Ali said.

"Good morning, Ali. There's something I need to talk to you about."

"Yes, what is it?"

"Remember when I asked you what side of the coin you're on?"

"Yes."

"It's important that I talk to you about your answer."

There was a pause before Ali replied in a lower tone, "Not over the phone, Raji. Are you home now?"

She answered, "Yes, I should be here for another few hours."

"Okay, I'm going to come over now."

"Right now?!" Raji asked in a more elevated and edgy tone.

"I'm just outside Tehran. I can be there in about twenty minutes."

Raji stammered a bit. "Uh . . . I have a guest with me," she said somewhat apologetically.

Ali chuckled. "I know, I got him the visitor's visa—remember? Hakeem is going to join us too."

"That's fine. I'll leave the door unlocked, so just come in when you get here."

# CHAPTER 34

Raji sat impatiently on the sofa in the great room. Her house had an open floor plan with the kitchen, dining room, and great room all opened to each other. The sofa faced a matching piece that sat perpendicular to an eight-foot linear fireplace. The wall of the fireplace had gray marble with veins of white that looked like lightning strikes running through it. The marble ran from the floor up to the top of the fourteen-foot ceiling. Raji couldn't sit still as she waited for Ali. She crossed her legs one way and then the other. As soon as she got comfortable in one position, she changed to another. When the time got near, she tried the other sofa and went through the same fidgety motions. Finally, she heard the chime of her doorbell ring followed by the sound of the large ten-foot glass door closing.

She heard Ali's voice call out, "Raji, we're here."

"I'm in the great room."

She saw Ali and Hakeem round the corner and stood. It had been over four years since she had seen Ali. And even then, it was just a polite wave as he sat in his car in her driveway waiting for Yasser.

Raji motioned with her hand. "Please have a seat."

Before sitting, Ali said, "This is my good friend Hakeem. Anything you want to discuss with me is safe with him."

Hakeem extended his hand. "It's nice to finally meet you. My condolences for your son, Yasser."

"Thank you," she said. "It's good to finally meet you too."

Hakeem stood a few inches shorter than Ali. His facial features were not as masculine and hardened as Ali's; they were much softer. He had wavy hair that was mostly gray on the sides.

Ali asked, "Okay, Raji—what's this all about?"

"There's something I'd like to share with you, but I have some very serious trust issues with you, Ali—on multiple levels."

He replied somewhat somberly, "Yes, I completely understand. I have made a lot of serious mistakes in my life, but my deception in getting you to marry me was the biggest."

Raji half smiled as her head slanted to the side. "Yes, that was an awful thing you did, but I didn't have you come here for another apology. Clearly, we have both moved on."

Raji noticed both Ali's and Hakeem's attention was drawn to the hallway leading to her master bedroom. She turned and saw Myk walking toward them.

She stood and said, "This is my friend M—" Raji stopped herself before she said Myk's real name. Her mind began to race, but she drew a blank. She couldn't remember the name on the passport Myk had used.

Without skipping a beat, Myk introduced himself in their Persian language, knowing full well that everyone spoke fluent English. "Lance Vaughn. It's nice to meet you."

Myk extended his hand as they both stood to shake it.

Ali said, "It's nice meeting you, Lance? Although, if you want to use your real name, you're safe to do so."

Myk chuckled. "Let's stick with Lance for now." He sat and couldn't control his huge smile that appeared across his face. He was struck by the enigma of the situation. It was a serious and life-changing meeting they were about to embark on, and yet the monumental paradox was not lost to him. An Iranian gay man and an outspoken and fiercely independent Iranian woman were meeting to discuss the take-over of a theocratic government that condemned their very natures.

Raji spoke up, "Ali, I'm still not convinced by your answer last night. I need you to elaborate. Which side of the coin are you really on—the regime's or the people's? You have always been one to toe the line for the regime, and you have a proven track record of lying—so why should I believe you?"

Hakeem looked at Ali and asked, "Ali, is it okay if I answer this?"

Ali shrugged with his shoulder. "Sure. Is that okay with you, Raji?"

She looked at Myk, whose eyes said yes, and then turned to Hakeem and nodded.

Hakeem crossed one leg over the other and began. "Ali and I have completely changed our beliefs since our younger days. You are one of the rare ones, Raji. From what Ali has told me, you've had your footing on solid ground since grade school. How in the hell you were able to do that while being raised by a father who was a notorious bomb maker baffles me."

*He was no father. He was selfish monster that used me, just like Ali did*, Raji thought.

Hakeem continued, "For our whole lives, we've been told by our parents and society to believe an archaic and dangerous set of morals, so it has taken Ali and me decades longer than it took you—but at least we know the truth now. Because of our relationship and our love, we could trust each other as we began to question everything that we were taught. There is no future for Ali and me in this country unless we want to continue to live a life in hiding that is a lie. That's why we can tell you with complete confidence that given the choice of being on the side of the regime or the side of the Iranian people, we are firmly on the side of the people. Unfortunately, because of our positions within the government, this is yet another lie that we perpetrate on a daily basis in order to live a comfortable life."

Raji asked, "Do you think there are very many others in the government that think the same way as you two?"

Ali answered, "It would only be a guess. As you are aware, this isn't something people can talk about openly. Every Iranian knows that a black van can pull up to their house anytime and take you away."

Raji's mind instantly flashed back to the scene of her best friend Meera being dragged out of school and stuffed into a black SUV.

"That being said, I wouldn't be surprised if thirty percent of those that work in the government have views similar to ours," Ali said.

"Hakeem, do you agree with Ali on his thirty percent estimate?" Raji asked.

"If anything, I'd say that's conservative."

Ali asked, "Okay, Raji, it's your turn. Where are you going with this?"

Raji turned to Myk and asked, "What do you think?"

Myk replied, "I think you're safe. You should tell them. Besides, you hold the cards that could destroy both of their lives." Raji's entire house was wired with hidden high-definition cameras that was recording the meeting.

Ali gave Raji a puzzled look and asked, "Tell us what?"

Raji shifted in her seat and paused before saying, "There's never been a better time for a movement by the people to oust this theocratic regime. Because of our government's own ineptitude and poor decisions, they have backed themselves up to the edge of a cliff. With just a little push, they'll fall."

"And you'd like to give them a push?" Ali asked.

"Yes, it's time. They've stolen billions of euros in aid that was meant for the Iranian people. They've bloated their bank accounts with cash from the previous American presidency. They've stolen elections. We have record unemployment. They stifle free thought, and they suppress women. They've made us dependent on the Chinese. Their lack of leadership killed thousands during the pandemic. They alone are responsible for decimating the beautiful country that once was Persia. It won't take much to unite the people."

"I don't disagree with anything, Raji. I have firsthand knowledge of their atrocities. But what are you suggesting? Or are you just venting?" Ali asked.

*Don't insult my intelligence, you weak-minded man*, she thought. "I am not *suggesting* anything, Ali. I am going to tell you about a revolution that is days away from starting. After hearing what I have to say, then you can decide if you want to be a part of it. Otherwise, I need assurances from you that you'll stay the hell out of the way because it's going to happen with or without you."

Somewhat bewildered, Ali said, "Wow! Okay, I'm listening."

Raji continued. "I have a studio here in the basement of the house that is an exact replica of the main studio in Tehran. I broadcast out of my home studio for about a month during the pandemic. I am going to tape a news broadcast at my home studio, and in that recording, I will expose the corruption of our government in detail during the hour-long segment. I will tell the people of Iran that if they want their country back, then they need to join one another in peaceful demonstrations and demand that the regime step down and cede their authority to a temporary transition government until a duly elected government can be voted into office. We have a technology team to hack into the live feed of my newscast and play my recording on a continual feed. We have plans for backup power already set up so that when the authorities try and cut the power, they will be unable to stop the feed. We estimate that it will take at least six hours before they'll figure out how to finally take down the transmission. By that time, it will be too late to stamp out the movement."

Ali and Hakeem looked at each other and nodded in unison. Ali said, "Pardon my cynicism, but when the military shows up and starts arresting people and dispersing the crowds with tear gas like they did during the Iranian Green Movement—then what?"

Raji shook her head back and forth. "C'mon, Ali—think! You know this is nothing like it was in '09. The regime has grown a hundred times more corrupt, and the people have grown a thousand times more angry. If I'm right, and I believe that I am, then the government won't have near enough jail cells or enough tear gas—or even enough bullets—to stop the tidal wave of people. Iranians are fed up—we can peacefully shut down the oil fields, blockade the airports, and bring the entire country to a screeching halt until the regime steps down. Then, they will see who truly runs this country—us or them! The sheer mass of people will be overwhelming. When the orders come down to you and Hakeem from the ayatollah to break up the demonstrations, ignore him. Instead, put the word out to the military and police to either join in the demonstrations or sit on the sidelines. The dissatisfaction of the Iranian people has reached its breaking point."

Ali interlocked his fingers of both hands and brought them to his face as if praying. He broke eye contact with Raji and stared blankly out the window. He inhaled a deep breath and said, "You are right, Raji—it is time." Ali set his hands down beside him and looked at Hakeem. "This is suicide for everyone in this room. The ayatollah will have us executed for this, but I don't care."

Raji replied, "I disagree with you. He can't have you executed if he's no longer in power. This movement will be unstoppable. The ayatollah will have to step down and will no longer have the authority to have anyone executed. Unfortunately, many of those that are ousted from power won't exactly disappear peacefully into the sunset. Because of my broadcast, I'll be their number one target. I know that I'll be hunted for the remainder of my days. And if you join us, then you will too."

Ali replied, "True, but because of our position in the military, Hakeem and I have more than just the ousted regime to look over our shoulder for. The Americans and Israelis would love nothing more than to see us dead or arrested."

Raji's eyes narrowed as she glared at Ali. "I have an idea that might help with that, but you'll get no sympathy from me, Ali. You've lived a life of luxury while the Iranian people suffered. My anger toward you almost kept me from bringing you in on the plan, but I would never let something like that get in the way of freeing the

Iranian people from this dictatorship. Having you on our side could be a game-changer—so what's it going to be?"

"Would you give me a moment with Hakeem?" he asked.

Hakeem spoke up immediately, "That won't be necessary, Ali. I'm in, and I know that you are too."

"Is this true, Ali?" Raji asked.

He nodded his head. "Yes, you can count on us. Tell me what you need."

Raji and Myk spent the next six hours unfolding the plan with Ali and Hakeem. Ali was able to fortify a few of the weaker points of the plan. When they were all satisfied, Ali thanked them and told them that he needed to leave to prepare for his weekly meeting with the ayatollah later that night.

# CHAPTER 35

Four days after meeting with Ali, Raji put the plan in motion. There was no turning back. Ten minutes before stepping into the unknown, Raji sat alone behind the locked door of her dressing room. Would her broadcast cause massive violent protests and death, or would the regime step down peacefully? The thoughts weighed heavily on her mind. She reached down to her leather handbag and pulled out two pictures—one new, the other faded and worn. She held the corner of the diminished picture between her index finger and thumb and smiled. Smiling back at her was the faded image of her mother, Nadine. She reflected for a moment and then replaced the picture of her mother's smiling face with another. Yasser's radiant grin looked up at her. She held the picture she had taken from the mirror of Yasser's hotel room in San Francisco. The picture that Habiba took at Yasser's championship soccer match where he stood with his arm around Raji. She stared at his happy face, shook her head, and then carefully placed the picture back.

She heard the familiar tap on her door. "Five minutes, Raji."

"Okay," she replied.

Raji was no longer nervous, she was determined. There wasn't a trace of fear within her. Instead, anger began to build. The puppet was minutes from cutting her strings from the regime. She checked herself in the mirror one last time. Her clothing, makeup, and hair were an exact match to the recording that would replace her live feed on the five o'clock newscast. The recording would put in motion an irrevocable movement, the likes that had not been seen since the revolution of '79. She spun in her seat, stood, and confidently walked out the door. As she slid into her chair behind the desk of the network studio, she stared blankly at the large studio cameras pointing directly at her. Raji smiled politely at her broadcast partner, Jalai, who was running his fingers over his bushy mustache. He had been her partner on the five o'clock news for the last three years, and not a week went by that Jalai didn't try to make advances toward her. He had groped her countless times and gotten away with it under the guise of accidently bumping into Raji. It had become so commonplace that she finally quit reporting it. He tried to make small talk with her as they waited for the signal from the director of the show, Khatchi. She ignored Jalai and pretended as if she was busy reviewing notes.

Raji looked straight ahead at the words on the monitor and then focused on Khatchi as he pantomimed a countdown with one hand held in front of him. Five, four, three, two, one—Khatchi's fingers disappeared into his fist one by one until his index finger pointed at Raji. The attention of the entire studio was drawn to the monitors as Raji began her newscast. The script on the monitor in front of Raji began with the lead story of the damage done by the recent storms, but the story that was actually being broadcast to the Iranian citizens would tell of an entirely different and much more destructive storm.

The prerecorded message began right on cue with the recording of Raji saying, "Good evening. Tonight's news will mark a pivotal point in our Iranian history. Tonight, I will expose the deep corruption of our Iranian government and I will uncover the truth behind the pernicious lies our leaders are hiding from the Iranian people."

Khatchi was the first one in the studio to take his eyes off of the monitors and notice Raji's empty chair. She was gone, and yet she was right there on the screen in front of him. With the entire studio's attention focused on the monitors, Raji had calmly stood and walked away from the studio desk the second the broadcast began. She walked past a sound technician in the hall that looked at her perplexed as he turned his head back and forth from Raji to the screen mounted on the wall that was playing the prerecorded message. The studio in the recorded message was an exact replica. The producer of the show yelled at Khatchi and the cameramen to stop the broadcast, but the cameramen shrugged and threw their hands in the air at the stupidity of the request—Raji's message was obviously not coming from their cameras. Within thirty seconds, the studio had turned into complete pandemonium. Every person in the studio asked the person standing next to them what was going on, but no one had answers.

The producer continued screaming at every technician within earshot, "Somebody stop this fucking feed!" He shoved the technicians off their chairs and began punching buttons and then finally resorted to slamming his fists on the large control boards. He screamed, "Stop the broadcast, you imbeciles, or they'll have us all killed!" But Raji's message to the Iranian people played on. Her message began with the billions of dollars that were embezzled by the Iranian leadership. Money that was supposed to go to the Iranian citizens who had suffered massive casualties because of the leadership's ineptitude in protecting its citizens from the coronavirus. The lead story on the recording would be followed by a more personalized story from Raji. She would tell the story of Levi, a Jewish man who risked his life to save her when she was a little girl. Decades later, that same Jewish man took a bullet and sacrificed his life for his mortal enemy: her father, Jaafar. The emotional and watery-eyed Raji was then replaced with the actual footage from Myk's safe house that showed Levi jumping in front of the bullet for Jaafar. The next story detailed how the Iranian regime cheated its citizens out of their elections—a story that pushed the hot button on all Iranians.

A smattering of workers ran around frantically trying to stop the recording, but most of the people in the studio were so shocked and mesmerized that they sat or stood, immovable, with their mouths gaping open. Iranian's beloved newscaster, Raji, was telling her fellow countrymen on live television the truth about their corrupt government. It was unprecedented and most in the studio ignored the chaos and remained glued to her message. Every phone in the studio began to light up. After fifteen minutes of futilely trying to stop the broadcast, the producer finally began to ask if anyone knew where Raji was.

In the meeting with Ali and Hakeem, Raji had asked both of them if they knew who would be loyal to the regime and who wouldn't. It was determined that it was too risky to make any effort in finding out who the regime's true loyalists would be. Instead, they took their best guess and organized a large-scale war games training exercise near the Pakistan border. Ali and Hakeem diverted a massive contingent of the military away from the epicenter of the demonstrations. Many of the most loyal to the regime would be nine hundred kilometers away from the demonstrations and unable to stop the movement from quickly erupting into a full-scale, country-wide overthrow of the government.

Iran's underground network had been in place for years. When Raji came knocking on their door with her plan, they were already well organized and ready to move into action. Raji's message was timed in conjunction with tens of thousands from Iran's underground Green Movement crowding into Baharestan Square in central Tehran where the Iranian Parliament met. In the village of Jamaran, they surrounded the ayatollah's residence. Raji's broadcast began at five o'clock, and by five thirty the targeted locations were already overwhelmed. The broadcast would conclude with Raji imploring all Iranians to join in the peaceful demonstrations for the transfer of power to a new government and demand an end to their sham elections.

Raji's recorded broadcast was halfway through airing when she pulled into her garage and shut the door. At the forty-five-minute mark of the recording, Ali would appear in the video and assure the Iranian people that he had instructed the military to stand down and allow the peaceful demonstrations. He stated that he could not guarantee that every soldier would obey his command, but that it was his wish that the demonstrations continue peacefully. Through a group email and text that was timed in conjunction with the beginning of the broadcast, Ali and Hakeem gave the orders to every leader under their command that they were forbidden to break up the demonstrations. It would take hours before the Iranian leadership would be able to decipher who was loyal and who was not. By that time, the demonstrations would morph into crowds that couldn't be contained and Ali, Hakeem, Raji, and Myk would be safely out of the country. It was a perfect storm. Ali stationed the most faithful of his inner circle at the Iranian border into Turkey. Just to be safe, Ali reached out to his long-time friend in Turkey that he had played soccer with in his college years, Turhan Tessir, who was the deputy prime minister of Turkey. Turhan told Ali he would assist them with whatever they needed. Ali agreed to help Raji and Myk get safely into Turkey. After that, they would need to be on their own.

Thirty minutes after Raji got home, Ali parked his Mercedes-Benz GLS SUV in her driveway and popped open the back hatch. Hakeem and Ali quickly entered the house and called out for her. There was no response. They entered the kitchen and called her name again. When they turned to enter the great room, Ali and Hakeem froze in their tracks. A gunman stood behind Raji with the muzzle of his Glock resting on the back of Raji's head. In his other hand, the gunman had a second gun pointed directly at Ali.

The gunman barked out, "Put your weapons on the floor in front of you, devilish traitors!"

Raji pleaded with tears running down her face, "Khatchi, please don't harm them. It was all my idea. Nobody needs to get hurt."

Khatchi quickly smashed the side of the Glock against the back of Raji's head and shouted, "Silence, you fucking whore! What are you traitors waiting for? I said put your weapons on the floor or I'll put a bullet through your skull!"

Ali calmly said, "Khatchi, this is the will of the people. Let it play out and see what happens. You can't trust our leaders anymore; they are all corrupt—every single one of them. Please don't do this."

The comment infuriated Khatchi. He yelled, "Stop your lies, you Zionist collaborator!" Khatchi aimed toward Ali and fired a shot. The sound was deafening. The large window behind Ali shattered and burst into a shower of glass like an eruption of water from a firehose. "I am warning you. Next time I won't miss. Put your weapons down now. The authorities are on their way!"

Ali and Hakeem eyed each other as they slowly reached for their weapons. As they bent over to lay their guns on the marble floor, Ali quickly stood straight and aimed his gun at Khatchi. He was too late. Khatchi squeezed off two quick rounds, striking Ali in the chest. Clouds of red mist exploded from Ali's chest as he spun and toppled to the hard floor. Hakeem managed to fire once before two of Khatchi's bullets struck him in the torso. He staggered toward Khatchi who shot him again. Raji smacked the other gun out of Khatchi's hand, leapt over the coffee table, and ran for the door. Khatchi swung his aim around to the back of his fleeing target and shot Raji once in the back. Her force kept her moving forward until she smashed unnaturally into the wall and slid to the floor. Khatchi took aim and put another round into Raji's motionless body. The white marble floor turned crimson red around the three bodies as pools of blood began to form. Khatchi stepped forward and stooped down to check Ali's pulse. He then stepped over Ali and nudged Hakeem's motionless body with the tip of his foot. He rocked Hakeem's body back and forth with his foot but there was no response from his flaccid body, so Khatchi moved to Raji and knelt down beside her. He lifted her limp wrist and searched for her pulse. Satisfied, Khatchi stood and took a step toward the front door before he heard a voice yelling in Persian from behind him.

Myk was standing in the hallway to the master suite with his arm extended and his Glock G34 pistol aimed directly at Khatchi's back.

He yelled, "Drop your weapon and then slowly turn and face me!"

The sound of metal clacking against the hard marble floor echoed as Khatchi let his gun fall. He put his hands above his head and then turned to face Myk.

When he saw Myk, he squinted and asked, "Who in the hell are you?"

Myk barked back, "I am the one asking questions, you blind zealot! Who sent you? How did you find out about this?"

Khatchi angrily answered, "I followed Raji from the studio today. I knew she was up to something. I've had my eye on her for years. How in the hell she got away with peddling her lies over these years I'll never know. But someone should have put a bullet through her skull long ago, before she could garner such a huge following and agitate the masses."

Myk yelled, "How's it feel to go down in history as the one who killed Iran's next national hero! Statues will be erected for the movement she started today, you moron!" Myk squeezed his index finger on the trigger. The shot struck Khatchi in the middle of the chest, causing him to spin and stumble. Blood began to spurt from his torso like the jet stream from a water toy. Khatchi hopelessly brought both hands to his chest in an attempt to halt the blood pouring out. He dropped to his knees and then fell over sideways.

# CHAPTER 36

Four bodies lay still, strewn across the white marble floor, which was slowly turning crimson red. Myk stayed in the confines of the hallway and avoided stepping into the large great room. He immediately pulled his burner phone from his pocket and dialed emergency services. He told the operator that four people had been shot and to send ambulances. He disconnected the call and surveyed the room. Myk stared at the massacre of bodies and paused. After thirty seconds, he asked, "Khatchi, are we good?"

Khatchi's stiff body suddenly came to life as he knelt on one knee and held his chest. "Damn, that hurt way more than I remember." He turned to the others and said, "Okay guys, well done! I think that will do it."

The three motionless bodies precipitously came to life, like stunned birds lying lifeless on the ground after striking a window and then instantly finding flight again. They all stood, almost in unison, and began peeling the bulletproof Kevlar vests from their bodies.

Raji bemoaned, "My back is on fire! That hurt like shit, Khatchi—I think your smack to the head was a little excessive!"

Khatchi grinned. "Hey, if you don't want to be looking over your shoulder for the rest of your life, we had to make this authentic. A bruised head and back now beats the hell out of torture if they ever came after you."

"Point taken."

"Too bad you couldn't see my performance. I saved the best

gadget for me—very theatrical. It shot out streams of blood."

Raji smiled. "We couldn't have done this without you." She stepped toward Myk then turned her back to him, lifted her shirt, and asked, "Would you check my back? It sure feels like I've got a bullet in me!"

Myk stepped closer and looked. "Damn! That's one of the biggest welts I've seen from these vests. I'll get some ice for you."

Both Ali and Hakeem lifted their shirts, pointed at the massive bruises on each other and began laughing. They both hugged each other and said, "We did it! Your plan was genius, Raji!"

Raji replied, "You can thank Khatchi. He's the filmmaker and guy with the fake blood."

Myk chimed in abruptly, "We need to get going. Every minute longer that we spend here makes it that much more risky crossing the border." Then he asked, "Khatchi, do you have everything you need?"

"Yeah, I'm good. You guys should definitely get going."

Raji approached Khatchi and said, "Thank you! I am going to miss you, my friend. You were the only person at that network that treated me as an equal instead of as an inferior woman!" She gave him a warm hug and then walked toward the garage door.

Khatchi replied, "I'll miss you too. Be safe."

The four of them loaded up into Raji's car and drove toward the border of Turkey. Khatchi stayed behind to pull all the recordings from Raji's security cameras. Prior to working at the network with Raji, Khatchi had been employed for more than a decade at the BBC filming studio in London. When he wasn't working at the news studio, Khatchi still dabbled in short films and had a complete gallery of costumes, makeup, fake blood, and everything essential to making a phony murder scene look very real. He would edit the recordings from Raji's security cameras and then leave one copy at the house for the authorities to find. He would send another copy to their studio to broadcast to the Iranian public—their new hero had been slain. The fake murder would allow her to live the rest of her life in peace. The hallway leading to Raji's master suite was the only location not covered by any security cameras—that was where Myk stood and watched the entire staged murder scene unfold. Iranian authorities would speculate for the next decade as to who the mysterious shooter was. Raji would be remembered as a martyr for Persia—their Kaveh that freed the country from a suppressive dictatorship.

# Istanbul, Turkey

Raji woke up the next morning with her back throbbing in pain. The swollen red welt left behind by the bulletproof vest was the radius of a small cantaloupe.

"How's it feel to finally be free?" Myk asked.

"Exhilarating! It feels like I'm starting all over—except I'm in my forties." She paused, and then in a more serious tone added, "It's difficult because I can't get past the feeling that I am abandoning my people."

Myk thoughtfully replied, "You need to chase that thought from your mind. You awoke the Iranian people to the facts about their government. If you stayed, it would have been suicide. If those in the regime get ousted from power, they would have spent their life tracking you down. You have given the Iranian people the opportunity for real freedom. What they choose is of their own accord. When they settle on a government, I have no doubt that Iranian women will set you apart. You have done more for the cause of Iranian women than anyone else in their entire history."

Raji grabbed Myk's hand and gave it a gentle squeeze. "Thank you, Myk. I think of how our paths crossed, and it makes me wonder.

There's something to be said of stepping out into the unknown."

"I agree completely. So many people take the safe route in life and never dip their toes into the pool of risk. Levi shared one of his favorite quotes with me. I think it was from Shakespeare. It was something along the lines of, 'Our doubts are traitors and make us lose the good we oft might win by fearing the attempt.'"

"That's beautiful. I wish we could have had more time with him."

Myk's lips tensed. "Me too."

Raji asked, "Can we turn the news on? I'd like to see what's happening."

"Of course." Myk stretched across the bed, reached over to the nightstand, and grabbed the remote. After surfing through a few stations, he landed on the news.

Raji sat up in bed and brought her knees to her chest. "Oh my God—look, Myk, it's happening!"

Raji stared at the television screen and tears welled up in her eyes. She saw the huge masses of Iranians that had poured into the streets. There were no police pushing back crowds, no tear gas, and no violence—just throngs of Iranian people that went for miles in each direction. It took her breath away to see such an incredible turnout. She had calculated an overwhelming response, but the actual number of Iranians that were peacefully demonstrating all across Iran was inconceivable. She had estimated that it would take six hours before the authorities would figure out how to take her recording off the air, but it was still running a day later. The truth about the Iranian regime was exposed to their entire country. The reaction of the Iranian people was so swift and all-encompassing that the regime gave up trying stop it. From the live feed of the news helicopters in Iran, there was not an inch of street pavement that could be seen—every street in every direction was packed with masses of people. Raji and Myk sat on the bed holding hands in silence. They watched in amazement as freedom-loving Iranians unified to oust decades of a leadership that practiced thuggery.

Myk glanced at the clock. "I have to meet Turhan down in the lobby. Do you want to join me?"

Raji shook her head, giggled, and said sarcastically, "And miss this? I've waited my life to see this day. I just wish I was there."

Myk shrugged, "Hey, I had to ask. I'm not sure how long I'll be. Can I get you anything?"

Raji continued to stare forward at the television. "No, thank you."

Myk was dressed casually as he sat and waited for the deputy prime minister of Turkey, Turhan Tessir, in the lobby of the Princess Palace Resort and Spa. The posh resort was located on the outskirts of Istanbul, with the Black Sea on its north side and the Sea of Marmara to the south. Myk stood when he saw a group of men enter the front lobby. One man, wearing the traditional Turkish salvar, was surrounded by a contingent of other men wearing black suits—no doubt, Turhan and his bodyguards. Myk approached and extended his hand, but he was quickly surrounded by Turhan's men, who began patting him down for weapons.

Ali had known Turhan Tessir since his college days of playing on the Iranian National Soccer Team. Turhan played for the national team from Turkey. During one summer, they both played on the same all-star soccer team. After a match with one of the European all-star soccer teams, Ali caught Turhan staring at him as he came out of the showers. Abashed, Turhan snapped his head in another direction. From then on, Ali paid more attention to Turhan and noticed that he seemed to be constantly paying attention to everything Ali was doing. Ali asked him if he wanted to grab a breakfast before practice one day. From that day forward, they became close friends, and they had remained close ever since. Ali was certain that Turhan was gay, like him, but he could never work up the courage to ask. They became inseparable that all-star summer. Ali forever regretted not having the courage to ask—neither man had the courage to ask the other. Societal condemnation was severe, and it would have meant the end of either man's career, so both men remained silent and missed the opportunity to have a lifelong friend to trust with their darkest secret.

Turhan turned to Myk and said, "I hope you'll understand protocol, Mr. Vaughn."

Myk quickly had to get his bearings after being called Mr. Vaughn. Clearly Ali had shared the name of Lance Vaughn on his fake passport. Myk replied, "Not a problem. I appreciate you taking the time to meet."

After his men gave him the nod of approval, Turhan put his hand out to greet him. Myk extended his hand and said, "Lance Vaughn. It's nice to meet you."

"It's nice to meet you as well." Turhan put his open palm forward. "I've reserved a place that's more private. Follow me."

They walked out of the back of the resort, which opened up to a crystal-blue lagoon with a white sandy beach. Wooden boardwalks were located on the left and right side of the lagoon. The boardwalks stood above the water of the lagoon and formed a massive U shape that began on one side of the beach, went out over the water of the lagoon about four hundred feet, and then returned back to the other side of the beach. There were four private cabanas, equally spaced apart, on the boardwalk that, on first sight, appeared to be floating in the middle of the lagoon. The cabanas were draped on all four sides with a white, see-through sheer linen. Turhan's men waited on the beach while he and Myk walked to the furthest cabana. Turhan parted the white linen with one hand as if entering a tent and asked Myk to take a seat on one of the two large sofas. Once inside, the two became shadowy silhouettes against the backdrop of a cloudless sky and sailboats skimming across an undulating blue sea.

Turhan asked, "Mr. Vaughn, I hope you appreciate how rare this is for me to part with the Zip drive without knowing a thing about you. But I trust Ali completely. There can be no doubt that you've had a hand in what's unfolding in Iran right now, so it's safe to assume that you are a man with good intentions. It's obvious you're involved in counterintelligence in some capacity. I'd ask who you work for, but I know you can't tell me. I would like to know what your plans are with the information on the drive."

"You're right; thank you for not asking. As you know, Iran's nuclear scientists as well as their leadership were decimated by the coronavirus. China's Communist Party approached the radicals in Iran and employed them to release a more deadly version of the virus that they had developed. Fortunately, the United States was able to contain it. Now, the Chinese want to try again. Because the CCP has such a heavy hand in social media, their juggernaut disinformation campaign has successfully clouded the world's judgement on the CCP's true intentions. With the hard evidence provided by you and Ali, it will be impossible for the world to turn a blind eye anymore."

Turhan nodded thoughtfully. He leaned forward with his elbows on his knees and said, "My grandfather said something very insightful while the whole world shut down because of the pandemic that the CCP tried to cover up."

"What's that?" Myk asked.

"He said that China's quick growth as an economic superpower reminds him of the Germans before World War I. Unified Germany enjoyed great economic growth and expansion, but they chose to go down the path of military expansion as well. Communist China is following an eerily similar path and has expanded their military to massive proportions. Hopefully, people will wake up to the developing danger. Turkey will have no part in their games. I'm not going to let our country get bullied by the CCP. There's no way in hell that we'll get sucked into their One Belt program." Turhan leaned back into the plush sofa and crossed one leg over the other.

"Was he upset that you wouldn't sign the contract?" Myk asked.

Turhan's eyebrows raised as he tilted his head slightly to the side. "Of course. They threatened to strangle us economically." Turhan shrugged and continued, "I believe they will follow through on their threat, but the country of Turkey will *not* be beholden to the Chinese."

Turhan handed the Zip drive over to Myk and said, "I would love to visit more, but I'm afraid that this is all I have time for. I trust you will use the information well. China needs to be reined in."

Myk smiled and said, "Thank you! With information like this, the day of reckoning is coming for China!"

When Myk arrived back in the room, Raji was still sitting on the bed watching the upheaval in Iran. The police and the military had already conceded and agreed to meet with the leaders of the movement to negotiate the terms of the transition of power. The mullahs, on the other hand, had locked themselves in their palatial palaces and were playing hardball. But, with the entire country of Iran against them, it was only a matter of time before they surrendered. Cries of Raji's name had begun to wake Tehran.

Two days later, Iran had turned from massive demonstrations to celebrations of the overthrow of their stifling and corrupt government. Schools, offices, and stores were empty as Iranian citizens reveled in the optimism of a new direction for their country. The new leadership that was forming by the hour wanted to hear from their heroine—Raji. Chants for her name grew louder in Tehran. After much deliberation, the producer at Raji's network interrupted the news hour with breaking news. An anonymous package containing the video footage of the murder of Raji and her husband had been sitting on his desk when he arrived in the morning. He waited until late afternoon to run the exclusive video. Rumor quickly spread that the mullahs were behind the massacre at Raji's home. Tensions flared at the barricaded residences of the mullahs. The "Millionaire Mullahs," a name Iranians had dubbed their corrupt leaders, were no longer safe in their palaces. Video footage of Raji's massacre went viral. Angry Iranians stormed through the barricades at every mullah's residence and forced them from their homes before burning them to the ground. The mullahs would atone for the blood of their Kaveh.

Raji turned away from the TV and looked at Myk. "I have just one piece of unfinished business—Jaafar."

Myk asked, "Are you sure you don't want to just turn him over to the authorities?"

Raji laughed. "I'm quite sure. His days are numbered, Myk. I've given it some thought. As much satisfaction as I'd get from shooting him, it would leave me with a mess to clean up and he's not worth the effort. Besides, I don't want to disrespect Becca by getting blood all over her guest house. This doesn't need to be dramatic. I'll put a pill in his food, and he will slip away and never wake up."

Myk nodded.

She asked, "What about you? Surely you're not going to run around being Lance Vaughn forever." A look of concern came over Raji's face. "What are you going to do about Rick Taft? Now that I've found you, I don't want to lose you to a bullet, a bomb, to jail, or anything."

"You won't lose me. I've got hard evidence on him that he slaughtered his entire FBI team, but I want more. I have friends in the agency still. They are digging through the forensics on Adelberg's assassination before any of Taft's dirty agents cover it up. Levi saved the bullets and took pics of my wounds. The bullet that killed Adelberg will match the bullets Levi dug out of me, and they'll clear my name. I'll put together a plan much like we did before. You seem to have a knack for toppling governments. The US government is almost as corrupt as Iran's. Maybe I should put you to work on that!"

Raji laughed and then asked, "How is that? Unlike Iran, your elections are still the will of the people. If it's so corrupt, why do they get voted into office?"

Myk's eyebrows raised. "Wow. That's a very astute question. In short, it's because they are the ones that have the loudest voices. Most Americans just want to live their lives and not get involved in politics."

"Makes sense. But you still haven't told me what you're going to do about Rick Taft."

"Kill him slowly."

.

# CHAPTER 37
## LEVI'S REPRISAL

# ISTANBUL

In life, Levi Miles had accomplished everything he ever wanted, except one thing—bringing justice to the murderer of his brother Mykel. In death, the seeds sown by Levi would come to fruition through his nephew Myk. Unbeknownst to Rick Taft, his days were numbered. His victims' lives had ended suddenly without warning, but recompense for Taft would be methodical and purposeful. Taft had managed to elude Levi and Myk's father when he absconded with the stolen Nazi gold from the lake in the Swiss Alps. Later, he escaped the fury of Myk's mother, Hannah, on the streets of London after he had killed Myk's father.

Myk's thoughts wandered to the man who had become his father figure, David Adelberg. Myk had the good fortune of thwarting Rick Taft's assassins, but not Adelberg. In Myk's mind, he would be completely justified in killing Taft. Two months prior, Myk wouldn't have given it a second thought, but some of Levi's qualities had rubbed off on Myk. He decided he wouldn't kill Taft physically—he wanted to assassinate him publicly. If he did kill him, Taft wouldn't suffer. Because of the evil that Rick Taft had gotten away with, Myk would make him suffer.

The pictures taken by Levi decades earlier, which he thought were ruined, would ultimately lead to the demise of Rick Taft. Myk reached for the Zip drive that Levi had given him as he was dying. He pulled the Zip drive from its container and then stared—Levi's dried blood formed a partial thumbprint on the drive. Myk reflected momentarily on the tragic night of Levi's murder and then slid the drive into the port, determined more than ever to expose the one responsible for the death of his father and the mass murder of an FBI team.

Two months later, Myk and Raji sat in the plush couch of their presidential suite at the Princess Palace Resort and Spa when they heard a knock at the door. Myk walked to the door and looked through the peephole. It was Khatchi with a shorter woman with wild ginger hair. Myk opened the door and Khatchi gently escorted the woman to the large dining room table. She was a trusted friend of Khatchi's that he had worked with at the BBC studio earlier in his career. Her name was Molly Murray. Molly worked as a journalist for a globally syndicated news organization. She was the youngest of seven children and the only girl. Raised on a dairy farm with six older brothers, she was as tough as nails, but being the only girl in the family, she was doted on by a mother that gave birth to six boys before capping the family at seven with her coveted girl. Molly's birth order was often her mother's "mic-dropping" argument against her sons: "You'd better thank God your sister came last, or you wouldn't, have been born!" Molly could drink most men under the table and when she wanted, could turn their heads walking down the street. She could stretch her height to five feet if she stood on her tippy toes. Molly had a thick mop of curly ginger hair, fair skin, and she spoke with an unapologetic heavy Scottish accent.

Myk and Raji sat at the large dining table.

In her thick Scottish accent, she said, "Jaysus, Khatchi. This clandestine theatrical bullshit had damned well better be worth it, lad!"

"It will be. The only question you'll need to answer when we're done is whether or not you think you'll be safe enough to publish your name on the story."

Molly turned and stared at Raji. She raised her index finger toward Raji and said, "I recognize this bonnie lass—I thought you were supposed to be dead, my dear. You've become somewhat of a national heroine in Iran."

Raji smiled. "Yes, I've been told that I look like her many times."

Molly's eyes squinted as she laughed. "Oh, I see. My mistake." She shifted back to Khatchi and said, "Okay, show me what you've got."

Khatchi glanced at Myk and said, "This is my friend, Lance Vaughn. He will fill you in on the details."

Molly took one look at Myk. "Lance Vaughn, eh? You look just like the American lad on Interpol that's gone missing. This is quite the group of Neds you're running around with, Khatchi!"

Myk laughed at how her Scottish accent made her sarcasm that much funnier. He replied, "All fun aside, what I'm about to share with you will undoubtedly endanger your life. As I'm sure you are aware, Rick Taft won the senatorial race in California by a landslide. We have irrefutable evidence that Rick Taft is a cold-blooded killer, if you're brave enough to take the story."

"I'm listening."

Myk's tone became more serious. "Rick Taft is evil to the core. The man is an empty vessel. He needs to suffer for what he's done. I want him to hang by a noose of his own making. He tried three times to kill me with hired assassins and is responsible for the death of my friend and mentor, David Adelberg. You will be putting your life at risk. Are you sure you want this?"

"Absolutely! And don't you fret, I know how to keep myself safe while this story runs its course."

"That's great!" Myk replied as he stood over the large table full of evidence. "Let's start here." He reached across the table and removed a cloth covering three gold bars. "These gold bars were removed from a secret gold vault deep in the mountains of the Swiss Alps. The serial numbers on the bars match the exact sequence of gold bars sitting in Fort Knox. Rick Taft murdered his entire FBI team that extracted the Nazi gold bars from a lake in Switzerland over forty years ago. Most of the gold was taken to Fort Knox, but Rick Taft stole four of the crates and created a story that he was the lone survivor of an ambush at the lake."

Molly asked, "How in the hell did you get his gold out of the vault? Those are the most secure places on the planet."

Raji cleared her throat and said, "I'll answer that." She turned to Molly. "During the Islamic Revolution in Iran in '79, anyone loyal to the Shah feared for their life. Most political and military leaders fled the country. One of the most influential bankers and an outspoken critic of the revolution, Hamid Farhadi, had to flee Iran for his life. He got out, but his wife and children never did. They'd had plane tickets for a flight the next day, but they were detained by haters of the Shah and he never heard from his wife again. Hamid had no intention of letting the billions he had made in the oil industry get confiscated by the incoming regime, so he fled to Switzerland and found a secure place to keep his wealth as well as a great business opportunity. He had slowly built up the name and reputation of his gold vault. Today, his vault was rumored to hold more gold than any other in the world."

Raji continued, "Lance knew that Taft had the gold; we just needed to find out where he took it. Lance's contacts at Mossad were certain that it was in Hamid's vault, so I requested a private meeting with him. Meetings such as this are not out of the ordinary for him, as most of his clients require anonymity. Lance and I met with him in a secure location." Raji thought of their first meeting. Once they were in the room with Hamid, she had removed her blonde wig. The blood had drained from his face, and Raji thought he was going to faint. Then the old sweet man had begun to cry, and reached out and grabbed Raji's hands.

Raji hesitated momentarily before continuing. "If you take anything away from this, please understand that it is literally a matter of life and death that my name as well as Hamid's remain anonymous."

"Of course! I would never put you in danger."

Raji went on with her story. "He recognized me, and the first word he said was 'Kaveh.'"

Puzzled, Molly asked, "What does 'Kaveh' mean?"

Raji answered, "Kaveh is a Persian figure from Iranian mythology who leads a popular uprising against a ruthless dictatorship."

Molly nodded. "Okay."

"He squeezed my hands and told me that his 'beautiful Persia' and family were snatched away from him during the Islamic Revolution. Hamid had very deep roots dating back to the beginning of the Persian Pahlavi Dynasty. We eventually came around to our reason for the visit. When we told him why we were there, he said he was certain that Rick Taft did not store any gold in his vault. From our intelligence gathering, we surmised that his deposit would have likely been one of Hamid's first clients. We asked if he had any recollection from forty years ago of someone depositing four crates of gold bars in his vault. He remembered the event, but he was confident it wasn't Rick Taft. Hamid said, 'It was the first and the last time I ever saw the young man that deposited the three and a half crates of gold bars.' We showed him a picture of what Taft would have looked like back then.

"Hamid kept meticulous identification records, so we asked if he would take a look at the original deposit to the vault in late 1979. He stopped taking pictures of clients in the early 1990s for security reasons, but he still kept all the files prior to that. The picture he had in his files is an exact match to a younger Rick Taft."

Molly commented, "I don't want to burst your bubble, lassie, but a forty-year-old picture won't be enough to even put a scratch on Rick Taft."

Myk stood and sauntered around to the head of the table, where he grabbed a purple-colored manila file and then gently slid it across the table to Molly.

Myk said, "You're right. But the information in front of you will.

It will do more than scratch him—there's enough in there to put him behind bars. But we're just getting started."

Molly flipped open the file. "What is this?"

Myk replied, "Those are the old iris scans that Hamid used for security before he switched to retinal scanning. The FBI building in Washington DC, where Taft worked for more than a decade, used an iris scanner for security. I have contacts in DC that were able to get me the iris scans of Rick Taft when he was a young FBI agent. They are an exact match. If you flip back a few pages, you'll see copies of the logs for his jet travel. Rick Taft's jet has been to the vault four times in the last ten years."

Molly chimed in, "Okay, let me be the devil's advocate. The only thing you've proved so far is that Rick Taft is a thief, not a murderer."

Myk placed a thumb drive in front of Molly. "My uncle Levi worked for Mossad when Rick Taft was a budding FBI agent. Levi recorded Rick Taft massacring his team after they extracted the Nazi gold from the lake."

Molly asked, "Why didn't this recording come to light earlier?"

"Everything got caught in a rainstorm, and they assumed it was ruined—and with their limited technology back then, it was. So, the file was saved and forgotten until my uncle Levi contacted Mossad a few months ago. Now they have the technology to restore much of the recording. It gets a little scratchy in a few parts, but there is no mistaking Rick Taft murdering his entire team."

Molly held the drive between her thumb and index finger and exclaimed in her heavy Scottish accent, "Geis! Dat's pure dead brilliant, lad."

Myk shook his head. "No—it's sickening."

Molly looked away and stared blankly out the window. "Aye, lads, you are swimming in some deep and treacherous waters. Are you sure you're safe?"

Raji answered, "We're fine. We're more concerned about your safety."

Molly shook her head back and forth. "Aye, I'm going to run this story. Right now, I don't see a plausible way of putting my name on it and staying above ground, but that's not the important thing. I'm going to expose Rick Taft for you. I agree with you, the right way to do it is to torment that shite and humiliate him publicly before we release the trap door and hang that huffy wee fuckbumper."

Myk laughed. "Can't say I've heard that term before!"

Molly asked, "You've got a lot more sitting on this table. What is it?"

Myk placed a handcrafted mahogany box in front of Molly and said, "We found this little gem in Taft's vault. Inside the box are all the documents of Taft's father's immigration to the United States. He was one of Hitler's leading rocket scientists that the US brought into our country to bolster our military. With the help of those same Germans, they started NASA and helped President Kennedy realize his dream of being the first country to land a man on the moon."

Molly asked, "Where are you going with this? That may have been unethical, but it was perfectly legal. Besides, this information is available to the general public."

"True. But there's documentation in that box for a very good friend of Taft's father that will shock the world."

Molly slowly opened the smooth wooden box. Her eyes narrowed as she looked at Myk and asked, "Who is it?"

"The US government was so desperate to get their rocket technology quickly up to par with the Germans that they gave Taft's father whatever he asked for. It turns out that he was good friends with Heinrich Mueller, who was head of the gestapo. Mueller was in the bunker with Hitler before he died and had been planning his escape. Six months before the war ended, Mueller began hording gold and other valuables. He is the highest-ranking Nazi that was never caught or confirmed dead. Taft's father successfully negotiated with the US government for a new identity and freedom for Mueller. The United States got their rocket scientist and his technology.

Heinrich Mueller got his freedom. Taft's father got a fortune, and fame at NASA, and Rick Taft got billions in gold."

Molly took a strand of her curly ginger hair and rubbed it across her lips as she shook her head. "Aye, that dafty bawbag Taft double-crossed Mueller as soon as his son got into the right position in the FBI!"

Myk nodded his head in agreement. "He sure did!"

They meticulously pieced together all the evidence that would destroy Taft. Then they sketched out a timeline of releasing the information that would inflict the most damage. Once they were all satisfied, drinks were brought out to the balcony and they spent the rest of the evening talking and laughing at Molly's jokes in her heavy Scottish brogue.

# Washington, DC

Rick Taft was sitting behind the desk of his posh senatorial office in Washington, DC. His phone lit up as his secretary said over the speaker phone, "Director Eastman is here to see you."

Taft replied, "Buzz him in, please."

Seconds later, Taft heard the remote-controlled electronic lock on his office door disengage. His administrative director, Chuck Eastman, entered the office and sat. "I apologize for stopping by unannounced, but one of the interns came across something that we need to get in front of."

"What is it?" Taft asked.

Eastman shook his head. "A paper in Scotland ran a story this morning that you were being investigated for illegal campaign contribution violations."

Taft's eyebrow furrowed as he clicked his tongue. "That's preposterous. Call over to the Federal Election Commission and see what this is about."

"I already did."

"And?"

"It's very odd. They told me that they just received the electronic copy of the complaint along with the corroborating documentation attached. Somehow the newspaper company got a hold of all the information before the FEC."

"Which paper ran the story?" Taft asked.

"A paper in Glasgow, *The Scotsman*."

A puzzled look came over Taft's face. "What did it say?"

"I forwarded it to your email. You can open it up."

Taft's fingers began to tap on his keyboard. He clicked on the article and began to read. The story in *The Scotsman* told about a beautiful blonde woman who stepped through the front door of the remote campaign office for Rick Taft, located in the obscure small town of Bodega Bay, California. The small town had a population of one-thousand people and became a popular stop along the beautiful California coast after Alfred Hitchcock filmed his movie *The Birds* at the location. The woman who identified herself as Tiffany Vaughn made a very substantial contribution to the Taft campaign. Apparently, the one-man campaign office became so distracted with the woman and her dazzling eyes that he paid no attention to the source of the three-million-dollar campaign contribution. The lead story in *The Scotsman* went on to say that Rick Taft would soon be under investigation for illegal campaign contributions.

Taft looked up from his computer and asked, "Who in the hell is Tiffany Vaughn?"

"A ghost. She's got no electronic footprint anywhere on our searches so far."

"How problematic is this?"

"Shouldn't be much of a problem at all. We can pay the fine and sweep it under the rug, so they won't need to start an investigation. However, there was bigger problem that was waiting in Tiffany Vaughn's car outside the campaign office."

Taft gave him a questioning look.

"Video from the CCTV outside the campaign office shows a man on the driver's side of the car that looks like Myk Miles. What would you like me to do, sir?"

Taft nonchalantly shook his head. "Nothing. I don't have time for this petty agitation from Myk Miles. It's time to send in the hounds!"

"What does that mean?"

"It means that I'll get all of his assets seized and freeze his bank accounts. By the end of the day, he'll have nothing left. Also, up the ante on the reward for his arrest."

"Will do."

# Istanbul

As Senator Taft finished up the morning meeting with his administrative director, Myk and Raji sat down for some late afternoon hors d'oeuvres on their balcony overlooking the Black Sea. They read about the first wound inflicted on Rick Taft—a mere paper cut, but the bleeding needed to start somewhere. They had just come back from a tour of Istanbul's most popular site, the Hagia Sophia.

Myk flipped open his laptop and found the website for *The Scotsman*. They read the "anonymous" story by Molly as they sipped their wine.

When they finished reading, Raji asked, "I don't mean to second-guess your decision, are you sure it was wise to expose your face on the CCTV at the campaign office?"

Myk grinned. "Quite sure! Taft spent many years in the intelligence-gathering world. He knows I parked in front of that camera for a reason. The message is crystal clear—I'm coming for him!"

"What do you think he'll do?"

Myk shrugged. "He'll pay a fine and put the story to bed before it grows legs. Then he'll try and flex his muscles somehow. Since he doesn't have a clue where I am, he'll try and go after everything else, but I've already shut down my bank accounts and transferred my assets."

Raji asked, "Will he go after *The Scotsman* and try to find the 'anonymous' writer?"

"I doubt it. As it stands, he probably thinks I filed the complaint and sent a copy to *The Scotsman*. We did exactly what we wanted—put him on notice and got his attention."

Myk held his glass up as Raji touched her wine glass to his for a cheers.


# Washington, DC


The following week, Senator Rick Taft sat down for breakfast at The Lafayette, where the powerbrokers of DC met to see and be seen. At the table with Taft were the Senate majority leader and a prominent senator from New York. The topic of discussion over breakfast was an offer from the Senate majority leader to Taft to fill a seat in the most powerful and prestigious Senate committee—the Senate Appropriations Committee. Taft was a rare asset to their party as he had managed to catch both the populist movement and the policy wonks of his party. In a weak bench of future presidential candidates, Taft was already their clear front-runner for the presidential election in three years. The Senate majority leader was no stranger to Washington politics. He would reward Taft with heading the most powerful committee in Washington, and his investment would give him a tenfold return.

Taft was sipping on a gourmet vanilla latte when he noticed his director at the entrance of the restaurant scanning the room for him. When eye contact was made between the two, Chuck Eastman walked hurriedly toward Taft. As he approached, Taft noticed the dire look of concern on Eastman's face—clearly the game of poker was not his forte.

Eastman bent over and whispered in Taft's ear, "*The Scotsman* published another article. This one claims that your father sheltered the Nazi war criminal Heinrich Mueller and that he got paid millions in Nazi stolen loot. Twitter is starting to catch fire."

Taft gently dabbed the corners of his mouth with his napkin to give the appearance of being completely calm. But inside him were the beginnings of a complete meltdown. He stood. "Gentlemen, I apologize for cutting our meeting short, but I have an urgent family matter that needs my attention. I am honored by your offer to chair the Appropriations Committee and I wholeheartedly accept."

Taft's limo was waiting out front of The Lafayette. Eastman joined him on the drive along Constitution Avenue back to the Russell Senate Office Building. Taft turned to Eastman and said, "Chuck, if you're going to survive in this town and stay on board the Taft Train, you have to learn how to mask your emotions. You should watch some *Star Trek* episodes and take your cue from Spock."

"I'm sorry. This is all new to me. I'll do better. I forwarded the article to your phone so you can read it on the drive."

Taft pulled the phone from his inside jacket pocket and began reading. The anonymous writer in *The Scotsman* claimed to have firsthand knowledge of a document between US authorities and Taft's father, Franz Weimer. The story detailed that Franz Weimer was part of the Project Paperclip which secretly moved over sixteen hundred German scientists and engineers to the US. Taft's father and Wernher von Braun were the top leaders in German rocket technology. Both were members of the SS, which was why Taft's father had his name changed from Weimer to Taft when he arrived in the US. Apparently, Weimer brokered the deal for a new identity for his

Nazi friend Heinrich Mueller as well as getting him in a specialized witness protection program. According to the article, Taft's father was paid millions in Nazi gold, stolen art, and jewels by Mueller in exchange for him getting a new identity and new life.

Taft slipped his phone back into his pocket and turned to Eastman. "We'll put together a response on Twitter when we get back to the office."

"Is it true?"

Taft laughed halfheartedly. "It's no secret that the US brought my father over from Germany along with thousands of other scientists. Everything else is fabricated. Our political foes can see the momentum we've started. The president's numbers are plummeting, and my numbers are sky-high. We'll put out a few tweets. The first one will vehemently deny that my father was ever associated with the monster Heinrich Mueller. My father became a prominent figure with NASA, so it's a matter of public record that he lived in a modest home and drove a standard car. Clearly, he never had millions of dollars lying around or lived an extravagant lifestyle. Included in our tweet will be a statement that if the Taft family ever had such stolen wealth, I would rightfully donate it. It is sad that anyone would use the Holocaust to score political points. I have complete confidence that Twitter will get behind us and label our opponent's tweets as unverified and then that will be the end of it."

Eastman nodded.

"We will also tweet that our previous political opponent, Susan Owens, was embarrassed by our landslide victory and that Ms. Owens thought that since she was a minority woman that she was somehow entitled to the Senate seat. Our sources have informed us that she is the one behind the story."

"Are you okay with the truthfulness of the tweet?"

Taft smiled as he shrugged. "Chuck, truth is a relative term around this town."

Always the master at disguising his true emotions, Taft was fuming inside. He was already formulating the calls he would make from his encrypted phone. He would put out a "name your price" incentive for the first person to identify the anonymous writer for *The Scotsman*. Next, he would contact the owner of his bank vault in Switzerland and verify everything was secure.

# Istanbul

Myk and Raji sat at their table drinking iced tea. They were somewhat sweaty from their morning fishing excursion on the Black Sea. They were reading Molly's recent article in *The Scotsman*. When they finished, Myk closed the laptop while Raji tapped her Twitter app to see if Taft had posted anything.

She handed her phone to Myk to show him what Taft had put on Twitter. She sarcastically said, "Apparently, Senator Taft would like to make a substantial donation to families of the Holocaust."

Myk continued scanning the Twitter post and then replied with a snarky look, "Perhaps we should help facilitate the Senator's desire to become a philanthropist."

Raji laughed. "I think so!" Myk handed her phone back as she took a sip of the iced tea. She said, "I assume this is more than a paper cut on Taft."

"For sure, this cut goes really deep. But it's not something he'd ever let on." Myk sipped his tea and then asked, "By chance, have you ever seen the movie *Monty Python and the Holy Grail?*"

Raji's eyes widened. "Actually, I have. Becca showed me a lot of iconic movies over the years. Why do you ask?"

"I guarantee you that Taft will be just like the Dark Knight in the movie who doesn't allow the seekers of the Grail to pass by him. We've just cut off Taft's arm, but he'll play it as ''Tis but a scratch.' When Molly posts her next article, effectively cutting his other arm off . . .'"

Raji finished Myk's sentence, "'Just a flesh wound' will be Taft's response." They both let out a laugh.

A few days later, Raji's phone lit up and began to vibrate from an anonymous caller. It could only be one of two people: Molly or Khatchi.

She answered, "Hello?"

Molly replied, "I just spoke to my editor. He's had several visitors peeping around and asking questions. They are offering crazy money for the source of the anonymous articles, but he hasn't budged."

"Thanks for letting us know. How are you doing? You're safe . . . right?"

"Aye. No need to worry over me, lassie. I'm fine."

"I figured as such. Remind your editor that we'll double every offer that's put on the table. Just stay strong."

# Washington, DC

Every other day, Molly posted a new story causing Taft to take more wounds. After ten days and five articles from the anonymous writer at *The Scotsman*, Taft received a call from the Senate majority leader who told him that he was being removed from the Senate Appropriations Committee. Throngs of reporters camped outside Taft's home as well as his office. He could no longer dine in public without being overwhelmed with aggressive reporters. Indeed, much like the responses of the Dark Knight in the Monty Python spoof, Taft's responses to the allegations in *The Scotsman* had become comedic.

*The Scotsman* told how Taft hired assassins to murder his friend and former FBI Director David Adelberg as well as his attempts to kill former military standout Myk Miles. While Taft was metaphorically hopping around armless on his one remaining leg and denying everything as scratches and flesh wounds, Molly was preparing the final swipe of the sword that would leave Taft limbless and screaming that he would bite the legs off whoever levied these false accusations.

There was so much pent-up demand for news coming out of the small Scottish paper that their server crashed. The paper could name their own price to advertisers that were clamoring to be a part of the once unknown paper. They had matched the last three-and-a-half years of revenue in just two weeks. Senator Rick Taft was among the millions of followers that were anxiously waiting to read the next article. He sat behind his desk, staring at his computer screen and watching the seconds tick away. It was 8:58 a.m. *The Scotsman* posted their news on the internet at 9:00 a.m., but Taft's opportunity to read *The Scotsman* would be delayed. He heard a lot of commotion outside his office. Before he could stand, authorities burst through his door. Seven officers with bulletproof vests and weapons drawn charged through his office and put him in handcuffs as they read him his rights. Reporters were shoulder to shoulder, shouting questions and blinding him with the flashes of their cameras. The Taft Train was derailed and was about to become the biggest train wreck in American political history.

# Istanbul

Myk and Raji sat on the balcony and read Molly's fatal blow to Senator Rick Taft. It was the first time she posted her name instead of being anonymous. Molly Murray's fame would skyrocket. The current issue of *The Scotsman* was almost entirely dedicated to the Taft case. All the prior allegations and stories about Rick Taft were backed by irrefutable evidence that was displayed on page after page in *The Scotsman*. Levi's pictures of a younger Rick Taft slaughtering his entire FBI team were on public display for the whole world to see. Secret bank accounts were exposed that showed funds being transferred from Taft to the assassin that killed David Adelberg, and there was a confession from the surviving assassin that had killed Raji's son. On the night before Taft's arrest, Myk called FBI Director Ross Fullmer and told him about the secure package delivery that would shortly be arriving at his door. It contained the video footage of Taft murdering his team at the lake decades ago and documents of the agreement between authorities and Taft's father, which included the new identity for Heinrich Mueller. There were iris scans from Rick Taft and his jet logs tying him to the vault.

It was the story the following week for which Molly Murray was awarded the Pulitzer Prize. Molly's story told the world how the love of an unknown Jewish man, who had resided by himself in a beautiful storybook-like cottage amidst the secluded woods along the Oregon coast, had changed the world. She told how both of Levi's brothers had been violently murdered in front of him. Molly wrote about Levi's risk to save an infant girl and her brother and how he paid the ultimate price by sacrificing himself for a man that was once his mortal enemy. Molly shared how Levi and his heart of gold had become forever woven into the fabric of the life of an insignificant little girl named Raji—the same little girl who had forever changed her country of Iran. It was the story of how love, not hate, cures the ills of an ailing world.

# PART III

# CHAPTER 38

# NORMANDY, FRANCE

When Raji and Myk landed at the Paris Charles de Gaulle Airport, a news story detailing the developments in Iran over the past several weeks was playing on all the airport televisions. Iran's national heroine, Raji, was now a martyr. She paused on their way to baggage claim to watch. As a picture of Raji flashed on the screen, she adjusted her blonde wig and returned to walking toward baggage claim.

Myk held her hand as they walked. "Your country loves you, Raji. I know it sounds trite, but you really are their Kaveh." He looked her in the eyes and asked, "Are you okay?"

"This is so hard. To see what's happening and not be a part of it. I know it's the right thing to do, it's just difficult."

Myk squeezed her hand in affirmation. "I can't even imagine. To go through what you've been through your whole life and then to be the one who was the catalyst for the change and not be able to be a part of it has to be tough. If you stayed, sooner or later, the radicals would find you and kill you."

"I know. I think that blonde Tiffany Vaughn may take a vacation or two to Tehran in the coming years though!"

Myk laughed. "I hope that Mr. Vaughn accompanies her."

Raji's pace slowed, and then she stopped. She looked up at Myk. Her eyebrows furrowed as her mesmerizing eyes became serious.

She asked, "Do you really?"

Myk nodded while never breaking eye contact and said, "Yeah, I do."

Raji wrapped her arms around him and gave him a warm embrace. When she broke, she said, "There's a little winery that Becca took me to on my second visit here. It's not too far from her estate. Can we stop in there on the way back?"

"Of course, that would be nice. When does Becca arrive in Paris?"

"I'm pretty sure she's arriving within a few hours of our flight. She didn't want to be there without us. Jaafar gives her the creeps."

Myk and Raji parked their rental car at the Acres of Sun Vineyard and sat inside at a table that had views of the entire Normandy coast. It had grown too cold and overcast for a table on the outside patio. They ordered a bottle of red wine from the local vineyard and a few hors d'oeuvres.

Myk asked, "What's on your mind?"

Raji smiled and shook her head. "What's not on my mind?! When you've lived a life where all your hopes and dreams always get smashed to the curb and then you wake up one day and you're living in the greatest dream that your mind could imagine—it's hard to believe. It's like I have an angel sitting on one shoulder whispering in my ear that this is real, it's safe to believe; at the same time, I've got a devil sitting on the other shoulder whispering that something will go wrong, it always does, you don't deserve this."

Myk's head tilted to the side as his eyes narrowed. "Why wouldn't you deserve this? You of all people are most definitely deserving. Believe it, Raji. You've created it."

Raji's voice cracked. "I should have been stronger. I could have been stronger."

Puzzled, Myk asked, "What are you talking about? You're one of the strongest people I've met."

"The bombs he had me wire . . . so many innocent lives were lost."

Myk nodded and paused in thought. Then he said, "Including yours." Raji gave him a puzzled look. Myk continued, "You were an innocent little girl that lost your childhood because of an evil man. You were strong then, and you're even stronger now. What if you took the section of dominos from your childhood out of the long string of dominos that comprise your life? Would Iran be replacing its totalitarian, theocratic government right now if that little girl didn't wire those bombs for her father and then grow up to despise her father and country with every bomb she wired? It made you who you are today. Without you, none of this would have happened." Myk looked affectionately at Raji and added, "Let it all in, Raji. It is safe to believe."

A single tear rolled out of the corner of her eye. "Yeah. I know. It's just going to take some time."

They both took a sip of their wine. Raji placed her glass down and asked. "How long will you stay, Myk? You've put your life on hold to help me while there's been a manhunt going on to find you."

Myk shook his head.

Raji asked, "What?"

"Why would you think my life is on hold, Raji? My life is not on hold. I chose to walk this path with you." He took another sip and then added, "And I'd like to continue on this journey with you and see where it goes."

Raji closed her eyes momentarily. She reached both of her hands across the table. "I was hoping you would say that."

The waiter appeared with their hors d'oeuvres. He placed a plate of caramelized brussels sprouts and another plate of cheese, mixed nuts, and crackers on the table. Both Myk and Raji took a bite.

Myk asked, "So what's your plan with Jaafar?"

"Ali had a container of pills in his gun closet that cause your heart to stop beating. I never want to see him again, even when we get back to the estate. I really don't give a damn about what he has to say about the overthrow of Iran's government. As far as I know, he probably thinks I'm dead, like the rest of the world. I'll slip the pills into his next drink or his next meal and that will be the end of him."

The two continued to talk until they finished their bottle of wine. Becca's estate was a twenty-minute drive from the winery. The sun had just begun to set when they pulled into the house. Myk noticed Becca's car and asked, "I thought she was arriving after us?"

Raji gave Myk a puzzled look. "That's what she told me."

Raji spotted Becca in the stables brushing down one of the horses, and quickly got out of the car to meet her. Becca looked up and saw Raji approaching. Her eyes got as big as saucers. "Oh my god! Who is this beautiful blonde bombshell coming to meet me?!"

They both embraced. Becca said, "I am so proud of you, girl! You are all over the news. You did it. I was so afraid I'd never see you again."

"Well, here I am. Now you'll never be able to get rid of me!"

"Where's that gorgeous man of yours hiding?"

Myk rounded the corner to the barn. Becca let out a small scream that qualified more as laughter than a scream. She put her hands to her mouth. "Good Lord, I hope that mustache is fake because you look like a damn pedophile with that mustache and nerdy hairstyle!"

Myk laughed as he pulled the wig from his head and gave Becca a hug. She said, "Let me see that nasty 'stache of yours." She reached up, grabbed the bottom corner of the fake mustache, and ripped it off his lip. "Ahh, now that's much better!" She gave Myk a kiss on his cheek.

Raji asked, "I thought you had a later flight?"

"I was antsy to get home, so I switched to the earlier flight. Let me help you with your bags."

Raji asked, "Where's all the ranch hands?"

"I told them they could clock out at noon since I was catching the earlier flight."

The three of them grabbed their things from the car and went into the house. Raji removed her blonde wig and said, "I'm going to go freshen up and slip into something more comfortable."

Myk said, "Okay, I'll meet you on the back patio."

Fifteen minutes later, Raji appeared on the back patio in a pair of comfortable jeans and a loose-fitting sweatshirt. She joined in the conversation between Becca and Myk.

Becca asked, "So what's next for you, Raji? I've known you for more than twenty years, and I don't think either one of us saw this day becoming reality. You have your health, you have money, and you have friends. I assume you'll have to find a new name. At the risk of being banal, you're not starting a new chapter of your life, you're starting an entirely new book!"

"I know. It's very exciting, but scary at the same time. Myk and I just talked about this. I'll have some time to think about it. One thing I know for sure," she paused and looked at Myk as she smiled, "the name Tiffany doesn't quite fit me unless I'm a blonde!"

Myk quickly interjected, "That's a deal breaker—I thought you were always going to be a blonde now!"

Becca cleared her throat in an exaggerated tone. "Excuse me. I think I'll fit the bill then. All-natural blonde right here!"

They all laughed, and then Raji winked at Myk and said, "Perhaps I'll go blonde tonight."

The temperature had begun to drop, so Becca reached for her phone. She had an app on her phone that controlled everything on her estate. She turned the patio heaters on with the press of a button. The three continued to skim along the surface of their conversation for forty minutes before slowly diving deeper.

Raji bottomed out her glass of wine and set it on the table. She asked Becca, "Any trouble with Jaafar while you were away?"

Becca shook her head. "None at all. I received an update twice a week. They said that Jaafar kept to himself. They said he went for a short walk every day and then never left the guest house."

"Have you heard from him since you got back?"

Becca hesitated and then replied, "He hasn't said a word to me."

"This may sound a little weird, but I picked up his favorite Iranian tea while in Tehran. He likes to drink it before he goes to bed. If I make him a cup, would you mind bringing it to him? I'm just not ready to see him yet."

"Of course, Raji. Although it's getting a little late."

Raji checked her watch and then stood. "You're right. I'll go make it now."

Raji left for the kitchen. As she entered the house through the back patio doors, Becca asked. "Is she okay, Myk?"

"As far as I know. You've known her much longer than me. Does she seem off to you?"

Becca paused in thought. "Perhaps just a little." She stood and then joined Raji in the kitchen. By the time she entered the house, Raji had already dissolved the heart-stopping pills into Jaafar's tea.

Raji handed Becca the tea and said, "Thank you. Thank you for everything, Becca. You've been my guardian angel."

Becca gave her a hug and said, "You are such joy, Raji. I'll bring this to Jaafar and then join you all on the patio."

While Myk and Raji conversed, Becca delivered the "poisoned apple" to Jaafar. Five minutes later, Raji saw Becca through the window carrying back the saucer and cup of tea that she dumped down the kitchen sink. *Damn, he's already asleep*, she thought. She watched as Becca walked to the patio doors and leaned out while she nervously said, "He's gone! I knocked three times and waited, so I entered the room and checked everywhere. There's no sign of him!"

Myk and Raji sprang to their feet and jogged over to the guest house. They turned every light on and scoured his room. Jaafar was nowhere to be found. Myk asked, "Do you want me to search the grounds?"

Raji answered, "No. Let the wolves have him if he's out there!"

Becca asked, "Do you want me to call the police?"

"Of course not. We're all fugitives," Raji answered.

Myk said, "If he left with someone, I doubt he'd leave everything here. We can look more thoroughly in the morning. Who knows, maybe he'll show up."

*I hope not*, thought Raji.

Myk scanned the room one more time. As he was about to leave, his eyes stopped on the side of Becca's boot—there was a blood stain. Myk looked up at Becca to see if she saw him staring. She was talking with Raji, unaware of Myk's gaze.

Becca announced, "It's been a long day. I think I'll get some shut-eye."

Myk nodded, "We will too."

As Myk sat up in bed, gathering his thoughts, Raji emerged from the bathroom donning her blonde wig, a negligee, and a devilish smile. "I'm afraid Raji had other business to attend to. She said you'll have to settle for the company of Tiffany Vaughn tonight!"

Myk grinned as he shook his head. Raji sat up in the bed next to Myk.

"You're fun!" he said.

"You make me fun!" She put her head on Myk's shoulder and asked, "Do you think it's any coincidence that Becca came home early at the same time Jaafar went missing?"

"Perhaps. When we were in the guest house, I noticed a blood stain on her boot."

"Do you think she killed him?"

"I doubt it, but you never know."

# CHAPTER 39

## BEIRUT, LEBANON, 1978

Nadine walked resolutely down the concrete ramp of the musty parking garage. Clutched in her right hand were the papers to her autonomy. She would hand the divorce documents to the monster who had become her husband, let her children say goodbye to a man they rarely saw, and then she would walk back up the concrete ramp to life anew. Her young toddlers, Malcolm and Raji, trailed behind her quickened pace, but that would give her the brief moment she needed out of earshot from the children. "You're a deceitful, murderous liar, and I am staying with my parents in Beirut," is the only thing she would say to Jaafar before handing him the divorce papers. Nadine would instruct her children to hug the stranger that was their father, and then they would turn around, exit the parking garage, and begin a life unencumbered by a religious fanatic. The doors to her six-year imprisonment with an overbearing misogynist had been unlocked and swung wide open. But the residuum of Jaafar's toll had come for its collection on her unknowing and undeserving family. The price for Jaafar's evildoing was about to be paid.

Nadine had met Jaafar at the University of Tehran. He was an electrical engineering major, and she was pre-med. Instead of using his electrical engineering degree to start a career in engineering, Jaafar began to make bombs for radical Islam. It wasn't until after her marriage that Nadine realized that everything about Jaafar was one big lie. He had completely deceived her. Jaafar had become a major player in the Islamic Revolution to overthrow the Shah of Iran, and he demanded that Nadine and the children move to Tehran. When Nadine finally shared with her parents the true nature of Jaafar, they told her they would help her out with her decision to go back to medical school and raise her kids as a single mom. It was with this hope in the future that Nadine's legs couldn't walk fast enough to deliver her divorce papers to Jaafar, who was waiting at the other end of the parking garage near his car. Little did she know, it would be the last time her legs would walk at any pace.

Nadine's mind was focused on the monster leaning against his car with a smirk on his face. She didn't notice that her children had fallen way behind her fast pace. She didn't notice the two Israelis hunched down in their car as she walked by. Nadine didn't hear the Israeli's car door swing frantically open as she neared Jaafar. What she did notice was the look of absolute terror that instantly come over Jaafar's face. Her first thought was, *How could he know that I'm handing divorce papers to him?* But that thought quickly vanished as she watched Jaafar turn and bolt toward the staircase as if the Grim Reaper had come to take him home. She turned and looked back in horror—a Jewish man with a blue kippah was sprinting toward Raji and Malcom. The mysterious man now had both of her children clutched under his arms. *No! Don't steal my precious children* was her last thought before Jaafar's car erupted in a massive explosion.


Nadine woke up to the smiling faces of her parents and her ten-year-old brother, Yasser. The swelling was so bad in her head that her neurologist was left with no other choice but to put her into a medically induced coma. She had been unconscious for two months. Her parents immediately stood and held her hands when Nadine opened her eyes. Before she could get her bearings or even utter a question, she watched her parent's eyes flood with tears of complete joy. When Nadine's mangled and bloody body, with its faint heartbeat from the loss of blood, first arrived at the hospital, there was little hope of her survival. But, with each passing day, hope grew.

Nadine squeezed her mother's hand and asked, "Where's Raji and Malcolm? Are they hurt?"

Nadine's mother sandwiched her hand between both of hers and said, "The children are unharmed, Nadine."

Suddenly, Nadine felt a sense of ominous doom—she tried to wiggle her toes but felt nothing. She tried to sit up and look down at her legs. With her hand that was free from an IV and heart monitor, she reached down and felt for her legs. Nadine's legs had been amputated from the hip down. She closed her eyes, put her head back on her pillow, and began to weep.

Between her sobs, Nadine managed to ask, "How long have I been out?"

"A little over two months. You had severe head trauma, which caused swelling that was almost fatal."

Nadine turned to her father and asked, "What happened?"

He answered calmly, "Authorities said that it was an attempt to assassinate Jaafar. Payback for his bus massacre outside Tel Aviv last year."

A memory from the event flashed across Nadine's mind. She said, "The last thing I remember was a man sprinting with Raji and Malcolm tucked under his arms."

Her father nodded. "Yes, he saved both of them."

Nadine smiled and then asked, "What about Jaafar?"

"He survived as well," her father answered.

Nadine closed her eyes again, and then drifted back to sleep. Her parents waited several weeks for Nadine to gain back her physical and mental strength. She would need all her strength in order to bear the weight of what they withheld from her—Jaafar had moved to Tehran and taken her children with him.

# CHAPTER 40

# NORMANDY, FRANCE

Myk and Raji arose early to take the horses for a ride and to gather their thoughts from the previous night. The blood on Becca's boot raised questions with Raji, so she planned to ask her if she was keeping anything from her about Jaafar's whereabouts. Raji sat atop her favorite horse, Penny, and gently eased back on the reins. After Penny came to a stop, Raji swung her leg over the top of the saddle and hopped to the ground. She slid the reins over Penny's head and began to walk her back to the stable. Myk followed suit with his horse, Buck. As they neared the stable, Myk glanced up at the house and noticed a newer model cargo van parked in front.

He asked Raji, "Is Becca expecting anyone?"

Raji shook her head and replied, "Not that I know of."

They brought the horses into the stable, unharnessed the saddles, and placed them on top of the stable doors. They unleashed the reins and fed the horses from the bucket of oats. Raji and Myk held hands as they came out the other end of the stable and walked along the path that led to the back patio of Becca's French farmhouse. Raji grinned as the memory of her passionate night with Myk in the stable flashed across her mind.

Myk asked, "What's so funny?"

Raji laughed. "Just thinking about the night we rolled around in the hay for three hours."

Myk squeezed her hand. Both Raji and Myk noticed them at the same time. There was a very elegant elderly woman in a wheelchair waiting at the base of the ramp to Becca's back patio. A man was standing behind the woman in the wheelchair. He had a large white bandage on the side of his head. The woman had thick hair, mostly gray, that was shoulder length. The closer they got to her, the prettier she became. Raji was the first one to notice that the beautiful elderly woman was missing her legs. Raji saw the woman raise her hand and point toward her, but she couldn't hear what she said to the man standing behind her. Raji and Myk kept their slow pace as they walked toward the woman who continued to look directly at them. When she was ten paces away, Raji began to feel a magnetic tug that seemed to be pulling her to the woman in the wheelchair.

Raji was three paces away when she noticed them. The woman in the wheelchair had Raji's same stunning iridescent eyes—a flood of emotion pierced her heart. Nadine tried to speak Raji's name, but she couldn't. She was completely overwhelmed. Nadine sniffled through the tears before she was able to articulate, "Raji, I am your mother, Nadine."

A waterfall of uncontrollable, joyous tears flowed from Raji's eyes. She clasped both hands over her mouth and sobbed out loud. "How is this possible? They said you were killed in the explosion." She managed to ask between her sobs, "Is it really you?"

Nadine outstretched both of her hands, beckoning Raji. "Yes, my child. I am your mother."

Raji stooped down and embraced her mother. Both mother and daughter hugged and sobbed. Nadine pulled back slightly as she quietly said, "Let me see your beautiful face."

Nadine cupped Raji's face with both hands, "Oh how I have missed my little girl." She touched her forehead to Raji's and audibly wept. Through her tears, she mumbled in a tone that was barely perceptible, "He took everything from me. He took everything from me. But now I have my daughter back."

Nadine reached up behind her and gently touched the man's hand that was resting on her shoulder. She looked up at him and asked, "Yasser, would you wheel me up to the patio out of this bright sunlight, please?" She reached out, squeezed Raji's hand, and said, "I'm so sorry for not introducing you, this fine man behind me is my brother, Yasser."

Raji replied, "This is my friend, Myk." She stepped toward Yasser and wrapped her arms around him. "My son's name is Yasser too."

"Let's talk on the patio out of the sun. I'm sure you have lots of questions," Nadine said.

As Yasser wheeled Nadine up the ramp, Raji fell into Myk's arms, squeezed him tight, and wept. "I can't believe it's her. She's here."

"This is unbelievable. I am so happy for you," Myk said.

Yasser pushed Nadine's wheelchair to the edge of the couch where Raji sat and turned toward her. They sat next to each other and held hands.

"I am still in shock. I have been told my entire life that you were dead," Raji said.

"The first two years after the bombing, I wished that I was." Nadine gently shook her head and said, "They kept me in a coma for two months because of the head trauma from the explosion. When I awoke from the coma, I wept when I realized my legs had been amputated. A few weeks later, my parents finally told me that Jaafar had taken you and Malcolm to Tehran. I was devastated and wished they had let me bleed to death in the parking garage. Recovering from my physical injuries was nothing compared to recovering from the loss of my children. Shortly after the bombing, the Islamic Revolution took place, and the Shah was ousted from Iran. After that point, communication or visitation to Iran was nearly impossible. About six months after the bombing, I was finally successful in contacting Jaafar. It was the one and only time I ever spoke to him—until yesterday that is."

Myk and Raji looked at each other but said nothing.

Nadine continued, "I tried every day for six months after the bombing to speak with Jaafar. When he finally did answer my call, I told him that I wanted you children back. That day of the bombing in the parking garage I was there to serve him with divorce papers. He would have gone to Tehran, and I would have stayed in Beirut and raised you and Malcolm. Jaafar turned into a murderous monster after I married him, and I tried to get out. But fate had a different path for me. My phone call with Jaafar was short. He told me in no uncertain terms that if I ever tried to contact him or either of you kids, that one of his bombs would find its way to me and my parents. Before he hung up, he said he was doing me a favor. He said I would never amount to a good mother without legs anyway."

Raji squeezed her mother's hand tightly. "I would have given up my two legs if it meant I could have had you in my life. He lied to us. He told Malcolm and I that you were killed in the bombing."

Nadine nodded. "Yes, I know. Eventually I found a way to bypass Jaafar's threat. The best I could do was to love you through a proxy."

Raji gave her a puzzled look. "What do you mean?"

"I had to do something. I couldn't put my family's lives at risk, because that lunatic most certainly would have followed through on his threat and bombed them, but there was no way I was going to give up on you either. So, I found an empathetic heart in a nanny that Jaafar hired."

"Habiba?" Raji asked.

Nadine nodded. "Yes. I spoke to your nanny, Habiba, almost every week. Every time Habiba gave you a hug, that was me hugging you. I have watched every one of your newscasts, Raji. You have no idea how proud I am of you. You couldn't know about me, but I have followed you as best I could your entire life."

Nadine wiped her eyes with the back of her hand at the same time as Raji. The two women with almost matching opalescent eyes filled them with tears.

Raji shook her head and whispered, "I don't know what to say.

I am overcome with happiness."

Nadine interlocked her fingers with Raji's and said, "And your last broadcast—you were so brave, Raji. What you've done for the Iranian people takes my breath away, and your story about that man, Levi, was very touching."

Raji smiled through the tears and asked, "What did you do with yourself after you were released from the hospital?"

Nadine gently patted the top of Raji's hand and answered, "It took me a few years in rehabilitation to fully recover mentally and physically. Sometime in my second year of rehabilitation, my parents gave me an article about a man in the US who had been struck by a drunk driver the night he graduated from medical school at Stanford University. He lost both legs because of the accident, but he didn't let that deter him. They told him he would have to switch his career path to becoming a family physician instead of pursuing his dream of being a cardiac surgeon. He ignored the experts and followed his aspirations. He became a well-respected cardiac surgeon and had a special hydraulic wheelchair made for him so that he could perform the surgeries."

Nadine paused and smiled lovingly at Raji. She continued, "That's all I needed. I wasn't going to let the bombing define me for the rest of my life. After a lot of hard work and some good fortune, I finished medical school. I specialized in surgeries for paraplegic children and eventually cofounded the St. Paul's Rehabilitation Center in London."

Raji's eyes widened. "Wow, that is really inspirational, M—" Raji couldn't quite verbalize the word that she got stuck on, so she tried again. "That's great—Mom." She paused, smiled, and then added, "That feels so good to call you Mom!"

"It feels even better to hear it."

Raji asked, "Which medical school in Beirut did you attend?"

Nadine shook her head and replied with a grin. "I didn't go to school in Beirut. The best medical school was actually in Israel, so that's where I wanted to go. When I wrote my application letter to the Bar-Ilan University of Medicine in Israel, I was shocked by their reply. An anonymous family in Israel knew about my story and they paid for all of my schooling and living expenses. Attending medical school in Israel was one of the best decisions I've made in my life, Raji. Some of my best friends for life were from my years in Israel. That single decision opened countless doors for me."

"That's beautiful—and ironic. I'm not sure I would have had the fortitude to let the country responsible for taking my legs educate me," Raji said.

Nadine shook her head. "No, Raji. There's no doubt in my mind. I've followed you as best I could your entire life. You are the most courageous woman I know."

The comment warmed Raji's heart. She paused as a puzzled look came over her. She asked, "Did I hear you right earlier? Did you say you spoke to Jaafar yesterday?"

Nadine didn't reply. Instead, she looked across to Yasser who was sitting next to Myk. Yasser made eye contact with Nadine and then gently nodded his head at her.

Nadine turned to Raji and said, "Yes. Actually, we came here yesterday in hopes of finding you."

A puzzled look came over Raji's face. She asked, "How did you find me? Nobody knows I'm here. The world thinks I'm dead."

Nadine shook her head affirmatively. "When I saw Jaafar's video message on Al-Jazeera a few months ago about becoming a 'peaceful man' and his plea for others to follow him, I knew it was finally my chance to find you without fear of me and my family being bombed. I reached out to Habiba and she told me that something very peculiar happened. Habiba said that you asked her to sneak you onto Jaafar's estate. At the same time, you were no longer on Tehran's nightly news, so I suspected that something was going on. I asked Habiba to contact your brother, Malcolm. He is the only one who knew about your friendship with Becca, so he shared the information about her *estate here in Normandy*."

Excitedly, Raji asked, "Does Malcolm know about you?"

Nadine smiled. "He does now. He said that he and his family would fly into Paris and meet us."

Raji looked over at Myk. She was radiant. "You said that you spoke to Jaafar yesterday. Do you know where he is?"

Nadine nodded. "I do. When we arrived yesterday, Yasser went to the front door and rang the doorbell several times, but no one answered. As Yasser was about to get back in the van, we saw Jaafar hobble out of the guest house. He asked, 'Can I help you?' Yasser told him that we were here to see you. Jaafar said somewhat belligerently, 'Don't you watch the news? Raji was gunned down at her home in Tehran.' Then Jaafar asked who we were. Yasser pointed to the van, where I sat waiting, and told him, 'Nadine is here to see her daughter for the first time since you left her for dead in the parking garage.' Jaafar was in complete shock and went pale. After he gathered his thoughts, he told Yasser that he wanted to talk to me. I told Yasser that was fine, so he wheeled me to the grassy area. Jaafar sat on the wall next to the cliff while I sat in my wheelchair."

Raji looked over to the area Nadine was pointing at. She hadn't noticed before, but now she saw it—huge swaths of blood stained the wall.

Nadine continued, "Jaafar sat on that wall and began to talk as if nothing had happened. If I had legs, I would have shoved him over the wall right then and there. I watched his mouth move as he talked, but I didn't hear any words—my mind was raging inside. I interrupted him and told him that I saw his pathetic message of peace on the Al-Jazeera network. Now that he was a 'peaceful man,' I didn't need to worry about his threats to kill my family. I told him I would not listen to another word he had to say. He took my precious children and the use of my legs, and he would not take another second of my time. I gave him an ultimatum—he could either call for a taxi and leave immediately, or I would call the police, and he could leave in handcuffs."

Raji asked, "What did he do?"

"The belligerent bastard continued to sit on the wall, so I pulled my phone out and started dialing the police. He immediately got his ass off that wall! He leaned against his cane and then began to hobble past us. As soon as he got to the other side of Yasser, he grabbed his walking cane with both hands and swung it as hard as his feeble body could. He cracked Yasser on the side of the head." Nadine pointed over to Yasser. "You see that nice bandage he's got on it now? Anyway, he knocked Yasser out and then came after me—but I was prepared this time. When he told Yasser that he'd like to talk to us, I had pulled Yasser's gun out of the glove box. When he turned and came after me, I didn't hesitate one second. I shot him twice right through the heart. Well—I should say I put two rounds where his heart should have been. That monster never had a heart."

Raji was riveted. "Where's his body at?"

"Well, I was in quite the predicament. The van is specially equipped for me so I can drive it. But obviously I couldn't get Yasser in the van by myself, so I had to wait. As it happened, Becca pulled in just as I was getting ready to toss some water on Yasser and wake him up. Your friend is quite the character! She was all too happy to help me toss that waste of flesh down that cliff into the ocean."

Raji looked up as if in thought. She said, "I'm not sure if I am supposed to have some feeling of loss, but I don't. I am actually a little happy."

Nadine replied, "Good! He was a monster." She wheeled herself toward Yasser and held her hand out motioning to him for a large leather bag he was holding. Yasser placed it on Nadine's wheelchair. When she wheeled herself back around to Raji, she said, "I'd like to share something with you. Open up the bag."

Raji leaned over and took the heavy bag. Inside, there were three large photo albums. Nadine said, "Open the tan one first."

Raji flipped open the photo album and began to look at the pictures. She methodically turned each page. They were pictures of Raji's childhood at Jaafar's estate. There were photos of birthday parties, photos of Raji smiling with missing teeth, photos of her karate competitions, and pictures of Raji at the shooting range. It was a complete documentation of her childhood.

Puzzled, Raji stared at Nadine and said, "I don't understand."

Nadine nodded and pointed to the photo albums. "That was my inspiration—what kept me going. Every week, I eagerly went to the mailbox to open the letters from Habiba. Without fail, I shed a tear over all the pictures she sent of you and Malcolm. Flip to the last page, Raji."

Raji folded over the bulging album to the last page. It was a picture of Raji and her son, Yasser, with his arm around her after his championship soccer match—the same picture that Raji had pulled off the mirror at Yasser's hotel in San Francisco.

Raji said softly, "This is my favorite picture too. It must have been Yasser's because he had it stuck to his bathroom mirror in San Francisco."

Nadine put her hand over her heart and asked, "Why is it your favorite?"

"Because of Yasser's smile. Just look at him—he's beaming! Jaafar got into his head shortly after that soccer match, and I never saw his glowing smile again."

"Do you know why it's my favorite?"

Raji thought for a second and then answered, "The same reason as mine—I suppose."

"Look closer, Raji—look beyond you and Yasser. What do you see?"

Raji pulled the picture up and examined it closer. She stared at the photograph while everyone on the back patio sat in baited silence. Suddenly, in swift unison, Raji gasped and covered her mouth with her hand—she spotted Nadine in the background of the picture. Nadine was in her wheelchair about ten feet behind where Yasser and Raji were posing for Habiba to take the picture. Nadine was *facing the camera and posing as well.*

Raji said, "I remember. Habiba was making such a fuss about people in the background of the picture. She kept waiting to take the right shot. She was waiting for you, wasn't she?"

A huge smile came across Nadine's face. "That's right. Habiba's letters and pictures of you and Malcolm helped to partially fill the huge void created by Jaafar stealing you from me. Every time Habiba would share stories of your loneliness, my heart would break for you. We all suffered because of Jaafar."

# CHAPTER 41

Raji and Nadine talked on the patio for hours. When Becca joined in, Myk made a sarcastic comment about the blood he saw on her boot. She quickly countered back that those boots were now in the bottom of the ocean along with Jaafar. Becca explained that when she discovered the stain on her boot, she walked to the same place that she had hoisted Jaafar's body over the cliff and tossed her boots in—she wanted no memory of the vile creature.

Nadine announced that she was getting tired and would need to leave soon to go back to her hotel. Becca insisted that she stay at the house and that she would have someone go retrieve her things. Nadine gladly accepted the invitation.

Nadine turned to Raji. "The video you put together about the corruption of the Iranian regime was absolutely amazing, Raji, but there was one story in that video that almost made my heart stop."

Both Myk and Raji gave her a questioning look.

Nadine continued, "Your emotion really moved me when you shared the story of how the Jewish man, Levi, saved your life when you were a little girl and how he recently took a bullet for Jaafar so that his message of peace would resonate. I am puzzled—how in the world did you ever cross paths with Levi?"

Myk eyed Raji. His look implied, I'll answer this one." He said, "Levi is my uncle."

Unexpectedly, Nadine gasped and went pale. She whispered almost inaudibly, "Oh my God, he didn't tell them."

Myk said, "I couldn't hear what you said."

Nadine paused and shook her head. "Levi didn't say anything to either of you two?"

"Say what?"

She shook her head again and said, "Oh my." Nadine turned her focus toward Myk and said, "About ten years after I had graduated from med school, I became curious about the family that paid for all of my schooling and living expenses. Through the use of a private investigator, I found out that the donation was from someone who worked in the Mossad agency. Eventually I learned the name of the man who made everything possible for me: Levi Miles."

Other than the sound of the leaves being moved by the coastal breeze, there was complete silence on the patio. Time seemed to stand still. Myk fought to stem the tide of emotions that welled up inside him. Finally, Myk said, "I think Levi saw this day coming and made the decision to take that story to the grave with him. He wasn't the type that liked the spotlight on him."

Nadine said, "I could have never imagined something like this. I am astonished. I hold no ill feelings toward Levi or the Israelis. I came to terms with this decades ago. Jaafar was an evil man who killed thousands of innocent people. He was a murderer, and I was caught in the middle. Levi chose to assassinate him in an isolated parking garage so that he could minimize any possible collateral damage. Had I not showed up unexpectedly to deliver Jaafar divorce papers, the world would have been rid of that murderous man and I would have kept my legs and my children. Your uncle Levi was a wonderful man. Were you close?"

"Sadly, I only knew him for a few months. There were a lot of secrets my mother kept from me. Unfortunately, Levi was one of them."

"I am so sorry to hear that, Myk. How about your father?"

Myk told Nadine how his father had been assassinated as well as some of his other history. They talked for another hour until Nadine's belongings from her hotel arrived. Nadine and Yasser retired to bed while Myk and Raji stayed on the patio next to the warm outdoor

352

fireplace. Myk's heart was touched as he observed Raji and Nadine. It made him think. There would be no joyful reunion for him—his father was gunned down before he was even born, and his uncle Levi was dead now too. Along with Levi's death, all of his memories of Myk's father were lost to the ages.

Both Myk and Raji stretched their legs out on the table and moved closer to the fire as it began to cool down. Raji crossed the bottom of her leg over the top of Myk's. He held her hand and interlocked his fingers with hers. He said, "I am so grateful I could be a part of this. To hear how Levi was so intimately woven into the fabric of your family and then realize I was part of it, too, it really shakes my cynicism."

Raji took his hand between both of hers and shook her head.

Myk asked, "Did she say when your brother and his family were arriving?"

"I don't think so. I got the impression she wasn't going to have him come until we met."

"That would make sense." Myk squeezed her hand gently as he shook his head. "What an amazing day!"

Raji smiled and said, "It has been extraordinary. My head is still spinning. I can't stop from reflecting on different memories when I was a little girl, a teenager, and a young adult. It's like all the pieces of the puzzle of my life that seemed so incongruent at the time, are all fitting together now. Everything has meaning. What didn't make sense then, does now."

Myk smiled warmly. "I am really happy for you." He leaned in and gave her a kiss. While the puzzle of Myk's life remained unfinished, Raji's was coming together. While it was true that the astounding emergence of Raji's mother finally gave her life more meaning and context, it couldn't erase her past pain and abandonment. At least now she understood why. And now that there was a *why* to her suffering, it made it all more bearable.

# The End

# ABOUT THE AUTHOR

Tom Fitzgerald is a graduate of Arizona State University and author of *Defector in Our Midst*. He began his career at a large accounting firm in Phoenix. With an itch to be more creative, Tom left accounting to found his own luxury home building company in Scottsdale in 1999. Tom is fascinated by the life stories that many of his multicultural clients have shared. The creative pining within Tom helped him to intertwine real life stories with fiction to create his second fast-paced thriller, *The Insignificant Girl*.